Romeo and Juliet of the Projects

WITHDRAWN
FROM THE
COLLECTION

Oakland Public Library
Oakland, CA
www.oaklandlibrary.org

Romeo and Juliet of the Projects

Krystal Jennel Armstead

www.urbanbooks.net

Urban Books, LLC
300 Farmingdale Road, N.Y.-Route 109
Farmingdale, NY 11735

Romeo and Juliet of the Projects
Copyright © 2022 Krystal Jennel Armstead

All rights reserved. No part of this book may be reproduced in any form or by any means without prior consent of the Publisher, except brief quotes used in reviews.

ISBN 13: 978-1-64556-391-4
ISBN 10: 1-64556-391-X

First Trade Paperback Printing September 2022
Printed in the United States of America

10 9 8 7 6 5 4 3 2 1

This is a work of fiction. Any references or similarities to actual events, real people, living or dead, or to real locales are intended to give the novel a sense of reality. Any similarity in other names, characters, places, and incidents is entirely coincidental.

Distributed by Kensington Publishing Corp.
Submit Orders to:
Customer Service
400 Hahn Road
Westminster, MD 21157-4627
Phone: 1-800-733-3000
Fax: 1-800-659-2436

Romeo and Juliet of the Projects

by

Krystal Jennel Armstead

Prologue

Bostyn "Easy" Reel

Fall, 2018

"He's waking up! Oh, my God!" A woman's voice awoke me from what felt like a deep sleep.

I slowly opened my eyes, blinking as they adjusted to the light. I squinted, looking to my left, into the unfamiliar yet welcoming faces. I looked around the room at a group of Caucasian people staring at me, watching me blink until my eyes finally focused on each and every one of their faces. I looked down at my tatted arms, eyed the IV needles that pierced my skin. Then I looked at the doorway as a doctor and two nurses entered.

I looked at the doctor as he pulled a stool up to my bed and sat down, resting his elbows on his knees. One of the nurses pulled a Welch Allyn pressure cuff system to check my vitals. The blond woman to my left burst out crying. I eyed her, watching the two children who clung to her legs eyeing me back with tears soaking their cheeks. A group of police officers entered the room with who looked like one or two reporters. I looked back at the doctor, watching him look my face over.

The doctor noticed the confused and frustrated expression on my face. "Good morning, sir. I'm Dr. Cooper. Do you know where you are?"

I tried to sit up in the bed, but it hurt like a muthafucka. The blond woman who was crying rushed over to my side to help me sit up as one of the nurses adjusted the bed. The woman helped the nurses fluff the pillows behind my head before she went back over to her children. I looked the blond woman in her flushed face as the other nurse continued to check my blood pressure. After the nurse finished taking my blood pressure, she signaled the doctor an okay, as if my blood pressure was fine or at least better than it was before. Before what, I couldn't tell you.

"Son, do you know where you are?" the doctor asked again.

I looked around the room at all the people standing around me. Then I inhaled the scent of the roses that were in vases all around the room. "I'm . . ." I cleared my throat. It hurt and was dry as fuck as if I'd just had a tube pulled from my throat. "I'm in a hospital, obviously."

"Well, he still has that smart-ass mouth of his!" An older woman—who stood arm in arm with two men—laughed and cried at the same time. "It feels good to hear your voice, honey!"

"What . . ." I hesitated. "What's my name?"

The older woman cried out and fell against the man's chest to her left.

"Bostyn Emilio Zachariah Reel," one of the police officers told me. "You're known in the streets as Easy, ya know, because your middle initials are EZ."

I eyed the tattoos on my arm. Some looked like fraternity tats, some looked like police tats, and others looked like gang tats. "Bostyn? With a y, right?" I looked up at the woman who was crying and the two men who favored her.

The woman nodded, drying her cheeks. "You were named after the group home that you were adopted from, honey."

"Who are my parents? Where are they? Do they know I'm in the hospital?" I asked.

The woman hesitated.

"I know this is a lot to take in." The doctor steered the conversation away from who my biological parents were to why and how I ended up in the hospital. "You're stable, which is a good thing. You went through a lot, but you're back and around the people who love you the most. What you're experiencing right now is temporary memory loss, but in due time, your memories will come back."

For some reason, I felt like someone was missing from the room. I shook my head in confusion. "How long have I been out?" I asked the doctor.

"A month. We had to put you in a medically induced coma. You were shot in the back of your head and in your spine. To slow down the swelling, we had to put you in a coma," the doctor answered.

I tried to remember what happened, but I was drawing a blank. "What happened to me?" I was kind of scared to ask.

"You were shot in the line of duty. Your father didn't make it. I mean . . ." The doctor hesitated to explain. "The man who adopted you—Jimmie Reel—didn't make it, son."

I leaned back in the bed, trying my best to remember being shot. *Line of duty?*

"Line of duty? Am I in the military?" I questioned, too stunned to ask about the man he mentioned who I had no recollection of.

The woman with the blond hair sobbed even louder, drowning out the cries of the others in the room.

"You're one of us." One of the police officers stepped forward. He was a tall white Richie-Rich-lookin' mutha-fucka. "Your father died trying to protect you," he told me.

I just looked at him, still trying to register it all. "Do you know who killed him?"

The police squad all nodded and mumbled among themselves.

"The man who shot your father is in police custody. He's alive, barely. We kept him alive to bring him to you, sir," the built dark-skinned man in front of the group of cops told me.

I looked into his face. "You look familiar."

He approached the foot of the bed, chuckling and crying at the same time.

"Muthafucka, are you crying?" I joked with him. I felt like I knew him. I felt like we were close, so I knew I could joke with him. "You ugly as hell when you cry!"

"Wigga, these are thug tears!" He laughed, drying his face. His crew laughed behind him. "Bostyn, we grew up together! We've been homies since we were in diapers! It's me, Claudius!"

I nodded. "Yeah, you look familiar. But if I had to guess your name, I would have to say Jody. You look like that crispy muthafucka from *Baby Boy*."

Claudius laughed out loud. "Ya white ass used to always say that shit!" He laughed with tears in his eyes like he wanted to start that crying shit again.

I frowned and looked at the other people in the room. It was killing me inside to see them crying over me, yet I couldn't remember who they were. The two little kids looked at me like they wanted to rush over to me, but their mother wouldn't let them. They looked about the same age, probably twins. I looked back at Claudius.

"We thought we'd lost you," he told me as he dried his face. "We'll help jog your memory, bruh. This woman over here is your mother, Lauryn Reel. She adopted you from the Bostonian Home for Boys when you were two. The two boys with her are Jaxon and Roxyn, your brothers. These men behind me are a part of your task force. They—"

"My task force?" I asked.

"You're the captain of our unit, sir," another officer told me.

I shook my head in confusion, trying to take it all in.

"Bostyn?" the shapely blond woman called out to me in the sweetest voice.

I looked over at her with my head spinning.

"Baby, these are your kids. Boss and Majesty. Twins. They're five." She whimpered as she approached my side.

I looked up at her. Her face was completely unfamiliar to me. "And who are you, pretty lady?"

She cried out before going over to grab the children, who were crying just as hard as she was. "I'm Mandy, your wife!"

I looked down at my left hand. I wasn't wearing my wedding ring. I looked up at her as she watched me looking up from my hand. I didn't feel connected to her. I didn't feel connected to my kids. She must've kept them from me for a reason. Why didn't I recognize my own kids? Why was she wearing her wedding band and engagement ring, yet I couldn't even remember wearing mine? I watched her grab our kids and leave the room. I rubbed my hands across my head in frustration, cringing in pain as the bandage on my head rubbed against the palm of my hand.

"Okay," the doctor told everyone, "I think we need to give Bostyn some room. Please come back later. This has to be confusing for him. Give him some time."

"How long?" Lauryn cried. "I want to talk to my son!"

"Your son, who doesn't even remember that you're his mother?" the doctor questioned.

"Mom, come on." The man introduced to me as Jaxon pulled on his mother's arm. "Let him be alone. He'll be all right. This isn't his first brush with death." Jaxon winked at me before taking his mom out of the room.

I watched my other family members and the other cops leave the room. Claudius stood right there at the foot of the bed, feet planted on the floor as if he dared the doctor to ask him to leave.

Dr. Cooper pushed his glasses back over the ridge of his nose. "Claudius, is it? You can leave right along with them."

"Were you there when he found out that he was adopted? Were you there when the woman who claimed to be his real mother was shot in the head right in front of him on his front doorstep? Were you there when he graduated preschool, kindergarten, eighth grade, high school, or the muthafuckin' police academy? Were you there with him when we lost friends, loved ones, and innocent civilians while we were undercover? Were you there when he got married? Were you there with him when his child died in his arms a few moments after birth? Nah, muthafucka! I was there, and I'm going to be there for him when you clock the fuck out and go home to your family who doesn't have to live through the shit we live through on a daily basis!" Claudius told the doctor with tears in his dark eyes.

"So, get the fuck out so we can talk," I chimed in, glad I at least had one person on my side who was willing to fight for me.

The doctor huffed, eyebrows connecting into a frown. "Maybe some things are better left unremembered." He shook his head, frosty hair glistening a little under the hospital room lights.

"Yeah, his family would love for shit to be that way, but I ain't about to let him go out like that," Claudius snarled as he watched the doctor and the nurses leave the room. Claudius sat on the stool that the doctor had just reluctantly gotten up from.

I looked around the room at all the balloons, flowers, and teddy bears scattered everywhere. “A lot of muthafuckas love me, I see.”

Claudius scoffed. “Most of this shit is death threats. You don’t wanna read the cards, trust me. Our cover was blown. What happened to you was a drug bust gone wrong, homie. But you’re gonna be all right, fam. We have guerillas all around this muthafucka.”

I looked at him and had a feeling that he wasn’t talking about zoo animals. “Like foot soldiers or some shit?”

Claudius nodded.

“The fuck do I need muthafuckas guarding a whole hospital for? What the fuck happened?” I asked.

Claudius shook his head. “Shit went wrong. Shit came out that they never wanted you to find out, at least not this way.”

““They? Who’s they?” I asked.

“Your family. The police department. We just came off suspension last week, but the entire unit is under investigation. News reporters are camped out all around this muthafucka waiting for you to wake up so they can grill you. Meelah’s okay, though. She’s in a safe place.” Claudius exhaled deeply. A frustrated look crossed his face when he said shawty’s name.

The sweetest face of a sexy brown-skinned goddess flashed through my mind. The name was familiar. I knew Claudius saw my face light up when I heard her name.

Claudius chuckled a little. “Yeah, I should’ve known you wouldn’t forget her.” Claudius pulled a picture out of his pocket and handed it to me.

I took the picture in my hands, holding it up so I could examine the details of the picture. It was a photo of the girl whose face had just flashed through my mind. She was sitting at a table in a restaurant with an older white man who looked somewhat familiar.

"Who's this old cat she's sitting with?" I asked Claudius, eyes still fixed on the picture and the dress that shawty was wearing.

"Ya pops," Claudius huffed.

"Jimmie? The man who adopted me?" I asked and watched Claudius shake his head.

"Nah. Not sure if you're ready to hear this shit, but if anyone is gonna tell you the real on your family, it might as well be me." Claudius exhaled deeply. "I'm not even sure where to start." He rubbed his hands across his fade.

I held the picture up, pointing at the sexy mama. "Start with why I know her and why her face flashed through my mind as soon as I heard her name. I have a whole family—wife, kids—"

"A dog, too. Can't forget ya dog and that big-ass muthafuckin' house you have with a three-car garage. Y'all muthafuckas living it up. We all are," Claudius let me know.

"I'm in love with her, ain't I?" I asked.

Claudius scoffed. "Love ain't the word. She's the reason you're in this muthafucka."

"Tell me about her."

"A'ight. Six years ago is the best place to start. Remember, you asked for it," Claudius warned me.

Chapter One

Meelah "Morning" Summers

Homecoming 2012

"'And then we'll walk right up to the sun, hand in hand! We'll walk right up to the sun, we won't land!'" I sang to myself as my boyfriend, Dinero, did line work to my new tattoo.

I watched him etch tiny footsteps up my arm until he got to the luminous sun that he had just finished on my bicep. It was beautiful. He was beautiful, but the nigga was crazy, which was why my daddy allowed him to come around. He was my protection. I wasn't quite sure how I felt about him, but I thought that I needed him.

"That shit is sexy, *mami!*" My sexy Puerto Rican friend, Sharita, eyed the tattoo as Dinero shaded in the feet. Her big brown eyes widened a little as she watched the tattoo gun needle vibrate against my skin.

Whitley sat up in the chair that was in the corner of my tiny room. She rubbed her pregnant abdomen. "Ya daddy is gonna come in here going the fuck off if y'all don't hurry up. We're supposed to be headed to the Dancehall in a few to get rid of these Rox. My nigga, Dash, is gonna pull up in a few, and if we're not ready, he's gonna leave us."

Rox—Rohypnol, oxycodone, and Ecstasy—combined into a very potent recreational drug. We (me and my crew) made thousands a night off the rich kids at the local hangouts. We made most of our money off the white kids who would take just about anything that was guaranteed to make them wake up the next day not remembering a fuckin' thing that happened the night before. Rox along with Sweet Tea (a liquid form of fentanyl and other opiates) allowed Dinero and his boys to gross about $15,000 a week.

I rolled my eyes. "Girl, Dash is all about paper. He wants that bread, so he'll wait for us. I have to look fly tonight for when I receive this homecoming queen crown."

I looked over at the beige sequined dress on the mannequin in the corner of my bedroom next to my bunk bed. When I was 13 years old, my mother and I worked for about a month on that dress. She used the cloth from one of her old dresses to create the timeless classic dress that I was now admiring. How we knew what size I would be at 17, I had no idea, but we got the fit just right.

The dress snatched my waist, cupped my booty, and hugged my hips. It had a thigh-high split and a train that floated over the floor for about four feet behind me. We had spent about a week placing the sequins on a pair of satin Prada heels. Mama would have been proud of the woman I'd become. She was the definition of trap queen, and my father bred me to follow in her footsteps.

My mother, Sadey Heinz-Summers, died when I was 14. She was arrested one night after being pulled over for a so-called blown taillight. After police found cocaine stashed in her bumper, they took my mother in for questioning, and she never made it home. Police claimed that she committed suicide in her cell, but we never received the autopsy report. The police were after my father, and since they couldn't get him, they got my mother. Killed her without hesitation, believing my father would give himself up. But he never did. And I thought I resented him for that. He never fought to get justice for my mother.

After she was murdered, he just went on about his life like he never had a wife. Like I never had a mother. Business went on as if the pretty, brown-skinned goddess never existed.

I took after my father, from the dark hair to the hazelnut brown eyes to his almond skin tone to his stubborn personality. I was my father's only child as far as he was concerned. Several teens at my school claimed to be his children, but my father never acknowledged them or their mothers, who he might have had a fling or two with whenever my mom pissed him off. Rumor had it that my bestie, Whitley, was his daughter too, but we never pressed the issue. She hated on me a little, but that came with the territory of being a big fish in a small pond.

My father kept us in the hood so I wouldn't forget where we came from, but we also had condos that he owned under pseudonyms to remind me that muthafuckas around us had nothing on us and couldn't be us if they tried.

My father had a big money scheme that no one could fuck with. My daddy, Emmanuel "Sable" Summers, was the mass narcotics distributor for Baltimore City, Baltimore County, Anne Arundel County, Howard County, Calvert County, and Prince George's County. He worked for an Italian man named Francesco Stefano Romano known in the streets as Stef. Stef had police units under his payroll. I mean, they had police officers robbing, killing, and dealing for them all over Maryland. Police corruption was at an all-time high, and everyone was caught in the middle. Even us teenagers. I tried my best to live a normal teenage life while I could, because there was really no telling when the crooked cops who worked for my father's boss would turn on us to save themselves. They were the law no matter how my father tried to put it. I was a teenager, but even I knew that you couldn't trust someone who could get away with killing you without any repercussions. The Baltimore City Police Department killed my mother. They were just waiting for the right moment to get to him. The only thing saving my father was the protection of the Howard County Police Department, and as soon as the police chief found out that Daddy was fuckin' his wife, we wouldn't have their protection either.

"Are you almost done with the tattoo, baby?" I asked Dinero, eyes tracing the stern look on his face as he looked over his line work.

Dinero nodded, his facial expression loosening up as he looked at me. "Yeah. I'm done, Meelah." He dabbed the tattoo with a damp cloth, wiping away the plasma that oozed from my arm. "I did that shit, yo."

"Yeah, you did, *hermano,*" Sharita agreed. She looked at the gold watch on her wrist, then rushed over and looked out the window. Her eyes followed a group of motorists who rode through our neighborhood. "Dash should be pulling up in a minute."

"Why are you looking at Stef's niggas riding through?" Whitley questioned.

"Because like clockwork, every night at seven thirty, those muthafuckas come riding through. It's like they're expecting to find somebody. My mother said that Stef took one of the police units off his payroll. I think it was the Anne Arundel County Police Department. Said he stopped fuckin' with them," Sharita told us.

Whitley rolled her eyes. "Just because your mama is fuckin' Stef doesn't mean she knows what the fuck is going on in his world. Do you think he'd really bring that kind of heat his way? Anne Arundel County police run this shit. Their district office is in the capital, boo. They distribute drugs from that muthafucka. That's his traveling unit. They steal from other gang members and bring their shit to us. Why would he let that unit go all of a sudden?"

Sharita smacked her lips. "Because my mother said Stef found out that Anne Arundel County is the unit responsible for Sadey's . . ." Sharita stopped talking when she saw that I was looking at her to finish her statement. She sighed. "*Lo siento,*" Sharita spoke softly in her sultry Spanish accent. "I'm sorry, *mami.*"

I shook my head and laughed it off. "I'm good. So, can we get into these dresses so we can get to the Dancehall? Boo, do you have your suit in the car or something?"

"We gotta move these Rox, ma." Dinero leaned back in his seat, looking at me from underneath his baseball cap.

I folded my arms. "Dinero, I live for this night, and you know it! I finally get to wear the dress I made with my mother, and you're worried about money? Money you're not even hurting for?"

Dinero looked at Whitley and Sharita, signaling for them to leave the room.

Sharita exhaled deeply. "We'll roll out with Dash and change over at his crib. I'll send my cousin, Krista, back over to pick you up. Be ready in thirty, Meelah. A'ight?"

Whitley eyed me, glaring at Dinero before she got up and followed Sharita out of the room, closing the bedroom door as they left.

"Baby . . ." Dinero pulled my chair closer to his. He eyed his tattoo before grabbing a cling wrap bandage to cover it until it stopped oozing. "Baby, look at me." He watched me roll my eyes looking everywhere but in his face. "Your pops is depending on us to get rid of these pills. Do you know how many of them rich niggas from Bay City High will be here?"

I looked Dinero in his face. Bay City High was a private school in Essex. They beat us every year at homecoming. They beat us every year at everything. Sports, academics, dance. Shit, they almost had us beat in the drug game, mainly because just about every student who went to that school had a family member who was involved in politics whether it was the local, state, or federal government.

Dinero's father, Miguel Rodriguez, was a senator for the Essex district. Miguel never acknowledged Dinero's existence. Before Dinero got in good with my father, he came from a poor household. His mother fell into a deep depression after her oldest son was killed in a neighborhood drug raid. She didn't work, didn't cook, didn't clean, didn't do shit but drink and get high. Shit got so bad that he had to drop out of school to look out for his younger siblings. After Dinero killed a few people who tried to break into our apartment one night, my father hired him to join his crew.

Dinero worked his way up from corner boy to my father's main supplier for the county. Daddy didn't play that high school dropout shit, so he made Dinero go back to school. Dinero got himself a crew of about ten to help him distribute whatever products my father hit him with. One night, Dinero got a call from a lawyer who needed something potent to get him and a few prostitutes he hired high as heaven. Dinero met up with the politician at a cheap hotel. When he walked into the room, he saw his father there. His father looked him straight in the eyes and didn't even recognize him. Told him to give him the shit and get the fuck out. Dinero carried that rejection around with him daily. He never let me or anyone else into his heart, and his father was the reason why.

"Baby, City High? At the homecoming dance? They have their own dance at their own school to attend. If Bay City is coming, then you already know Claudius's crew will probably be in the spot," I had to remind him.

Claudius was Dinero's brother and Miguel's son with a district attorney, Leanne Crosby, who often attempted to prosecute the men who worked for my father. Rumor had it that Claudius and Dinero had the same birthday. Around the time that Miguel was questioned for being involved with illegal drug activity, I was told that he slept with the DA to get his case dismissed. Apparently, that was around the same time that he fucked around with Dinero's mom, Jaylah. Claudius was raised by his aunt, Marilyn Crosby, who was a judge and couldn't have kids. Either way, whoever raised that nigga, he was set for life. He was one of those rich kids who hung in the hood because he could, not because he had to.

Claudius was everything Dinero pretended he didn't want to be. He was at the top of his class and was the star quarterback of the Bay Broncos, who beat the cleats off our asses the night before at the homecoming game. He scored a damn near-perfect score on both his ACTs and SATs and got accepted to universities all over the country. He kept his hands clean. He wasn't involved in the drug game and didn't have to be. His mom made a six-figure salary a year, fuckin' her way to the top like most women in the area who were in politics. Claudius's popularity and lack of need to ever struggle his way to the top made Dinero push harder to outdo his brother. Homecoming dance was the last thing on his mind, mainly because he knew his brother would show up.

"Man, fuck him. Ain't nobody worried about him. I'm worried about selling out." Dinero clicked his teeth, and the bottom row glistened in blue chrome. "The fuck is you worried about that nigga for?" Dinero looked at me as he put his tools into Ziploc bags so he could clean them up later.

I scoffed. "Who said I was worried about Claudius? I was just sayin'. You get like this every time that nigga comes into town. Like you said, fuck him. He ain't got shit on you. They're only coming to the spot to rub their trophy in our face. And you already know he won homecoming king without even having to show up to their dance!" I watched Dinero's nostrils flare as he put his tools up. I huffed. "You know how the tradition goes, Dinero—the homecoming king of our opposing school shows up to the homecoming dance to dance with the queen of that school! If I win homecoming queen, then—"

"Then what?" Dinero slammed his Glock 37 down on the table that sat beside us.

I looked down at the pistol before looking back into Dinero's frown. I shook my head, grinning a little. He tried his best not to love me, but I knew he did. That gun was a part of his 'staying over at yo' crib' starter pack. Next, he was going to pull out his extra clip, his charger, his durag, and his brush. "Aww, how cute." I laughed a little. "Is that thing even—"

Dinero picked up the gun and quickly cocked it back.

I gulped. "I just want one dance with you before the drama, Dinero, damn."

Dinero just glared at me, watching me stand from the chair in my Pink shorts and tight cropped top. His eyes traced my tattoos, all free styled by him. "Don't play with me. You dance with that nigga, and—"

I slid my shorts down, revealing the fact that I didn't have on any panties.

That angry expression on Dinero's face switched up real quick. Normally, there was a houseful of mutha-fuckas, but that night, Daddy and his crew were over at his house in Bethesda, keeping clear of the raids that he had caught wind of. Dinero's crew stood watch outside of my apartment, waiting for him. I was supposed to be getting into my dress, but I had to calm Dinero's soul. And the quickest way to that nigga's soul was through my pussy.

I picked up my phone from the table. Going to my playlist, I quickly put on Keri Hilson's "Slow Dance."

"Remember the first time I let you inside?" I reminded him, pulling my shirt over my head and showing him that I didn't have on a bra either, though I was sure he noticed my nipples poking through my shirt.

Dinero's eyes traced my hips as I slid onto his lap, throwing my legs over his and straddling his waist. He gripped my hips, knowing that I was trying to distract him from being mad about me bringing up his brother.

"'I don't want to come on too strong, but something happens when we slow dance,'" I sang with Keri.

Dinero smacked my thighs, looking into my face as I wrapped my arms around his neck, titties all in his face. I lifted my booty a little, looking down at him as he grabbed the Gold Wrapper (or as he called it, the Golden Ticket) from his pocket. We had started having sex about a year earlier. Though I talked to my father about everything, that was one thing that I didn't bring up. But he wasn't stupid. He told me that if I was going to give up the goods to a nigga to make sure I played it smart. He told me that all men dipped their dick in more than one female, no matter how much he claimed to love a bitch. It was the nature of a man to need more than one bitch for validation. He said under no circumstances to trust a nigga, no matter how loyal he claimed to be. "No glove, no love," was my daddy's motto.

I wasn't with Dinero twenty-four seven, but whenever he wasn't trappin' out, he was with me. And whenever I wasn't with my girls, in school, or helping my father with both his legit and street businesses, I was with him. It was a lust thing between the two of us, but damn it if it didn't feel like a sure thing to my young heart.

I watched as Dinero unzipped his dark denim Alexander McQueen jeans. I bit my lip, giggling as I watched him pull his erection through his jeans. He looked into my face as he bit the condom wrapper open. He gave me a tender yet passionate peck on the lips as he slid into the condom. I didn't have any other dicks to compare his to at the time, but that thang was the juiciest thing my 17-year-old eyes had ever seen. I desperately wanted him to love me. At that point, I just knew that Dinero was going to be with me for the rest of my life.

Whenever we were together, I felt like a queen. All the other girls—even the girls I kicked it with—hated on us. Though we both played it hard, we needed each other. The chemistry between us was crazy, though we pretended that it was just sex between us. We both claimed to be single, but damn it if we didn't fuss, fight, and fuck like we were a couple.

Dinero held my hips, gliding me down onto his dick. My thighs knocked against his waist as I eased onto it. Dinero grunted a little, holding my hip with one hand, then reaching for my phone to change the song on the playlist.

"Red dogs at my trap got me for a half a stone. See, I'm trappin' all day, can't wait to get home." I sang along with Lloyd and Jeezy to "Tear It Up."

Dinero bit his lip, groaning as I started to wind my hips and grind on him. He looked down, watching my pussy go up and down on his dick. I knew he wanted to pull out of me and snatch the condom off, but that nigga wasn't crazy. He kept track of my period better than me. I had just been put on depo, but he didn't trust it. Said nothing was 100 percent. He wasn't ready to be a father, and I knew I wasn't ready to have his child. But the dick was so good, and I was sure the way my pussy slid up and down the condom had him ready to get all in them guts raw as fuck.

"Nah." Dinero moaned, gripping my hips and sliding to the edge of the chair. "Nah, we ain't doing this slow grinding shit. We gotta roll out in a few. Grab the chair, ma." He lifted my body up and off him.

I stood from the chair and backed away so he could get behind me. I got down on my knees, gripping the seat with both hands and bracing myself as he got down behind me. I sighed as he got on his knees, pressing the small of my back down as he slid back inside of me. Before he started to stroke, he slid his hands between my pussy lips.

"That thing is wet as fuck. Am I the reason that pussy is so juicy?" Dinero questioned, more like dared me to say that it wasn't.

I nodded, sighed, and looked back at him as he rubbed my clit. "Yes, baby."

My body melted as the nigga grabbed the back of the chair and rammed into me, shoving his dick to the very back of my cervix. I screamed, body immediately breaking out in a sweat. Then he had to go and put a little umph in it. I swore my soul left my body as I listened to the sound of his pelvis clapping against my booty. I tried to throw it back, but the way he worked my soul relaxed my body. He had my mind in a trance, and my body had no choice but to follow.

"You dance with that nigga tonight if you want to." Dinero gripped the back of the chair with one hand, then gripped my neck with his other. "You let that nigga anywhere near my pussy and see what happens. This pussy is mine. This good shit belongs to Dinero. Do you fuckin' hear me?"

"Yes, baby!" I squealed, regaining my senses enough to bounce back. His warm hand around my neck felt amazing. I started to grind and bounce on his dick, causing him to slow his pumps a little, enough to feel my rhythm.

"Shhhhit," Dinero hissed.

I looked back at him, watching him watch me lose it. I pounced on his dick until he started to pounce back. He beat that thang up, biting his lip as he gripped my neck until I fell down on the chair, just taking the dick. He had me crying, begging him to stop, no, keep going. I reached behind me, pressing my hands back against his chest.

"Put your goddamn hands down!" he growled. "Now throw that ass back! Ride this dick. Ya nigga had a long day!"

I cried out. "Oh, my goodness, this shit feels so good!"

My arms fell to my sides as he released my neck and grabbed the back of the chair again. His stroke got deeper, faster, and stronger as my entire body began to convulse, shiver, and shake under his. I came just as he came, all his weight on top of me, grunting and breathing heavily in my ear.

My knees burned as Dinero pulled out of me. I remained in that position, ass still in the air. Dinero smacked my booty before he kissed it then licked from my clit all the way through my pussy up the crack of my ass. I giggled, screaming in delight.

"Oh, my Goddddd, Dinero!" I cooed, sitting down on the floor and watching him breathing heavily as he pulled the condom off.

Dinero grinned and went over to the trashcan in the corner of the room to throw the condom out. "Get'cha ass up. Shower and shit before your ride gets here. Oh, yeah, I got something for you to go with your dress." Dinero nodded toward the closet.

I held up my hands for him to help me up.

Dinero zipped his jeans, then came back over to help me off the floor. He looked down into my face before kissing my forehead. I wanted him to wrap his arms around me, but he didn't. He walked over and grabbed his plaid shirt. I sighed as I walked over to the closet. I opened the closet and looked on the floor. Alongside my shoes were a bouquet of yellow daffodils, a card, and a small Fendi shopping bag. I smiled and bent over at the waist to pick up the bag.

"Shit. You're lucky I gotta get rid of these Rox tonight, or else ya ass would be in so much muthafuckin' trouble. Have ya ass going in that homecoming dance pigeon-toed," Dinero joked.

I grinned, picking up the flowers, card, and bag from the floor. I peeped in the bag to see a sequined clutch purse and a velvet box that looked like it contained a tennis bracelet. Typical gifts that my dad probably told him to get. That was the kind of thing my dad did. I opened the envelope, peeping the card and the fact that it was custom made. My eyes watered at the picture on the front of the card. It was a picture of me and my mom on Myrtle Beach. I loved that picture. We were so happy.

I opened the card and read Dinero's handwriting out loud. "'Your mother would be so proud of you tonight. You're beautiful. You're smart. You're fine, and you're mine. I know I don't say it enough, but you mean the world to me. Whether you win the crown tonight or not, you are already a queen. My queen.'" I cried out loud, barely able to get the last few words out.

"Aww." Dinero chuckled and walked back over to me. He finally wrapped his arms around me and kissed my neck.

I held his flowers, his present, and that card in my hands. "Thank you, boo," I cried.

"No time for tears. We gotta move out," Dinero whispered. "Good luck tonight."

I nodded, looking up into his face as he let go of me. "Good luck to you too, Dinero."

Chapter Two

Bostyn

"Don't you look handsome tonight." Our Colombian housekeeper, Donna, smiled in the doorway of my room the night of Meade Senior High's homecoming dance.

I grinned at Donna's reflection in the mirror as I buttoned my crisp, beige Burberry dress shirt. I wasn't really in the mood to go to a homecoming, especially since it wasn't my shit. I was homeschooled, for my safety, according to Pops. I was one of three children in the Reel household. It wasn't until I was about 13 years old that I learned that I was adopted. And that was only after my birth mother showed up at my front door and barely got the words out that she was my mother before she was shot in the head.

Donna walked up to me. "Your father is downstairs, honey, in his office."

I looked into Donna's face as she adjusted my tie. According to my birth mother, Donna was my aunt. My parents never answered my question about Donna being my aunt, and neither did she. After my parents explained that I was adopted, they left the subject alone and never brought it back up. They told me to appreciate the fact that I was brought up in a better life than I would have been if I were left with my birth parents. Though I really didn't see how.

After Donna fixed my tie and I grabbed my jacket, I headed out of my room, down the mansion halls, and down the spiral marble steps toward my father's office. As I made it to the office, one of the maids came out, giggling and pulling her dress down. She cleared her throat when she caught the frown on my face and scurried past me as I walked into the office.

My father stood at his liquor cabinet drinking Scotch from a glass before slamming it down on the counter. He flashed a mischievous grin before saying, "It's not what you think."

I shook my head, clicking my teeth. "It's always what I think, sir."

Pops shook his head. "You and this thuggish, bad-boy demeanor. No one would have ever thought I raised you in my image."

"Well, judging by shawty who just walked out of here with her dress stuck in her panties, looks like you're not too far from being a bad boy yourself," I growled. "Does Mom know the maid is dusting off more than she thinks? Where's ya wife, Pops?"

That stupid grin was wiped from his face real quick. "At one of her club meetings. Book club, cry on another bitch's shoulders club, old hag club, who knows, son?"

I frowned, watching him pour himself another glass. "What did you call me in here for, bruh?"

"I heard you were going to Meade's homecoming dance," Pops answered.

I nodded. "Yeah, Claudius wants me to roll with him. Not really feeling it. I'm just interested in the after-party."

Pops nodded, taking a sip from his class. "I'm interested in that party too. Your 'boy' is in."

I looked at him. "In what?"

Pops walked over to his desk and pulled out what looked like a wire device from his drawer. "The kinds of drugs these kids get a hold of during these parties needs to stop. At every major party this year, one of these kids has gotten in a car accident or ended up OD'ing on that shit."

"What shit?"

I inched closer to his desk and watched him pull out several little bags of assorted colored pills, crystals, and weed. Shit, some of that weed was pink as fuck. I picked up one of the bags of weed from the desk, popped open the bag, and took a whiff. When I tell you I felt like I was floating on cloud nine from just barely inhaling that shit, I ain't exaggerating.

"Goddamnnnn!" I laughed as my father snatched the bag away from me and resealed it.

Pops frowned. "I need to know where they get this shit from. Who's supplying this shit to these kids?"

I looked at him. "You really think I'm going to find out who supplies this shit just from a school dance? I might find out which kids are selling, but that doesn't mean I'm going to find out their distro, Pops."

"Make friends with these kids." Pops watched me as I clicked my teeth. He huffed as he handed me the wire. "Just take it."

I shook my head. "A white boy going to an after-party with a bunch of black kids? Yeah, wearing a wire is smart. They already think I'm five-o enough as it is. Every time I go anywhere with Claudius, they assume I'm a cop's son."

Pops smiled. "You are a cop's son."

I shook my head. "No, I'm not."

Pops's smile faded. He exhaled deeply. "While you're here, I might as well have this talk with you now."

"What talk?" I asked him.

"About Mandy," Pops answered.

Mandy Wineyard lived a few mansions down from us. We grew up together. Our mothers were best friends.

Our fathers were best friends. We went on family vacations together. We were both homeschooled, and our parents only wanted us to become friends with other children who were homeschooled, which was how I met Claudius, who was a little more rebellious than I was. He did what he wanted, and I soon became the same way. Once his aunt (who raised him) discovered how good he was at sports, she ended up putting him in public school. He started attending Bay City High freshman year. He made new friends and refused to leave me out. So, his homies became my homies, and, man, did we stay in trouble.

Mandy wasn't as good as her family thought she was either. She started hanging out with a few Catholic-school girls she'd met at the mall. Mandy and I weren't boyfriend and girlfriend, but every now and then we had sex. Great sex. Leg-jerkin', "eyes rolling to the back of my head," "dick throbbing when I had flashbacks" type of sex.

"What about Mandy?" I hesitated to ask.

"She's pregnant," Pops told me and watched me sit down in the leather chair in front of his desk.

I slouched back in the chair. "Nah, man. We use condoms every time!"

"Did you blow in the condom to check for holes like I told you?" Pops huffed, his peach skin flushing over a little.

I hesitated. "Nah."

"You know you can't trust these women. That girl loves you! She knows you're going to meet a lot of other girls when you go off to the police academy." Pops barely got the words out before I sat up in my chair, shaking my head.

"Police academy? Nah, we discussed—"

Pops shook his head. "We discussed that if you kept your grades up, I'd let you go to any college of your choice. I also told you that if you stayed out of trouble, I wouldn't press you about joining the military or the police force. Your grades aren't up to par, and you can't seem to keep your dick in your pants. You're going to the police academy after graduation. I don't want to hear shit else about this."

"This isn't in my plans, Pops," I hissed.

"Plans change. That's life. Mandy is just like the other girls around here. She sees a young white handsome man who could have any girl he wants, and she went for it. Her parents want you to marry her." Pops watched me stand from the chair.

I shook my head. "Hell nah, Pops! You gotta do something!"

Pops nodded. "I am. I'm paying for the honeymoon."

"Nah, homie. Fuck this shit. I don't even know who I am, and y'all muthafuckas are trying to marry me off to this bitch! What's my real last name? Who are my parents? Who am I?" I yelled.

Pops walked around the table and stood face-to-face, toe-to-toe with me. "You are a Reel. This is your fuckin' family, and don't you forget that shit. You need to forget about the past and appreciate where you are now. Look around you. You have everything a child could ever hope for. I didn't have any of this shit growing up! I worked my ass off to get my family to where we are today! I do whatever it takes, by any means necessary, to provide for my family, and you're about to do the same thing for Mandy and your child. And I don't want to hear shit else you have to say about it!" Pops shoved the wire into my chest. "Wear this shit tonight. Your other friends will have one on too. You like fitting in, don't you? Well, everyone is going to be wearing one of these, so fit in, Bostyn. Have a good night."

***

"Yo, Easy, the fuck is wrong with you?" Claudius scoffed as I slid into the back seat of his Hummer that night.

"Nothing." I closed the door behind me and slid into the back seat alongside my brothers, Jaxon and Roxyn. "The fuck are y'all doing in here?" I nodded at Keith, Claudius's homeboy who went to school at Fort Meade. "What up, Keith?"

"Pops said we needed to roll wit'cha, bruh." Jaxon imitated the way me and my homies talked.

I huffed, having no time to babysit them muthafuckas at Fort Meade High. My brothers were college freshmen, going to school at the University of Maryland College Park. They were preppy *Saved by the Bell* Zack-type muthafuckas. And to them I was a mix between Eminem and Mark Wahlberg with just a pinch of 50 Cent. They always told me that I was too black to be white.

I wasn't trying to be something that I wasn't. I was just being myself. I never fit in with them. It didn't take my real mother showing up on the front porch when I was 13 to let me know that I didn't belong. You should have seen the "one of these kids is not like the other" looks on our guests' faces whenever muthafuckas came to visit.

"I ain't about to be babysitting you muthafuckas tonight, man," I let them know.

"How the fuck are you babysitting us when we're older than you, son?" Roxyn clicked his perfect white teeth, mocking me.

I looked at him. "Keep ya distance. Stay the fuck away from me tonight. Grab you a girl—don't be in here on no R. Kelly shit—grab you a girl who's at least seventeen, dance with her, whatever, just stay the fuck away from me. Y'all gonna make shit obvious."

"Y'all dad came to you with that wire, huh?" Claudius laughed.

"I ain't wearing that shit," I hissed.

"Me either. My aunt thought I was gonna be in on that shit too. They have been trying to get a hold of the distro to this area for years. They better do their job and leave us out of that shit. Muthafuckas expect me to snitch. I'm the son of a fuckin' lawyer, and my aunt, who's a judge, is raising me." Claudius scoffed. "Niggas don't trust me as soon as I step in a building. The only people I want strip searching me are the girls at this after-party! Anyway, man, we won the homecoming game last night. I came here to stunt on muthafuckas. The team is meeting me at the dance. Yo, ain't we missing somebody? Where's ya girl, boss?"

As soon as he said that shit, my cell vibrated in my pocket. I huffed, already knowing that it was Mandy. She'd been trying to get a hold of me all day. I wasn't ready to talk to her, and I damn sure wasn't ready to be a father. All I wanted to do was get high and drink that night. I wanted to get away from my family, but there the two of them were, grinning ear to ear, knowing I knocked up Mandy, and they couldn't wait to tell Claudius.

"Oh, he's been avoiding baby mama all day." Jaxon's snitching ass started laughing.

Claudius looked at the glare on my face through his rearview mirror. "The fuck is he talking about? Mandy's pregnant?"

I didn't even want to talk about the shit. "Yeah."

"How far along is she?" Claudius asked.

"Muthafucka, I don't know, shit. She didn't even tell me that she was pregnant. Pops told me about the shit tonight. Talkin' about her parents want us to get married and shit after I graduate from the fuckin' police academy!" I told them. "I don't even know what I wanted to do with my life, but I knew I didn't plan to be a husband or father before I was twenty!"

"Man, our parents did that shit, so you gonna do it too, sad to say," Roxyn told me.

"They're not my parents, homie," I reminded him.

"They are your parents!" Jaxon was offended. "Stop saying that shit! Pops puts more effort into raising you than he's put into raising us! When we graduated Chesapeake, what did he get us? Furniture for our dorm room. When you graduate high school, guess what he's getting you? A fuckin' Jag! So what, he wants you to go to the police academy? That means he believes in you. He believes you can handle being out there in those streets. He has bodyguards following me and twin around everywhere we go, but not you. He knows you can handle yourself.

"I'm going to school to be a forensic scientist, and bro is going to school to be a lawyer, because he knows you'll probably need one of us when you become captain of his unit someday! He's retiring in a few years, and who do you think he wants to fill his shoes? Not one of us, but you! You, a person who doesn't even consider us family! You're ungrateful like a muthafucka, Bostyn! I love you, but I swear I fuckin' hate you! You think I wanted to come with y'all tonight?"

"Hell yeah," Roxyn interrupted. "Them bitches are hot as fuck. That's all you kept talking about was that Bay City and Meade Senior High had some of the hottest bitches around!"

Jaxon hit his twin in the shoulder. "Man, shut up. I'm trying to make a point!" Jaxon looked at me. "Just do what Pops says. He knows what's best. He wants y'all to tell him who's dealing these drugs tonight. Just keep an eye on who's doing what. Have fun. Take Mandy off your mind. Don't think about her tonight. Matter of fact, turn your phone off. If Pops wants to get in touch with you tonight, he'll call us."

I exhaled deeply and slouched back in the chair.

There were no words for the way those females looked that night in their homecoming dresses. Fine as fuck would be an understatement. Dresses so tight you're wondering how the fuck did they fit into that shit. I just stood outside next to Claudius's ride, watching them stroll in. Claudius's crew showed up dressed to stunt on muthafuckas in their Gucci and Armani attire.

Most of the dudes who Claudius went to school with were children of drug dealers, but they made chump change compared to the muthafuckas Pops was after. He wanted the muthafuckas on top. Bay City kids were flashier than Meade Senior High kids. They only came out to dances in their expensive attire but kept it simple out there on the streets. Their gang members didn't even wear gang colors anymore: they didn't wear any colors that represented any gang. But they had particular tattoos and rode in certain cars. They dated the baddest chicks who were often daughters or nieces of the drug distributors.

The kids of these heavy hitters went to public school, though they could afford to go to any private school in the area. Most of them even lived right there in the hood so you couldn't tell them apart from anyone else. Though I didn't claim to be a Reel, being in that family had taught me to pay close attention to detail.

"Y'all see this? Yeah, we won this shit!" Claudius's homeboy Texas held his team's trophy up to the sky, as we watched the girls walk up the red carpet leading to the front door of the Dancehall. "Come home with me tonight. I'll let you touch my trophy, too."

We laughed at his stupid ass while the girls walked by checking us out just as much as we were looking at them. Bay City athletes were hated on because they were the best at whatever they did. I wasn't allowed to play sports or do shit to bring too much attention to myself. Pops said it was to keep me safe because he helped to put a lot of criminals away and didn't want them to take their rage out on me. But I had a feeling it was more than that.

"Oooohh, shit, look at this one." Keith nudged Claudius as a group of girls in tight sequined dresses passed us by.

I made eye contact with one of them and stood up from leaning against the car. My eyes traced every inch of her curvaceous frame. She was a tall brown-skinned girl with the prettiest face I'd ever seen. Her body was shaped like a thick mannequin. You know the big-booty mannequins they put in the windows of stores to get everyone to notice the clothes? Yeah, that was her. She strutted her stuff down the carpet in her floor-length sequined dress, heels, and matching purse. Her long hair trailed down her back, grazing her skin. The backless dress revealed the tattoos that trickled across her back and up her arms. She was bad, and she knew it.

Claudius grunted. "Man, fuck her."

"Exactly. That's exactly what I wanna do," I mumbled.

Claudius shot me a quick glare before looking back at the girl and her friends as they entered the Dancehall. "That's Dinero's girl."

I looked at Claudius. "Dinero? Your brother?"

Claudius nodded.

Claudius didn't talk about his father much, but his father was a senator who liked to get around. Fucked around with all types of women in both high and low places. The senator didn't acknowledge either of his sons, but damn it if they weren't beefing like he was playing favorites. Dinero was big in the streets. He ran with CMC—the Clean Money Crew. Shit, it was no wonder his girl looked like a bag of money. He hustled so hard and had so much money circulating in his hood that there was no way the police could keep up with where he was getting his products from. Claudius hated that muthafucka, but he wasn't a snitch. Rich or hood, that wasn't who we were. Snitching was something that would get you killed. Pops knew that.

"Shawty is fine as fuck," I had to say out loud.

"Man, she's off-limits," Claudius warned me.

"Off-limits to yo' ass. He ain't my brother, shit. Fuck you talkin' about?" I reminded him.

Claudius shook his head. "You got a wife and a baby at home, nigga."

I looked at him, watching him and my brothers chuckling. "You trippin', man."

"Nah, you trippin'. Stay the fuck away from her, I'm telling you. We're here to show off our trophy, get a few dances in, then head to this after-party tonight. If she's here, her nigga isn't far behind. If he doesn't show up here, he'll be at the after-hours spot. It's a Rox kind of night. Muthafuckas are going to be celebrating our homecoming victory. That's why she's here. To distract us. Her crew is fine as hell. Stay focused. Stick with us. Don't go wandering the fuck off, Bostyn," Claudius told me.

Man, fuck him. As soon as we got in the spot, I went off on my own. I made my way around the ballroom where the dance was taking place, and pills were already in rotation. They already had the pills, it seemed. So, whoever dished them out gave them that shit before they got there. Girls were standing along the walls of the Dancehall, popping the pills and chasing them down with some dark liquid in these tiny bottles. Shawty in the sequined dress stood alongside the wall with her friends. She wasn't partaking in the drug activities, but she was keeping watch. As a matter of fact, she was watching me watch her.

"You obviously like what you see, but I'm telling you that nigga doesn't play about her," Claudius said over my shoulder.

"Man." I wasn't trying to hear him. "Ain't you supposed to be over there with ya crew eating? The cooks in the back prepared an entire feast for y'all thick-backed muthafuckas. Why you over here grillin' me, man? I'm just admiring the merchandise, shit."

Claudius laughed. "Whatever, man. I see that predatory look in your eyes. Little does she know, he's bangin' her friend over there." Claudius nodded toward the pregnant cutie alongside her.

I shook my head. "What would make him cheat on someone like her?"

"Because he can. Because she lets him. Who knows why females put up with our shit? Niggas cheat, that's what we do. Soon as you and Mandy get married, you'll be fuckin' around on her too. Watch." Claudius took a swig from the Mountain Dew twelve-ounce bottle that he held.

"Our parents are making us do this bullshit, man. I don't love her, and I doubt she loves me," I told Claudius.

Claudius disagreed. "That crazy muthafucka has always loved you, Bostyn."

"Man," I changed the subject, "you ready for that call? You already know Bay City is about to text you with the homecoming court pics."

Claudius watched me smirk.

"Yo, you see how fine Dinero's girl is?" Keith dug in. "You already know shawty is gonna win that crown!"

"I ain't dancin' with her." Claudius shook his head.

"I'll do it," I spoke up. "When we get those homecoming results and they call you out for that first dance, I'll step to her."

Everybody laughed out loud, clowning me as usual.

"Yo, Eminem," Claudius laughed, "she'll laugh ya ass off the dance floor."

"A'ight, Jody," I joked back. "We'll see. I got more sauce than you, homie. You already know I put it down on the dance floor."

Claudius's laughter subsided a little. "Seriously, leave her alone. Her nigga will show up just when they announce the winners and dare anyone to dance with her. He's expecting me to be here and take that chance. I'ma fall back, break the tradition. I'm just here to floss on 'em with this trophy."

"Well, I'ma floss on 'em with Dinero's." I nodded toward the beauty queen.

In a few minutes, the dance floor was filled with asses shaking and hips swinging. Cutie and her friends made their way to the dance floor, stealing the show in their flashy gowns and expensive shoes. She knew I was watching her, and the longer I watched her dance, the higher she lifted her dress, showing some skin.

Claudius wasn't lying. The closer it got to the time to announce the homecoming court, the more of who looked like members of the Royals and the CMC trickled into the club. They were dressed in all black, but you could tell by the purple accents in their clothes, jewelry, and shoes who they were affiliated with.

Keith nodded toward the door when Dinero made his entrance. Just in time for the school vice principal and SGA president to hit the stage.

Applause and squeals filled the room as Meade Senior High's homecoming court was announced. Dinero Rodriguez was announced as homecoming king. The crowd paused, waiting for them to announce the queen.

"And the crown for homecoming queen Class of 2013 goes to . . ." The vice principal smiled and clenched her teeth as she paused. "Meelah Summers!"

The crowd went wild as shawty made her way to the stage. She hiked up her dress a little as she moved. Traditionally, at a homecoming dance, the queen takes her place on the stage beside her king. It used to be that the king crowned his queen, but since athletics had become a show for the media, the battle between football teams clamoring for their territory called for drastic measures. The opposing team always showed up to the dance anyway, so schools around the state began to incorporate the opposing school into the tradition. The losing team's king crowned the winning team's king. And the winning team's king in turn crowned the losing team's queen.

I nudged Claudius, watching him watch Meelah make her way onto the stage, the train of her dress trailing behind her and glistening under the ballroom lights. She stood there, pretty as could be, glancing over at Dinero, who stood in the doorway waiting for shit to pop off.

The president of the SGA checked her cell phone, awaiting the text from the SGA president of Bay City high. She whispered in the vice principal's ear.

The vice principal smiled nervously before saying, "And the Bay City High homecoming king crown goes to Claudius Rodriguez!"

There were a few squeals from the ladies, but other than that, the crowd was quiet, awaiting Dinero's response. Dinero didn't bust a move, and neither did Claudius. Dinero looked at Claudius as if he dared his muthafuckin' ass to even attempt to make his way toward that stage. I couldn't believe my man was going to back down. Claudius never admitted it out loud, but he felt guilty that he was privileged. He wanted to know Dinero, though Dinero never wanted shit to do with him. I had to do something. Had to bring the two together. What better way than to start some shit?

"Man, fuck this shit," I said and stepped up from the wall.

My homeboys tried to grab me back to the wall, but I pulled away and made my way across the dance floor toward the stage.

I adjusted my jacket and straightened it out, feeling like the Man as I walked through the crowd.

"Who in the hell is white chocolate right here?" I heard one of Meelah's friends comment as I strolled over to the stage.

"Excuse me, young man, but—" The vice principal started to ask me what the hell I was doing.

I grabbed the mic from the vice principal, already having my lines rehearsed. "How is everybody doing tonight? My name is Easy."

I hated the fact that I had four names to write down on paper whenever I was asked to write my real name. Bostyn Emilio Zacharia Reel. After a while, I just started writing "Bostyn Easy Reel." It took some convincing, but my parents allowed me to legally change my name. "Easy" was the name I used when I went out with my boys. I never gave my real name because I didn't have time for muthafuckas sizing me up. "Easy" gave them something to laugh at but something to question at the same time. Made them curious as to who I was and what I wanted. I wanted the crowd to know that I wanted Meelah.

"Claudius looks like he'll stomp a muthafucka, but when face-to-face with his brutha, his own flesh and blood, neither of them busts a muthafuckin move," I pointed out. "Look at this fine woman standing beside me."

I turned to Meelah, watching her look me over the same way that I was looking her over. The SGA president scoffed as I snatched the crown from her hands. I placed the glistening crown on top of Meelah's head. Her eyes traced my lips. When I licked my lips, she kinda bit hers. I grinned before turning back to the audience.

"Easy, you are breaking a homecoming tradition," the stuck-up SGA president let me know.

"And so are them two clowns," I told her. "If they don't wanna dance with her, shit, I will. Y'all muthafuckas made shawty get dressed up for no reason. I'm not about to let all this fine go to waste. Ay, DJ, play this girl a love song." I grabbed shawty's hand and led her down the stage steps.

"Ay, Marky Mark," the girl called out to me as I pulled her along through the crowd and they parted the way for us. "You're crazy!" she squealed, following me to the dance floor. She was telling me how crazy I was, yet I didn't feel her pull away from me once. It was as if she wanted to see how crazy I really was. She was about to see, too.

A little while earlier, I heard one of her friends mention that "Please Excuse My Hands" by Plies featuring Jamie Foxx and The-Dream was one of her favorite songs. They mentioned the fact that she was hoping Dinero would show up so they could dance to the song. Apparently, it was the first song they slow danced to. I happened to slip the DJ $200, telling him to play that song for the king and queen dance. And that was what the fuck he did, too.

You should have seen Meelah's eyes as soon as the intro to the song came on and I turned to her, grabbing her by her waist and gripping it in my hands. Man, she smelled good as fuck. Her skin looked kissably soft. That ass and those hips in that dress made me wanna snatch that shit off right there on the floor, or better yet, just slide that shit up, hold her up against a wall, and fuck the sequins off that dress.

Meelah started to tell me how crazy I was, until I opened my mouth and started singing along with Jamie Foxx.

"Please excuse my hands. They just wanna touch. They just wanna feel. They don't mean no harm. Baby, just excuse my hands," I sang to her as I grinned.

Meelah hesitated a little, but she slid her arms over my shoulders, hands cupping my neck a little. She glanced at her girlfriends as they grabbed a dance partner and made their way onto the dance floor. Claudius's football team cheered me on, hyping me up like a muthafucka. Meanwhile, Dinero's crew stood alongside the wall, close to Dinero, watching him to see what his next move was about to be. He was pissed like a muthafucka. He didn't appreciate me dancing with his girl to "their" song.

"I have never seen you around here before," she told me, "but you look so familiar."

I shrugged as I swayed with her to the music. "I guess I have one of those faces."

Meelah shook her head. "Nah. I don't forget faces. Easy, that can't be your real name. What's your real name?"

"Eric Wright," I joked. "Why do you think they call me 'Easy'?"

Meelah pursed her lips. "Really?"

I shook my head. "Nah."

"You look like a Mark or a Justin. Maybe a Robin." Meelah grinned.

"So, you got jokes?" I asked her.

"You're one to talk, Easy." Meelah rolled her eyes. "Playing my and my boyfriend's song. I know that was your idea. My girl Sharita said you walked by them when they were talking about it. Why would you do this? Dinero and all his niggas have Glock 45s on 'em, and they will blow your head off right here in front of everyone."

I shook my head off. "Nah, he would've done that shit by now. I think he'd rather you dance with me than his brother, Claudius, over there. Who was too scared to take the risk. Punk ass."

"You weren't scared?" Meelah asked.

"I'm holding you close right now, ain't I? I know you feel my dick digging into your belly button," I whispered in her ear.

Shawty giggled. "You be tearing pussy up with that thang, huh?"

"Damn right. If ya man ain't careful, I'ma be tearing yours up pretty soon. You're fine as fuck, shawty," I told her.

"And you're white as fuck, Easy," she told me with the quickness. "And dead as fuck if you think for a second Dinero isn't going to make his way over to us as soon as this song is over. I hope you got ya strap on you."

"That's what you feel diggin' into your belly button," I told her. "My nine goes 'pow' too, shit."

I watched her eyes search my face a little before she rolled her eyes and grinned. Her eyes widened a little as my hands slid down a little farther, inching their way toward her ass cheeks. I just wanted to get a little feel, but she quickly placed her hands over mine.

She shook her head, looking over my shoulder, just before I felt someone shove me in it. Meelah looked back in my face before I turned around and saw Mandy standing there with her arms folded.

Mandy was dressed in Old Navy sweats, a T-shirt, a hoodie, and gray Adidas. "What the hell? I've been calling you all night!" She watched me let go of Meelah. After she glared at Meelah, she looked back at me. "You didn't receive any of my calls?"

"Yeah, I did," I told her.

"And?" she asked.

"And I'm here with my crew. You shouldn't even be here," I said. "Get the hell on, Mandy."

"Oh, it's like that? Who the fuck is this?" Mandy asked, stepping in front of me and facing Meelah.

Mandy was about five feet tall, looking up at Meelah, who had to be about five seven. "Bitch, are you fuckin' my man?"

Meelah laughed. "Easy, you better get ya girl. She doesn't know who she's talkin' to. Malibu Barbie will get her ass stomped into the ground."

Meelah barely got her words out when at least six girls made their way over to us, ready to back her up.

"And you must not know who my man is. He—"

I grabbed Mandy away before she blew every fuckin' thing. I had to pick shawty up and throw her over my shoulder, kicking, screaming, acting a fucking fool as usual. I couldn't say Mandy couldn't fight, but she was definitely about to get her ass beat. Meelah's girls were probably strapped. Mandy's ass wasn't strapped with shit but a mouth that ran entirely too much.

"Mandy, what the fuck, yo?" I put Mandy's ass down as soon as we got outside the Dancehall. She was always causing a scene. Couldn't take her ass nowhere.

Mandy shoved me in my chest, her blond hair blowing in the wind behind her. "Why haven't you answered any of my calls?" she yelled at me, then took something out of her sweatpants pocket and threw it at me.

I looked down at the ground and saw that she'd thrown a Clearblue pregnancy test applicator at me. I exhaled deeply as I looked back at her.

Mandy's bright blue eyes sparkled as she frowned at me. "I'm pregnant, Bostyn!"

I nodded. "Yeah, Pops told me. He also said that your parents wanted me to marry you."

Mandy looked up at me, her frown softening a little. "What do you have to say about that? Do you want to marry me?"

I didn't even hesitate. "Nah, not really."

Mandy punched me in my chest before turning around to walk away.

I grabbed her back to me. "Mandy, come on now, be realistic. We're seventeen! The fuck do we look like getting married this young, man?" I grabbed her arm and pulled her along with me as we walked toward her blue BMW parked on the other end of the parking lot.

"Like we're handling our responsibility like fuckin' young adults!" Mandy screamed, pulling away from me.

I shook my head. "The adult decision would be to coparent. I'm not running from responsibility, but at the same time I'm not ready to be a father."

Mandy yanked my arm as we stepped in the middle of the parking lot. She faced me as she folded her arms. "So, what you're saying is when you took your dick out of my pussy and I told you to put it in my mouth, I guess you're saying I should have swallowed your kids instead of jumping back on the dick, huh?"

I shrugged. "Well—"

Mandy punched me in the chest again.

"A'ight, shawty, put your hands on me one more time," I warned her.

"If you don't marry me, I'll tell my parents that you raped me!" Mandy threatened.

I looked at the bitch like she had lost her mind. "What? Man, ain't nobody going to believe that shit. We both know that shit didn't go down like that."

"I will tell my mother that I wasn't ready to have sex and that you forced me. That you raped me in front of your friends when I was drunk," Mandy went on to say.

"You wouldn't do that shit, Mandy," I told her.

Mandy looked at me, blue eyes searching my face. "Who the fuck is that bitch you were dancing with?"

"I don't know. Pops wanted me to come here, blend in, and find out what's going on in this community. That's all this is. You know he's always having us do his undercover work. I'm not trying to have muthafuckas knowing my name and shit, and then here you come about to blow the whole thing. How the fuck do I even know this baby is mine? Every time me and you had sex, we used condoms!" I told her.

Mandy nodded. "And every time we had sex, I saved them."

I just looked at her. It took everything in me not to wring her fuckin' neck. Man, never trust a bitch who takes actual notes while watching *Law & Order: Special Victims Unit*.

"Mandy, we have been friends since we were fuckin' babies! Why the fuck would you do some shit like this to me?" I asked her.

Mandy laughed in disbelief. "What? How could you make love to me all those times, but when I told you how I felt about you, you didn't say shit? You don't fuck a girl the way that you fucked me, then turn around and tell me that it was only sex! It didn't feel like only sex! We had sex so loud and good that even the neighbors smoked a blunt after they heard us fuckin'! You had my legs above my head, my ass up, pounding the shit out of me! You fucked the soul out of me every time we had sex, then have the nerve to say that it was just sex, nothing else!" Mandy shoved me, not giving a fuck about the people who passed us as they left the Dancehall probably on their way to the after-party.

"You weren't the only girl I was fuckin', just like I wasn't the only dude you were fuckin', Mandy, let's just be clear about that," I told her. "You knew what it was when you signed up!"

"You knew what the fuck it was from jump too, Bostyn!" Mandy pushed me.

And I pushed her back into the trunk of the car behind her.

Mandy's eyes widened when I got in her face. She was scared, but she was still talking shit. "I only fucked them other dudes because I knew you were fuckin' other bitches! If you had told me that I was the only one you wanted, I would've chosen you and only you! And you know it, too!"

"Go the fuck home, Mandy." I gritted my teeth.

"Go get that ring, Bostyn. I swear I'll act surprised." Mandy gritted hers back.

I shook my head at her. "This is fucked up, Mandy."

"This will teach you that you can't play with every bitch, because every bitch ain't playin'." Mandy pushed me out of the way as she walked to her car.

I stood there, hands in my pockets, watching her.

"Man, what the fuck was that all about?" I heard Claudius's voice over my shoulder.

I exhaled deeply, not really feeling like hearing his shit. I turned around to see Claudius and his homies from the football team approaching me.

"Man, you already know Mandy be with that bullshit," I reminded him.

Claudius frowned and stepped up to me. "Nah, I'm talking about that shit that you pulled in the Dancehall."

I grinned. "Oh, you mean having the balls to step to Dinero's girl? I thought you said ya dick was bigger than mine, muthafucka. Well, I can't tell."

Claudius's homies laughed until they peeped the pissed-off expression on his face.

"Ya brothers think you're crazy. Do you have any idea who Dinero works for? Because even ya brothers do!" Claudius snarled at me. "That nigga could unload his clip on ya ass in front of everyone, and no one—not even the fuckin' police—would move because of who he works for!

Shit, rumor has it that half the niggas on your father's unit used to work for the same nigga Dinero works for!"

I wasn't backing down. "Pops sent me down here to figure out who's distributing the Rox. The only way we're going to find out who's supplying that shit seems to be through ya brutha."

"We need an invite to get up in that after-party tonight, bruh," Keith let us know.

Claudius glared into my face, about to say something when we were interrupted.

"Yo, Easy!" a female voice with a strong Spanish accent called out to our left as several footsteps approached.

We looked up to see Meelah's group of girls approaching us.

"Aww, shit. All this ass stampeding toward us," Keith muttered as the girls walked up to us.

"Ladies." I nodded, looking the Spanish chick over as she stood before me.

"Fellas." The Spanish chick looked me over before looking back at my friends. "Y'all lookin' fine in y'all suits and shit," she told us before looking back at me and opening my jacket a little so she could check out the shirt that I was wearing. "Nice patch work. You got a little swag, *chico blanco*. I'm Sharita."

I nodded. "What's up wit'cha, Sharita?"

Sharita looked my face over a little. "You have a lot of nerve stepping to Dinero's girl like that. He doesn't play when it comes to her."

"And I promise I won't either," I told her.

Sharita laughed a little. "*Ella no lo admitirá pero le gustas. A ella le gustas mucho, chico blanco.* (She won't admit it, but she likes you. She likes you a lot, white boy.)"

I just looked at her, wondering why the fuck she looked so familiar to me. "I don't speak Spanish, *mami*," I told her.

"You got too much flavor to just be white, honey." Sharita smirked. "You need to shake your family tree a little. You never know what might fall out of it." Sharita shoved a yellow envelope it into my chest before she walked past me.

I looked at the envelope, then looked at her girls as they followed her. "What's this?" I called out to Sharita.

"An invitation. Party starts in an hour. Bring ya friends." Sharita looked back at me over her shoulder and winked before walking away toward a Hummer that pulled into the parking lot.

The team surrounded me, peeping over my shoulder at the envelope as I tore it open. It was an invitation to the homecoming after-party. I grinned back at Claudius as he huffed over my shoulders.

"We're in that muthafucka, homie," I told him as I watched him shake his head at me. As you can see, I was the risk taker of the crew.

Hey, we got a good thing
Don't know if I'ma see you again
But is that a good thing?
'Cause, girl, I can't be your man, no ma'am

J. Cole's lyrics burst through the sound system in the basement of a muthafucka named Dash's condo. Seemed like everyone who stayed in Meade Village Apartments (which were located right behind the condos) were at the spot. Nothing but ballers were in the spot, and their girls accompanied them.

Claudius was heated with me for putting him on the spot in front of his brother, so he didn't come with me. His crew did, though. They weren't letting all that ass go to waste. I needed to clear my head, get Mandy off my mind. She was crazy as a muthafucka, she'd always been, but I never thought she'd do me dirty. Who the fuck saves sperm? Where the fuck did her nasty ass keep it? My family would rather believe I'd forced her to have sex with me than to believe the bitch set me up. So, there was really no point in talking to my family about it.

Meelah was in the basement, dressed in tight, ripped jeans and a tight pink T-shirt that cupped her breasts just right. She may have changed her clothes, but she kept that homecoming crown on top of her head. She chilled by her friends, peeping me looking at her. I looked at her every now and then, at the same time peeping just about everyone around me getting high as fuck. Blunts were passed. Sweet Tea was poured. Powder lines were on tables. And I saw a few girls popping Rox. I didn't plan to report back to my pops.

Claudius wasn't slick. He left the scene so he wouldn't be obvious. He looked up to my father. If his football career fell through, his ass was going to have a seat right next to me at the police academy. I wasn't telling on shit. I was just making sure the football crew didn't participate in the festivities. Their coach was no joke. That muthafucka was sure to drug test their asses the following Monday when they went back to school. It was funny because I felt right at home with those teens: the children of some of the heaviest drug dealers on the East Coast.

I chilled to myself in the cut, watching from the corner of the basement. That was until the fourth Heineken got to me, and I had to pee. Meelah watched as I made my way out of the basement chilling area and down the hallway toward the bathroom. The door to the bathroom was cracked open a little. I could hear cheeks clapping, groaning, and moaning and shit from the hallway. The muthafuckas who lined the hallway were too fucked up to even notice.

"Yo, I gotta pee like a muthafucka, shit." I tapped on the door.

After a few seconds, Dinero's head popped through the doorway. Homie closed the door behind him before I could get a chance to look over his shoulder to see who shawty was in the bathroom with him. It definitely wasn't Meelah, because she was chilling in the basement with her friends.

Dinero swiped his nose, trying to play off the fact that he was nervous. "There's like four bathrooms in this bitch. You couldn't have taken your ass to one of them?" he questioned.

I scoffed. "There's four bathrooms in this bitch. You couldn't have taken shawty to one of them? Especially since ya girl is just down the hall, muthafucka?"

Dinero stood a few inches taller than me, looking down into my face like I was supposed to be scared of him. All I saw when I saw him was Claudius with a fucked-up attitude. "The only reason I haven't put a hole in the middle of your head is because Sharita told me to keep my bullets to myself."

I frowned. "Sharita?"

"Shawty says you're her family, which is why you got an invite, homie. Keep your muthafuckin' hands to yourself and off my girl," Dinero called himself warning me.

I laughed a little. "The one in the bathroom or the one in the basement?"

It didn't take dude two seconds to draw his gun on me and point it right at my temple. "I didn't hear you, nigga. What the fuck was that you said?"

"I said, which girl were you talking about? Shawty in the basement or shawty in the bathroom?" I repeated, feeling him digging the gun farther into my face.

Sharita came around the corner just when Dinero had his finger over the trigger.

"Ay, amigo, what the fuck? I told you to play nice." Sharita walked up to Dinero. "I don't think my mom would appreciate you putting bullet holes in her favorite nephew," Sharita told Dinero, her eyes wide as saucers. She looked at Dinero, watching the anger in his eyes. "Put it down, Dinero, please."

Just then, old pregnant girl stumbled out of the bathroom. She was high as fuck, giggling as she fell up against Dinero, her panties still around her ankles.

"Whitley!" Sharita gasped, trying to catch her friend as Dinero tucked his gun back in his pants. The nigga was still glaring at me as Sharita tried to help her friend pull up her panties.

Whitley was knocked out cold. She was supposed to be Dash's girl from what I heard, and there she was, fuckin' another nigga in her nigga's crib. Sharita yelled for someone to go get Dash. He was smoking in his two-car garage with his crew, having no idea of what was going on with his girl and his man. It didn't take long for Meelah and her girls to rush to Whitley's rescue. And moments later, Dash came rushing in.

"What happened?" Meelah got down on the floor in the hallway, hovering over her friend, smacking her in the cheeks a little to wake her up. Meelah glanced at me before looking up at Dinero and Sharita for answers.

Sharita glanced at me before looking at Meelah. "Girl, she just came stumbling out of the bathroom. She must've taken something! What has she been drinking? Someone come bring me her cup that is sitting on that coffee table. Tajha, go dig in old girl's purse, too!"

"We have to call 911!" Meelah squealed, putting Whitley's head in her lap.

"Nah, bruh. Moms is out of town. She doesn't know I'm throwing this shit, man!" Dash disagreed. "We over here getting high, fucked up, and shit! We're all going to jail, even if we flush our shit."

"Which one you gonna worry about, nigga—your girl or going to jail?" Meelah questioned him.

Dash frowned at Meelah as everyone in the basement flooded the hallway to see what was going on with Whitley. Dash looked around at everyone with cell phones in their hands, ready to call for help if they had to. Dash shook his head. "She's all right. Just fucked up."

"She shouldn't be 'fucked up,' muthafucka!" Sharita squealed. "She's pregnant!" Sharita looked up at Tajha as she rushed back over to us with the cup that Whitley had earlier and a handful of pill bottles. "What is that?" Sharita asked.

Tajha sniffed the cup, cringing. "Smells like Sweet Tea and vodka, maybe cough syrup, too. Then she's got oxycodone, Rox, and misoprostol pills."

Meelah and her friends gasped.

"The fuck? Misoprostol? I learned about that in health class." Sharita snapped her fingers, trying to remember what the pills were for.

"They help induce an abortion," I spoke up.

Everyone looked at me, then back at Whitley as she lay nearly lifeless on the floor.

"We have to get her to the hospital!" Meelah exclaimed, looking at both Dinero and Dash for help. "Y'all are worried about the police running up in here when you need to be worried about Whitley! Someone please take her!"

"My ride is outside," I responded. "Well, it's my homie Ace's ride, but homeboy has been drinking too much to drive. He gave me his keys. Y'all can put ol' girl in the back seat. I'll take her."

Dinero looked at me, his temples twitching.

"Dash, help put her in the car!" Sharita cried out.

Dash finally decided to scoop his girl off the floor. He carried her outside, down the hallway, and through the back door of the basement. Meelah was crying over her friend, having no idea that her nigga was just fuckin' the shit out of her in the bathroom.

I jumped in the front seat of Ace's Chevy Malibu. Sharita and Tajha slid into the back seat, holding their friend in their arms to comfort her as she seemed to slip further and further away. And Meelah jumped into the passenger seat next to me, tears sliding down her face. I didn't think we even made it a mile down the street when Sharita hollered that old girl's water broke. Ace was going to curse me out about his custom seats.

Chapter Three

Meelah

"Why would she do this to herself?" I sat in the waiting room, leg shaking anxiously.

We had been waiting in the maternity ward waiting room for hours. Once Whitley's family made it to the hospital, they kicked me and my homegirls out. We weren't giving them the answers that they needed, so they were going to rely on the hospital drug-testing technology for answers.

"Ain't no telling." Sharita glanced at Easy as he slouched back in his seat sipping on a cold Gatorade. His boys had been blowing his cell up trying to see what was going on and what the damage was to the back seat of his homeboy's car.

What kind of name was Easy for a boy who looked like he came straight out of *GQ* magazine? I wasn't even into white chocolate like that, but damn it if he didn't look good enough to eat. He looked like he was something else besides white, like he was of Latin descent. He was more than eye candy. That muthafucka was straight-up soul food. He was cocky as a fuck and had every right to be. I couldn't get the way he held me on that dance floor out of my head. I knew he was trouble from the moment I spotted him in that parking lot outside of the Dancehall.

I was shocked that Dinero would even let me anywhere near him, but my homegirl, Sharita, played it cool when she told Dinero that Easy was her family. Made up a whole backstory on the nigga, telling Dinero that Easy was her cousin. That her mother, Jimena Gonzalez, was his aunt, and she hadn't seen her cousin in years. That his mother was killed by a man hired by the police when he was about 13 years old. Her fabricated story seemed so authentic that even I believed the lie a little.

"When they find those drugs in her system, we're fucked!" Sharita muttered. "She had no business taking that shit. We were supposed to be getting rid of that shit, not getting high off our own supply! Any of you other bitches high off that shit?"

"Hell nah," Tajha scoffed. "I sold out of the Rox that I had. I made about 3 Gs tonight. Just enough to pay Mom's rent, her car note, and my sister's daycare bill. Not to mention the new Giuseppes I saw online."

"Them Giuseppes are gonna look real good with that orange jumpsuit." I rolled my eyes. "Y'all are worried about the wrong shit. I keep trying to tell y'all. Your mama needs to get off her ass and pay her own bills. The only income in y'all house is your little sister's SSI check. Yet y'all all have iPhones. Y'all got a Benz and a Lexus parked out front. You just bought your mom a new wardrobe, a bedroom set, a stand-up washer and dryer, a living room set, and a fuckin' purebred huskie! Could you make it any more obvious that you're in the game, Tajha?"

Tajha rolled her eyes over from Sharita to me. "Look, Princess of the Hood, we don't all have it like you. My daddy ain't running shit. Hell, I don't even know who the muthafucka is! I take care of my family the best that I know how! I'ma fuckin' ball 'til the day I fall, okay, bitch?"

"We're all gonna fall if your ass has anything to do with it!" I told her. "Lie low. Be inconspicuous! Save your money for college! Find a legit way to launder this money we're making! Daddy has all kinds of businesses to mask what's really going on! You can do hair. Start a hair business when we graduate. Sell bundles to these bald hoes who are running around instead of doing bald ho shit like flossing money that you're not supposed to have! Wait 'til tax season to splurge, bitch. Not now in the midst of all of these police raids!"

"Is there a reason why you're talking about all of this shit in front of Marky Mark over there?" Tajha shook her head at me and glanced over at Easy.

"He's harmless." Sharita rolled her eyes.

Tajha shook her head. "Nah. I don't trust him. He could be the Feds." She watched him as he spoke on the phone to someone. Tajha looked back at me. "He looks like a cop's child."

"No, he's not," Sharita spoke up quickly.

Tajha and I looked at Sharita.

Sharita hesitated. "I mean, you know, according to the story that I told Dinero. That's my cousin. He's one of us. Easy seems cool, that's all I'm saying. He didn't have to bring us to the hospital. You saw how his girl was clowning at the Dancehall. He could be somewhere snuggled up with old girl, *mami,* yet he's here with you."

I rolled my eyes at Sharita. "Bitch, he's here with Whitley."

Sharita shook her head. "He's here with your friend. Your friend who I never trusted. I don't trust none of these hoes you kick it with." Sharita rolled her eyes at Tajha as hard as she could. "Y'all hate too hard for me. Meelah is over here telling you how to conduct business, and instead of listening to her, you're throwing shade."

"Trick, you have it just as easy as she does. You don't even live out here in Anne Arundel County. You live way out there in Howard County, living in luxury. You're using Meelah's address so you can go to school with us peasants." Tajha sneered. "Y'all are faking a life so that no one knows how y'all really live. Both of your fathers have these fuckin' cops on payroll. If your family ever goes down, they'll be out in the streets in no time while we all get Fed time if we don't so-called snitch on muthafuckas they already know about." Tajha stopped talking when she saw Easy get up from his seat and make his way over to us.

I looked up at Easy as he sat down on the chair in the row across from me. He rested his elbows on his thighs, tatted hands intertwined. "That was my homeboy Ace. He said the police were over at the crib. Said the neighbors called the cops."

"And?" Sharita asked, her hazel eyes widening.

"Said they found some bags of Rox in the sewage drain alongside where Dinero had his car parked. They took him in for questioning." Easy looked at me for a reaction.

I ran my fingers through my hair. "Fuck."

"And what about Dash?" Sharita hesitated to ask.

"They got him too." Easy sounded as if he hated to tell us that. "And about three of Dash's crew members."

"We're all going down if they question Terk. That nigga is going to tell it all. Y'all know this is his third strike. They just killed his brother in his cell a few months ago," Tajha reminded us.

Sharita looked at Easy as if she wanted to ask him something but was afraid to in front of me. "What happened in that bathroom?" she asked anyway.

I looked at her. "What do you mean?"

"I caught Easy and Dinero exchanging words in the hallway in front of the bathroom in Dash's basement just a few seconds before Whitley stumbled out, panties around her ankles," Sharita admitted.

"What?" I looked at the "I don't know shit, I ain't seen shit" look on Easy's face. "What is she talking about?"

Easy leaned back in his chair, slouching, separating his legs at the knees. "I don't know what shawty's talking about."

Sharita pursed her lips at Easy. "Ummm-hmmm, Easy. Lie for the nigga."

Easy scoffed. "You think it's him I'm lying for? Why would I lie for a nigga who wouldn't even break tradition and dance with his own girl? I wasn't about to let all that ass go to waste. If he didn't wanna hold it, I sure as hell was."

Tajha let out a hateful smirk.

Sharita rolled her eyes playfully.

I couldn't help but gaze at his bold ass a little before Whitley's mother made her way into the waiting room.

We all stood from our seats, anxiously waiting for what Miss Glenda was about to say.

Glenda shook her head, letting out a long painful sigh. "She had the baby."

"And?" Sharita hated to ask.

Glenda shook her head. "The doctor said the baby had been gone for days. That she'd been taking medication to kill the baby for at least a week."

My heart sank in my chest as I fell back down in the seat behind me. "Why? Why would she do such a thing? We just gave her a baby shower! She seemed so happy!"

Glenda dried the tears that ran down her chestnut cheeks. "I don't know. She's stable. She said she wanted to talk to you, Meelah. Just you."

I looked at Sharita and Tajha, who nodded for me to go on without them. And I looked back at Easy as Miss Glenda pulled me away to go talk to her daughter.

Whitley sat up in the bed, her cheeks stained with tears. She dried her cheeks with her fingertips as she caught sight of me walking into the room.

"Ma, I need to talk to Meelah alone," Whitley spoke out as soon as Miss Glenda stepped into the room.

Miss Glenda was reluctant to leave the room, but she left me alone with her daughter.

"You must think I'm weak, huh?" Whitley laughed a little, crying at the same time.

I shook my head and sat in the chair next to her bed. "No, boo, not really. I just don't understand why you'd do something like this. Why would you kill your baby?"

Whitley's eyes overflowed with tears, her plump lips trembling. She looked at me and quickly dried her face. "I'm your sister, and you never acknowledge that."

I looked at her, sitting up straight in the chair, wondering how the subject switched from her killing her own blood to me. "The only reason why you're not going down for killing your own baby is because of that gray area between the rights of a fetus and the pro-choice laws that exist in this country. You just took drugs that could have killed both of you! And you're sitting here about to go in on me like you always do about what my father chose to do with every woman who caught his eye! This is so typical of you!"

Whitley shook her head at me. "Our father won't even look at me when he comes into the room. He's never called me his daughter. He's never so much as said hello to me, yet he speaks to Dash on a daily basis. He's all about money and nothing about family! Your own mother died, and he didn't even shed a tear!"

My nostrils began to flare. "We're not about to go here today, Whitley."

"Look at you, sitting there with your diamonds and pearls. Your expensive shoes. Your expensive jeans. Your nine-hundred-and-fifty-dollar jacket. Your silk press, your facial, your Mac lipstick." Whitley sneered. "Everything on your body was given to you because your father loves you, because that nigga he hired is in love with you. Dinero doesn't show it often, but he loves him some you."

I exhaled deeply and let the girl vent. She was feeling some type of way about what she did, and she was deflecting her feelings toward everything she saw as unfair about my life.

"I see the way he looks at you like you're the finest thing he's ever seen. He plays hard, but you're the girl he wants to give his last name to. I know because he had me and Sharita go pick out a ring." Whitley glared at me and watched my eyes widen a little.

"W . . . what?" I hesitated.

"He was planning to propose to you on New Year's, your birthday." Whitley rolled her eyes a little.

"You don't seem happy for me," was all I could think of to say to something like that. I didn't think Dinero even considered me his girlfriend, let alone someone he wanted to spend the rest of his life with.

"Why should I be?" Whitley scoffed. "Your father has houses in your name up and down the coast! He's planning this huge birthday party for you on New Year's. I heard he's getting your ass a Porsche and a Jag. And what do I get? A nigga who didn't even care enough to bring me to the hospital because he planned to meet his side chick! If he didn't get arrested tonight, that's where he would have been! I could have been in a coma! I just delivered a dead baby, a baby I didn't want to kill!"

"Then why did you?" I had to ask.

Whitley barely let me get the question out. "Because he didn't want me to have it!"

I looked at her, glaring at her in confusion. "Dash didn't want you to have his baby?"

Whitley laughed a little. "No, dummy. Dinero didn't want me to have his baby."

I just looked at her in shock, not really sure how to react, so I didn't.

Whitley's big brown eyes searched my face for a reaction. When she saw that I was in shock, and didn't know what to say, she kept digging to get the reaction that she wanted. "We have been fuckin' off and on since the tenth grade. Whenever you pissed him off, he was at my door. It was nothing but sex. We were on a 'fuck me, nigga, then leave' thing. He didn't love me, didn't give a fuck about me. He just had a hard time admitting that he was in love with you. He didn't want to be in love with you, but who wouldn't love a dope princess? You're every thug's dream. Beautiful, talented, rich, smart, and would fuck a bitch up over her nigga. So what are you waiting for, trick? Hit me."

I gripped the edge of my seat. I knew she hated me. Shit, everyone but Sharita hated me. They hung around me so they could copy my every move or meet the niggas in my nigga's circle. But Whitley was my flesh and blood. Different mothers, but the same father. My father wasn't the most loving father, but he kept me close because I was all he had left of my mother, a woman down to ride with him through whatever.

I felt for Whitley. I was there for her when her mother's boyfriends would abuse her mentally, physically, and sexually. She lived with me for months at a time, and she was right, my father didn't acknowledge her nor care to get to know her. And there she was, high off drugs that reigned in his kingdom. Once the complete tox screen came back, and the complete concoction of drugs she'd taken was revealed, shit was about to get real. Every bone in my body let me know that she was going to give us up. She had nothing to lose.

I was more worried about my father than Dinero's infidelity. Even though my father had most of the criminal justice system working for him, when it all came down to it, they were still cops, politicians, lawyers, and judges. And the law was on their side, meaning they could flip the script whenever they wanted. My father told me not to trust the people closest to me, and I wasn't surprised that Whitley would cross that boundary.

I stood from the chair. "I'm not even mad at you. I'm not even mad at Dinero. As a matter of fact, I'm not even going to confront him about it. Thanks for telling me, though. I appreciate it. I'm just going to let the nigga continue to cheat in peace, like he's been doing. When he proposes to me with that big-ass ring that I'm sure he had y'all pick out for me, I'm going to act surprised. I'ma have every last one of you bitches watch me strut my fine ass down that aisle. As a matter of fact"—I laughed a little—"consider this your invite to be my maid of honor. That is, if the state doesn't find a way to press charges on you for killing your baby. That was a dumb move. If it were me, I would have kept his baby and used it to blackmail his ass. Whenever he started acting funny, I would have threatened to tell his girl. But nah, you were so hung up on hurting me that you only hurt yourself. Dumb ass. I ain't about to beef with you over a nigga. These niggas ain't loyal. He was fuckin' you and had you picking out my ring. Yo' mama raised a dumb-ass bitch. I'ma let you rot in hell because that's exactly what your life is about to be."

I couldn't get out of that room fast enough. I didn't want that bitch to see me crying over her or Dinero. I didn't want her to know how bad I was hurting. Sure, I wanted to choke the shit out of her, but I didn't. I told her how I felt, then got the fuck out of her room. She was going to hurt herself. I was the wrong friend to lose, especially when her way of life depended on her connection to me. But what I told her was real. I wasn't going to tell Dash the baby was Dinero's. I wasn't even going to tell Dinero that I knew about the baby. I was going to go about shit as normal, act like I didn't know.

Dinero was a huge part of my father's operation when it came to the youth of the community. Dash was Dinero's main distributor. His crew was ruthless. They demanded respect, posting up in every neighborhood on every block. Claudius didn't know his mother and the aunt who raised him were dirty. That they kept the drug flow within the community going right along with us. They helped to arrest the ones who weren't within The Chain (what my father called his operation). We didn't trust the so-called justice system either, but for the time being, everything was running smoothly. As long as Dash and Whitely kept their mouths shut when it came to the cops who actually did their job, then The Chain would remain unbroken. So, I remained as calm as I could. For the time being, anyway.

"Boo, what happened? What did she say? Hold up!" Sharita grabbed me as soon as I tried to walk past the waiting room like my friends weren't sitting there waiting for me.

I exhaled deeply, peeping over at Easy and watching him sit up in his seat. I looked at Sharita. I looked around the room for Tajha. "Where's Tay?" I asked.

"Her mom is downstairs to pick us up. Her mama is paranoid about them picking up Dash. She's here to take us home." Sharita handed me my cell. "I think ya dad's been calling you, boo. There's a hell of a lot of calls from an 'unknown' caller. I think your father's driver is pulled up outside for you, too, boo. But what's the word? *Que pasa?* What happened?"

I shook my head. "Her stupid ass just didn't want the baby. She could have aborted the baby the right way from the beginning, before the baby had a heartbeat. Before the baby had a face. And damn sure before I spent ten grand on her baby shower! That muthafucka was lit like a wedding!"

Sharita nodded. "I told y'all we should have had that shit at CeCe's Pizza and called it a day, but nah, y'all wanted to rent out the convention center at the Marriott and lace that baby with Gucci, Fendi, and Prada. It's a goddamn baby. All babies want is *Paw Patrol* shit! Correction: *was* a baby. She's a fuckin' fool. Anyway, fuck her. You need to get downstairs before your father's niggas come up here looking for you."

I looked at Easy as he stood from his chair. "I'll go downstairs in a minute. Go ahead, boo. Tell the driver I'm coming, okay?"

Sharita hugged me tight. "Everything will be okay, boo," she told me as if she knew I was hurting inside. "Take ya time. I'll stall them."

I nodded as Sharita let me go. I watched her leave the waiting room as Easy approached me. I pushed my hair from my face and looked up into his. Them damn bright hazel-green eyes had me dazed from the moment I looked into his face earlier that night.

"You good, babe?" he asked me.

I shook my head. "No. It's been a long night. But I'm not even ready to go home. Can I roll with you?"

Easy looked at me, stunned a little that I wanted to kick it with him. "Word? Where you wanna go? I gotta bring my boy his car back though in a few."

"Can we just go to a park or something? We can get some coffee and just talk. I don't want to go home right now," I told him.

He nodded. "A'ight. Let's roll."

Easy took me to No Doze, this twenty-four-hour coffee spot in Pasadena. It had to be around 2:00 in the morning and I was wide awake. My father was blowing up my phone to make sure that I was okay. Sharita told me that they'd let Dash and Dinero go. Dinero claimed to have gotten the drugs from some "white boy" who showed up with his crew from Bay City. He gave Easy's description to the police, according to Sharita, who got her information from her mother.

After I told Easy, he was unbothered. We sat on the hood of his boy's car in a small neighborhood park in Glen Burnie. He looked as if he wasn't ready to go home either. His phone was vibrating off the hook in his pocket.

"Malibu Barbie is blowing ya phone up, huh?" I smirked and sipped from my extra-large cup of white mocha with two shots of espresso.

Easy smirked. "Yeah. She is."

I rolled my eyes as the warm white chocolate fluid slid down my throat. "She doesn't seem like your type. I'm sure your family set that up for you, huh?"

Easy frowned a little as he ate a vanilla bean scone. "Something like that."

I looked at Easy, eyes searching his profile. Man, he was beautiful. "I feel your pain. It's kind of like that with Dinero too. He's the exact type of guy my father wants me to be with. He does whatever my father asks him to do at the drop of a hat. A ride-or-die type of nigga. I'm sick of this life, though."

Easy peeped my Giuseppe open-toe denim boots. "Not rockin' those Roxies on your feet, you're not. This is your life. Can't escape it."

"I desperately want to," I told him. "I want to just go off to college, maybe join the military. Travel the world. What about you? What do you wanna do?"

Easy swallowed his food. "Just live normal. Rich kids don't have it all. You know how it goes. I don't know my parents. They're always busy, and they keep me busy too."

"I never seen you around before," I mentioned.

Easy looked me in the face. "I'm homeschooled."

"What does your daddy do?" I grinned a little.

Easy shrugged. "I told you, I don't know my parents. Enough about me, though. I want to know about you. Why did you trust me enough to come here with me?"

I just looked at him.

"You don't know shit about me," Easy told me.

"You can't be any worse than the people I already know," I responded. "Like Whitley . . . and Dinero."

On that note, Easy took my drink from my hands and started drinking it.

I shook my head. "What happened in that bathroom? Were they fuckin'? Is that what you walked up on?" I asked him.

Easy looked at me as he drank from my cup. He lowered it from his lips. "This shit is good."

I rolled my eyes. "Don't act like this. Tell me what you saw."

"I ain't see shit," Easy told me and handed me back my cup. "And even if I did, I ain't no fuckin' snitch. Tired of muthafuckas thinking I'm a snitch. That's the story of my life. I hate being in the middle of shit. Don't put me in that shit. That's y'all shit, bruh. Take up whatever type of way you're feeling with that muthafucka and that bitch, not with me."

I just looked at him. He looked hurt that I'd even ask him to tell on Dinero. "Sorry. You're right. Forget I said anything."

Easy wiped the crumbs from his pants.

"I like your style, white boy. It's authentic," I told him, changing the subject.

Easy looked at me. "Why do you keep addressing the color of my skin? I identify with you. Why can't you identify with me without noticing what color I am? Close your eyes."

I laughed a little. "What?"

"Close 'em. Now, shit. Just do it," Easy told me.

I closed my eyes, heart already speeding up a little.

"Can you hear me loud and clear?" Easy asked me.

I nodded. "Yes."

"Do I sound white?" he asked me.

I shook my head. "Nah, not really."

I felt him gripping my waist, pulling me closer to him. I felt his hands sliding up my shirt a little, sliding across my waist. I gasped, feeling his pulse beating against my skin.

"Do I feel white?" he asked me.

I shook my head, exhaling deeply. "No."

I felt his breath against my cheek before I felt his lips on mine. He got about three gentle strokes in before I shied away.

"The fuck do my lips feel like?" he asked me, looking into my face as I opened my eyes.

I hesitated, not really sure what to say but, "Damn."

"Exactly. Don't underestimate me, ma," he told me. "Use your heart and not your eyes. I'm not white. I'm human. You're not a black woman. You're just a beautiful woman who deserves more than Dinero. Our worlds are so different, Meelah, but I want to be in your life in some way."

I looked into his face. "You're here, aren't you?"

Easy exhaled deeply, looking my face over, from my hair to my chin then back to my eyes. "Barely. Your dude ain't going to let us be friends. And my family damn sure wouldn't let this happen. Not to mention Claudius."

I looked at him. "How do you know Claudius?"

Easy looked at me and hesitated. "My uncle coaches his football team. When he didn't step to you tonight, I stepped in."

"Oh, I thought y'all were homeboys or something," I assumed.

Easy shook his head. "Nah. I barely know him."

I nodded. "Oh, okay. So, where your friends at?"

Easy shook his head. "I'm a lone wolf. It's just me."

I shook my head back at him. "Not anymore. It's just us."

Easy laughed a little, shaking his head. "Only in a dream, baby girl. So you go to Meade Senior High, huh? What was your SAT score like?" He changed the subject.

"A 1350. Not bad, but not what I wanted it to be. But at least I got into UCLA. Dad wants me as far away from here as possible when 'shit goes down,' whatever that means," I slipped up and told Easy.

Easy looked at me. "What you mean?"

"They're still trying to find out how my mother was killed in police custody," I said.

Easy's eyes searched my face. "Which police department?"

"Anne Arundel County," I told him and watched him frown. "She was killed when I was thirteen. She was beautiful inside and out. Helped me make that dress that I wore tonight. I took a picture in that gown tonight. I just wanna . . . Can we go to her and give her the picture?"

Easy nodded. "Yeah, if that's what you need to do. Let's go, ma."

Easy put the address to the gravesite in his GPS and flew down the highway toward the Holy Cross Cemetery in Baltimore. It took me a minute to prepare my nerves to get out of the car. I was shaking so badly that the shaking in my legs was causing the entire car to shake. Easy got out of the car and walked over to my side. He opened my door and held out his hand for me to grab.

I took his hand, and he pulled me out of the car. I hadn't been to see my mother since her funeral. I still dreamed of her funeral. Watching them throw dirt on her casket was the most painful thing I'd ever been through.

I cried until my lungs caved in, whereas my father was conducting business during her funeral. He stayed on his cell the entire time the preacher prayed over her. My mom was being laid to rest, and no one cared but me. And it hurt.

Easy—a boy who didn't know anything about me—walked me through the cemetery until we reached the tree that my mother was buried underneath. As soon as we got to my mother's tombstone, I dropped to my knees, staining my Everyday Blue Bon Bon Up skinny jeans. The day the principal called me to her office to tell me that my mother was dead flashed through my mind. She told me that my mother was dead like she was telling me that I didn't make the cheerleading squad. It didn't matter to her. To her, I was just some rich kid who had the world at my fingertips. She probably thought I didn't know my mother anyway. That my mother was one of those mothers who partied hard and spent long vacations away from me.

Principal Patty Brooks didn't know that my mother spent long hours with me making dresses or drawing or dancing. My mother ate breakfast with me every morning before school and cooked dinner for me every night. Whenever she visited the trap houses or visited our family businesses that cleaned our money, I was right there with her. And when she couldn't be there with me, she paid people to watch me. She was my everything, and she was gone. I was her only child. All I had left of her was . . . me.

"Hey, Sadey," I told her and placed my homecoming pictures alongside a few fresh flowers that someone had recently left there for her. "Mommy . . ."

Easy got down next to me, deeply rubbing the small of my back.

"I won homecoming queen." I took the crown off my head and placed it alongside the picture. "Mommy, it was crazy! You know how the king of the opposing school is supposed to crown the queen of the losing school? Well"—I glanced at Easy before looking back at Mommy's tombstone—"a white boy named Easy shut that shit down! You know Claudius, Dinero's brother? His team—Bay City—won the homecoming game. And he won the king's crown at his school, too. When they announced his name at homecoming, the nigga just stood there. And Easy spoke out, walking up to the stage. He crowned me, then took me by the hand, leading me out on the dance floor. My heart was shaking so hard in my chest, Mommy, I was afraid that he could feel it! Dinero watched from the wall, but he didn't move. He just watched like everyone else. I know I won't hear the end of it, but . . . tonight was all right. Whitley killed her own baby because she's not woman enough to own up to her shit. It won't be long before the police are on our ass, or even worse, the niggas daddy works for. I knew from the moment I looked into Easy's eyes that my world was about to change. But not like this. I don't think I'm ready for all of this change."

Easy's eyes traced my profile, and he watched as the tears started to bubble then slide down my cheeks.

I rested my butt on the ground, my body falling against Easy's, my head falling to his shoulder. "Mommy, I miss you so much. Life hasn't been the same since you left. Daddy went from the man who showed me how a man was supposed to treat a woman, to a man I never see. He used to have me get dressed up in my best clothes to take me out to dinner then a movie. He used to cook breakfast for us in the morning, remember? All that's changed since you've been gone. I barely see him. He spends most of his time at his house in Philly or his house in DC or his spot in Richmond. He's got a houseful of niggas watching me at our place in Odenton over in Pioneer City! His hittas look out for me more than he does. When I need money, his man Arcen throws me a few stacks. I don't even know Daddy's phone number! He's low-key from everyone, including me! I hate this life, Mommy! I'm so tired!"

Easy surrounded me with his warm arms. Before I could even turn to him, crying in his arms, we heard footsteps behind us. Easy pulled his gun from his pants, and I grabbed his arm. He looked into my face before we turned around to see my father's crew walking toward us, guns already drawn on Easy. We stood from the ground. There Arcen was, ready to unload on Easy. Arcen was like family. He raised me from birth, even gave me the nickname Morning because he said I always woke up everyone with the sun, crying before my eyes even opened.

"Morning, who the fuck is this cracker-ass nigga?" Arcen asked as the crew approached us, guns drawn on Easy.

I swear, he made up curse words. As a kid, he'd threaten to whup my ass. He'd say shit like, "I'ma beat the hot fuck out of you if you don't get ya hardheaded ass over here." I would mutter, "I didn't know fuck had a temperature, but okay, I'm coming."

"It's cool, Unc," I told him. "This is Sharita's cousin, Easy," I tried to lie.

"Easy who?" Arcen sneered, watching Easy hold the pistol grip of his gun.

"Gonzales. He's Jimena's nephew," I told them and watched them all hesitate before lowering their weapons.

"What's ya pops's name, Gonzales?" Arcen asked Easy.

"None of your fuckin' business," Easy answered. "You run up on a muthafucka ten guns drawn down on him then expect him to have friendly conversation?"

Arcen grinned a little, and his crew laughed a bit behind him. "Morning, tell the little nigga to get out of here before he ends up looking like Swiss cheese. I don't give a fuck if he's a Gonzales. I don't think they'd appreciate the li'l mixed-breed nigga with you. And Dinero's about to get out. We got our people getting him out now. I don't think he'd appreciate you out here in the dark with this muthafucka, either. He looked the wrong way when he looked your way, Morning, and you know it. So, tell him to get the fuck on," Arcen snarled.

Easy glared at Arcen, hand gripping the fuck out of that gun.

I patted Easy on his chest, and attempted to push him back a little, but he wouldn't budge. "Easy, hey, you gotta go, okay?" I looked up into his face.

Easy glared from Arcen and his crew down at me. His angry expression softened a little, but he still wasn't backing down. "I don't feel right letting you get in the car with them. You came with me. You leave with me."

I hesitated, looking back at Arcen, who wasn't about to let me leave with him. Arcen wasn't playing. But for whatever reason, he didn't clown. I didn't believe Sharita's story because that's what it was: a story she told Dinero so he'd ease up his jealousy a little. But Arcen somewhat believed the story. Gonazaleses were always on their shit. Rumor had it they were related to Stef, the Italian my father worked for. I didn't believe it, but the Gonzales family was respected in the streets like they were related to that family, so no one tried them. Stef didn't acknowledge them as family, but he employed most of them. Come to think of it, Easy looked a lot like that muthafucka. Easy was white with dark features, so you knew he was mixed with something, which was why Sharita thought that it was a good idea to say that he was one of her people. Spanish or Italian—yeah, that fit him.

I slid my hand into his pants pocket, taking out his cell phone.

"30908," Easy said, giving me the passcode to his screen lock.

I gasped, looking up into his face.

Easy frowned a little, eying not only my expression but the expressions of my father's crew when he gave the password. "What?" he asked all of us.

"March 9, 2008 was the day my mother died." I exhaled deeply.

Easy's frown softened as he eyed the date of death on my mother's tombstone. He shook his head to himself. "I didn't even peep the date, shawty."

"Why is that your passcode?" I hesitated to ask.

Easy looked at me. "My mother was shot in front of me when I was thirteen, on March 9, 2008, on my birthday."

So that part of Sharita's story was true. Something was tearing me up inside realizing that Sharita's story may not have been a story at all.

"We gotta go, Morning." Arcen glanced at Easy, then back at me.

I quickly put my number into Easy's phone before giving it back to him. Easy gripped my hand in his, hesitating before letting it go. Arcen pulled me away from Easy.

The ride back home was quiet, but my thoughts weren't. My head was spinning. Who was Easy? Why was Sharita's story starting to match his story? He didn't know Sharita, but damn it if she didn't know him or want him to know me. Usually she pushed away any nigga who wasn't Dinero, though she wasn't his biggest fan either. Easy did look familiar. He did kind of remind me of Sharita a little, with that mouth of his, but there was something else familiar about him. I didn't have time to put my memories back together, and that unknown number kept blowing my cell phone up. And I continued to ignore it, and maybe I shouldn't have.

As soon as we pulled up in Arcen's Escalade with his crew trailing behind us, there were several black Rolls-Royces pulled up to the curb outside of my place. We all kind of looked at each other before Arcen and his crew made sure they were locked and loaded before we got out of the car. Arcen always covered me in the front with a few members and had the rest of the crew having my back. He never left me out in the open. So I thought.

When we got inside our townhouse, Stef's crew was sitting in my living room. Stef's 23- year-old son, Cristobal, sat in the center of my father's leather love seat, glaring at us as we stepped through the front door.

"Y'all might want to put that shit away," Cristobal told Arcen and his men.

"The fuck are y'all doing up in here? Who the fuck gave y'all a key to get in this muthafucka?" Arcen asked.

Cristobal laughed. "We have a key to every one of your houses. Every one of you standing in this living room has no privacy. You all remember that." Cristobal looked at me. "Your girl, Whitley, is being questioned by the police after her boyfriend was brought in for questioning. Dash told the police that he's been getting drugs of all sorts from a nigga named Emmanuel who gets his shit from an Italian named Stef. Of course, the police know about us—shit, we pay them to stay out of jail! They are the main suppliers of the shit that we sell! But what they didn't know about is the shit that we manufacture in Mexico: the Rox, which they are getting no cut from. The police don't give a fuck what we do on these streets as long as they get a fuckin' cut!" Cristobal got off the couch and came over to where I was standing in the middle of the floor. "The dead baby your friend gave birth to was Dinero's. Whitley told us."

I looked up into his face, my nerves on edge. "What did you do to her?"

"I couldn't touch her. She's in the hospital! They'd know it was us! The police were guarding the hospital, waiting on us to get to her. They questioned Dinero, who denied everything, like a loyal soldier does. They're questioning her now. And what do you think she's telling them?" Cristobal snarled in my face. "Why didn't you kill the bitch when she admitted to you that she had your nigga's baby? So, guess what we had to do? Dinero is going to take care of the job that you didn't. He has no problem killing his side bitch." Cristobal laughed a little.

"Arcen, call my father now," I told Arcen.

"Emmanuel is in California conducting business. It's best he doesn't know about any of this. It's best that my father doesn't know shit about this either. If my father finds out that you little teenagers fucked up our Chain, it's a wrap. Everything and everyone involved will be eliminated. This money keeps this community moving. Your future depends on our operation. As long as we eliminate the witness before the court date, then we're good. No witnesses, no crime," Cristobal told me. "Those kids at that party at Dash's house, I need them taken care of."

"The fuck? Killing kids?" Arcen scoffed, and his crew muttered behind him.

"Nah, getting rid of evidence," Cristobal told him. "It's either them or maybe your wife and teenage son who both know what you do for a living. Every one of you has family members who know what the fuck we do and where the fuck we get our shit from. Maybe we should get rid of that evidence." Cristobal looked at Arcen, then back at me. "Tell your dogs to leave, Meelah."

Arcen started to step in front of me when one of his crew members grabbed his arm. Arcen frowned as his phone rang in his pocket.

"Answer it. Put it on speakerphone," one of Cristobal's men spoke out.

Arcen hesitated before taking his phone out of his pocket. He pressed the speakerphone icon after looking at the display to see that it was one of his kids.

"What's up, Chuckie? Why are you up this late?"

"Daddy, there's a man with a gun sitting in my bedroom. And there's a man in Mommy's room. She's in there screaming for help. I think he's slapping her or something," Arcen's 5-year-old son cried through the phone.

The anger mixed with fear in Arcen's eyes stung. He wanted to shoot Cristobal right in his face then, but he knew the wrath that Stef would bring if anything happened to his son.

"Get ya niggas and get the fuck out of here." Cristobal looked at Arcen, then back at me. "I'll tuck her into bed. You don't have to worry about that."

My heart stopped in my chest as Arcen's men left my father's living room one by one. I grabbed Arcen's arm, and he yanked from me, leaving my father's house without a fight. There I stood in my living room, wishing I had answered that unknown call. It was probably Daddy telling me not to go home. The only thing I could do at that moment was pray to God that I made it through whatever hell Cristobal was about to take me through.

Chapter Four

Bostyn

That Monday after homecoming, I sat on Claudius's back porch staring at Meelah's contact information in my phone. I'd tried to call shawty at least five times that weekend. I looked her up on social media. Luckily her page was public, so I wouldn't have to wait for her to respond to a friend request. Apparently, I wasn't the only one who hadn't seen nor heard from her over the weekend. Most of her friends were looking for her, Sharita being one of them.

She hadn't gone to school that day. Whitley wasn't among her friends looking for her, and I couldn't help but notice that her dude hadn't tagged her in any comments or any posts looking for her, which meant the muthafucka either knew where she was or didn't give a fuck where she was. It was killing me not to be able to reach her. I was worried. Shit didn't feel right.

"Ay." I heard Claudius's back door slide open before I heard his voice over my shoulder. "My aunt said your pops is on his way over."

"Yeah," I muttered under my breath.

Pops had been looking for me all weekend. Once I brought Ace back his car, I stayed over at his crib the whole weekend. I didn't want Pops questioning me about the party, and I knew it was the fuckin' talk of the station.

Them muthafuckas lived a double life. Moms didn't know shit about what went down out there in the field, and Pops damn sure didn't bring it up. I didn't want to be involved in anything that had to do with the cops, but he was determined to make me follow in his footsteps. I wasn't the best academically, and my parents wouldn't allow me to join any of the sports teams in the area. I stayed out most nights all night. The streets felt a lot better than home. The police academy was Pops's way of keeping me out of trouble, or maybe getting into trouble. Who knew when it came to that man's intentions for me?

Claudius hadn't said a word to me since I got us into that after-party. The only reason I even went to old boy's crib that afternoon was because I needed answers. Claudius came over and sat on the bench across from me in his aunt's expensive outdoor set. He watched me swiping through Meelah's mobile uploads. Man, that girl was beautiful inside and out. I wanted to get to know her. Something inside of me was telling me that I needed to get to know her.

"So, has Mandy's mom started planning y'all engagement party yet?" Claudius called himself snapping me back to reality.

I looked up from my phone into Claudius's shadowy face. I always hated that sneaky-ass grin of his. "Why do you wanna know? So you can make sure the stripper's G-string matches the string on the invitations?" I watched Claudius laugh out loud and shook my head at him. I wasn't playing with that muthafucka. "I'm telling you, if you throw me a bachelor party, I'm fuckin' you up! I'll knock all those pearly white teeth out of your mouth. The groupies don't like snaggletoothed muthafuckas, ladies' man."

Claudius's laughter subsided, but that stupid smirk was still on his face. "You over here lookin' at old girl's picture like you done fell in love with the bitch."

I looked at Claudius, ready to smack him in the face with my phone. “Say something else, muthafucka, and this phone is going down your fuckin’ throat.”

Claudius’s smirk finally disappeared. “You don’t know this girl you’re crushing on, B. You need to just mind ya own business and stay out of Dinero’s shit.”

“She gave me her fuckin’ number. She put it in my phone. I’ve been calling her all weekend, bruh,” I told Claudius.

Claudius shrugged. “Maybe shawty gave you the wrong number.”

I shook my head. “Nah, it went to her voicemail. Her voice was on that muthafucka. Shawty gave me her number before these muthafuckas in all dark purple took her.”

Claudius looked at me. “Where were y’all?”

“I took her to her mother’s grave so she could leave her homecoming picture and her crown with her mother. A mother she missed. A mother she needed. I could feel her pain. I wasn’t going to tell her that I couldn’t take her when Lord knows I wish I got the chance to say more than, ‘Who are you?’ to my mother before she was shot right in front of me,” I told Claudius.

Claudius shook his head. “You shouldn’t have involved yourself with that girl, man.”

“Something ain’t right, yo! I’m not just gonna leave it alone,” I responded.

“Let Dinero handle the shit. He’s been handling shit with shawty this long,” Claudius scoffed.

“At least forty students from Meade Senior High are lookin’ for shawty except Dinero, a muthafucka who’s fuckin’ shawty’s best friend. He doesn’t care about her. He ain’t lookin’ for her, homie!” I told Claudius, speaking loudly but whispering at the same time. “Where the fuck does Dinero stay?”

Claudius laughed out loud. “Nigga, what?”

"What's his address? I wanna talk to him." I looked Claudius in his face. "I know you know where he stays. He's your brother."

Claudius frowned. "That doesn't mean I know or care where the nigga stays. Stay the fuck out of this shit, because that's what the fuck I'm going to do."

"Boys, how are you?" I heard Pops's voice coming through the back door.

I didn't take my eyes off Claudius.

"Son?" My father tried to get my attention. "Where have you been? Your mother's been worried sick."

"I stayed with Ace this weekend. I needed some air. Y'all know he stays in Annapolis. Just enough distance to get away from the bullshit on this side of town," I responded.

"So, how was the party? I heard some shit went down. A girl named Whitley went into labor at the party, high off the drugs that were distributed at the party, and now that same girl is missing," Pops told me. "Her boyfriend is missing too. Someone named Da'Vius Saver also known as Dash in the streets."

Both Claudius and I looked up at my father as he came over to the table, straightening out his silk tie. Pops always talked about his caseload as if he were talking about the Sunday comics in the paper. I didn't care how brutal the crimes were, he never showed any remorse or concern. The day my mother was shot in my face, he told me to suck that shit up and take my ass to school. He wouldn't even let me go to her funeral.

"Y'all know anything about that?" Pops asked, standing before the table.

"Nah," I responded.

But Claudius said, "Yes, sir."

I looked at Claudius. I could've sworn the muthafucka just said he was staying out of it.

Claudius couldn't look at me. He just concentrated on my father's eager stare. Claudius cleared his throat. "Emmanuel Summers's men killed Dash a few hours after he left the police station. There's no body because they cut him up, shipping the packages off to warehouses in Europe. At least that's the rumor."

Pops nodded, rubbing his goatee. "Whose warehouse?"

Claudius shrugged. "Probably Stefano Romano. They say he's in Paris."

"Where the fuck did you find out this shit?" I clicked my teeth.

"Every crew has a snitch," Claudius scoffed.

"The fuck happened to staying out of it?" I shook my head. "You telling this man shit based off rumors."

Pops looked at me just as his iPhone chimed in his pocket, letting him know he received a text. He took his phone out of his pocket, running his hand through his hair as he frowned while reading the message. "Fuck!" he yelled.

"What's going on?" I asked, watching Pops put his phone back in his pocket.

Pops exhaled deeply before saying, "Housekeeping at the Red Roof Inn said they found a hand with a purple 'CMC' tattooed on it in the dumpster in the back of the hotel. That purple cursive 'CMC' tattoo is the same identifying mark that Whitley's mother gave us when she reported her daughter missing today."

Claudius looked at me. "Just rumors, huh?" Claudius scoffed. "My boys are telling me that more and more teens are coming up missing. That the same muthafuckas who got to Dash are taking them out one by one. And the teens who are coming up missing are the ones who were at that party the other night, the ones who took the Rox, Sweet Tea, and a few other pills from The Chain."

"Since you know all that shit, where the fuck is Meelah?" I asked.

Pops looked at me. "Who is Meelah?"

"Dinero's girlfriend, who your son is crushing on," Claudius mocked. "She's Emmanuel's daughter."

Pops looked at me like I'd lost my mind. "How did you get mixed up with a notorious drug distributor's daughter?"

I shrugged. "I don't know what you're talking about. Claudius is just running his mouth as usual."

"So, you didn't just tell me that you took old girl to visit her mother's grave?" Claudius kept pressing my buttons.

"Yeah, I did tell you that shit. But what I didn't tell you was that her mother was killed on the same day that my mother was killed." I looked from Claudius over to Pops. Meelah told me that her mother was killed at the Anne Arundel Police Department where my father was commanding officer.

Pops's entire facial expression changed. "I'm headed back to the station. Thanks for the info, Claudius. And, Bostyn, stay the fuck away from this girl. You need to call Mandy, concentrate on her and that baby instead of trying to get mixed up with a rich hood girl you have nothing in common with."

"Obviously we do if our mothers were killed on the same day, yo," I told my father, talking to his back as he turned around and walked back into Claudius's house.

"Stay away from her, Bostyn, before you get that girl hurt." Pops slammed the door behind him.

Claudius looked at me, already seeing "I ain't staying out of shit" written all over my face. "Yo, don't go digging for shit, Bostyn. So what the dates match? That doesn't necessarily mean anything."

"Her friend Sharita made up this entire story about me being her cousin. That I'm her people. What if she's not lying? I don't know shit about my mother's side. The day my mother came to my door, she said she was looking for her aunt Donna. All I know about my mother is that my father's maid is my aunt, and he scared her into not talking to me. What if Sharita is my people for real, bruh?"

"So what if she is?" Claudius rested his forearms on the table, intertwining his fingers and clenching his hands together.

"Then I can get some answers to who I really am. Who my real family is," I told Claudius.

"This is your real goddamn family!" Claudius got up from the table, frustrated as hell, and I didn't understand why. "You have everything at your fuckin' fingertips! A mother who worships you, brothers who look up to you, maids, butlers, cars, clothes, savings accounts and shit!"

"Everything but the truth," I told him and stood up from the table.

"My own fuckin' mother gave me to her sister to raise because she couldn't deal with the fact that my father didn't want her! Dinero's mama might have checked out on him mentally when Miguel said fuck her, but physically, she was there for him! She still raised her son! Yes, I'm from a rich family who could buy the air that we all breathe, but so what?" Claudius yelled.

"Exactly my point. Fuck this money. I'd give it all up to have a mother. To have a father. To know and to have a family," I tried to tell Claudius.

"You have all of that! You have a family!" Claudius tried to tell me. "You don't know them niggas you're looking for, and maybe it's best that you don't."

I looked into Claudius's face, watching his temple twitch. He knew more than what he was telling me. "Claudius—"

"Leave this shit the fuck alone. Go be with Mandy and stay away from Meelah. Mind your fuckin' business!" Claudius pushed past me and walked into his house.

***

"You have to eat something, *señor*." Donna came into my room that night.

I looked up from Meelah's picture that I saved in my phone. I lay on the floor in my room, head rested on my oversized pillow in front of my forty-two-inch television where I normally played video games with my brothers or my homies, sometimes even the staff and their kids. All I could think about was Meelah and what happened to her.

What happened to Whitley was all over the news. The reporters speculated that the person who killed her may have been after revenge for her killing their baby. They assumed it wasn't Dash's child because he was killed before she was. That weekend, eight teens in total turned up dead around the county and in the city of Baltimore. The autopsy reports were in the making, but I was sure the crew responsible for killing those teens had enough power to get the reports shielded from the public.

It was 10:30 at night, and there was still no sign of Meelah. The fact that she wasn't one of the teens who came up dead was the only comfort I had. Emmanuel wouldn't have his own daughter killed. Or would he? A man on top would do anything to stay there.

"I'm not hungry, Don," I said, sitting up from the floor.

Donna sighed and set the tray of food on the nightstand. It was taco night, and Donna always hooked my shit up with just the right amount of cheese, tomatoes, and sour cream. I just couldn't eat knowing baby girl was in trouble.

"What's on your mind, baby?" Donna asked me.

I turned the picture I was looking at toward Donna. It was a picture of Meelah hugging her girl Sharita. The picture was captioned Daytona Beach. They looked happy. Out of all the girls who were with Meelah at that dance, I could tell that Sharita really cared about her. There was no hate, no envy, no jealousy. Just straight love.

Donna's eyes lit up when she saw the picture on my phone, but she looked shocked, not because I had a picture of a black girl but a picture of Sharita. It was someone she obviously knew.

"Who is the girl with the *pequeña niña negra?*" Donna hesitated to ask.

"You tell me. She says I'm her cousin. Her mother is named Jimena Gonzales." I could barely get the words out before Donna tried to turn around and walked toward the door. I grabbed Donna's arm. "Aunt Donna!"

Donna looked at me, her round face flushing as tears rushed to her light brown eyes. "Yes, *sobrino?*"

"We have never talked about my mother. Who she was or why she left me in that group home. Tell me something, anything," I asked, more like begged.

Donna looked back at my room door as if she suspected someone would walk in. She looked at me, shaking her head. She mouthed, "I am wired."

I frowned at her and let her go.

Donna went over to my cherry-wood computer desk and grabbed a piece of notebook paper and a pen. She quickly scribbled down something, then rushed back over to me. She cried as she shoved the piece of paper into my chest before rushing out of the room.

"Who is it?" a voice called through the newly painted front door of a blue townhouse in the Provinces, a townhouse community not too far outside of Fort Meade.

"Easy," I answered as crickets chirped all around me.

"Easy? I don't know no goddamn Easy. And anyone who knows me knows better than to knock on my fuckin' door at 11:30 at night!" the woman yelled at me, turning on the porch light so she could get a better view of me.

I laughed a little. "Ummm. I went to the homecoming dance last Friday. You know Bay City beat the brakes off Meade Senior High. Dinero Rodriguez won the king's crown for Meade Senior, and Claudius Rodriguez won the crown for Bay City. Neither of them wanted to approach the stage to dance with Meelah Summers, so I did."

The front door cracked open a little. "Sharita told me about you. She said *Tía* Donna says Maria Alejandra is your mother." The woman opened the door all the way and stepped into the doorway.

I was stunned when I saw the woman at first. She was the spitting image of the woman I saw get shot in front of me four years earlier. I hesitated, looking her face over.

"We used to call her MA, you know, because her name is Maria Alejandra. She was my twin. I'm Jimena. I'm Sharita's mother. And you're—"

I cut her off. "Easy."

Jimena scoffed. "That's your street name that your parents just so happened to let you legalize. Your first name was originally Emilio, but that cop changed your name to Bostyn when his wife picked you out from that group home. I wanted to bring you home with me, but that cop and all his political power outweighed my street affiliation. Your mother didn't give you away. You were taken from her. She was sixteen when she had you, and she had a drug problem. Your father and your adoptive father were both in love with your mother."

I frowned, heart speeding up in my chest.

"You sure you want to hear this?" Jimena asked, watching me nod. She signaled me to come into her house.

I stepped through the doorway into that house. I know it sounds crazy, but I could feel my mother from the moment I walked through the door. As I followed Jimena down the hallway, I eyed the picture frames on the wall. There were pictures of Jimena with my mother from birth until around the time of my mother's murder.

Jimena stood alongside me, watching me stop to gaze at the photos.

"Nice house," I said as I looked around.

"It's not my house. It belongs to one of my bosses. We stay here from time to time to serve our products. Our home is in Howard County. Most of us have multiple homes to throw off our enemies," Jimena told me.

"So, you're my aunt, huh?" I asked her.

Jimena sighed, watching me look the pictures over. "Your father was in love with my sister, and so was that man you live with now. But there is a thin line between love and hate. If Jimmie Reel couldn't have her, no one could. Your father is untouchable, brings this state too much revenue both on the streets and in the business world. But your mother, my twin sister, wasn't anything but a Guatemalan girl from a poor family. No one cares about us." Jimena turned to me.

I turned to her. "Who is my father?"

Jimena shook her head. "It's not time. No one knows Jimmie adopted you, and it's best we keep it that way. I'm just glad you're alive!"

The knob on the front door jiggled, and the lock turned. Both Jimena and I looked back at the front door as Sharita stepped through, her face full of tears.

Sharita quickly dried her face when she saw me standing there with her mother. "Easy? What are you doing here?"

"Aunt Donna gave me the address." I hesitated.

Sharita cried out loud. "I can't find her. Kids are coming up dead left and right, and I can't find my friend!" Sharita rushed up to me, burying her face in my chest. "Please, help me find her!"

I hesitated, watching Jimena rub her daughter's back. "Have you been to her house?"

Sharita let go of me, looking up into my face. "Her block is lined with Links in The Chain."

I frowned. "Who?"

"The men who work for Emmanuel. They've been taking muthafuckas out left and right all week. The police won't even go on that block!" Jimena told me.

I nodded. "Let's go."

"What?" Sharita shoved me in the shoulder. "Did you not just hear me tell you that these muthafuckas have been taking everyone out these past few days? They killed Whitley before she could snitch! They killed her boyfriend because he did snitch! They don't know whose son you are. They're gonna kill you too if you step foot near Meelah's house! They don't know shit about you, and it's best we keep it this way! Your real father doesn't know who you are, and right now that's protecting you. And trying to help Meelah might hurt everyone involved. I love her, I care about her, but we have to think about our families."

I shook my head, turned around, and headed back to the front door.

Sharita caught up with me. "Bostyn!" She called me by the name on my birth certificate. "Dinero will kill her before he lets you have her!"

I looked back at her as I pulled my arm from her. "Not if I get to him first. Where the fuck does that muthafucka stay then?"

Sharita hesitated. "He . . . he's hiding out. Lyin' low since what happened to Dash and Whitley. Everyone thinks he killed Whitley because he thinks she told Meelah the baby was his."

"Are you going to give me the address to ya girl's house or not?" I frowned at her.

Sharita sighed. "You can't go by yourself, Easy!"

"Who said I was going by myself?" I responded.

Sharita gave me the address to where Meelah lived, which wasn't but a few minutes from Jimena's trap in Pioneer City. I had a few homies in the area who were members of the Bay City Hustlas, a ruthless gang which originated in Baltimore City. We called my homies the Guerillas. These gang members were only brought out when it was time to fight. The police force would often hire these young thugs to take out rival gangs.

I knew enough about Emmanuel Summers to know that his crew ran far, wide, and deep as a muthafucka. But even he had a boss whose reach was further than his. The killings that went down over the weekend had to be approved by his boss. There was no way he'd draw all that attention without direction from his boss. They were hiding Meelah for whatever reason, and I had to see why. Something in my heart wouldn't let her go. I knew that getting to know her would help me get to know who I really was.

Before I even got to Meelah's spot, my soldiers were already in place scoping the neighborhood. Turned out, one of the men in Emmunuel's crew was my man Ace's cousin. I parked my car a few blocks away and hopped in my boy Lorenz's ride. Ace was in the car, riding shotgun with his AK-47 in his lap, ready to unload on the muthafuckas if his cousin chose The Chain over his blood. There was always that one muthafucka in your crew who was down to do whatever, and that was Ace.

"There her house goes right there," I told them, spotting a townhouse with the number on it that Sharita had given me earlier.

Lorenz had barely pulled his burgundy Chevy Impala up to the curb when I jumped out of the back seat, heading up the sidewalk leading to Meelah's house with my chopper drawn down on the big dudes standing in front of Meelah's front door.

They had their guns already aimed our way as soon as we pulled up on the curb, but I didn't give a fuck. They could've shot me, but the dude at the front door was Rickie, Ace's cousin. He had his finger over the trigger ready to shoot until he saw Ace jump out of the passenger seat.

"The fuck y'all niggas doing here?" Rickie snarled, watching my crew jump out of Lorenz's ride.

"Cuz, we don't want no problems," Ace told Rickie, coming down the sidewalk, gun drawn on his cousin.

"It looks like you're looking for trouble, pulling up to the spot with your gun drawn down on a nigga!" Rickie aimed his gun from me over to his cousin as he stood alongside me.

"Where is shawty? Let her out now," I told him, holding the pistol grip in my hands. "I ain't fuckin' around! Let her out!"

"Who the fuck is 'shawty'? And why do you sound like my boss, nigga?" Rickie hesitated. "You Sharita's cousin?"

I wasn't going to let him distract me from doing what I came there to do. "I'm only going to ask you one more fuckin' time—let her out!"

"You really think we're the only niggas around this muthafucka? Every house in this neighborhood has one of our niggas inside of it, posted up, ready to take all of y'all out. Even cuz." Rickie nodded toward his cousin. He looked back at me. "You sure you wanna see what your people did to her?"

I glanced back at my crew before looking at Ace, who stood alongside me, signaling me to lower my gun but still to keep my finger over the trigger. I lowered my gun but stayed focused on shooting him if I had to. "My people?" I asked.

Rickie grinned a little, shaking his head and lowering his weapon. "We haven't been in this house since Friday night. We were told to make sure no one gets in this muthafucka and no one gets out. But the fact that you're here must mean your people changed their mind."

I frowned at Rickie in confusion as he and his partner moved from in front of the door.

Ace nudged me to go into the house.

I opened the door and stepped through it. The sight of blood trickling down the hallway caused my heart to tremble in my chest. Ace followed close behind me, eying the trail of blood. He nudged my shoulder, pointing at the trail of blood that led up the steps.

"Fuck!" I yelled, eying the stains on the steps that looked like a body had been dragged up the stairs.

"Who is this girl we're looking for, man? Whose house is this anyway?" Ace questioned, tripping over the blood just like I was.

"Meelah Summers," I answered as I made my way up the stairs.

"Yo, Dinero's girl?" Ace hollered. "Shawty you danced with the other night? That's who you have me ready to blow my cousin's head off for? I thought you ain't seen Mandy, so you were looking for her or some shit! I didn't know you were looking for another nigga's girl!"

"Well, she ain't really his girl if she's been locked up in this muthafucka for three days and no one has come in this muthafucka to get her, is she?" I snarled back over my shoulder as Ace stayed at the bottom of the staircase.

"This shit doesn't look good, man. You sure you wanna see what shawty looks like?" Ace called out to me as I reached the top of the staircase.

I wasn't paying him any mind as I walked through Meelah's crib, eying the smeared trail of blood that led to a closet at the end of the hallway. I made my way to the closet, pulled the door open, and there shawty was, bloody, bruised, and naked, balled up on the floor of the linen closet.

"Shit!" I grabbed a sheet from one of the shelves and kneeled, wrapping the sheet around her. Her face fell against my chest. The left side of her face was so bruised and swollen, as if her jaw was broken. There was a big gash on her scalp and blood under her fingernails as if she had fought a few muthafuckas. She was breathing but barely. I wrapped her arm around my neck before wrapping my arms around her and picking her up from the floor. I carried her down the hallway and down the stairs.

"The fuck, Bostyn?" Claudius exclaimed, looking over my shoulder at Ace and his crew posted up in his front yard. Claudius looked at me like I was crazy as fuck as I stepped through his front door holding Meelah in my arms. "Yo, why is she here?"

"Ya uncle is a doctor. Where he at, yo?" I asked, stepping through the doorway with shawty wrapped in my arms.

Ace followed me, followed by Keith.

Claudius scoffed, closing the door behind us as we stepped into his mansion. "What happened to her, and why isn't she in the hospital?"

"We can't take her to the hospital. Shit is crazy right now. We probably shouldn't have even taken her from her crib, but Bostyn wouldn't leave her. I don't really blame him. Look at her. Her own father doesn't even know what happened to her." Keith shook his head as he watched me walk down the hallway and over to Claudius's staircase.

"Where the fuck are you going with her, bruh?" Claudius called after me.

"Taking her to one of y'all guest rooms. Y'all got three of them muthafuckas in this bitch. She can stay in one of them until we figure things out," I responded as I carried Meelah up the staircase.

"Where is her nigga at, shit?" Claudius scoffed, following me. "If my aunt comes home and finds shawty in our house, I'm dead, son!"

"Man, ya aunt ain't never home," Ace scoffed behind us. "The bitch probably fuckin' somebody's husband."

I couldn't turn around to stop Claudius from running up on Ace—because I had shawty in my arms—but Keith stopped him. He didn't want to hear the truth, but that was what his aunt Marilyn and his mom, Leanne, did, shit. They fucked their way up the criminal justice system by fuckin' the niggas who controlled the votes and who signed their paychecks. I even heard that Marilyn—a respected judge—fucked some of the defendants she was supposed to be trying.

Most of the money she made was off the books. The mansion she lived in was paid for by some of the biggest drug dealers in the country from what I heard. Claudius refused to believe that his family was crooked. He kept his head in the game to keep his mind off his family.

"Say something else, Ace!" Claudius growled as Keith pushed him up the steps.

"Man, chill!" Keith laughed. "We gotta get shawty some help. Call ya aunt's ex-husband. Tell him shawty is here and she needs help. We'll pay him whatever we have to so he can help shawty. Man, look at her! Ace's cousin said them niggas whupped the fuck out of this girl for hours because of what her friend's man did! They held a gun to the girl's head before they beat her. They called her father up and had her tell him that she was staying with Sharita for the weekend and not to reach out to her while this investigation is going on!"

I took shawty into the first bedroom of the house and laid her on the bed, leaving her wrapped up in the sheet. I frowned as I sat beside her on the bed, looking her bruised face over. "We can't take her to the hospital. You already know whoever did this to her will think she's gonna snitch them out. She's not going to admit them muthafuckas did this shit to her."

Ace hesitated. "Are you really Sharita's cousin? Do you know who her people are?"

"Nah." I shook my head, looking at Ace and Keith standing in the doorway.

Claudius went over and sat in the recliner that was in the corner of the room.

"Nah to which question? That you're Sharita's cousin or that you don't know shit about her family?" Ace asked.

Claudius cut me off before I could even say anything. "Yo, why does it even matter?"

"Because if he's related to the Gonzales and Romano families, they'll kill this nigga too for helping her!" Ace responded.

"Nah, he's not related to them muthafuckas. His father is Jimmie Reel, captain of the narcotics unit at the Anne Arundel County Police Department who's about to be the captain of the UAD (undercover affairs division). How the fuck is he related to that family when his father is a cop? His father ain't Italian, and his mother damn sure ain't Hispanic. They're white as fuck, probably German or some shit!" Claudius laughed to himself.

I looked at Claudius before looking at Meelah, who lay damn near lifeless on the bed. "Claudius, call ya uncle. Please."

"How are we going to explain this shit?" Claudius shook his head at me.

"Tell the truth, that we don't know shit," I told him.

Claudius reluctantly called his uncle Tiger Stabler. Tiger and Marilyn were divorced but whenever Claudius called Tiger for anything, he was right there. Marilyn hated it, said Tiger spoiled Claudius. Tiger loved his nephew, but coming over was his way of checking up on Marilyn to see what she was getting into, or should I say, who was getting into her.

Claudius looked away while Tiger looked Meelah over, but my eyes were glued on every bruise, every scratch, every swollen area. Tiger made Ace and Keith go back outside with their crew.

"So, what happened?" Tiger questioned, looking over her scalp and feeling for lumps.

"We don't know," Claudius answered.

"Did one of you do this to her?" Tiger questioned.

"The fuck?" Claudius looked at his uncle.

"Do you think we'd call you if we did this shit to her?" I asked.

"I had to ask." Tiger shook his head. "I'm just wondering why this girl isn't at the hospital and why you called me instead of calling Jimmie. Y'all called the Guerillas. Whatever happened, whoever did this must be some high-profile muthafuckas. She needs to go to a hospital. The way she's breathing, the slow pulse, the fact that her skin is pale tells me that there may be extensive swelling in her brain. Her jaw is broken, and a few of her ribs appear to be broken too. The swelling and bruising between her thighs, vaginal area, and anus lets me know that she was sexually assaulted. They need to do a rape kit."

My blood immediately started to boil. "What?" I clenched my fists.

"If we take her to the hospital, they are going to kill this girl." Claudius hated to admit it.

"Who is she?" Tiger asked.

"Meelah Summers," Claudius answered.

Tiger looked at me, then back at Claudius. "Emmanuel's daughter? The drug distributor they call Sable? You brought this man's daughter to your aunt's house? Marilyn tried him in court! She left me because she found out that I tampered with medical evidence to help Sable's attorney."

Claudius and I looked at Tiger.

"Does he know she's here?" Tiger watched the both of us shake our heads. "There's no way he knows what happened to her."

"He thinks she's staying with a friend. That everything's cool." I exhaled deeply. "Rape? These muthafuckas raped her?"

Tiger nodded. "It looks that way, Bostyn. If her father thinks she is with a friend, then you need to call that friend and have her meet you at the hospital. When she gets there, tell her to call Sable and tell them that his daughter was beaten, raped, and left in a dumpster. Don't involve yourself, Bostyn."

"Then how do we explain how she got to the hospital?" Claudius asked.

Tiger looked at me.

"It's cool, Tiger. We got this," I told him.

"Are you sure? Do you know what kind of people we're dealing with? Where did you find this girl? As pretty as she is, I know she has a boyfriend. Where is he?" Tiger asked.

"You think that muthafucka is involved?" Claudius growled.

"He sure hasn't looked for his girl in three fuckin' days," I muttered.

"Come up with something. We gotta get her some help." Tiger frowned, looking Meelah over. "Damn."

***

"Which dumpster did you find her at?" Officer Zel Neddleman questioned me that night in the waiting room of the Baltimore-Washington Medical Center. We'd been waiting for hours while Meelah was in surgery.

I sat in the waiting room with Ace, Claudius, Sharita, Tajha, and Jimena. I looked up at the officer from where I was slouched in my chair. "I found her in the dumpster behind 7-Eleven," I told the officer.

"And what were you doing behind 7-Eleven?" Zel questioned.

Claudius looked up at the officer. "The fuck is that supposed to mean?"

Zel and the other officers with him looked at Claudius. "Watch your mouth," Zel told him.

"Nah." Claudius stood from his chair. "Y'all are here questioning us like we did this shit to her! We found shawty naked behind a dumpster! She's been missing for three days, and no one bothered to look for her! We were hanging out and heard a noise. When we went to check it out, we found shawty."

"Meelah Summers, daughter of a known drug dealer, is found unconscious behind a dumpster, naked, and her parents aren't looking for her?" Zel scoffed.

"He thought she was with me. He doesn't know." Sharita dried the tears from her eyes.

"And you're her friend. You didn't look for her? When is the last time that you saw your friend? Why didn't you call the police?" Zel asked.

"Man, don't do that. Don't treat us like we did this shit to her, bruh. From the looks of things, right now we're the only ones who give a fuck about her!" I told the officers.

"We're going to have to swab you, Easy, is it?" one of the other officers told me.

I looked at him. "What?"

"We're going to have to swab you. Can't you hear?" Zel told me. "Your story isn't adding up. You're not telling us everything. All three of you need to be swabbed to see if your DNA matches what the doctors found in that rape kit. It won't take long. It's real simple. Test results won't take long to come back."

By the time the results of the rape kit and our swabs came back, Pops and Mom had shown up. As usual, Pops played it cool in front of strangers, as if he didn't know me. He questioned me in front of Meelah's friends as if he was just an officer questioning me. Ace and Claudius were cleared. They were mad as fuck for even being put in that position after all they did to try to make sure that Meelah was taken to get help. They were put out of the hospital. The doctor wanted to talk to my parents and Officer Zel alone.

"So, what are the results? Was my son involved in this bullshit?" Pops was so mad his olive skin was turning red.

Dr. Lonni Max hesitated and pushed her glasses back over her nose. "Ummm, no, he wasn't. But his DNA proves he's related to one or more of the men who raped Meelah Summers."

We all looked at the doctor.

Pops looked at Zel.

"One of the suspects is named Cristobal Romano." Zel hesitated.

Pops's skin went from bright red to damn near snow white. "What did you say?"

"According to the DNA, it appears that Cristobal Romano is a close relative of your son, probably a brother. And—"

"Get rid of that rape kit," Pops cut her off.

Dr. Max gasped. "What, sir?"

"If you want to live, get rid of that shit!" Pops yelled.

"I can't do that, sir. I took an oath, and so did you." Dr. Max's eyes watered.

"The son of Stefano Romano raped the daughter of a man who works for him! If her father finds out what happened to his daughter and who did it, it's going to cause a war!" Pops screamed.

"Pops?" I spoke up. "Who is this muthafucka? Is he my father?"

Pops hesitated. "No."

"But the doctor just said that Cristobal is—"

Pops cut me off. "I'm your fuckin' father!"

Mom hated when he yelled. She tried to soothe her husband by rubbing his arm, but he pulled away. "Okay, honey, we need to go home. Bostyn, go home."

"Home?" I scoffed. "Where is that?"

Pops pointed in my face. "Leave that girl alone. Stay the fuck out of this! Doctor, get rid of that shit. And, Zel, if this shit gets out to the press, your career is over! Keep this shit in this office!"

Pops left the office, pulling Mom behind him. The doctor hesitated to follow them.

Zel stood there, not really sure what to say to me except for, "Go home, son."

I shook my head. "I didn't find out I was adopted until four years ago! I didn't find out until I was thirteen that Jimmie wasn't my father and Lauryn wasn't my mother. Their maid happens to be my real mother's sister, who helped to raise me all these years! Then, tonight after finding a girl—who I just met a few days ago but can't stop thinking about—naked and beat the fuck up, come to find out I'm related to the muthafucka who did this to her! My father knows the muthafuckas who did this! I'm piecing all this shit together in my mind, and I still can't figure out how Jimmie ended up with the son of a drug lord!"

Zel exhaled deeply. "When your father was younger, before the police academy, he used to run with *La Catena,* Italian for The Chain. He worked side by side with Stefano. They were like brothers. That was until they fell in love with the same girl. A girl from Guatemala. She was sixteen, beautiful, and down to ride. She had a drug problem that Stefano supplied. Her addiction to that drug outweighed any love she may have had or may have not had for your father. When she was pregnant with you, they put her in a rehab clinic. The State ended up taking you from your mother and putting you in that group home for boys and your mother in a foster home until she was eighteen. The Shones family took her in."

I looked at Zel. "Shones? That's Mom's family. They took her in, knowing her affiliation with my father?"

Zel shook his head. "As far as they were concerned, she was a girl who didn't speak English and needed a home. Jimmie told his parents that the child was his. He was twenty-one at the time. His father didn't want to get his son in trouble, so he convinced a friend of the family—his best friend, Patrick Shone—to take the young girl into their home. Jimmie got to know Lauryn with the intention of keeping an eye on Maria Alejandra. Stefano was after her, so Jimmie joined the police force, trying to protect her. He convinced Lauryn to adopt her child. They changed your name to protect your identity. As soon as Maria Alejandra was eighteen, she went back to Guatemala, only to be kidnapped and end up back in *La Catena.* After all Jimmie did to try to secure her safety, she told Stefano that Jimmie raped her, that you were Jimmie's son."

I frowned, looking into Zel's face. He stood there like he couldn't believe he was telling me all that information, more like he wished he hadn't said shit.

"So, Stefano thinks I'm Jimmie's son?" I asked.

Zel hesitated. "The day your mom showed up to tell you the truth about who she was, she was supposed to kill you to prove to Stefano that you weren't his son. Instead, your mother was killed. In order to save your life, we ended up creating a crime scene with your mother's body and one of the young John Does we found dead in the alley that night. We fabricated an entire story and told the media that Maria Alejandra killed her son Emilio Gonzales before killing herself."

"Who killed my mother? Tell me. I wanna know," I asked.

Zel hesitated. "Emmanuel, the father of the girl you're worried about in the room down the hall. Her father started off as a contract killer. He was hired to kill you, broke into your house one night while Jimmie and Lauryn were away on business. Donna—your father's maid who came up from Guatemala to try to help her niece—stopped him from killing you in your sleep by telling him that you were Stefano's son. Instead of killing you, he hid out in the shed, waited for Maria Alejandra to reach into her pocket for the gun and shot her. Once Donna admitted to telling Emmanuel the truth about you, Jimmie made her spy on the Gonzales family and the Romanos, since Jimena—Maria Alejandra's twin—is still in the gang. There is so much more to this story, son. I shouldn't even be talking to you about this shit. But your father's right."

"He's not my fuckin' father!" I yelled. "You just said so yourself!"

"Just leave!" Zel shoved me, though I planted my feet on the ground and didn't budge an inch. Zel laughed to himself. "So, you want to be stubborn, huh? Fine, stay. Create another murder scene. I can just see the headlines now. Son of a cop turns out to be son of a drug lord. Daughter of a drug lord raped by the man who employs him. Both families at odds until there is no one standing to tell what really happened." Zel shook his head. "You're looking for answers that you're not ready for. Let the past die."

"Like my mother?" I asked, not believing for one minute that she would kill me to save herself.

Thirteen years had gone by. Why would he wait thirteen years to tell her to kill me? Why not when she was kidnapped back into The Chain? After Emmanuel found out that I was his boss's son, what kept him from telling Stefano about me? Was I a bribe? Pops didn't have any gang tats, but was he still affiliated with The Chain?

"There's no way Stefano doesn't know about me by now! That girl in the room with Meelah knows she's my cousin! Her mother is my mother's twin sister!" I told Zel.

"Emmanuel didn't tell your father about you. He bribed Jimmie, told him he'd keep you a secret in exchange for immunity. And . . . there's more," Zel started to say.

There was a knock at the doctor's office door before she peeped back in. "Umm," Dr. Max said. "Meelah's aunt is here."

I looked at Zel before walking out of the office.

Zel followed me. "All right, Bostyn, I warned you to stay out of this. We all did."

"Yeah, whatever." I peeped back at Zel, watching him stop in his tracks.

I walked to Meelah's room where her aunt stood crying over the bed. I tapped at the door lightly, watching the middle-aged woman dry her face. She was beautiful, looking like an older version of Meelah.

"I'm Easy. I'm the one who found your niece," I told her and walked up to shake her hand.

She nodded and shook my hand. "I'm Troy," she told me. "We're waiting for them to prepare a helicopter."

"Helicopter?" I asked.

Troy nodded. "I will be taking her with me to live in Richmond, Virginia. The social worker was trying to get a court order to take Meelah away from her father, who they can't get in touch with due to the fact that no one ever knows how to reach him other than the men he runs with. This isn't the environment for her. I'm taking him to court for custody, and he'd be a fool to fight me on this. This isn't the life for her. Sharita just left here crying her eyes out when I told her that I was taking her best friend away."

"Is she stable enough to leave Maryland?" I asked.

Troy shook her head. "She'll never be stable enough to leave Maryland."

I looked over at Meelah, watching the ventilator help oxygen flow throughout Meelah's lungs. She was put in a medically induced coma so her brain could rest while the swelling went down. I looked back at Troy, who stood there with tears running down her face. "What is your address? Or a number where I can reach her?" I asked.

Troy shook her head. "No. I don't want her to have anything to do with anything in this area, including my brother-in-law. I should have taken her after her mother was killed."

"I'm hurt, I'm man enough to admit that. I just met her, ya know? Whoever knew I'd be feelin' a girl this much who I just met?" I admitted.

Troy looked my face over, staring at me like I looked familiar. "What did you say your name was again?"

"Easy," I told her.

"I'll tell her that you were asking about her," Troy responded and pulled her purse strap over her shoulder, looking bitchy and boujee.

I laughed a little when I really wanted to curse her out. "That I asked about her? I risked my life to bring shawty here. Everyone kept telling me to leave her. And you're not gonna mention the fact that I was the one who brought her here?"

Troy just looked at me, clearing her throat like she was ready for me to leave the room.

I shook my head before going over to the stool that sat alongside the head of the bed. I sat down on the stool, looking at Meelah's swollen face. "This isn't goodbye, sweetheart. It's 'see you when ya aunt stops acting like I didn't save your life.' She doesn't know how to see with her heart either. She must think I'm like Dinero, the same person who let you go missing for three days. I ain't worried about her though. I'm worried about you. I'm coming for you, baby girl. Ya hear me?"

I stood from the bed and kissed her on her forehead. I didn't want to leave her, but the way things were going, I really had no choice. I just hoped that when she woke up, she'd look for me and ask about me.

Chapter Five

Meelah

I smelled pot roast and vegetables simmering and cornbread baking before I opened my eyes to see a bedroom I hadn't slept in since I was a little girl. I struggled to sit up in the bed, my side and face in excruciating pain. I felt like I'd been asleep for two months, and that was because I basically had. I didn't remember much but waking up in the hospital and being told that I was waking up from a three-week-long medically induced coma. When I woke up from the coma, my jaw was wired shut. The only thing I remembered from the past eight weeks was having my wires removed, a doctor connecting bands to the metal brackets that were on my teeth, my aunt and father arguing over me, and being questioned by a social worker for a few seconds while I could keep my eyes open.

What I didn't remember was being questioned by the police about what happened to me. Shit, I could barely remember what happened to me, and I didn't want to either. Broken jaw, broken ribs, and my aunt hated to tell me that I was raped. That was where the strong medication was needed. I didn't want to remember anything. All I wanted to do was sleep.

Outside of not wanting my memory to recover, I needed to sleep through the excruciating pain of my jaw healing around the metal plates and screws in my mouth. I don't think I stayed awake longer than half an hour during those eight weeks. The moment I smelled the food cooking was the only time I'd been in my right mind. The last full memory that I had was the night of the homecoming, sitting at my mother's grave with Easy. Everything after that was a blur.

There was tapping at my room door before it opened. Aunt Troy came into the room carrying a blended drink. She smiled slightly when she saw me sitting up in the bed propped up on three pretty, pink pillows.

"Hey, baby. It's dinnertime." Aunt Troy came over and sat down on the edge of the bed next to me. "Sorry you can't eat what I cooked, but here." She handed the drink to me.

I hesitated to take the drink, slightly opening my jaw and slipping the straw through the bands in my mouth. I slurped the drink. It was pretty good. Tasted like bananas, strawberries, and blueberries.

"The swelling has gone down drastically in your face and your hands." Aunt Troy pushed my bangs from my face. "There's that pretty face that I've missed so much."

"Where is . . ." I coughed a little as I removed the straw from my mouth. "Where is Dinero?" It suddenly dawned on me that the one face from that night that I didn't remember was Dinero's. "Has he called about me? Has he come to see me?"

Aunt Troy hesitated. "He mailed your cell phone here."

I looked at her, my head spinning in confusion. "How did he get my phone? I haven't seen him since the homecoming!"

Aunt Troy shrugged. "I don't know."

I leaned back in the bed, rubbing my cheeks. "What about Sharita?"

Aunt Troy rolled her eyes a little. "She's been calling my cell nonstop. Your father gave her the address, but she hasn't shown up yet. That white boy has though."

I looked into my aunt's face. "What?"

"Easy. He's shown up five times in the past eight weeks trying to see you. Said Sharita gave him the address." Aunt Troy exhaled deeply. "Meelah, he's bad news."

I shook my head. "Did you let him in to see me?"

Aunt Troy's eyes glistened as she continued trying to play hard. "That hardheaded daughter of mine let him in while I was at work. I swear, Zara never listens. I came back from work about four weeks ago after a long day and found him in your room. He was helping the nurse give you a sponge bath. I started to yell at him for being in my house, but . . ." Aunt Troy choked back the tears. "The way he washed your feet and combed your hair, I could tell he really cares about you. So, I asked Sharita about him."

"And?" I asked her.

"He is related to the man your father works for. He's a known mobster's son!" Aunt Troy exclaimed.

"So? I'm a drug mobster's daughter!" I responded.

Aunt Troy shook her head. "There's a difference and you know it. Whether he knows who his father is personally or not, he's trouble. Sharita said her mother was his mother's twin. Said the woman was shot in front of him on the same exact day that my sister was killed in police custody! This is too much of a coincidence! This is trouble! I told your friends to stay away. Dinero knew better than to show his face. Easy is the most persistent one. Here it is, Christmas Eve, and—"

I gasped. "Christmas Eve?"

Aunt Troy nodded. "Yes, honey."

"My . . ." I choked back the tears. "My birthday is in a week!"

Aunt Troy nodded. "Yes, it is, honey. You have more than enough credits to graduate on time. After Christmas break, you'll return to school if you're ready."

"School here?" I asked and watched her nod her head. "What did my dad say?"

"It doesn't matter what he says. Your father is in no position to tell me how to raise my niece!" Aunt Troy snapped at me.

"I'm the only one he has left!" I argued. "I'm his only daughter!"

"He had you selling drugs for him! Your boyfriend kills and deals for him! Easy told the police this bogus-ass story about finding you behind a dumpster! The doctors did a rape kit on you, but mysteriously, the specimen was lost, and the technician couldn't find her report! When I asked them to redo the exam, they claimed that you had been cleaned up and there was no way they could collect another sample! I'm not stupid. Someone who was involved with your father hurt you, Meelah!" Aunt Troy tried to reach for my face, but I pushed her hand away. She laughed a little. "I'm trying to help you."

"Then let me see my friends!" I shouted. "Where is Whitley? You mentioned Sharita, but you didn't mention the girl who is supposed to be my sister!"

"She's dead, sweetie," Aunt Troy didn't hesitate to say.

I sat up in the bed, heart thumping in my chest. "Dead?"

"All the students who took the drugs at that party that you went to after homecoming have come up dead. And their autopsy reports are missing. Your father claims no connection to this, but we both know he's lying."

Aunt Troy watched me cringe in pain, feeling sick to my stomach.

"Can I call—" I started to say when my aunt cut me off.

"No! You need to move on from that life, Meelah!" Aunt Troy hollered. "I took your father to court for full custody. I really don't give a fuck if you're about to be eighteen! The fact that you're about to go to college next year means I'm still your guardian until you're twenty-one and a senior in college! Fortunately, I found out they're offering you a full scholarship, so the only thing I'm responsible for paying for is for your meals while you live on campus. And while you're in school, just to make sure you don't try to run back to Maryland, I'll be moving to Los Angeles too. Zara will be okay here without me for a few months."

I shook my head. "You can't do this."

"Baby girl, I already did," Aunt Troy assured me. "You were beaten within an inch of your life and left for dead for almost three days. The only one brave enough to look for you was a white boy who you know absolutely nothing about! Which is why . . ." Aunt Troy watched the tears sliding down my face. "Which is why your cousin invited him over for dinner tonight."

I gasped, looking up at my aunt as she got off my bed.

"Do you need me to help you wash up, sweetie?" Aunt Troy cried too as I nodded.

After Aunt Troy helped me get dressed and comb my hair up into a bun, she helped me down the stairs. When we got to my aunt's dining room, there my cousin Zara was laughing at whatever Easy was saying to her. When I saw that boy in my living room, all I could do was thank God for him. I stood there in the doorway, unable to move from the shock of seeing him sitting there. Zara looked over from him to me once she noticed me in the doorway. Easy looked over at me before standing up from his chair. There he stood, looking fine as ever in his slim-fit, long-sleeved gray and blue checkered shirt, black pants, and white Nikes. Tattoos swerved around his hands and up his forearm. He didn't have to do much to clean up, but when he did, goddamn.

Aunt Troy hesitated a little. "Zara, baby, let's get the table set. We have family members coming over for dinner in about thirty minutes."

Zara grinned at me, her soft brown eyes sparkling a little. "Hey, cuz, nice to see you up and moving around. Have you met my boyfriend, Easy?" she joked, getting up from the table and coming over to me. She hugged me around my neck before going to the kitchen with her mother.

Before Easy could open his mouth to say anything, I made my way over and threw my arms around him. He hugged me back, his face buried in my neck.

"Feels so good to see you, baby girl," he told me. He squeezed me as tight as he could without hurting me before letting go a little and helping me over to the chair that was next to the one he was sitting in. He helped me sit down, and then he sat next to me, pulling my chair as close to his as it could get. Then he turned to me, hands gripping mine in his. He looked at me like he was genuinely happy to see me okay.

"How did you get my mean-ass aunt to invite you to dinner?" was all I could say.

Easy laughed. "I've been coming up here damn near every other day. I brought my boy Ace with me. Your cousin Zara started feeling him. Once Zara saw I was cool, she convinced your aunt that I was cool. That I didn't mean any harm. Ace showed your aunt footage from the homecoming dance. I guess your aunt was impressed that I had the courage to overstep my boundaries with the CMC. But I think what really got her is when she came home and I was giving you a sponge bath with your cousin. That shit broke me down, Meelah. I hated seeing you like that. I guess my persistence and determination to not give up trying to see you with your eyes open is what got to her. She's not feeling your friends. And to tell you the truth, I'm not either."

I just looked into his face, listening to him talk.

"That story that Sharita told everybody about me, turns out it's true. Her mom is my mother's twin sister. And my father . . ." Easy shook his head to himself. "You don't want to know who he is."

"Whitley's dead," I whispered as he looked my face over.

Easy nodded. "I know. All the kids from that party who ya father's crew sold their product to are dead. Shit, some of their family members too. There are rumors of the CMC wrecking shit, but no one has gone to the police. No witnesses, no case."

I looked at Easy just as Cristobal's voice rang in my ear, uttering the last words that Easy had just said. An image of Cristobal pinning me down on the floor and pouring liquor down my throat flashed through my mind. In that flash of memory, I felt like I was drowning. I *was* drowning. He was just pouring gin down my throat.

"What's wrong?" Easy asked, watching me slip my hands from his.

"I . . ." I hesitated. I had to think smart. Cristobal was relying on me not remembering anything. So, I had to play the part. I didn't want the memories to come back. "I look horrible."

Easy shook his head. "Nah."

"Yes, I do. These metal braces in my mouth. The swelling. The bruises." I tried to cover my face, but he moved my hands away. “My aunt won’t even let my father see me.”

“She’s just trying to keep you safe,” Easy assured me.

“Dinero hasn’t come to see me,” I let him know.

Easy’s dark eyebrows connected into a frown. “He’s trying to miss the moon, too busy counting stars.”

I shook my head. “It’s more than that.”

“The men who did this to you—”

I cut Easy off. “What men?”

Easy’s eyes searched mine. “The men who your father work for.”

I shook my head. “I don’t remember anything.”

Easy hesitated for a minute, not sure if he should tell me what he knew. He was the one who found me. My aunt said he claimed that he found me behind a dumpster, but she knew that was a lie. I didn’t want to hear how he found me. I didn’t want to know.

“I don’t want to remember anything. Please,” I begged him.

Easy nodded. “Okay.”

I exhaled deeply, trying my best to not let the memories seep into my mind. The thing about the human thought process is that your mind is a separate entity from your brain. Your mind takes over your brain at times, reprogramming you like a person sitting in front of a computer. Once your eyes encounter something, it’s etched in your mind forever. Maybe you can’t recall the memory, and then boom, out of nowhere, something as simple as a fragrance can trigger the most painful memory.

As soon as Easy leaned in a little closer to dry the tears that started to escape from my eyes, the smell of his Tom Ford Tuscan Leather cologne filtered through my nose, and I was back there in the center of my living room, hands tied behind my back, legs tied at the ankles, face down, ass up, someone fucking the shit out of me while Cristobal laughed and held a gun to Dinero's face.

I gasped, standing up from the chair. Cristobal wore that exact cologne. I knew when I saw Easy that he looked familiar. He was the perfect blend of Stef and Jimena. His mother had to be Jimena's sister. Sharita was telling the truth. He was her cousin. Did he really know who his biological father was? I was afraid to ask. I didn't know Easy all that well, but I knew he pried into my business.

Easy stood from his chair, pulling me close.

"Why did you come here?" I questioned him.

"Because I care," Easy told me.

I shook my head. "Why? No one else does! Dinero watched those men . . ." I stopped myself from revealing the nightmare that was starting to come back.

Easy frowned. "So, you do remember?"

I shook my head frantically.

Easy exhaled deeply. "Word around town is the doctors lost the results of your rape kit. They're saying the rape never happened. That what happened to you was the result of gang violence."

"Well, wasn't it?" I cried with my lips quivering.

"I'll get you the answers you need. I'll find out why ya dude—"

"I don't want to know shit about Dinero!" I yelled. "Fuck him!"

"Is everything okay?" My aunt came back into the living room, carrying a plate stacked with slices of sweet cornbread.

Zara followed her mother, eying Easy as he sat back down in his chair and helped ease me back down to mine.

"Yes, ma'am, everything is fine." Easy cleared his throat.

"Good. My niece has been in that bed for eight weeks. I let you come over, hoping you'd cheer her up. You were the only one brave enough to weather my storm, young man. Don't disappoint me." Aunt Troy forcefully set the plate of cornbread on the table.

"Aunt Troy, it's all good. I'm just in some pain. That's all." I was so upset my hands were shaking.

Easy grabbed my trembling hand in his, intertwining his finger with mine. "I got you, Meelah. I'm here, okay? When you're ready to talk, I'm here. Whenever you need a friend or a protector, I'm here for that, too."

I looked at him. "For how long?"

"As long as you need me to be." Easy gripped my hand in his. "I mean, I gotta be home for Christmas—Pops will kill me—but I'll be back for your birthday. I promise."

I couldn't figure out why Easy was so determined to meet me. Why, all of a sudden, I looked up and there was this cool-ass white boy smiling down into my face on the dance floor. He came out of nowhere. I'd never seen him before, but when I met him, I was instantly drawn to him. I should have hated him, knowing who his family was, but I couldn't. He didn't know them. He was nothing like them. Whoever raised him taught him how to treat a lady. Dinero was my boyfriend, but Easy was about to be something more.

"Why are you here?" My heart thumped in my chest.

"Don't you need somebody to love you, Miss Meelah?" Easy grinned. "Let me do me for a few hours, if that's all right with you."

I blushed a little as Zara giggled to herself.

My aunt rolled her eyes, still not convinced. It wasn't too often she'd seen me with a white boy. In fact, she'd never seen me with a white boy. None of my guy friends were white. Other than the Romanos, there were no white men in our circle. And we didn't even see color when it came to that family. They were ruthless as fuck, so they pretty much fit right in with us. Pretty much like

Easy did. Everything in me kept telling me that I was making a mistake by letting him into my world, but I just couldn't let go. Not just yet. I had lost everything already. I couldn't get the horrified look on Dinero's face out of my head, and I desperately needed to.

"Dinero is going to show up sooner or later as soon as he finds out my aunt let you come over," I told him.

White boy looked at me like I had him fucked all the way the fuck up. "You're stressing about that muthafucka like he's promised to you forever. I'm here. He's not. Focus on that. Prioritize because that's what that muthafucka is doin'. If he cared about you, he would've tried as hard to get through your aunt's front door as I did. Plain and simple. Fuck him."

Aunt Troy scoffed, impressed a little. "Well, damn."

Zara laughed out loud, watching me look Easy's face over. "Well, he got Mom's stamp of approval!"

The doorbell sounded.

"The Heinzes are in the building!" Zara squealed excitedly, scurrying past her mother to go to the door.

Aunt Troy grinned at me as I tried my hardest not to blush. "Thanks for coming by, Easy. You think I'm tough? Meet my sisters."

We sat at the dining room table. I hated being around all that food and not being able to eat it. I didn't have much of an appetite anyway. And who could eat with my boujee aunt Louise looking at Easy like she'd never seen a white person before? He was the elephant in the room that no one wanted to address. He sat there eating everything on his plate, no objections to anything until he drank Aunt Winifred's Sweet-Ass Tea. She sold her Sweet-Ass Tea in stores and made a killing, literally. That shit would send you into a diabetic coma if you drank more than one glass.

"You want some more Sweet-Ass Tea?" Aunt Cynclaire reached for the tea pitcher, noticing Easy's glass was half full.

Easy shook his head. "Nah. I'm good. Can I just fill it halfway with water? It's too sweet."

Everyone looked at my Aunt Winifred, who usually went off on anyone who insulted her recipe. But instead of trippin', she grabbed a water pitcher and stood from the table to go around to the side where Easy was sitting and poured him a glass.

"So, you can't handle something so dark and sweet, huh?" Aunt Winifred teased him.

"Ain't nothing better than dark and sweet, ma'am. But sometimes you gotta add a little bit of unsweet to tame the taste a little. Too much of a good thing can be bad," Easy clapped back.

Aunt Winifred backed off and went back to her seat, straightening out her pleated skirt as she sat down. "So, how did you meet our baby?" she asked.

"He stole a dance from the homecoming king!" Zara chimed in. "It's on Bay City High's Facebook page."

I rolled my eyes over at Zara and watched her giggling at my aunts staring at Easy.

"And Cash Money Millionaire didn't feel some type of way?" Aunt Troy commented.

I exhaled deeply. "If you're talking about Dinero, you already know he felt some type of way about it."

"Why isn't he here on Christmas Eve with you?" Aunt Cynclaire questioned.

"Mom won't let anyone see her," Zara responded.

Aunt Cynclaire looked at Easy. "She let Mark Wahlberg in."

"He didn't really give Mama a choice. He's a persistent little somebody," Zara huffed. "Barely knows anything about my cousin, but dammit if he isn't protective over her. Look how close they're sitting. Don't try to scoot over now!" Zara laughed, watching me try to scoot away while Easy pulled my chair back.

"He's brave," Aunt Troy spoke through the laughter. "We all know what happened to baby girl was a result of some shit that went wrong in her father's organization."

"Aunt Troy—" I tried to stop her from downing my father, but she cut me off.

"The fact that the police aren't involved in this tells me that they know who did it. Either the police are working with these corrupt muthafuckas or they have dirt on one another. Either way, the court awarded me guardianship until you finish high school. Turning eighteen doesn't make you grown, little girl," My Aunt Troy let me know. "Going to college at UCLA doesn't grant you approval to run wild either. I retire next summer, so I'ma be on your ass like corn on a cob!"

My aunts gave out a unanimous, "Umm-hmm."

I rolled my eyes and grabbed my smoothie from the table. "This some bullshit," I muttered.

"What was that?" Aunt Winifred snapped.

"I said I smell biscuits," I responded quickly.

"Ummm-hmm, that's what I thought." Aunt Winifred peeped Easy chuckling to himself. "Where are you from, little boy?"

Easy took a few sips from his glass of tea before looking back at my aunts and cousin, who were looking at him. "I don't know."

Aunt Louise frowned in confusion. "You don't know?"

"I mean," Easy said, shrugging, "it wasn't until I was thirteen that I found out that I was adopted. As far as I know, I was adopted from the Bostonian Home for Boys. I was adopted by a family who thinks they're protecting me by keeping my identity from me."

I slurped loudly through the straw.

Easy looked at me before looking back at my Aunt Louise. "All I know is that I feel out of place. It's funny because when I came around your niece, I felt right at home. It was like I knew that with her is right where I'm supposed to be." Easy looked back at me as he watched me lower my cup onto the table.

My aunts were stunned to silence for a few seconds. They'd never heard anyone talk about me that way. And neither had I. The sweetest thing that Dinero had ever said to me were the words on that card that he'd given me on homecoming night. It was the first time he'd openly expressed how he felt about me, but turned out he was fuckin' my so-called friend.

"What do you have to say about that, Meelah?" Aunt Winifred helped herself to another slice of ham. "I'm sure you two haven't even established if you're even friends, and here he is proclaiming his love for you in front of your aunts. He's so smooth-talking you'd almost forget he was white. Your daddy wouldn't approve of him at all. Your father likes men for you who he can control with money, and Easy doesn't seem like the kind of man you can control with anything."

"Look," Easy spoke up. "I'm just here as a friend, nothing else. I'm not here to get cut with the jagged pieces of your niece's broken heart. I was worried about shawty, so I came to see her. I just met her, and I wasn't ready to lose her. I didn't find her behind a dumpster."

We all looked at Easy.

Easy exhaled deeply. "I found her in her apartment, beaten, bloody, swollen, naked, and balled up on the floor of a closet upstairs. The men who worked for your father were outside of that apartment, guarding it, none of them going in to check on you. They were just focused on keeping everyone out. It took me and my crew to go in and get you. Your aunt is right, Meelah. Ya dad is involved in some type of way. And from the looks of things, my real relatives might be involved too, though you're forcing yourself not to remember. I don't know who I am. I need to know. I know you're hurt, Meelah, but so am I. I need you to find out about me. Help me help you."

I just looked into Easy's face as my aunts went off.

"I knew we should have taken this girl from that nigga when Sadey passed! I told her about that nigga from jump!" Aunt Cynclaire went off.

"Nah, I told her to stay the fuck away from him, but y'all were like, 'Go on and get the money from that muthafucka!'" Aunt Troy told her sisters. "She died, and the nigga didn't even push the investigation! They forgot about my sister! I filed for full custody of you, Meelah, and your father was in California, not even bothering to show up for the court date. He responded to my court motion with a letter, explaining his presence in California, how he was starting a hotel chain and was there on business. I mentioned the assault in my motion."

I looked at my aunt.

Aunt Troy's eyes watered. "Money is all that matters to him."

I shook my head. "That's not true."

Aunt Troy huffed. "What type of father knows his child was beat the fuck up, left to die, and not show up to see what's wrong with her? Two months have gone by, and the only people who tried to contact you was your friend Sharita and Easy. Once your father found out that the swelling in your face went down, your jaws were wired, your ribs were healing, and you would probably suffer temporary memory loss, he left you to my care. This stranger right here is the only one who fought his way to you. That says a lot about the people in your life, sweetheart."

I exhaled deeply, sitting back in my seat. Yeah, my dad was all about the money. He knew money before he knew me. That was his favorite line. If I fucked with his money, he was fuckin' me up. I should've been hurt about him not coming for me or fighting my aunt in court, but I wasn't. Easy was right. I needed love.

"So, Easy," my aunt Cynclaire said, changing the subject from my father to my friend, "what you drankin'?"

Easy chuckled a little, looking at my aunt like she was crazy until he realized that she was serious. He looked back at me. "She serious?"

I rolled my eyes a little and nodded. One thing about my aunts, they let us drink or smoke as long as we did it with them and no one else.

Easy looked back at my aunts and nodded. "Shit, what you got?"

"Ya aunts cool as fuck." Easy laughed as he sat next to me in the window seat of my bedroom.

I laughed to myself, hearing the muffled sound of my aunts laughing downstairs. "Yeah, they like you too." I watched Easy take a sip of pineapple tequila from his glass. "We do this every year," I told him. "There are usually more people than this. My aunt's sons and daughters are probably spending time with their baes' families. Usually we're deep in this bitch. We meet the day before Christmas to exchange gifts. I usually get twice the amount of presents as everyone else since my birthday is January first. When is your birthday?"

Easy licked his lips a little. "March ninth," he reminded me.

I smacked my forehead, feeling stupid. "Duh. I'm so stupid. You already told me that. Sorry, Easy."

Easy shook his head. "It's all good. Oh, and it's Bostyn with a 'y' before the 'n'."

I looked at him, glaring in confusion. "Huh?"

"My name. It's Bostyn," Bostyn told me. "Easy is my middle name. My middle initials were actually EZ until I legally had it changed to Easy."

I looked his face over. Yeah, that kind of fit him. "Well, it rhymes with Justin, so I guess I was kind of close. Why did you have to give me a fake name? Now I know how niggas feel when me and my girls used to give niggas fake names at the club!"

Bostyn scoffed. "Fuck you mean? You know good and well muthafuckas will Google your ass and call your cell phone right in front of you these days! We tired of y'all shit, man."

I laughed out loud, side aching a little. I held my side, laughing at Bostyn, watching him smirk a little. "You're right about that one. 'Easy' kinda grew on me, though. I like it, Easy-B."

Bostyn looked at me. "For safety reasons, I don't give out my real name. Only my crew knows my real name. But you seem cool enough to know the real me, so I guess I'll let you in on the secret."

I exhaled deeply, looking out the window at the starlit sky. "I know all about secrets. The drug world is full of secrets, lies, and deceit. I just need something real."

Bostyn looked at me. "I'm right here. Levitate with ya boy."

I grinned a little, watching him take out a dime bag of Buddha Haze, which was my favorite. Sharita got me high with that shit on a weekly basis, so I knew he hit her up.

"Roll up," I told him before pulling the window up to vent my room because that Haze smoke was thick and lingered like a muthafucka.

Halfway through smoking that joint, Bostyn's head was in my lap, and my fingers were running through his hair. I watched him take in the vapors, holding it in, choking on it a little before releasing the smoke through his mouth and nose. My cell phone rang, vibrating against the bookshelf that it sat on. I reached for the phone and peeped the display. It was Dinero. The only way he'd know that I was awake was if Sharita called him. I'd texted her earlier to let her know that I was awake and spending time with family. After I told her that Dinero hadn't reached out to me once, I should've known that she'd hit him up with the "Nigga, you ain't shit" text.

I exhaled deeply and set the phone back on the bookshelf.

Bostyn handed the joint back to me.

I shook my head. "Nah, I'm good. I'm already high enough, boo. I feel like I'm on my way to heaven right now."

Bostyn sat up. He backed up against the wall of my window seat and faced me. He peeped the frustrated expression on my face. "What's up, ma? Who was that?"

"Nobody," I muttered and watched Bostyn put out the joint in my crystal ashtray.

"You don't wanna talk to ya dude?" Bostyn frowned at me, eyes low.

"He doesn't want to talk to me," I told him. "He's only calling because I'm sure Sharita told him that you're here. I texted her and told her that my aunt let you in. And I'm sure she rubbed it in Dinero's face that her cousin got in and he didn't not only because he didn't try, but because he couldn't get in. My aunt hates him. He reminds her of my father. I thought that was what I wanted, until . . ." I stopped, trying my best not to cry. "I woke up a few times throughout the last eight weeks. As soon as I opened my eyes, the pain hit me. Then the memories hit me. I'd scream for the nurse my aunt hired to come in and dope me up with meds. Today is the first day that I've gotten out of that bed. The only reason I don't have bedsores is because of the masseuse my aunt hired. She would turn me every hour in the bed. The memories of what happened to me have been flashing through my mind all night. And in those memories, Dinero is watching me get beaten, raped, beaten, raped, and beat some more! I understand that there was a gun pointed at his head, but why did it take him until person number three choked me damn near unconscious before he said, 'Okay, all right, muthafucka, I'll do it'?"

Bostyn frowned, watching my lips tremble as I fought off the tears.

I laughed a little. "I'm not about to blow my high talking about him. He isn't ready for me. He's never been ready. He's out there living his life, and I'm stuck with these demons."

"Trust me, baby girl. He's got demons too. Knowing he saw those muthafuckas torturing you, I think he stayed away because he couldn't face you after what happened. I know I would've gone out shootin' muthafuckas if it were me. I couldn't watch no shit like that, but everyone loves different." Bostyn watched the tears start to slide down my cheeks. He started to say something, but his phone chimed in his pocket before his ringtone started to play. And he rapped along with DMX's voice seeping through his pants pocket.

"See there, something can go wrong, it does. Loved it, let it go, but it came back. That's how strong it was. But you belonged to 'cus, couldn't belong to me. You had two kids by this n.... It was wrong for me."

I smirked, loving the fact that he was smart enough not to let the word "nigga" come out of his mouth. "You're really just gonna rap to the song and not answer the phone?"

Bostyn clicked his teeth. "Hell yeah, this is my shit. Fuck who's callin'. It's just Ace. I told him to hit me up at nine thirty to remind me that I need to be making my way back to Maryland. Moms is real big on getting up at like four in the morning to help the staff cook. I mean, she makes food for Santa and shit too. I hate to be coming in with the sun and running into her. Not trying to hear her mouth."

I looked his face over with so much admiration. "The family you're adopted into is nothing like your real family. I know who your family is all too well."

Bostyn frowned a little.

"Do you want to meet your f—"

Bostyn cut me off quickly. "Hell nah. After these last few months, I've been through enough with so-called family. I don't wanna know the muthafucka. I met my cousin. I met my mom's sister. I'm good on that. Pops would kill me if he knew I was around any of y'all. This is our secret, ya heard me?" Bostyn reached into his pocket and pulled out this little silver box. He opened it before placing it in my hands.

I looked into the box before I reached inside of it to pull out the prettiest hair comb barrette I'd ever seen. It was silver with diamonds and pearls scattered all over it. It was heavy. The real thing. I looked into Bostyn's face as he took it from my hand.

Bostyn held my arm, pulling me closer to him as he scooted closer to me, surrounding me with his legs.

I blushed as he slid the comb through my hair.

"You have money, so I knew you wouldn't be easily impressed. The day my mom died, after the police came and scraped her body off the pavement, I just stood there watching. Her brain matter was all over my shirt. I was covered in blood. And when I lowered my head that day to cry over her, I looked down on the ground to see that hair comb. When I showed it to my maid, who turns out to be my mom's aunt, she told me that it was my great-grandmother's wedding comb. That it had been passed down through the family. This comb symbolizes the last thing I remember about my mom. It means something to me," Bostyn told me.

I exhaled deeply. "Easy-B, you didn't have to do this."

Bostyn nodded. "Yeah, I did. You lost a mother that day too. Our paths crossed two months ago for a reason, little lady. And I'm glad they did. Dinero isn't ready, but I knew the second I saw you that you were the one. I know I can't have you like I want to, but it's the thought that counts, right?"

I was speechless, not really sure what to say as I watched Bostyn stand from the seat. I stood before him, holding that silver box in my hands. "Thank you for coming to see me," was all I could think of to say. "Thank you for looking for me. When gangstas' daughters get killed or beaten, the police never stay involved. Soon as they find out who's involved, the charges are never even filed. If you hadn't saved me, then—"

Bostyn wouldn't even let me finish. "But I did, so let's just leave it at that. You're here now, your aunt is taking care of you, and I'll pop in from time to time. You already know." Bostyn pulled me closer to him by my arm. He looked down at me. "Your braces and shit are kind of cute. You can barely notice the rubber bands and shit."

I rolled my eyes. "The rubber bands come off in a couple of days, but these braces will be in for a while. I look ugly as hell. I hate that you have to see me like this."

"I'm just glad I get to see you. Ya aunt was pissed at me the day I gave you that sponge bath." Bostyn shook his head.

"You just wanted to see me naked," I teased.

Bostyn frowned. "Fourteen."

"Huh?" I asked.

"I counted ya bruises. You had fourteen huge bruises all over your body. Ever since then, I've been looking for at least fourteen muthafuckas from the Romano family to get at." Bostyn frowned.

I shook my head. "That's your blood!"

"I don't know them muthafuckas," Bostyn told me. "You were hurt, and I felt guilty because I knew in my soul that night that I shouldn't have let you go with your father's crew." Bostyn held my waist in his hands.

"Do you want to kiss me?" I asked, looking up at him.

"I can't stick my tongue through all those rubber bands and shit." Bostyn chuckled a little. "But yeah, I wanna kiss you." Bostyn gave me a gentle kiss on the lips. Then another. Then another.

At that point, I was gripping his shirt in my hands. "Thank you," I whispered after the last peck. And that was when the doorbell rang. My heart stopped for what felt like forever.

"Meelah, girl!" After a few seconds of silence, Zara came racing into my room. "Ya nigga is downstairs!"

I looked back at Bostyn, watching him straighten his collar before sitting back down in my window seat.

"Go see what the muthafucka wants." Bostyn leaned back in the seat.

I exhaled deeply before following my cousin out of the room and down the stairs. I didn't see Dinero in the corridor. "Aunt Troy, where is Dinero?"

"On the porch. You know I don't let dogs in my house," Aunt Troy growled from the living room. "You better get rid of his ass, Meelah."

I rolled my eyes before walking down the hallway, grabbing my cousin's hoodie from the coat tree, and walking out the front door.

There Dinero was, standing tall and handsome on my aunt's porch. He stood there with his hands in his sweatpants pockets, looking down at me as I slid into my cousin's hoodie.

"Ya aunt is really gonna make a nigga talk to you in the cold?" Dinero scoffed, looking my face over.

I smiled at him so he could see the metal bars, braces, and rubber bands in my mouth. "She doesn't like you. You know she thinks you ain't shit," I told him.

Dinero tried to hold my hand, but I pulled away from him. "Babe, come on. Don't—"

I cut him off. "You were there. I have been asleep for two months, and the moment my memories come back, they have you in them. How could you let them do that shit to me?"

Dinero frowned, shaking his head. "How did I let them do that to you? Do what to you? Sharita said you don't remember shit that happened!"

"Nigga, they held a gun to your head while they fucked the shit out of me!" I shoved him in his chest. "How many of them were there, huh? How many niggas raped me?" I shoved him again. "You sat there and watched?"

"It's not what you think." Dinero's temples twitched.

"It's not?" I couldn't believe he was defending his actions.

"When I rolled up on ya crib, ya father's crew was there, trying to guard the door, telling me that I couldn't go in. I made my way past the niggas, and when I got inside, Cristobal and them had you tied up on the floor, watching his cousin Ricardo shoving his . . ." Dinero couldn't bring himself to tell me what happened. "They said we fucked up when we let Whitley OD off her own supply. They told me her boyfriend snitched on us to the police, letting them know about the Rox that we hadn't let them in on. They told me to kill Whitley. Them niggas wanted me to kill you too! It was either I kill you or watch that shit! What was I supposed to do?"

"You weren't supposed to leave me there!" I shoved him as hard as I could, then started punching him in his chest until he finally grabbed me. "You just left me!"

"They told me to go kill that bitch!" Dinero shook me a little. "When I left that house, they told me that they'd get you to the hospital!"

"Did you check on me to see if they actually sent me there?" I pulled from him. "No, you didn't! Did you tell my father what happened to me? Did any of you?"

Dinero looked at me, his nostrils flaring and his temples twitching, chest heaving in and out. "No."

"Why?" I asked, eyes searching his face. "Because you were worried about the money. You didn't want to stop your money flow to worry about what happened with me. You helped get rid of the problem. They used me as an example. If they'd do that shit to me, the daughter of the man who brought in most of their profit along the coast, what do you think he'd do to you? The son of a senator who doesn't even acknowledge him? Dinero, I am always down to ride for you! And I thought you'd do the same!"

"Shawty, I have a little brother, little sister, and a mother to take care of. I'm good out there on the football field, but I doubt I'll get a scholarship. The scouts don't even check for anyone at Meade Senior High, too busy hoping to catch one of the niggas at Bay City High at our games. The streets are my life. I'm sorry that you got hurt, but this is the way the game goes!" Dinero tried to tell me. "You got a few broken ribs, a broken jaw, some internal bruising. Those kids at that party are fuckin' dead! Your sister is fuckin' dead!"

"You mean your baby mama is dead?" I hissed, correcting him.

Dinero's frown softened a little as he peeped the angry, hurt expression on my face. "She was just sex, shawty. You have my heart."

"That sounds so fuckin' stupid, Dinero!" I squealed. "What did I do to push you to her? Huh?"

Dinero shook his head at me. "She made time for me away from the hustle. A place to go where I could forget about the pressures of weighing up to expectations that are not realistic in my world. I'm not the man for you, Meelah."

I cried out, shoving him in his chest, "You fuckin' asshole!"

"Ay, what's good?" Bostyn's voice roared over my shoulder.

Dinero's entire remorseful stance changed to defensive. "The fuck is he doing here?"

I looked into Dinero's face. "Sharita didn't tell you that he was here?"

Dinero shook his head, glaring at Bostyn as he stood alongside me. "She told me that you were finally awake and that you wanted to talk to me. She didn't tell me that Robin Thicke was here. I let you dance with shawty. That doesn't mean I'm cool with you kickin' it with my girl."

"Your girl?" Bostyn scoffed. "Was she your girl when you left her to die? A real muthafucka would have gone out shooting to get her out of there! You let them muthafuckas do some shit to her that I wouldn't wish on my own enemy, and you have the nerve to stand here and ask why the fuck I'm here? Muthafucka, where were you? Why weren't you here?"

"Nigga, you don't know shit about the life we live. As soon as I came in her crib, they took my guns from me. What the fuck was I gonna do? Fight my way through some bullets to get to her? I help her father move weight all around the country! A fuckin' eighteen-year-old millionaire, nigga! She'll get over this!" Dinero told Bostyn.

Bostyn shook his head. "No, she won't. Shawty is hurt, man. Her own father hasn't come to see her. If I didn't get her from her apartment that day, what would've happened to her? Who would have helped her?"

Dinero shook his head at Bostyn. "Mind ya fuckin' business, nigga. All you did was dance with her. You don't know shit about her."

Bostyn agreed. "True, I don't know her, but I knew her well enough to know that she needed that dance that night. That she needed you, but you weren't there. I'm sure you've known shawty for a minute."

"All my life, muthafucka," Dinero snarled.

Bostyn scoffed. "Word? Then you should've taken her from me on that dance floor that night. There's no way Whitley should've ended up with you that night in the bathroom. Dash wouldn't have given her those drugs to take. You gave her that shit, huh? You're the reason all this shit went down, muthafucka."

Dinero reached in his pants for his gun.

I stood between the two. "Dinero!"

"Tell this muthafucka to get the fuck outta here before I splatter his brain all over your aunt's pretty rosebushes," Dinero growled. "Tell him to mind his muthafuckin' business and stay out of our shit."

I looked over my shoulder at Bostyn, who really didn't want to leave, but his phone kept going off in his pocket.

"You better get on your job, muthafucka." Bostyn grinned and stepped off the porch. "I'll holla at'cha, baby girl."

Dinero watched him leave. "Who the fuck is this nigga? And who the fuck does he think he's talking to?"

My heart pounded in my chest. There was no way I was going to tell Dinero that Bostyn was Stef's son. I knew as little about Bostyn as he did, but what I did know was that when no one else cared enough about me to risk their life for me, he did.

"You have to go," I told him.

Dinero turned around, facing me as Bostyn rode off in his black Chevy Monte Carlo. "I better not see that muthafucka around you again."

"You just said that I deserve better. That you're not the man for me. What if he is?" I asked.

Dinero looked at me like I'd lost my mind. "I know you're mad at me for the way things went down, but I'm not playing with you, Meelah. Don't get Zack fucked up. Nice barrette." He noticed the shiny comb in my hair. "Give that shit back to the nigga. Let him know he's overstepping his boundaries. If you don't tell him, then I'ma show 'im. Get rid of him, Meelah, before I do."

Chapter Six

Bostyn

"Yo, boss!" Jaxon shook the shit out of me Christmas morning.

"What, muthafucka?" I turned over in my bed.

"Mom said get'cha ass downstairs! She wants us to help her with breakfast before Dad gets home." Jaxon stood before me.

"What time is it?" I mumbled.

"Six. Dad should be home by seven. Come on, man, shit." Jaxon shoved me again.

I grumbled to myself and sat up in my bed, hair probably sticking up like Sonic the Hedgehog's. I watched Jaxon race through my doorway, and Donna entered my bedroom. I sat on the edge of my bed, dressed in a T-shirt and loungewear. As soon as I got back to Maryland from visiting Meelah, I went over to Ace's crib. I had a few drinks, then brought my ass home. I had to talk to someone about Meelah. Claudius would think I was fuckin' crazy for visiting her. He'd already thought ya boy was obsessed with her, and I was to an extent. I tried to find out as much dirt on the Romano family as I could, but there was nothing on them in the system. No one in my biological family's crew had a record. The only way I was going to find out about that family was if I snuck my way into it without them knowing who I really was.

"I thought Moms gave you the day off," I said to Donna as she walked in.

Donna nodded, walking into my room. "Yes, I'm about to leave. Jimena is cooking breakfast over at her house this morning. The Gonzales family will be there," she told me before mouthing, "You're welcome to come."

I shook my head. "It's kind of awkward, Auntie. I'm good."

Donna nodded, exhaling deeply before handing me an envelope. "*Feliz Navidad,*" Donna whispered.

I hesitated before taking the envelope.

Donna kissed me on my forehead before leaving my room.

I opened the envelope and pulled out a folded piece of paper. I could tell by the watermarks before I opened it that it was a Maryland birth certificate. I unfolded the certificate, and a picture fell out. I held the picture up to see my mother holding me in her arms at the hospital. She looked happy, yet sad at the same time. I looked at the birth certificate. "'Emilio Zachariah Gonzales Romano. Mother: Maria Alejandra Ruiz Gonzales. Father . . .'" I exhaled, frustrated. "'Father: unknown.'"

"Bostyn?" Mom's voice shook through me.

I hid the birth certificate and picture behind my back though she'd already caught me looking at something. "What's up?"

Moms glared at me suspiciously. "Wha'cha got there?"

"Oh, acceptance letters from colleges I won't be going to next year because Pops already planned my whole fucking life for me," I told her.

Moms folded her arms. "Your pops likes to feel needed and in control, you know that. He runs everyone's life. And the life he's molding for you isn't such a bad one."

I shook my head in disagreement. "How would you know? He doesn't even talk to you about any of his cases. He's so numb to the shit that he's exposed to that he doesn't lose sleep at night. I still can't get the image of shawty I found behind that dumpster outta my head. Bloody, beaten up, choked out, raped. And Pops is just going on like it's just the way the game goes. Her own father isn't even pressing the issue! I already know someone told him about what happened, and he hasn't even called to check on his daughter. Sick of these muthafuckas taking on the responsibility of having a child but don't even take the time to raise or look after them like they're supposed to! She's dying in Virginia, Mom! She doesn't wanna be there."

Mom's hands were on her hips as she walked into my room. "What?" she scoffed. "How would you know where she is unless you've been going to see that girl? Bostyn, your father told you to stay away from that girl!"

"Since when do I listen to him?" I clicked my teeth.

Moms shook her head. "I heard you come in late last night. Is that who you went to see? Huh?"

I just looked at her.

Moms shook her head, running her fingers through her dirty blond hair. "The Wineyards are coming over for breakfast." Moms rolled her eyes at the frown on my face. "She's due on June seventh. She's sixteen weeks, Bostyn. Have you been to any of her appointments thus far?"

"Hell no," I told her.

Moms shook her head at me. "Well, it's about time you start going. Those babies will be here before you—"

"Babies?" I exclaimed.

Moms covered her face before she could stop herself from telling me that the crazy bitch was carrying more than one baby. "Shit. She was supposed to tell you that she was having twins today at breakfast. I'm sorry. Act surprised when she tells you, okay?"

I just sat there on the bed, heart sinking to my stomach as Moms headed out of my room.

"Get dressed. Your father is on his way home!" Moms yelled back over her shoulder.

Man, I didn't wash my face or brush my goddamn teeth that morning. I didn't even give a fuck. I didn't feel like faking and fronting for Mandy's stuck-up ass parents, Josh and Melissa Wineyard. My brothers, parents, cousin Bradley, aunt Tachina, Mandy, Josh, Melissa, Mandy's younger sister Malia, and her younger brother Rex sat at the table laughing like we were already one big, happy fucking family. They were all dressed up, on some suit-and-tie shit, whereas I was on my "Man, it's fuckin 7:15 in the goddamn morning, and I don't even like none of you muthafuckas" shit. I sat slouched in my chair, not touching a goddamn thing on my plate. I just sat there fuckin' with my Samsung Galaxy when my phone chimed with a message.

I opened the message, grinning to myself at the selfie Meelah had sent me. Good morning, white chocolate, she captioned it. Shawty was laid up in her bathtub, skin glistening, lips shining, hair wet. Braces, metal bars, rubber bands in her mouth, and all, she was still the cutest.

Before I could even respond, my mother cleared her throat loudly. "Bostyn, that's rude. We have guests. It's bad enough that you're not even dressed for the occasion, but you're sitting there on the phone at the table. Put that phone away now," she muttered through her teeth like she wanted to whup my ass for embarrassing her.

I slouched back in my seat, turned the phone over, and placed it on the table.

Mandy peeped that I turned it over, and she smacked her lips. "Bostyn." She nudged me. "I have something for you."

I frowned at her. I still wasn't on good terms with that bitch. Now getting her pregnant was one thing, but her setting me up to get her pregnant was another. The bitch got her own self pregnant to try to keep me in her life. I wasn't feeling her, but I knew my family would believe I raped her over believing that she'd set me up. So, I played along for the time being.

Mandy slid a silver box over to me. "I know we haven't exchanged presents yet, but I thought you'd like to see this."

I looked at her, watching her open the box. She took out a sonogram photo that revealed that she was having not one but two of my babies.

"Twins! We're having twins!" Mandy squealed as Pops nearly spat out his orange juice. "A boy and a girl! Aren't you excited?"

"Nah, not really," I muttered.

Roxyn nudged me in the side to my right. I glared at him before looking up at my parents, who were glaring at me to say something nice to the girl. I couldn't come up with shit to say to her because I was mad as fuck about how everything turned out.

"Bostyn, don't you have something that you want to give to Mandy?" Pops cleared his throat.

I looked over at him.

"Oh, yeah, Pops, he told me to hold it for him," Roxyn spoke up and took a tiny blue velvet box out of his pocket, then slid it over to me.

"Oh, my goodness!" Melissa squealed and placed her hand over her heart.

"Aww shit." Jaxon muttered my exact thoughts.

Mandy's eyes widened as she grabbed the box. She damn near fell out of her seat at the sight of the rock on that ring. "Bostyn, it's beautiful!"

"It was my mother's," Moms spoke up. "Tiffany Legacy engagement ring with a beautiful center stone, surrounded by diamonds." Moms showcased the ring to her in-laws-to-be. "Go ahead and put it on her finger, Bostyn."

Everyone was looking at me, expecting me to put that ring on shawty's finger. They could tell by the look on my face that I wasn't feelin' none of it. I stood from the table. "Pops, can we talk?" I grabbed my cell from the table and put it in my pocket. "Now?"

Pops straightened his tie and got up from the table. "Excuse us."

I went into the kitchen and waited for my father. I paced back and forth, prepping my nerves to tell him what I really thought of him and everyone sitting at that fuckin' table. Pops came into the kitchen, face flaming red.

I stopped pacing and faced him. "Pops—"

"Take your ass back in that fuckin' dining room and propose to that girl." Pops got in my face, standing there in front of the marble island in the center of our kitchen.

I shook my head. "This isn't the right thing to do, Pops, and you know it! She set me up!"

"So, you didn't have sex with that girl?" Pops questioned.

"Yeah, I did, but she—"

Pops cut me off. "Then how the fuck did she set you up? You run the streets twenty-four seven with your boys from the hood! I can't tell you how many times your mom has called me crying because the maid found an earring or a pair of panties in your bed! Smoking, drinking, tattoos all over your body! Skipping out on your homeschool teachers! Marrying this girl and joining the police academy is going to teach your ass some fuckin' discipline!"

"Did it teach you discipline?" I asked him. "Did marrying Mom when she was pregnant with Jaxon and Roxyn teach you discipline? Did it stop you from fuckin' other females or make you stay your ass in the house at night? Did it teach you to be faithful? Nah, the police academy taught you to be just as dirty as the people you put away. What happened to Meelah's mother? It happened at your unit, the same night my mother was killed in my face. Don't tell me that you don't know, because you do. What the fuck are you hiding? You're talking about being a man. Why don't you be one now, muthafucka!"

Pops laughed away his hurt as he rolled up his sleeves, the way he always did before he beat the fuck out of his sons Roxyn and Jaxon. I can't tell you how many black eyes Moms helped them to cover up. If he thought he was about to put his hands on me, he was in for a wake-up call.

"You trying to square up, Pops?" I asked him, looking him in his face, ready to take out all my pent-up aggression on his ass. "You think I'm about to let you do me like you do my brothers? Like you do Moms?"

"Someone needs to beat some fuckin' sense into you!" Pops shoved me. "I risked my life to raise you because even though your mother loved him, I loved her! You are the only part of that woman that I have left!" Pops shoved me again. "I loved her so much that I got my wife to adopt her child! You are the son she had with Francesco Stefano Romano she was supposed to have with me! I am protecting you, whether you see it or not! Marrying into Mandy's family is a business move! It will not only secure your kids' future, but it's securing your future too! You will be set for life! I don't want you to have to do the things that I have to do to stay afloat! When you become a police officer, I want you to keep your hands clean. I don't want you to get in too deep like I did. This family is your way out of the life. You don't want the life that I live, son. And you definitely don't want the life that the Romanos live. Marry this girl. Get your family out of here." Pops's angry expression changed to remorse.

I shook my head. "I don't love her."

Pops agreed. "But I promise you, you're going to love those beautiful children. When I married your mother, I wasn't in love. But when I held my sons in my arms and I realized I was their father, I knew I had to do what I had to do to provide for them. I thought marrying into your mother's family would get me out of the life, but it sucked me further in. I don't want this life for you, but it seems to me that you're getting in deeper than I am. Your mom said you came in here late last night, or should I say early this morning."

I shrugged. "And?" I clicked my teeth.

"*And* where were you?" Pops questioned.

"Minding my own business," I snarled in his face.

"You mean Emmanuel's business? You mean that gangsta Dinero Rodriguez's business?" Pops scoffed. "That girl is going to get you killed! Stay the fuck away from her!"

"What happened to her mom?" I asked him, not backing down.

"The same thing that happened to yours. They were just casualties of war. Get over it and move the fuck on," Pops snarled in my face.

I frowned. "Did you move the fuck on? You're holding on to me like my mom owed you something, muthafucka!"

"She did! She owed me her life after all I've done for her! After I saved your life!" Pops shoved me back against the island countertop.

"You didn't save shit! Emmanuel kept me alive!" I yelled at him.

Pops looked at me like I wasn't supposed to know that. "What did you say? Who told you that?"

"Don't worry about it," I told him. "Just keep worrying about what you've been worrying about—yourself."

Pops shook his head. "Stay away from that family. They don't know you're alive, Bostyn. They think you're dead. I am trying to protect you. Joining the police force is the perfect shield. Fuckin' around with that black bitch is going to make you a walking target!"

I stood up from the island counter. "Callin' shawty out of her name is going to make you a walkin' target."

Pops laughed to himself. "So, what makes you think this girl feels anything about you that you feel for her? Her boyfriend is a teenage millionaire. He moves more weight than we can keep track of! We can't get our hands on him because he's smart. The money circulating in his neighborhood is clean because of the neighboring businesses that he invests in. And what do you have going for you? You're a boy who has to hide who he is to even have a chance with her. Does she know about Mandy? Does she know you're getting married? Does she know about the babies? Does she know you're the adopted son of a cop whose unit was involved in the death of her mother?"

I glared into my father's face as he backed away from me.

"Stay in your place, Bostyn. Go back out there and welcome your pregnant fiancée into the family, ungrateful ass," Pops scoffed, then turned around to walk out of the kitchen.

"What did you get for Christmas?" Claudius asked me the afternoon of December 31. We were chillin' at the food court in Arundel Mills.

I picked over my pizza. “Man, I don’t know. I ain’t even open none of that shit,” I muttered. “Supposedly one of the boxes had a card in it with a check for two hundred thousand dollars, which was supposed to be part of the money to start building my house. Or should I say Mandy’s house. They want us to get married before she starts showing more than she already is. We were supposed to get married after police academy graduation. I don’t want none of this shit. Do you know the bitch told me that she saved my sperm and that’s how she got pregnant? The bitch said she used a syringe and put that shit in her!”

Claudius shook his head. “I told you that you can’t trust a bitch who takes notes when she’s watching *Law & Order: SVU, Snapped,* or *CSI*. You should’ve stopped fuckin’ around with Mandy. I don’t care how fire the head game is. When is the wedding?”

I shook my head. “We’re supposed to go to the courthouse on February fourteenth, fuckin’ Valentine’s Day. They made me propose to the bitch over Christmas breakfast. This shit is killing me.”

Claudius felt for me. “Man, that’s fucked up. Man, fuck them muthafuckas. We’re about to get fucked up tonight, boss. Ace is throwing a party tonight in Alexandria, at the Marriott. His aunt works at the hotel. She reserved us a few rooms. Grab you a shawty and take your mind off some shit.”

I shook my head, running my fingers through my hair anxiously. “I’m not in the mood to party, man. I got too much shit on my mind, dawg.”

“Ay, yo, cuz?” I heard a familiar voice over my shoulder.

Claudius and I laughed a little to ourselves as Sharita and her crew approached our table dressed like they were about to hit up a party or two or three that day.

“Sup, cuz?” I dapped her. “What’s good wit’cha?”

Sharita glanced at Claudius, then back at me. "You tell me."

"What you mean?" I frowned in confusion.

"Meelah's Aunt Troy decided to let her niece hang out with us. I can't believe her aunt is letting her niece out of the house after everything that's happened. You must have made a big impression on her. She doesn't like anybody. Her daughter Zara said some nigga named Ace invited her to some party in Alexandria." Sharita watched me grinning back at Claudius.

Claudius shook his head. "The fuck? How the fuck did Ace get caught up in this shit? Who the fuck is Zara?"

"You coming to the party, Easy?" Sharita asked me.

"I am now," I told her.

"A'ight, bet. Party starts tonight at—"

Claudius cut her off. "Nine thirty. We know, shawty."

Sharita glared at Claudius a little before looking back at me. "Thanks for looking after my girl. We appreciate you for that. All I'm asking you to do is be careful. You might be Panamanian, but you look white, and white doesn't fit into her world. Trust no one."

"Even you?" Claudius scoffed.

"Especially me," Sharita told us. "See y'all tonight."

"I don't trust them hoes," Claudius snarled as the group of girls pranced off, walking back through the mall. Claudius looked back at me. "I told you to leave old girl alone! I don't know what strings that nigga Dinero pulled, but at least five of my top schools sent me letters saying they are unaccepting my admissions application! When have you ever heard some shit like that? Then muthafuckas has the pull to get them muthafuckas to revoke both academic and athletic scholarships! These are the kinda niggas you wanna fuck with? This shit you doing ain't got shit to do with me, yet that nigga is fucking up my life because he heard that we rolled together! That girl is gonna fuck up your life. I'll be damned if she fucks up mine."

"So does that mean you ain't going to the party tonight, Jody?" I smirked.

Claudius frowned at me. "You think everything is a fucking joke, don't you?"

"Yes or no, muthafucka?" I clicked my teeth.

Claudius shook his head at me. "Fuck you, nigga. You know if Sharita is there, then Tajha is gonna be there. I've been trying to holla at shawty for the longest. Besides, someone has to watch your back. Make sure you don't do anything stupid and shit. Ace is just as retarded as you. He'll let you walk right into some dumb shit. Nigga, you got new tattoos and shit?"

I peeped the tats on my hand and arms. Ace gave me my official welcome into the Guerilla unit the week before. The Guerillas were like a fraternity. They looked out for one another, bailed each other out of jail, sent money to their homies in prison, looked out for the families of our deceased soldiers, and pulled up on muthafuckas in their time of need. I needed people like them on my side. A badge wasn't going to protect me. The fuck was Pops thinking? Cops got killed every day out that muthafucka. Pops should've known I wasn't going to leave Maryland. He wanted me to take Mandy and move, but I wanted to get to know Meelah and stay. If I wanted to keep my family safe, I needed to blend in with everyone else.

"Don't worry about my shit, muthafucka," I told Claudius.

"Ummm-hmmm, don't let Ace get you fucked up out here in them streets. They're used to this shit, and you're not. They're into some of everything. Do you know how many bodies that nigga has on him? Maybe not going to the school of my choice happened for a reason." Claudius hated the fact that he wasn't going to the college of his choice, but he hated the fact that he was leaving me behind even more.

"What are you trying to say?" I asked.

"See you at the academy in June, homie." Claudius grinned.

I shook my head. "Nah, man, fuck them colleges. There are more colleges all over the country. Don't let that muthafucka fuck up your shit. You've wanted to play football forever! You're gonna give it all up to play New York undercover?"

Claudius shrugged. "Shit, why not? Ain't you about to be doing that shit? C'mon, we'll talk about this later. Let's get to this party. I gotta find something to wear."

I could feel the bass from the ballroom speakers vibrating through my soul as I stepped through the ballroom doors at the Marriott that night with my crew. Nobody threw a party like Ace. The baddest females were always in place. The DJ had the hits in rotation. Food was served. Drinks were filled. Asses were shakin'. Blunts were rolled, lit, and passed.

I promise you Mandy wasn't on my mind that night. I didn't even want to think about shawty or my family. All I was focused on was catching up with Meelah. I couldn't believe her aunt let her out to play. My crew spread out, and I made my way out onto the dance floor. I don't think I made it halfway through the dance floor when I felt a tap on my shoulder. I looked over my shoulder to see Meelah standing there. I turned around to face her.

Meelah grinned at me. Her hair was braided back in two loose French braids that went down her back. She had on a tight black sheer spaghetti-strap shirt and tight jeans that made me wonder how she got all those ass and hips in them muthafuckas. Black and red stilettos lifted her a few inches off the ground. She stood before me, looking me over from my fresh white Jordans to my white and black baseball cap. I wasn't trying to be too flashy. I just sported a black Nike jacket, white tee, and fresh dark jeans. I didn't take much to clean up. My entire crew rocked labels that none of us could pronounce, and for what? To impress who?

"Doesn't take much for you to clean up, Easy-B," Meelah told me.

See?

I grinned at her. "You neither, Meelah."

"You lookin' for me?" Meelah asked as the song changed.

I nodded. "You already know."

"This song is for the birthday girl in the building. Where you at, Meelah? My man, Easy, said this one's for you." DJ Scribble gave me a shoutout that night.

I told him as soon as he spotted me in the building to play one of my favorite R&B songs. A song that made me think of the person I needed in my life. When I first heard the song, I knew I wanted to slow dance with someone I loved. When I met Meelah, I knew she was the one I wanted to dance to the song with.

"'Don't wanna make a scene. I really don't care if people stare at us.'" Jagged Edge flowed through the speakers, and the females in the spot went wild. That was everyone's song, they just couldn't admit it. It was hard enough to still feel like a man if you sang it to your girl, but soft enough to let her know that you were feeling the fuck out of her.

Meelah blushed, her light skin flushing over as I grabbed her close by her waist. She exhaled deeply as she slid her arms over my shoulders, locking her hands behind my neck. She rubbed the back of my neck a little as she looked into my face.

"'Is it real? What I feel? Could it be you and me 'til the end of time?'" She mouthed along with the song, her eyes sparkling under the ballroom lights.

"When did y'all get here?" I asked her, speaking over the music, hands gripping her tightly.

"About an hour ago," Meelah spoke over the music.

"How long are you staying?" I asked her.

"How long are you staying?" she asked me back.

"Until the morning. I'm not trying to go home anytime soon," I told her.

Meelah nodded. "Zara reserved me a room. My aunt knows I'm here. She believes her daughter will keep me out of trouble. She doesn't know Zara like I do! She thinks my cousin is sweet and innocent. She doesn't know Zara busted it wide open for your boy a few weeks ago."

I smirked, looking back over my shoulder at Ace, who had Zara bent over twerkin' on him out on the dance floor. I looked back at Meelah. "Word? You got a room?"

Meelah nodded. "You comin' up?"

I nodded. "Hell yeah."

"How about now?" Meelah's eyes traced my lips. "Just for a little while, until the countdown."

I hesitated a little. I wasn't stupid. I knew Dinero wasn't too far behind. Sharita was Meelah's homegirl, so I didn't think she'd tell Dinero where the party was, but that shawty named Tajha wasn't feeling me. I knew she was going to hit Dinero up as soon as she saw me leaving the dance floor with Meelah.

"What's wrong, white chocolate? You scared? You act like you scared or somethin'." Meelah grabbed my hand.

I frowned a little, looking down into her pretty face. "Hell nah, I'm not fuckin' scared. You don't bite, do you?" I grinned at her.

Meelah grinned. "A little. C'mon." Meelah held my hand and led me off the dance floor.

We walked through the crowd of spectators whispering and pointing at the two of us walking through the room hand in hand, but none of that mattered to Meelah. She just wanted to get out of there.

We got to her room door. She took her room key out of her purse, then slid it through the slot. She turned the knob, walked inside, and I followed her. The door closed behind us. Her cousin hooked her up with a two-bedroom suite. Full kitchen. Living room. Jacuzzi tub in the bathroom.

I took off my jacket, hung it over a chair, and watched her as she slung her purse onto the kitchen counter, then proceeded to make us drinks. I watched her slice four fresh strawberries. Then she cut up one frozen banana. She then sliced a peach and an orange. She threw it all into a blender. She added ice cubes, then poured half a can of Red Bull energy drink into the blender. She blended the ingredients until it was smooth, then she poured the drink into margarita glasses and slid a glass over to me.

All it took was one sip to get me hype as fuck. "Goddamn!" I told her. "That Red Bull got me feeling like I can fly! All it needs is a little bit of tequila and it'll be hittin'!"

Meelah giggled a little bit as she slid into the seat next to the one that I was sitting in at the bar. "Next round, I'll add some alcohol. This is my special recipe. I call it Mee-Mee. With the tequila, I guess we'll call it—"

"Meelah." I chuckled.

Meelah liked the sound of that. "Yeah, Meelah but spell it M-í-l-a. The i with an accent over it."

"You always gotta be extra." I shook my head at her drinking more of her drink.

Meelah rolled her eyes playfully. "Sure am, goddamn it."

"I see you got those rubber bands off," I told her. "How you been? You're good?"

Meelah nodded and set her glass back down on the counter. "I'm doing good." She kicked off her heels one at a time.

Her goddamn feet were just as pretty as her face. She giggled a little as I pulled her chair closer to mine, and she wrapped her legs around one of mine. She looked into my face.

"You sure?" I asked, eyes tracing her lips.

She nodded, trying to act like she was shy when she and I knew that she was feisty like a muthafucka. "I'm good, boo. My side doesn't hurt much anymore. My jaw isn't aching as much. I get at least four hours of sleep a night before the nightmares hit. Then I'm up for the rest of the night, crying most nights."

"Why don't you call me? Or text. Something, shawty," I told her.

Meelah shook her head at me, her bright brown eyes sparkling. "It's not your problem."

"It is my problem," I disagreed.

"You have a life of your own, Bostyn. You have a life where you can't even use your real name most of the time. I bet Bostyn isn't even your birth name," Meelah told me, looking my face over. "Stef doesn't even know you're his son, does he?"

I hesitated. "Supposedly, he sent my mother to kill me, not knowing that I was his son. He thought she was killing his enemy's son. Before she could even kill me, my mother was killed. Supposedly, it was your father who killed my mother."

Meelah's eyes widened as she attempted to get up from the chair.

I grabbed her arm and shook my head at her. "It's not even like that. This thing I have for you isn't a revenge thing, ma, I promise."

Meelah exhaled deeply. “So, my father knows who you are?”

I shook my head. “I doubt he remembers my face. A few years ago, I was a scrawny little muthafucka. My hair was a little lighter. I was thirteen, ya know? I hadn’t even hit puberty. We lived in Baltimore City then. We moved. Going to homeschool was supposed to protect me. My life is complicated. You don’t wanna know about my life. I hate it. Being around you helps me forget about my problems.”

“You look a lot like your Panamanian side. The dark features, the hair, the hazel eyes, the tan complexion. But you got that cool Italian side to you, too,” Meelah commented before she took a few sips from her drink. “My father tried calling me the other day. I can’t bring myself to talk to him. Dinero said he knows about what happened. He found out that Cristobal did this to me.”

I looked at her. “Who the fuck is Cristobal?”

Meelah looked at me. “He’s Sharita’s brother. Jimena’s son. Your brother, too.”

I just looked at her. The doctor who came back with the results of the rape kit told me the results showed that at least one of the muthafuckas who raped Meelah was a close relative, like a brother. They mentioned Cristobal’s name. Jimena was fuckin’ with my father too?

“My father won’t kill Cristobal. He’s the one who gets corpses filled with opiates of all kinds through the border. He’s a part of The Chain that my father can’t afford to lose. What happened to me is just considered an occupational hazard.” Meelah frowned, fighting back the tears. Meelah laughed to herself to mask the pain. “My aunt was right about him.”

I exhaled deeply, watching her eyes swell up with tears. “Tupac Shakur. ‘Smile’ by Scarface.” I quoted from one of my favorite songs.

There's gon' be some stuff you gon' see
That's gon' make it hard to smile in the future
But through whatever you see
Through all the rain and the pain
You gotta keep your sense of humor
You gotta be able to smile through all this bullshit
Remember that!

Meelah nodded, tears slipping down her cheeks. "What are you doing here with me?" Meelah asked me.

"Where else would I be?" I asked her, squeezing her thigh.

Meelah shook her head. "My father hasn't told Stef about you for a reason. You're some type of leverage. It's best my father doesn't find out about me talking to you. I'm sure if we keep this up, Dinero is going to tell my father about you, and then my father will come snooping his nose in my business." Meelah rolled her eyes.

"So, I am your business? This isn't just a one-night stand or some shit?" I asked her. "You ain't gonna just get the dick, then start curving a muthafucka, are you?"

Meelah laughed out loud. "You're the one who's got secrets. My shit's out here in the open. You know all about me. You know about my friends. My father. What school I go to. Where at least one of my houses are. You know about what my father does for a living. You know about my boyfriend. You . . ." She cut herself off when she realized that she still called Dinero her boyfriend.

"Oh, so you're still fuckin' with him? After finding out he was fuckin' with ya girl? That she was pregnant with his baby? That he killed her?" I asked her.

Meelah sighed deeply. "By killing her, he thought he was protecting me. Every time he tried to leave her alone, she threatened to tell me about the baby. He's not big enough to kill the Romano family, but he will be one day. My father plans to leave everything to Dinero someday. He's even in my father's will! Our house in Baltimore City, our house in DC, our house down south on Myrtle Beach, and our house in Raleigh, North Carolina, have Dinero's name on the deeds! He's a part of my family. He's not a bad dude."

I frowned at her. "Then what are you doing here with me?"

"You're not a bad dude either," Meelah admitted. "He does his thing, and I'ma do mine. And I'm sure you got a girl. What happened to old girl who was about to get stomped at the homecoming dance?"

I just looked at her. Shit, who was I to question her? At least she was honest. She was right. I had a whole girl who was pregnant as fuck back home. I was getting married on Valentine's Day. We were having the wedding reception on graduation day. My babies were due on June 7, a week after graduation. I had some fuckin' nerve worrying about her boyfriend when I had just slid a ring onto Mandy's finger a few days earlier.

"She doesn't mean anything to me." That much I could admit to her. "She's the girl my family wants to see me with."

Meelah nodded. "Yeah, I can definitely relate to that." Meelah watched me kick off my Jordans. "How was your Christmas?" Her eyes traced my hands and forearms. She rubbed her thighs against my leg a little.

"It was a'ight," I told her. "Got the usual gifts. Clothes, video games, season game tickets, money. What about you?"

"My aunt ordered me a bedroom set for my dorm room at UCLA. It's sitting in storage until this summer. She deposited money into my account for a Toyota Camry 2013 that I won't be getting until I touch down in LA next year. My father sent me some designer clothes from Europe. Dinero got me these diamond earrings. Oh, and he did this tattoo for me." Meelah got up from her chair, pulling her braids over to one shoulder so I could see the "Boss" tattoo that she had tatted on the back of her neck. She sat back down, facing me.

"'Boss'?" I questioned.

Meelah nodded. "I have just enough tattoos on my back, so I couldn't put your name on my back, so I put in on my neck."

I grinned a little. "You got that tattoo for me? Quit playin'."

Meelah frowned a little. "I'm not playin'. I couldn't put 'Bostyn.' That would be too fuckin' obvious. I mean, everyone knows you by Easy, but Bostyn with a y would have my nigga questioning me. You had my back when everyone else was scared to. And that's real."

"So, what you tryin' to do, ma?" I asked her.

Meelah stood from her chair, turning around, her back facing me. Not to mention that booty, that big ol' booty. She looked back at me over her shoulder. "Unzip me, please."

I grabbed her by her shirt, pulling her back to me between my legs. I unzipped her sheer shirt. She pulled it from her arms, tossing it on top of the counter. I unsnapped her bra. And I kissed her spine, gripping her waist in my hands.

Meelah sighed as she pulled her bra from her arms, tossing it onto the counter too. "Let's get in this Jacuzzi tub. Can't let it go to waste." She tried to walk toward the bathroom, but I pulled her back to me by the waist of her jeans.

I stood from my chair, turning her around so I could see her.

Meelah looked into my face, arms across her breasts.

"Move ya arms, shit," I told her.

Meelah shook her head, cupping her breasts with her hands.

I attempted to kiss her forehead, but she kissed my chin instead before soaking her lips in mine. We kissed and nibbled on each other's lips a little. Only a little while until midnight. It wouldn't be long before both of our crews tried to hit us up. I pulled my lips from hers, taking my phone from my pocket. I turned that bitch on vibrate, then tossed it on the counter on top of her shirt. I pulled my T-shirt and wife-beater over my head at the same time. Meelah licked her lips a little, eyes tracing my tattoos. She looked into my face before turning around to walk toward the bathroom. I followed her as I unbuckled my pants.

We walked into the bathroom. Shawty faced away from me, unbuckling her jeans. She peeled the jeans down her legs, bending over at the waist. Shawty had on sheer black panties. As she bent over, I could see that she had a diamond barbell piercing vertically through her clit hood. Fuck swole—my dick was on brick hard. She slipped out of her sheer panties, and that pussy was staring at me. That pussy was so pretty and pink. I was about to fuck shawty like I was never going to get that chance again.

Chapter Seven

Meelah

I knew I was crazy, being there with Bostyn that night, but I really needed him. No one else really took the chance to listen to what I wanted and needed, but he did. He didn't want me for my money, because he had money. He just wanted to spend time with me. Our worlds collided that night in that bathroom in more ways than one. I went over and started the water, going for the hot tub. I didn't wait for it to fill. I stepped down into it, facing Bostyn. I sat down in the tub as he eyed my body from head to toe.

"Are you coming in?" I asked him, giggling at the way that he stood there gawking at me instead of undressing. I was turned on as I watched him pull his 9 mm from his pants and set it on the sink counter.

"I'm hard as fuck," Bostyn told me, unzipping his pants.

"Let me see it." I bit my lip, watching him pull his pants down.

The mound in his Joe Boxers looked promising. My heart beat steadily in my chest as he approached the tub, kicking off his jeans. I scooted to the edge of the tub, reaching for his boxers.

Bostyn grinned as I pulled on his waistband, tugging on his boxers.

I smiled devilishly as I pulled them down, my eyes glued to his dick as it stared me in the face. I backed up in the tub as Bostyn stepped inside of it. I wasn't expecting a tan thick, long penis. I was expecting raw meat, like my friends always claimed to encounter whenever they slept with white boys in school. Maybe it was his Latin blood that left him well-endowed and pigmented. Whatever the reason, that curved dick was beautiful to me. When he pulled me on top of his lap, pulling my legs around his waist, I didn't hesitate to press my breasts up against his tatted chest. I felt like I was right where I needed to be.

I looked down into his face as he started to unbraid the two French braids I had in my hair.

"You like him?" Bostyn grinned.

"Does he like me?" I asked him back, feeling like a cat who was getting rubbed behind the ears as he slid his fingers through my scalp to loosen my braids.

"You look like you were expecting something else. You thought I didn't have a dick, huh?" Bostyn joked.

I giggled as my hair fell to my back, and Bostyn slid his hands around my neck. I felt his dick poking my pussy lips as I straddled his waist. "I just wasn't expecting it to have color, that's all. My girls said white boys have raw meat," I told him.

"I ain't your typical white boy. Turns out, ya boy is half Panamanian," Bostyn responded, eying my body from my hair to my waist. "Life is crazy, ma."

I agreed, watching as he kissed between my breasts. "It is." I ran my fingers through his dark, straight, yet really thick hair.

"Relationships are hard enough as it is, but being in an interracial relationship is going to be that much harder," Bostyn told me.

I grinned, stuttering a little. “So that’s what this is? A relationship?”

“In my mind that’s what this is, damn it. Don’t kill my fantasy.” Bostyn kissed me, biting my bottom lip a little. “I just want to cherish this while the moment lasts. A white muthafucka with a beautiful Nubian queen? Nobody wants to see this happen, you know that. And you’re right. We’re both in situations that our families both set up. I wish I could be with you for more than just a moment.” Bostyn pulled on my hair a little. “You smell so good,” he told me.

“You do too,” I cooed as Bostyn started sucking on my neck, his dick growing harder between my legs.

“You wanna ride this wave?” Bostyn growled in my ear.

I grabbed his dick, raising up a little so I could slide it through my pussy lips. I eased into his dick, taking a deep breath. I exhaled as Bostyn pressed down on my booty, pressing me down onto his dick like my body was sliding down a pole. I calmed my nerves, holding on to him as he continued to suck on my neck. I reached behind him and cut off the water. My pussy fit snugly around his dick. As I started to grind on his dick, water started splashing everywhere. Bostyn and I laughed out loud.

“Hell nah.” Bostyn chuckled, grabbing me. “Hold on tight, ma.”

I held on to him as he rose from the tub, holding me tight as he stepped out of the tub. We barely made it out of the bathroom. He held me tightly against the hallway wall just outside of the bathroom door.

“You sure you want to do this, baby girl? You been through a—”

As soon as he stepped out of that tub, I started kissing on his neck.

“Fuck, ma, damn,” he hissed, gripping my booty in his hands.

I squealed out in delight as he carried me over to the wall and pressed my body against it. I wrapped him up in my legs as he braced me against the wall. I sighed, feeling his dick throbbing inside of me before he started to grind into my soul. I promise you I did not expect him to have any rhythm. I didn't expect him to have the strength and stamina to support my weight, pump in and out of me, and concentrate on sending the both of us into orgasm. I didn't expect him to pump into my soul like he was trying to dig out whatever it was he was searching for. He was in complete control of the depth and pace, but he paused for a few minutes to let me grind with him too.

Once my rhythm matched his, he pulled my body a little farther from the wall, then went back to work. His hands were gripping my booty so tight as I tightened my thighs against his waist. I rocked my pelvis back and forth. After a few minutes of pumping back and him digging into me, he effortlessly lowered one of my legs to the floor, and I hooked my right leg over his inner elbow. He pulled my body away from the wall, until only my shoulders were resting against it. I gained more momentum and control. I circled my hips, throwing my head back in pleasure. I guessed he gave me too much control, and he wanted it back.

Bostyn pulled out of me, effortlessly turning my body around as if I was as light as a feather, gripping my waist.

"Damn." I sighed, looking back at him over my shoulders.

Bostyn watched me panting and gasping for air for a few seconds before kissing on my neck and shoulders. "Put ya hands on the wall."

My hormones soared as he pressed down on the small of my back, motioning me to bend over. I straddled his waist, pressing him back against the wall with my butt.

"Shit," Bostyn moaned as I slid back down on his dick, bracing my hands on the wall in front of me and my feet on the wall behind me. He grabbed my thighs as he began to work me slowly, digging his spoon deep into my bowl. He worked me slowly for a few minutes, until he had my pussy dripping wet. Once he got her wet, playtime was over. He pulled out of me, letting my legs back down to the floor.

I sighed as Bostyn grabbed my hair, twisting it into a ponytail, grabbing it like he was about to drill the fuck out of me. To be a growing young man, he was a pretty good size. He was about seven or eight inches, hard as wood. Didn't have the biggest dick, but damn if he didn't fuck me like he did. Bostyn bent me over so that my torso was at a ninety-degree angle to the wall. As I got on my tiptoes, he slid back inside of me.

And when he started to work, I swear it took everything to fight off the urge of my knees giving out on me. The way he gripped my hair with one hand and gripped my booty with the other was a turn-on in itself. Then he had the nerve to work the pussy like he was digging for buried treasure. I promise you, my head was spinning in circles. I knew at that moment that he'd won my heart, body, mind, and soul. I guessed he wasn't getting me back for all those white boy jokes that I made, shit. Dinero was going to kill us. But it was going to be a good death.

"Goddamn this pussy is so fuckin' juicy," Bostyn grunted, stroking deeper and a little faster. "Warm and tight. Fuck!"

"Work this pussy, Easy, shit." I sighed, grinding my hips as I arched my back.

Bostyn stroked the pussy so good that, after a few minutes, it sounded like he was stirring tender pasta. My pussy was dripping wet with each stroke. When he finally busted inside of me, he was still hard as hell.

I stood up straight, facing him, backing up against the wall as Bostyn grabbed me close, looking into my face. I felt his semen leaking out of my pussy, sliding down my thighs. I wasn't even thinking of the consequences of fuckin' around with Bostyn. All I knew was that the sex was so good that I wanted to celebrate the fact that we fucked by fuckin' again.

"What are we doing?" I asked him as he pushed my bangs from my face and unraveled the ponytail that he'd twisted my hair into.

"Each other." Bostyn kissed my forehead.

I exhaled deeply. "There are dangers to this. You know this. I know this. If they find us here, we're both—"

Bostyn pressed his lips against mine, lifting me up, wrapping my legs around his waist before carrying me away from the bathroom, grabbing his gun from the sink along the way. He carried me down the hall to one of the bedrooms. He worked my body into a sweat that night. Needless to say, we didn't make it downstairs to the countdown until my birthday.

I woke up that night to the sound of a gun cocking in my ear. I looked up to see Bostyn getting out of bed, naked as fuck, walking toward the room door, arm extended. I sat up in bed, covering myself with the blanket.

Bostyn looked back at me. "Stay back," he said once he got to the door. He started to turn around and face me when he saw me about to get out of the bed. "Shawty, I said—"

Before he could even get the sentence out, a shot was fired, and he was shot in the shoulder. As I screamed out his name, Bostyn dropped to the floor. Before I could get up from the bed, Bostyn looked up at me, shaking his head. He frowned a little on his knees, pressing on his wound with one hand and gripping his gun with the other hand.

Bostyn sat there in the dimly lit room, awaiting the shooter to make his way down the hall, and just when the shooter made it to the door, Bostyn quickly turned around, letting his gun off three times, shooting the nigga in his chest. The nigga he shot was Evan, one of Dinero's boys. Evan was Arcen's son. My father was somewhere in the building.

Bostyn got up from the floor, arm extended, still aiming at Evan, watching him bleed out on the floor.

The hotel phone rang. I glanced at Bostyn as I grabbed the phone. I placed it to my ear, and before I could say anything, my father's voice was yelling through the phone. "Meelah, the fuck do you think you're doing?"

I looked at Bostyn, watching him walk over the body and down the hallway toward the bathroom where we left our clothes.

"What do you mean?" I stuttered.

"If you don't come out of that muthafuckin' room with that nigga, then I'm coming in," Daddy warned me.

"You already sent someone in to get me!" I squealed. "Evan is lying in a pool of blood right now! If you come in this room with that shit, Daddy, I don't think he will care about shooting you either!"

Just then, I heard the door to the room fly open.

I hopped out of bed, dragging the sheet and wrapping it around me. I dropped the hotel phone and ran out of the room. There Bostyn stood in the hallway in his boxers, arms extended, aiming his gun at my father and the three niggas he had with him.

"Tell this clown either he can leave this muthafucka now on his feet or leave the muthafucka in a body bag like that muthafucka on the floor over there," Bostyn howled.

My father eyed me slowly approaching them, sheet wrapped around me. "Daddy . . ."

Bostyn frowned, shaking his head at Daddy. "The fuck, man? Ya daughter is in this bitch and you gonna send someone in here shooting? You don't give a fuck about her!"

"Meelah, your friend here is going to get himself killed. He needs to back the fuck off. I sent Evan in here to scare the little muthafucka, not shoot him. But, of course, Arcen won't see it that way. I don't think he'll appreciate you murdering his son," Daddy told Bostyn.

"I was protecting your daughter, muthafucka," Bostyn hissed.

"You mean fuckin' my daughter?" Daddy's voice boomed throughout the hotel suite. "After all she's been through, you wanna put her through more?" Daddy stepped farther into the room toward Bostyn. He looked into Bostyn's angry face. "Easy, is it? What's that, a nickname?"

"Nah, muthafucka, it's my name. Step the fuck back!" Bostyn yelled.

I was sure at that moment that Bostyn was picturing the day his mother was shot in the head in front of him. And right there, he was face-to-face with the person who killed her.

Daddy didn't say anything at that point, but he looked at Bostyn as if he looked familiar. As if he recognized Bostyn's face but couldn't remember where he knew him from. Daddy glanced at me, then back at Bostyn. Before my father could say anything, Aunt Troy came barging into the room with Zara.

Aunt Troy pushed past my father and his friends. She looked back at my father and his crew, rolling her eyes at them before eying me standing in the middle of the living room. Zara stood in the doorway, looking at me remorsefully as if she was the one who told where I was.

Aunt Troy gasped at the sight of Evan's dead body in the middle of the living room. She looked back at Bostyn, who had just lowered his weapon at the sight of my aunt.

"Self-defense, Aunt Troy," he told her, nodding toward my daddy.

Aunt Troy shook her head. "Zara, go downstairs and call 911 now!" She looked back at my father. "You sent one of your killers in to find your daughter? Ugh, I knew I shouldn't have called you when she wouldn't answer her phone!"

My father shook his head at the sight of me wrapped in my sheet. He looked back at my aunt. "You were supposed to be watching her. This shit is your fault."

Aunt Troy scoffed, "My fault? Nigga, this shit is your fault! She wouldn't even be living with me if you didn't live this lifestyle! I was worried about her! When she didn't answer her phone when I called, I thought something happened to her! I had no idea she was here with Easy! I thought . . ." Aunt Troy choked back tears, not to mention probably vomit from seeing a dead body, something she didn't see all too often. "I thought something happened to my baby girl."

I looked at my aunt. She wasn't mad at seeing me there with Bostyn. She was scared. "I'm sorry, Aunt Troy. My friends kept calling me, and I put my phone on vibrate."

Aunt Troy glared at me. "Get your clothes. Let's go now!"

"She's coming with me," Daddy demanded.

Bostyn gripped his gun as if he was about to extend his arms toward my father again, but Aunt Troy spoke up.

"The judge granted you with visitation during the summer and whenever else I agreed to, Emmanuel. If it were up to me, you'd never see her. And right now, it is up to me," Aunt Troy told my father in his face. "She's not going anywhere near you after you let this happen to her. After your friends here watched what happened to her. Yes, Zara told me that her friend Ace told her that these niggas you employed knew what happened to your daughter! That his cousin told him that they watched what happened to her!"

My father frowned back at the three niggas who were with him. He shook his head at my aunt. "I didn't know shit. I don't know what you're talking about. Watched who do this shit to my daughter?"

"I don't know, nigga. Ask them!" Aunt Troy shoved Daddy in his chest. "Regardless of whatever it is that you claim you didn't know, you're not going anywhere near my baby! Do you hear me? My sister died because of you. I'm not about to let the same thing happen to her daughter!"

Daddy looked at me, his dark brown eyes glossing over, though he had a frown on his face. Saying sorry was something that my father never did. He looked at Bostyn. "Nigga, you have five minutes to get the fuck out of here. The police are on their way up. We got the body."

"I'm good. I ain't never run from my problems, and I damn sure ain't about to pick today to start runnin'," Bostyn told him.

Daddy scoffed, looking back at my aunt. "This is the type of muthafucka you'd let come near my daughter? She's standing here with a sheet wrapped around her! The nigga just shot my man's son!"

"He was protecting her, something you've never done for her! You've been placing her in dangerous situations all of her life!" Aunt Troy yelled, pointing over at Evan. Aunt Troy glanced at Bostyn as he went over and sat on the couch and slouched back, gun in his lap. She looked at me. "Get ya shit, Meelah. Let's go."

***

"Girl, ya goddamn cousin is a snitch." Sharita rolled her eyes as I sat across from her at the cafeteria in Arundel Mills Mall, February 13, 2013.

It was the day before Valentine's Day, and I hadn't heard from Bostyn since New Year's Day. Not because he hadn't attempted to call me, but because my aunt took my phone and told Zara that if she even thought about letting me use the phone, she wasn't going to get her that car she wanted for her birthday. Bostyn attempted to stop by and see me, which let me know he didn't go down for Evan's murder. But talking to Sharita that day let me know that shit was hectic in the neighborhood after what happened that night. Dinero found out about the incident, though my father told him to stand down.

Valentine's Day was reserved for our baes, but Pre-Valentine's Day was reserved for me and Sharita. Pre-V Day lunch at the mall was something that Sharita and I did every year since the mall had opened. There was no way that I wasn't going to show up that evening to see her no matter what. I just took the bus to the mall, hoping she'd be there, and she was. I hadn't gotten the chance to really be alone with her to try to talk to her about what happened to me.

Dinero told me that my father knew what happened to me, but the look on my father's face told me otherwise. I didn't want to know whether Sharita knew what her brother had done to me. I was sure she'd heard that it was her brother who raped me. She wasn't close to her brother at all. Jimena pretty much let Stef and his wife raise their son. Sharita and her mother did as Cristobal told them without any questions. He was their protection as long as they never questioned shit that he did, including what he did to me. We both avoided the conversation for the time being.

I sighed, sipping from my cup of ice-cold Sprite. "This isn't Zara's fault. I knew better than to be there with Bostyn. My aunt is the one who panicked and called my dad when she couldn't get in touch with me. He called Zara, and Zara told him where I was. Old scary ass, ugh. She's always been afraid of Daddy." I looked at Sharita, watching her slurp from her cup. "So, how is everyone? How's Tajha?"

Sharita shook her head. "Doing Tajha shit. You know she's fuckin' around with not only Claudius, but his nigga Keith, too. She's playing with fire. Them two have been boys forever from what I heard. Claudius seems clean, but his crew is dirty, and you know Tajha loves 'em dirty. She loves them dope boys. I'm one to talk, though." Sharita reached into her purse and pulled out a small Dollar General shopping bag.

I looked up at her. "What's in the bag?"

Sharita exhaled deeply, putting the bag back in her purse. "Girl, four one-dollar pregnancy tests. My period is like eight days late. My mama would kill me if I'm pregnant, Meelah." She watched my eyes widen. She shook her head. "I'll be a'ight. I have money. If I need to get rid of it, I will. God knows I don't need no baby. I can't even remember to feed my dog, and I had that dog since I was two. Just think what I'd do to my baby. I'd probably leave him or her at home and forget about it like I do my phone sometimes!"

I nearly spit out my soda. She was always forgetting shit. "Girl, who is the potential father?"

Sharita looked at me. "You can't tell anyone. You know if CMC found out that I was fuckin' around with anyone from Bay City, they'd be pissed. Tajha isn't officially one of us. They just fuck the bitch. If they knew I was fuckin' with Ace—"

I gasped. My cousin was fuckin' that nigga. Thought he was her man, and he was fuckin' my friend. My best friend. I didn't know how to tell her. "Ace?" I gulped. "How long have you been seeing Ace?"

Sharita shook her head. "I'm not seeing him. It only happened once. We were drunk. It was on New Year's."

I exhaled deeply. He must have fucked her as soon as my aunt got us from the hotel that night. I shook my head. "Damn."

"So, I have four tests. Take one with me?" Sharita asked.

I scoffed. "Bitch, what? I don't need to take a pregnancy test. I get the depo shot, bitch. You're the one who isn't on birth control."

Sharita smacked her lips. "Come on, please."

I went with Sharita to the bathroom to take the test with her. My period had never been normal, and the shot threw it off even more. A late period wasn't anything new to me. And I'd been spotting since the day that I got the shot. So, when Sharita and I decided to pee on the sticks together, I didn't expect to see two lines cascading down the window of the cheap pregnancy test applicator.

"Whew-hoooo!" Sharita squealed from the stall next to mine. "He might have put the cream in my cupcake, but nothing is baking in this muthafuckin' oven! Hell muthafuckin' yeah!" She was so excited not to be pregnant. "What does yours say?"

I sat there on the toilet seat in shock, staring at the applicator. "Dinero is going to kill me. That's what it says."

Sharita couldn't get out of her stall fast enough. "What, bitch?"

I slowly got up from the toilet and tossed the applicator in the toilet before flushing it. I was too much in shock to cry. I opened the door and slowly walked out.

"That night, at the hotel, I heard that ya father caught you and Easy fuckin'. That wasn't a rumor? That shit was true?" Sharita watched me slowly walk over to the bathroom sink to wash my hands.

I washed my hands, shaking my head to myself.

"You slept with him, *mami?*" Sharita asked. "Answer me!"

The door to the bathroom opened, and in came a group of white girls. They looked like a group of cheerleaders, coming into the bathroom dressed in Pink from head to toe, their blond hair pulled up into ponytails. I recognized one of the girls. She looked like that chick who confronted Bostyn about dancing with me at homecoming. We made eye contact. When it registered in her head who I was, she grinned and walked over to the sink to primp in the mirror alongside me.

"Amy, do you have my lip gloss in your purse?" she asked one of her friends.

"Mandy," her friend Amy called her, "yes, I do. Nobody wants your dick-sucking lip gloss, bitch." Her friend shoved the lip gloss at her. "We're supposed to be headed to a movie tonight. We're not going in every store tonight for this dress of yours. Find something cute and simple to wear. Nothing tight either. Everyone at the courthouse doesn't need to know you're almost six months pregnant."

My heart slammed in my chest as I watched a smirk slide across Mandy's face when she peeped my distraught reflection in the mirror.

"Umm, excuse me." Sharita peeped my expression before speaking up to the group of girls. "Hi, I'm Sharita."

"And?" one of the prissy white girls scoffed.

Sharita rolled her eyes from Mandy over to the bitch, then back to Mandy. "And I believe I met you at the homecoming dance last year. What was your name again? Becky?"

Mandy laughed a little. "No, it's Mandy. What was your name again? Marisol?"

Sharita laughed along with her. "No, *puta,* it's Sharita. If I remember correctly, you confronted my cousin the night of the homecoming. You felt some type of way because he was dancing with Meelah."

Mandy made a face. "Cousin?"

Sharita folded her arms. "Yes. Easy is my cousin, on my mother's side."

Mandy's mischievous glare moved from Sharita to me. "Meelah Summers, is it?"

I looked at her, eying her round abdomen before looking back into her face. "Yes?"

"Homecoming queen and rape victim—what a combination," she scoffed, looking me over. "Drug distributor's daughter found beaten and raped in an alley days before nearly twenty people who went to a party where people associated with her father's distributed drugs were murdered. What a headline."

Sharita started to step forward, but I pulled her back. Obviously, the bitch felt threatened by me or she wouldn't have thrown insults so soon into the conversation. She looked my name up, which meant that Bostyn must have brought me up to her.

Sharita looked at me, then back at Mandy. I knew Sharita wanted to smack her in the face with the results of my pregnancy test, but she didn't say anything about it. Thank God, because Sharita was not one to give a fuck about breaking someone all the way down to size.

"Mandy, we have to get going. I told you that my friend has been holding this dress for you since New Year's." Amy pulled on Mandy's arm.

"New Year's? Isn't that about the same time that you saw Easy back at the hotel, Meelah?" Sharita asked me but was staring Mandy in the face.

I'd never seen a smirk wiped cleaned away from someone's face as fast as I saw it leave Mandy's face that evening. Mandy looked like she wanted to choke Sharita, but instead, she took a deep breath while digging into her purse for something. She pulled out a little card-size envelope wrapped in a pretty purple bow and handed it to Sharita.

Sharita looked at the envelope in confusion. "The fuck is this?"

Mandy spoke to Sharita, but she looked at me. "Sharita, since you're family, I thought you deserved an invitation. Come on, girls, let's go."

Sharita and I watched as Mandy and her groupies left the bathroom. We looked back at the envelope as Sharita tore it open and read it aloud.

"'You are formally invited to attend the wedding ceremony for Bostyn 'Easy' Reel and Mandy Wineyard at three thirty p.m. on'"—Sharita paused, eyes widening—"'February 14, 2013.' That's tomorrow! He's marrying that bitch tomorrow?"

Chapter Eight

Meelah

"Get rid of it," Daddy snarled at me that night in my aunt's living room.

I don't even know why I used Sharita's phone to call and let my daddy know that I was pregnant. He rarely gave me his attention, so I was always trying to get it. I don't know why I expected him to hug me and tell me that everything was going to be okay. That he backed any decision that I wanted to make. He never comforted or supported me because he didn't even know how. So, I don't know why I expected it that day.

My aunt sat on the couch, face buried in her hands, not even sure what to say to me. She had big dreams for me, wanted me to go to college and do something big with my life. My aunt wanted me to become an officer in the Navy or just to go to medical school. The last thing she wanted was for me to follow in her sister's or brother-in-law's footsteps. But there I was, pregnant by a boy I barely knew. I didn't tell them that Bostyn was getting married. Hell, I didn't want to think about it, much less talk about it.

"Aunt Troy?" I whimpered, watching her start to cry. "What should I do?"

Aunt Troy lifted her tear-drenched face from her hands. She hated to say that she agreed with my father, but she did. "I . . ." She hesitated, looking up at my father, who stood there pissed off at me. She looked back at me. "I mean, what other choice do you have?"

"Plenty!" Sharita screamed.

My father and aunt looked at her like she needed to stay out of our business. I brought Sharita with me for backup since I was already in trouble for leaving VA that day to be with her. There it was, almost nine at night, and I was just coming in after ignoring my aunt's calls all day. After finding out that Mandy and Bostyn were getting married, I was in no condition to take public transportation back to Richmond. Just a month and a half ago, I watched Bostyn's dick burst out of his boxers like it was hooked to hydraulics. I never imagined I'd be pregnant by him, let alone him having another bitch pregnant at the same time. A bitch who he was just a day away from marrying. 17 and married? Of course, his parents put him up to that bullshit, but still, he could have told me. My head was spinning in all sorts of directions.

"Why does she have to kill the baby?" Sharita questioned.

"Why are you even here?" Daddy questioned her back.

"Because she is my friend! And I'll always have her back, unlike you!" Sharita told him. "I'll help her raise the baby! She doesn't need y'all. She's got me! It's her body, so y'all can't run shit!" Sharita shouted at both my aunt and father.

Zara sat at the foot of the stairs watching as Sharita defended me.

Aunt Troy rolled her eyes at Sharita before looking at me. "You better get your friend, Meelah."

"She's right, Aunt Troy." I tried not to sound like I was begging, but at that point, I was. I didn't know much about Bostyn Easy Reel, but I wanted to. I was about to give birth to a part of him. I couldn't kill a part of him. "Aunt Troy, I can do this."

Aunt Troy folded her arms. "You can't be serious! Assuming that you're still dealing with Dinero, how do you plan to break this to him?"

My father looked at me for an answer while shaking his head in disgust. He knew like everyone else in that room that I hadn't seen Dinero since Christmas Eve. The last person my aunt and father caught me with was Bostyn.

I hesitated.

"What were you thinking? Did you fuck that white muthafucka to pay Dinero back for what happened with your friend Whitley?" Daddy questioned.

I shook my head. "No, Daddy!"

Daddy shook his head at me, his dark skin glowing red. "Who the fuck is this muthafucka? Your friend Tajha told Arcen that Easy is Sharita's cousin." Daddy looked at Sharita. "That he's Cristobal's brother."

Sharita frantically shook her head.

Daddy wasn't backing down. "Tajha said that you told her that Easy is your brother's brother! She said that you told her that Stef is Easy's father."

Sharita rolled her pretty, hazel-brown eyes. "Ugh, I ought to slap that two-faced ho in both of her faces! That bitch is lying. I didn't tell her shit. I told Dinero that Easy was my cousin so he would back off Easy the day of the homecoming dance. I didn't tell her shit else. Anything else she's making up." Sharita glanced at me.

If Tajha knew anything, she went prying into Easy's life on her own. Or my father knew more about Easy than he let on, and he was playing us to see if we'd crack. I couldn't let my father get his hands on Easy, especially when Easy was supposed to be dead. I did a little prying of my own, investigating the day that Easy's mother was killed. I Googled the article about her so-called suicide.

The article claimed that Easy's mother had killed him, then killed herself.

As far as my father knew, he killed Easy's mother and someone else killed Easy. The article stated that the police found Easy's body. I had a little talk with Jimena, Sharita's mother, who told me that Easy's birth name was Emilio Zachariah Gonzalez Romano. The police were in on covering up Easy's true identity, which led me to believe that my father spared Easy as collateral against the police department. I had to cover up Easy's true identity for as long as I could before my father went prying.

"The ho is lying!" Sharita told my father and my aunt. "Easy is just some white boy who hangs with the black crowd. He doesn't even go to school with us. I found out that he hangs around Claudius, Dinero's brother. Easy is harmless."

"Harmless?" Daddy scoffed. "How could a harmless muthafucka get between my daughter's legs?"

"Things happen, Emmanuel." Aunt Troy tried to take up for me. She was mad at me, but she wasn't about to give me a piece of her mind in front of her brother-in-law, whose very existence she couldn't stand.

"'Things happen'? The fuck do you mean? Do you think that 'things happen' bullshit is going to fly with Dinero? Do you know the type of nigga my daughter is dating?" Daddy yelled at Aunt Troy as she stood from the couch to approach him.

Aunt Troy got in his face. "Do you know the kind of nigga your daughter is dating?"

I rushed up to my aunt, pulling her away from Daddy. He wasn't the kind of man who let a woman talk to him any type of way. No woman checked my daddy without him checking her ass in her face. There was so much to my father that I didn't understand or even want to understand. He made money where he could make it, and he would sell me if he thought he would make a profit. And he would choke a bitch to death and not think twice about it, myself included, if he thought I crossed him.

"My daughter is fuckin' around with a nigga who would kill her while fuckin' her! I've seen that nigga make a bitch suck his dick right before shooting her in the head!" Daddy screamed, his voice causing my body to shake.

Aunt Troy looked back at me, watching me pull her away from Daddy. She shook her head. "How could you date someone like that? He sounds like the type of lunatic who thinks you're his forever! How do you think this is going to go over with him?"

"I don't care how this goes over with him!"

My aunt pulled her arm from my hands. "Well, you should!"

"Does that white boy know you're pregnant?" Daddy snarled.

"He doesn't know. We barely know, shit. We just found out today," Sharita spoke up.

"How many times have you slept with that boy?" Aunt Troy sounded as if she hated to know.

"Just that one time," I admitted.

"Well, then, based on the night things went down with Easy, you're only about six weeks pregnant." Daddy looked down at me as he snatched me away from my aunt. "Get rid of that muthafucka."

I cried out, pulling from my father and pushing him away from me. "No!"

"Ace said that Dinero went to Meade looking for Claudius. He said that Dinero heard about what happened on New Year's." Zara got off the last step and walked into the living room.

Sharita frowned, looking at Zara like she didn't like the way she said Ace's name. "Ace? I've been meaning to ask you, how the fuck do you even know Ace?"

"How the fuck do you know Ace?" Zara clapped back. "From what I heard, y'all not even supposed to be around them niggas. The Clean Money Crew doesn't fuck with them, so that means that you're not supposed to either, right? Uh-huh, Dora, thought so."

Sharita glared at my cousin like she wanted to snatch her ass bald.

"But, to answer your question since you're writing a book about my life, Ace used to come over with Easy while cuz was in the coma. You saw me dancing with Ace at the party. You know I know Ace, Sharita. I'm the one who told y'all that he invited y'all to that party. Why you in ya feelings about a nigga you aren't even supposed to know?" Zara rolled her eyes, ignoring Sharita's glare. "Anyway, Dinero knows what happened or at least he heard the rumor of what happened in that hotel room. Ace said they've been beefing all month. The Clean Money Crew has been looking for Easy for weeks because of what happened to Evan. They know Easy killed Evan. They also know that Easy got away with killing him. The police barely questioned him."

"The nigga was shooting at us! What was Easy supposed to do? Daddy sent him in the room after me! Easy was protecting me!" I squealed.

"No one sees it that way. Arcen sure as fuck doesn't see it that way," Daddy let me know. "Arcen sees it as Easy being where he wasn't supposed to be. I had to call the muthafucka off killing your white boy. Told him that Evan went in the room, no questions asked, and shot at Easy. I told Evan to hold up, and he didn't listen to me. He thought he had the situation handled. He didn't expect the cracker-ass nigga you were with to be strapped. Your friend seems to be prepared for this shit. He killed Evan and is still free, no jail time, and just like Zara said, no one questioned him from the police department. Why is that? What do you know about him? Who is his family?"

I hesitated. "I don't know."

"Exactly." Daddy shook his head, looking at me like he taught me better, and he did. "I saved your friend because I heard what he did for you. He got you to the hospital after finding you beaten up while I was away. Your friend is smart. He didn't retaliate, which was in his best interest."

I just looked at my father. "Why are you telling me this? What does this have to do with anything? You're telling me that you called off your dawgs because Easy helped me, but then you're telling me to kill his baby?"

"It's better you do the shit than Dinero do it!" Daddy told me. "The shit you do affects other people, Meelah. Dinero isn't in his right frame of mind right now. He hasn't been able to really function with you being here, away from him. Dinero's mother died this morning from a drug overdose. He said he called Zara's phone a few times to leave a message for you."

Zara hesitated. "Mama told me to block all calls from Meelah's friends."

My heart dropped in my chest. Everything Dinero did was for his family. He had already lost a brother, and he had to provide for his drug-addicted mother and younger siblings. With his mother dead, where would his sister and brother go? With my father's help, Dinero went from being a high school dropout to not only going back to school, but becoming a star player on the football team. I was in a coma during his birthday, which was December 5, but I was sure my father paid for an elaborate party for him. My father played a major role in Dinero's life. My father was the only thing standing between Easy and the barrel of Dinero's gun. Dinero hated Claudius, and it turned out Easy was Claudius's friend.

"Dinero was going crazy at that hospital! His little sister and brother found their mother passed out in the shower and called 911. If these kids go into foster care, you know the police are going to be on their asses, asking them all types of shit about our Chain. They've seen a lot of activity going on in that house." Daddy was more concerned about his own well-being than anyone else's, as normal.

"Daddy, you're worried about your business when you just said Dinero's mother died from a drug overdose? Must be some of your shit that she overdosed on, huh?" I scoffed.

Daddy looked at me like I was crazy. "Nah, it's our shit, little girl. The entire East Coast profits off shit that we bring across the coast, and don't you forget that shit. If they bust me, it's only to get rid of me so they can have all the money for themselves. Everyone is fuckin' dirty! Everyone is out here trying to make a profit, including Dinero, who won't appreciate you fuckin' with the friend of his enemy. You can't just cut Dinero off like he never existed! He was there for you when you didn't even know Easy existed! So, you think you're just gonna have Easy's baby, huh? It's that simple, huh? Do you think his family would appreciate their son having a baby with a black ho?"

I gasped a little as my father snatched my body back to his. "Daddy, how could you just call me a h—"

"That's what all black women are to white families!" Daddy snarled in my face. "You're not the type of bitch white muthafuckas bring home to Mama! You're just the type of bitch these white muthafuckas fuck and forget about! You're that muthafucka's best kept secret! You're just like your mother! She didn't listen, and look what the fuck happened to her! Keep playing games, and that's exactly where you'll end up! In a casket next to hers!"

Daddy shook me as hard as he could before Aunt Troy snatched me away from him.

"That is enough, Emmanuel!" Aunt Troy screamed, calling my father by his government name.

"You didn't have to do her like that, Sable!" Sharita yelled at my father. "You have yet to acknowledge what the fuck happened to her!"

I looked at Sharita, who hadn't even talked to me about what happened to me.

"Neither has she!" my father yelled back.

"The son of the muthafucka you worked for raped and beat her!" my aunt screamed out in anger.

I looked at my father for some sort of angry reaction about what happened. I didn't see any look of revenge in his eyes. He kept his poker face as expected. He did know exactly what happened to me. The night my father and aunt caught me and Easy together, my aunt told my father what happened to me—about the fact that I was assaulted, but not the details. It was the first time I actually heard my aunt mention that Stef's son raped and beat me. And it was the first time that I saw the look on my father's face when my aunt told him who raped me. He didn't look the least bit surprised, which led me to believe that he'd found out exactly who did what to me.

"Rumors are going around that it was more than one of them!" Aunt Troy went on to say. "What are you going to do about it, huh?"

"He'll dig his own grave. Don't worry about that. Let someone else worry about that, Troy," my father let her know.

Troy shook her head. "So, you do know exactly what happened to her, and those muthafuckas are still breathing? You're going to do Meelah like you did her mother? Let muthafuckas get away without pressing any issues? Deal with that shit now! Meelah needs your support right now, not your 'money over everything' bullshit! She's been through enough!"

"And it looks like she's ready to go through more if you ask me!" Daddy howled at my aunt before transferring his glare from her over to me. "If you don't kill this baby, you better find a way to make this baby Dinero's. Opening your legs for niggas doesn't seem to be a problem for you." Daddy straightened his jacket.

Sharita scoffed. "This muthafucka," she muttered.

I shook my head at the man who sure as fuck wasn't acting like a father. "I'm not a ho."

"Then stop acting like one!" Daddy barely let me get my sentence out. "I raised you to respect your body, and your behavior proves that you don't. As long as you are my child—"

Aunt Troy cut him off. "Well, right now, Emmanuel, she's my goddamn child! Don't come here trying to run shit when you've been missing in muthafuckin' action for months! Say what you have to say, then get your street niggas from out in front of my yard! This is a white neighborhood. They already think every nigga who comes up in here is selling fuckin' dope."

"Muthafucka, I am," Daddy snarled.

Aunt Troy rolled her eyes, growing impatient.

Daddy looked at me, watching me dry the tears from my face. "Save ya tears for the funeral. Jaylah's funeral is tomorrow at three thirty."

"Tomorrow?" Sharita gasped.

"I had to pull some serious strings to get that woman's body from the medical examiner before the tox screen came back. I had my nigga Dr. Newborne from the mortuary perform her autopsy. He convinced the police department and the media that she OD'd off one of our rivals' products. And I had one of the embalmers at one of my funeral homes embalm her a few hours ago. The wake is tomorrow at eleven. The funeral is at three thirty. Your boy should have his insurance check posted to his account by midnight tonight." Daddy sounded cold as ice, but then again, funerals were a part of his everyday life. "Sharita, you might as well stay here with my daughter tonight so you can drive her back to Maryland in the morning."

Sharita frowned at my father. If it weren't for her family's affiliation with my father, she probably would've had my father killed. She didn't trust nor like him and said he always treated me like I wasn't his own flesh and blood. She never saw him hug, kiss, or console me. All she ever saw him do was treat me like one of his employees. And she was right.

"Take her out. Buy her a nice, pretty, black dress online. Somewhere local so she can pick it up in the morning. Pay for her shoes, purse, jacket, hair, whatever. Make sure you get her something that Dinero would like." Daddy pulled out his wallet and slipped out an American Express Centurion Card.

Zara's eyes lit up at the sight of the Black Card as my father held the card out for me to take from his hands.

Sharita shook her head at my father. "We don't need your money. I'll buy her a dress." She smacked her lips, rolling her eyes and her neck at Daddy. "You can't buy her like you do your other hoes."

Daddy glared at her before looking back into the hurt expression on my face. "I'm sure your friend here will cancel whatever plans she thought she had with Archer Wright—street name Ace—tomorrow. I'm sure she'll sit by you tomorrow at the funeral."

Sharita rolled her eyes, but she knew the fact that my father knew Ace's real name meant that she needed to stay the fuck away from him before she got his whole family killed. I bet she was glad that pregnancy test was negative as fuck.

"A funeral on Valentine's Day, Daddy?" I asked him.

"Love, flowers, marriage proposals, funeral, same fuckin' thing," Daddy muttered. "It's all a death sentence."

He was right about that much.

"Do you want the card or not?" Daddy's nostrils flared. He didn't give me enough time to respond before putting it back in his wallet then the wallet back in his pocket. The muffled sound of Daddy's cell phone ringing came from in his jacket pocket. "I have to get going. You have a lot to think about, Meelah. Life as you know it is about to change for you regardless of what decision you make about that mistake growing inside of you. What about college in August?"

"I can still go," I told him.

"The hell you can!" Aunt Troy scoffed. She couldn't wait for my father to leave so she could give me a piece of her mind. She looked at my father, folding her arms, weight shifted to one leg.

Daddy smirked at my aunt before looking at me the same way he did when he caught me with Easy. He looked at me like I was making the worst mistake of my life. "What you gonna do when that black-ass baby pops out and that pale muthafucka doesn't want shit to do with you? How many days have you spent with the muthafucka? One? Two? Maybe three? How many years have you spent with Dinero? Eighteen muthafuckin' years! Easy has a life that you don't fit into and vice versa! You don't know shit about him, and he doesn't know shit about you. It's not smart to kick a nigga who you have known all your life to the curb for a nigga you just met a few months ago. Do the right thing, Meelah."

I wasn't sure what that was. I sobbed to myself, watching my father go out the front door of my aunt's cozy house. Before I could turn to my aunt and apologize for the situation, she was already digging into my feelings.

Aunt Troy put her finger in my face. “You were in a coma for two goddamn months, Meelah! Soon as your ass gets up out of that bed, you’re back to that shit that your father lets you do while you’re at home! I trusted you! The only muthafucka I let around you was that little white boy, and you couldn’t keep your legs closed a good week! You only just met the boy! You have been dating Dinero damn near all your life, and never once have I heard your father say that you had a slipup! You let that white muthafucka go in raw for the first and the last fuckin’ time, I promise you that! Either you get rid of that baby, or like your father said, you’re going to have to figure out a way to make Dinero believe the baby is his!”

“You want her to lie to Dinero’s crazy ass?” Sharita exclaimed.

“What else is she going to do? Do you have any brighter ideas? That muthafucka isn’t about to drive by my goddamn house and unload them choppers on me and my daughter all because my niece wants to ruin her life!” Aunt Troy shouted at the top of her lungs. “If you decide to keep this baby, your ass is going to finish high school! Your ass is going to go to college! Your ass is going to get a job and not depend on anyone else’s money to take care of this baby! You are not about to pass up any opportunities because of this baby! This isn’t the end of the world, but change is going to be necessary, Meelah! Being with Easy isn’t an option. I don’t know him, but judging by the way he looks, his family has his entire life mapped out, and you are nowhere in their plans for him. Stay away from him! If I catch you near that muthafucka again, I’m sending you to live with my cousin in Los Angeles, and you won’t be a three-hour drive away from your friends.

You'll be a seven-and-a-half-hour plane ride away! Do I make myself clear?"

I nodded. "Yes, ma'am." My lips trembled as I fought back the tears. "Aunt Troy, I'm so sorry! Easy is the only one I've ever met who listens to me even when I'm not even saying anything. I love him so much, Auntie! I don't want to do this! I don't want to be with Dinero. All I want is Easy!"

My aunt fought back her tears too. "Oh, baby. Why did you do this to yourself?"

"Auntie, I love him. I really do." I started crying.

My aunt grabbed me close and wrapped me in her arms. "I know, honey. I know. But it's over."

Sharita let me use her phone that night to call Dinero. He played hard on the phone, but I could hear in his voice that he was hurting inside. Social services couldn't wait to take his 10-year-old brother, Landon, and 6-year-old sister, Cordey, away from their house. I wanted to hate Dinero for what went down with Whitley, but when it came down to it, Dinero had been down with me since day one. I knew what I signed up for when we made it official. He'd always had hoes. It shouldn't have surprised me that one of my friends was one of them.

Sharita was friends with just about every manager at every store that sold Gucci in Anne Arundel County and Howard County. We found a few cute outfits and matching shoes online and had her friends take the outfits and shoes over to her mother's place for us. Jimena agreed to do my hair for me in the morning. Sharita sat next to me messing with her phone, trying to ignore the muffled sound of my aunt in the room next to mine, gossiping about me to my other aunts on the phone. Lawd, my aunts were going to rip into my ass when they saw me again.

"Lord, how many aunts do you have? *Dios mío!*" Sharita rolled her eyes as she sat on my bed in my Old Navy pajamas. "She's gonna have the whole church talkin' shit! I think I just heard one of your aunts say she was tired of being a freak for the pastor! Your aunt Louise is fuckin' the pastor?"

"Ain't no tellin'," I sighed, sitting alongside her with a hot cup of cocoa in my hands. "Sharita?" I hesitated.

"Oh, my goodness, I swear that big bitch from my chemistry class does not need to wear plaid! She looks like a fuckin' picnic table!" Sharita laughed out loud as she scrolled down her Facebook timeline before looking at the distraught expression on my face. Her laughter subsided. "Yes, boo?"

I exhaled sharply before asking her about her cousin and brother. "What do you know about Easy?"

Sharita scoffed. "That he's a liar."

I shook my head. "He didn't lie to me."

"Well, he didn't actually tell you the truth either! The nigga was dickin' you down, knowing he had Stephanie Tanner pregnant! He knew he was about to play *Full House* with that bitch! Did he tell you about her?" Sharita exclaimed.

"We saw that bitch about to turn up on us at homecoming. I knew the bitch existed," I told her.

Sharia rolled her eyes. "Did he tell you the ho was pregnant?"

"That's not the point," I muttered.

"That's exactly the point!" Sharita snapped.

I shook my head. "His family is obviously planning his life for him," I told her. "What muthafucka you know gets married at seventeen years old? His family is making him marry that girl because she's pregnant, I know it."

Sharita shook her head at me. "Don't get caught up with him, I'm telling you. I didn't agree with your punk-ass daddy before, but he's right. Either you gotta abort this mission or you gotta play this baby off as Dinero's, which is gonna be hard. What if the baby turns out white as snow with blond hair and blue eyes? Dinero's not stupid!"

I rolled my eyes. "I guess I'll cross that bridge when I get there."

"Girl, you need to just forget about everyone and join the military like you've always wanted to do." Sharita locked the screen on her phone, then put it down on the bed.

"Easy is your cousin. Cristobal is your brother, but I heard that Easy and Cristobal are brothers too," I told her. "Your mama and your aunt were fuckin' the same dude! Easy and Cristobal are cousin-brothers! Did you know that your brother is one of the guys who raped me?" I had to ask her.

Sharita looked at me, her light eyes searching my face. "Let's get something straight. That muthafucka and I might have the same mother, but he is not my fuckin' brother. He treats me and my mom like we're beneath him. We work for him as far as he's concerned."

I looked at her, watching the look of hate and disgust form in her eyes.

Sharita frowned at the thought of Cristobal. "The muthafucka chased away all the boys who liked me in middle school. And why do you think that is?"

I didn't even want to think of the reason why, but she told me anyway.

"So he could do what he wanted to do to my body." Sharita was too angry to cry about what she was telling me. "So he could do what he wanted to me, his own fuckin' sister! The things he made me do to him and his friends, trust me, you don't want to know. From the age of ten until I was seventeen."

"You never told me any of this!" I squealed under my breath.

Sharita shrugged. "Wasn't your problem."

"What the fuck? Yes, it was! How could I not know? How could I not see what was going on? Was I too busy? Was I—"

Sharita cut me off. "Boo, it wasn't your fault. Nobody knew."

I shook my head. Someone had to know. "Did Jimena know?"

Sharita scoffed. "The bitch didn't want to know. But we're not talking about me. We're talking about you, *bonita*. I'm sorry for what he did to you, I really am, but if you want to live, you need to forget that shit ever happened. The shit that he did, and the shit that Easy did."

"I really like Easy, ya know? I thought he was different. When I talked, he listened. He really saw me, the real me. When my aunt told him no, he made her say yes. He made my aunts like him, and he made me love him. And now he's getting married, and I'm pregnant just like his wife-to-be." I was so hurt.

Sharita was hurt with me. She wrapped her arm around me and rested her head against mine. "I know there has got to be nothing worse than meeting the right person at the wrong time, boo, but if you don't want any trouble, you need to forget about everything that happened from the night you met Easy until now. As far as you should be concerned, that baby inside of you is Dinero's. He's vulnerable, he's hurt, and he needs you. Fuck the shit out of that nigga, and three weeks later, tell the muthafucka you're pregnant." Sharita peeped that my hot chocolate in my mug was getting low. "You want some more hot chocolate, *chica?*"

I shook my head.

Sharita sighed heavily. "Well, I'ma go make me some. We have a lot to talk about, like why you didn't tell me your cousin was fuckin' Ace." She rolled her eyes.

"Shit, why didn't you tell me that you were fuckin' Ace?" I rolled my eyes back at her. "I had no idea that y'all even rolled with them. As far as I knew, Dinero told us to stay the fuck away from anyone who rolled with Claudius. I just went to the party to chill and hopefully run into Easy. I had no idea you were hooking up with Ace, someone my cousin has been seeing since I was in that coma! Bitch, you caught me off guard too!"

Sharita shook her head. "Well, if it hadn't been for me with them damn pregnancy tests, you wouldn't have known that you were pregnant. My intuition never lies, boo. I knew one of us was fucked up, shit. Wish I would've never entertained that nigga, and I'm sure you wish that Easy never wasted your time. But I'll be in the guest room if you need me, boo. We have a long day tomorrow. Try to get some sleep."

Sleep was the last thing on my mind. I sat outside on my aunt's front porch that night, looking up at the stars. I wished at that moment that I could talk to my mother. She'd know exactly what to do. She always did. I sighed heavily as I stared up at the sky.

"Mama, can you hear me?" I whispered. "I'm lost, and I don't know what to do. If you happen to run into God or Jesus while you're up there, could you ask Them to do me this one favor and make this pain go away?" I sniffled. "Ya sista is mad at me." I laughed to myself. "All ya sistas are mad at me! They can't believe that I got caught up with a white boy who I know nothing about. The sad part is I think they really like Easy. If this was really Dinero's baby, Aunt Troy would have driven me to the abortion clinic tonight to get rid of it!

"Aunt Troy knows I'm not going to get rid of the baby. She's talking about moving with me to LA and practicing law again. She wants what's best for me, unlike your husband, who only seems to be thinking of himself. I don't know what to do, Mama. I don't want to kill this man's baby, but I don't want to lie to Dinero either. He did wrong, I'll admit that, but two wrongs don't make a right. Or do they? Dinero would kill me in front of Easy if he ever found out that this baby was his."

I silenced my talk with Mama as soon as a dark car sitting on twenty-twos came gliding into my aunt's driveway. It was one of Daddy's luxury rentals. My heart palpitated in my chest as I watched Dinero step out of the car dressed in dark sweats and a hoodie. Whenever he was stressed the fuck out, he worked out, so that explained the attire. He walked up the walkway that led to my aunt's front porch, holding a bag from Neiman Marcus in his hand.

I sighed as Dinero sat down next to me, his sweet, masculine cologne saturating the air around us. Neither of us said a thing to the other, but as soon as I laid my head on his shoulder, he let out a long, quivering sigh.

"Ummm." Dinero cleared his throat, his voice shaking a little. "My aunt from LA flew down about an hour ago. She plans to adopt my li'l brother and sister. You know they ain't trying to leave a nigga." He laughed a little.

I nodded. "I know, but staying with her is better than them getting caught up in the foster care system. Not to mention the family business."

"I did a lot of bad shit. This is God paying me back." Dinero continued to laugh through his pain.

I shook my head while looking up into his face, my chin resting on his shoulder. "No, Dinero, this has nothing to do with anything that you've done. Your mom has been addicted to drugs since we were kids, boo."

"She knew we needed her, man. Why did she do this shit to us, yo? My sister and brother didn't deserve to find my mother drowning in her own vomit and shit! That image will be engraved in their memories for the rest of their lives!" Dinero howled. "How am I supposed to explain to them that our mother died from the drugs that I help to distribute? How many other people have been murdered off the shit that I profit from? I'm getting rich off taking people's lives, Meelah! And the sad part is that I have no plan to stop anytime soon." Dinero exhaled deeply. "Ya pops plans to make me Numero Uno on the East Coast as soon as I graduate."

I looked into Dinero's face. Numero Uno was the term we used for the head distributor. That meant he'd have access to all my father's assets both foreign and domestic. Something big was going down if my father was giving Dinero that title.

Dinero handed me the bag that he had in his hand. He watched me peep inside. "It's a black Givenchy dress. Tight, knee-length, sexy. You'll like it."

I peeped inside the bag, eying the black velvet box. "What's in that box?"

"A necklace," Dinero told me.

I looked up at him. "Sharita and I already have our outfits and accessories picked out. You didn't have to do this."

Dinero nodded. "Yeah, I did. I missed ya birthday. I wasn't invited to the party." Dinero frowned at me.

I shook my head. "I know you heard about—"

Dinero cut me off. "I didn't want to hear about the shit then, and I damn sure don't wanna hear about it now. I want to kill that nigga, and you know it."

I swallowed hard.

"He's been in your face ever since the homecoming, and niggas are saying that your father caught him in your hotel room. Did you fuck that muthafucka, Meelah? Be real with me. I don't really want to know, but at the same time, I have to know." Dinero looked me in my face.

All I could say was, "Dinero, you really have no right to question me about anything or anyone after what you did with my friend. I know better than to fuck with Easy. I'm not crazy. I got a little drunk, and Easy brought me to my room. As he was leaving, Evan burst into the room, and that was when Easy shot him. Nothing happened. I thought about it—I wanted to pay you back for what you did—but nothing happened."

Though Dinero looked relieved, he wasn't totally stupid. He knew I wasn't telling him everything that happened, but I'd never lied to him before, so he had no choice but to take my word for it. I didn't want to lie, but if I was going to have that baby, I needed to learn to get good at lying at all costs.

"I was wrong, and you wanted to pay a nigga back. I get it—you can get any nigga with no problem. I can be replaced. You made your point loud and clear. I'ma be real wit'cha. The only reason I haven't offed that nigga Easy is because of ya daddy."

I nodded. "I already know."

"My own brother had enough sense not to dance with you that night at homecoming, and then this nigga comes up and dances to a song that was meant for you and me." Dinero scowled. "Shawty, we all knew to keep our distance from you that night that Cristobal was on his rampage. We all knew to back the fuck off. After Stef found out what his son did, he gave me all of his son's territories because I didn't retaliate."

"Was it worth it?" I hated to ask.

Dinero's frown softened. "Was what worth it?"

"Watching them niggas fuck me?" I had to know.

The frown wrinkled back onto his face. "The fuck?"

"You want to kill Easy for what? For rescuing me?" I asked, about to get back on the porch.

Dinero yanked me back down by my wrist.

"You watched Cristobal violently assault me! You sacrificed me so you could put a guilt trip on the muthafucka's father? Gaining all that money was worth it to watch me in pain? You got what you came into my life for, huh?" I yelled at him.

Dinero shook his head, digging into his pocket. "We all know how the game goes, shawty. We fucked up when the police raided that party on Christmas Eve. They did what they did to you to show us a lesson. Did I like seeing you like that? No. But when we fucked up, we knew they'd blame you, the boss's daughter."

"I want out of this," I told him. "Get me out of this shit!"

Dinero frowned at me. "And then where would I be?"

"With the next ho who has a father running shit!" I exclaimed.

I was so busy cussing, fussing, and shoving him that I didn't even notice that he was pulling out the diamond ring that Whitley mentioned to me the last time I saw her in the hospital. Once I stopped cursing him out enough to notice the diamond sparkling under the porch lights, I started crying.

"I never meant to hurt you. I didn't mean to leave you, but I had to. They threatened to kill my li'l sister and my brother!" Dinero tried to explain. "I wanted to kill that nigga Easy because he got to the best part of me. You're the best part of me, Meelah. I saw the way you looked at him that night on the dance floor. You wished that it was me out there with you. I let you down and I'm sorry." Dinero grabbed my hand and slid the cold ring onto my trembling finger. "Life is too short. I lost my big brother, I lost my mama, and they took my little siblings away from me. Meelah, I can't lose you, too. I promise that I can give you a life that you won't need a vacation from."

I just looked down at the ring, watching it sparkle like it had magical powers.

"Please, Mee-Mee." Dinero called me something that he hadn't called me since elementary school.

I looked into Dinero's handsome face. Like I told Easy, Dinero wasn't a bad guy. Or at least he wasn't meant to be one. He hadn't been the same since he lost his older brother. Losing someone you love fucks with your mental state. And the fact that his father wasn't around didn't help him either. If a boy doesn't have a father figure in his life, he needs that male role model. That was what my father was to Dinero, shit to every black boy growing up in the hood.

Daddy was the ghetto king version of Uncle Phil. He taught the young black men of the ghetto that just because they were in the ghetto, it didn't mean they couldn't prosper. Dinero and the other young men were rich beyond the wildest dream of any man in any neighborhood. It was their choice to stay in the hood to hide their assets. I didn't want to be a part of that life, and that was what really had me shook when he asked me to marry him.

"We just turned seventeen, Dinero," was all I could say.

"So what? I don't want anybody else, Meelah." Dinero held my hand in his.

"Are you sure?" I questioned him.

Dinero exhaled deeply. "I talked to your father about this. He said it was cool. He welcomed me into the family last night and inducted me into one of the highest seats on The Chain, ma. I'm in there. We're in there. This shit is ours. I don't want anybody but you sitting next to me. I'll fly back and forth to visit you in LA when you go to school. You wanna join the military after college, then you can do that, too. I won't make you stop your life. I just want to be a part of it."

"So, I'm just supposed to forget about Whitley like that shit with her never happened?" I had to ask.

Dinero frowned again. "You forget about her, and I'll forget about that nigga Easy."

"Dinero, I just told you that nothing happened."

Dinero scoffed. "I'm not stupid, Meelah. That shit he was talking that day at your aunt's house let me know that if he hasn't gotten in between those thighs yet, he's going to continue to make his move. You keep entertaining the nigga, which is why he keeps coming around. See, Whitley's gone. You won't ever have to worry about her. But your man Easy is still around. For now."

I gulped. At that moment, I realized that Dinero wasn't asking me to marry him. The nigga was telling me that I was going to marry him. I'd given him a dose of his own medicine, and he didn't like it. Yes, a part of me wanted revenge, but Easy wasn't a part of that plan. I had played with fire, and I was getting burned. Dinero was making sure that he wasn't the only one taking that medicine. I was swallowing that pill too. Easy was getting married to a girl he'd known a lot longer than he'd known me. We'd never be able to be together. There was no way.

"We doing this thang or not?" Dinero saw me thinking hard about my answer.

Shit, do I really have a choice?

Chapter Nine

Bostyn

"You ready, son?" Pops tapped on my bedroom door that Valentine's Day of 2013.

I huffed, fumbling with my tie, as I stood in front of the full-length mirror. The house was buzzing with guests. We were supposed to have a small courthouse wedding, but it seemed like my mother and Mandy's mother had invited everyone in their fuckin' family tree. Mandy wasn't feeling well at all that week and didn't want to have a reception that day, but I couldn't tell by the way the house was packed like "ladies free before twelve" night at the club. Who'd have ever thought they'd be so happy to celebrate two teenagers who hadn't even turned 18 years old yet getting married only because the bride-to-be had gotten knocked up? You would've thought we were Bey and Hova by the number of gifts that were stacked on our dining room table downstairs.

Mandy was already at the courthouse with her mother and father, and I was at home with my family and the other guests who were going to follow us to the courthouse in Annapolis. Pops was going to have his boys from the precinct lead us down Route 50 to Annapolis. Talk about drawing too much attention to myself. I just wanted to get the shit over with. I stood in the mirror, struggling with my tie, when Pops entered my room.

"Having trouble?" Pops laughed a little as he closed the door behind him.

I glanced at his reflection in the mirror before tossing the tie on a chair that stood alongside my mirror. I was like fuck it. I didn't want to wear a goddamn tie for this bullshit anyway. I peeped my reflection in my window, eying myself in my black Alexander Wang button-down shirt and black pants. I went over and sat on my bed, pulling my black-and-white Alexander Wang Adidas box from under my bed.

Pops shook his head at me as he watched me slip my feet into my sneakers. "On top of wearing all black, you're going to wear sneakers to a wedding?"

"Shit feels like a funeral anyway. Might as well wear black," I muttered, looking up at my Pops like he had lost his mind trying to tell me how to dress for some shit he knew I wasn't down with. Little did he know, I already had my divorce papers signed and in my safe deposit box at the bank. I'd gotten the paperwork from the law library at the very courthouse that Mandy and I were about to get married in. I was prepared for that shit when the day came because it was coming. I was going to do whatever I had to do to make that bitch leave my ass.

Pops cleared his throat before coming over and sitting beside me on the bed. He looked my clothes over a little before he helped to adjust my collar. "I know you're upset with me—"

"Upset?" I barely let him get the sentence out when I cut him off. "Pops, upset isn't even the word."

"Image is everything. You'll learn that as you get older, son. You're young. You'll live, and you'll learn from your mistakes," Pops tried to tell me.

"Did you learn from your mistakes, muthafucka?" I muttered to myself as I bent over and tied my shoelaces. "The way you talk, you act like you never made any."

Pops exhaled sharply before saying, "Oh, I've made plenty of mistakes. And I'm looking at one of them right now."

I stopped tying my shoe and sat up on the bed, looking Pops in the face.

Pops grimaced, looking at me like I had no idea of the shit he'd gone through for me. "I'm trying to teach you about life, and you're mad at everyone else for the mistakes that you made! While you're living under my muthafuckin' roof, your fuckups are my responsibility! You fucked up when you started having sex with a girl who is obsessed with the ground you walk on. No matter what lengths the crazy bitch went to to get pregnant, those kids are still yours! If you don't marry this girl, she will make your life hell.

"Marriage these days is just a business venture. Her father's brother is head of the Street Safety Squadron. It's a secret police academy in Texas that trains undercover cops. No one will know you're a cop. When people try to look up your information in the computer to check if you're a cop, nothing will come up. Your shield will be invisible. With your street credibility, you can help bring down some of the biggest drug lords. That little girl you care about so much is in for a world of trouble, and she doesn't even know. This can help her, and as long as you keep your feelings in check, we can all benefit from this."

I looked at my father as he stood from the bed.

"When you go in this courthouse today, when you say, 'I do,' kiss that bitch like she's the most beautiful woman in the world. Her father will thank all of us tremendously," Pops told me as I stood before him. "You ready?"

I just looked into his face, feeling like I was about to face my sentencing. "Walking the mile, walking the mile, getting right with Jesus." I exhaled deeply, thinking about one of my favorite scenes in Stephen King's *The Green Mile.*

My father laughed out loud as he shoved me toward the door to my room. "You came in the world crying and fussing, Bostyn, and you haven't stopped. Time to lie in this bed you made. Your brother has the rings."

Everything happened so fast that morning. I don't even remember saying, "I do," but apparently, I did. We got married on the third floor of the circuit court for Anne Arundel County. My father had the entire floor blocked off so no one could come in the huge hallway to see the event. Family from both sides—mine and Mandy's—stood by and watched me sign my life away to that girl before God and the court magistrate.

Claudius stood by as my best man. He couldn't care less about the wedding. He was just there as his excuse to miss school that day. He hated Valentine's Day. That was the day that his mother, Leanne, tripped the most because his father would post videos and pictures all over social media of his new wife and children. She couldn't take it, and she let the stress seep into the way she carried him. His aunt Marilyn wasn't much different than his mother in that, though. She took Claudius in, and she still catered to her sister's needs. Claudius just needed an outlet that day, and my walk down the Green Mile was his way out.

My mother looked so proud. Her tears of joy were real. I wasn't her son biologically, but she never treated me like anything other than her baby boy. The twins were right. Our parents did give me a little more leeway than they gave their own biological kids. Jaxon and Roxyn wouldn't have gotten away with half the shit our parents let me get away with. Jaxon and Roxyn smirked all the way through my wedding, glad that our parents were finally making me pay for fuckin' up.

"Congrats, bro!" Jaxon patted me on my back after the ceremony as everyone cleared out of the courthouse on their way back to the Wineyards' house for some of their bland-ass food. You'd have thought with all them Haitian cooks they had that they'd have known better.

I frowned at my brothers, watching them laughing at me. "Man, if it weren't for the strippers y'all got me last night, I would curse y'all the fuck out right out now." The night before was lit like a muthafucka. Claudius had some of his groupies from Chesapeake High roll through and give us a show. Took my mind off Mandy, but the way they moved them hips only reminded me of Meelah even more.

Just when I started to ask Claudius what he was getting into, as the crowd dissipated, there stood Sharita right in the middle. I was shook for a minute, watching my cousin standing there in her blue polka-dot dress and hair pulled up into a perfect bun. She grinned and flipped me the bird before signaling me to come over to her.

Claudius peeped me looking at her before he looked around at my family members leaving the church and Mandy over in the corner of the hallway by the steps, bragging to her friends about the honeymoon we were supposed to go on that weekend. Her folks had this huge house on Myrtle Beach that they gave us as a wedding gift.

"Boss, c'mon, man. Fuck ya cousin. She's trying to start some shit." Claudius nudged me.

I shook him off and walked over to Sharita. How she heard about the wedding, I had no idea. I doubted Donna would have told her anything. Sharita was the messy type, yes, but I had a feeling she'd come to deliver a message. I stood before her as she waved an invitation to the wedding ceremony in my face. As soon as I saw my mom's stationary, I knew that Mandy had given that shit to her.

I exhaled deeply, shaking my head at Sharita looking at me like I had her friend fucked up. "Where did you get that?" I asked, though I already knew the answer.

"I was meeting Meelah at the mall yesterday, and ya bitch gave me the invite when we ran into her in the bathroom." Sharita watched me anxiously rub my head.

"Meelah was with you? Meelah saw this invitation?" I asked and watched Sharita nod. "So, she saw Mandy's stomach?"

"Duh, dummy." Sharita shoved me in the chest.

"Was shawty mad?" I hesitated to ask, just knowing the answer was going to be yes.

Sharita shrugged a little. "More like hurt."

I shook my head. "I didn't mean to hurt her."

Sharita nodded. "I know, cuz."

"I didn't plan this," I told her.

Sharita rolled her eyes. "That ho looks like one of them bitches to save the sperm and shoot it in her pussy with a turkey baster!"

Sharita could read old girl like a muthafucka. I grinned a little. "All I'm saying is my family planned all of this. Pops calls himself securing my future, but I don't want any of this shit."

Sharita looked around at my family. "My mom told me a little about you but not much. I don't know who your adoptive family is, but they gotta have some money. These muthafuckas look like cops." Sharita looked back at me. "Tajha was right. You are five-o!" Her eyes landed on Pops, and she looked back at me like she'd seen a ghost. "Which one do you call Pops?"

She seemed like she really didn't want to know the answer to the question that she'd just asked. One thing

I was learning about Sharita was that she liked to play stupid.

I shook my head. "None of your fuckin' business."

Sharita shook her head at me. "Well, while y'all playing Barbie and Gangsta Ken, Dinero put a ring on ya girl's finger last night."

"What?" I couldn't believe the muthafucka had proposed at the perfect time. Just when shawty found out I was getting married to Mandy, that muthafucka proposed to Meelah. "What did she say to the muthafucka?"

"What do you think she said?" Sharita scoffed. "His mother was found dead in her apartment yesterday morning, and everybody is at her funeral today. Dinero is using the money that he's getting from her insurance to go into business with Meelah's father and open a casino in Baltimore. I don't know when their wedding is, but I'm sure it's not until the summer."

I was so pissed off that I was sure my face was red as fuck.

"Your life isn't the only one getting planned out, Easy." Sharita peeped over at a few of my father's family members. "I just asked you a question, muthafucka. I saw the invitation. I peeped the last name. Who is your adoptive family? That last name Reel sounds real familiar."

I shook my head. "Nah, you don't know my people."

Sharita assured me, "Oh, I know a lot of things, *chico blanco*. More than I want to know, trust me."

"My family is about to dip." I watched Sharita eying Pops leaving with Mom. "I'm supposed to go over to Mandy's people's place for a light dinner and then out to dinner at Soul Fusion, that new restaurant downtown."

Sharita's eyes lit up a little. "I think Meelah and Dinero are going there too at eight tonight."

I just frowned down into Sharita's face, shaking my head. "Oh, word?"

Sharita nodded. "Yup. If you want, I could get one of Dinero's boys to call him up for some business, and I could get Mandy's cousin, who is a nurse, to call her to the hospital and tell her some shit about they found something in one of her blood tests. I sell Rox to her cousin, Klarissa. She'll do what I want. Better yet, I'll have Klarissa throw a surprise party for your girl at her crib."

I shook my head. "Nah, they'll let Mandy drink. I don't give two fucks about her right now, but she is carrying my baby. I mean, babies. Twins."

Sharita's eyes widened. "That bitch is having two of your kids? *Dios mio!*" Sharita looked like she wanted to cry.

I exhaled deeply. "Mandy is my problem, not yours, Sharita."

Sharita looked at me like I didn't have a clue. "I don't think you know how much my boo really likes you."

"Oh, yeah? Then why the fuck is she marrying Dinero?"

Sharita folded her arms. "The fuck? Muthafucka, why are you marrying Kelly Clarkson over there?"

"I didn't have a choice," I told her.

"Neither did she!" Sharita exclaimed through clenched teeth. "Dinero is about to own these streets. You don't know shit about your family—the one in the streets or the one who planned this wedding for you. Little do you know, the Reels aren't much different from the Romano family."

I knew she knew about my family even though she played like she didn't. I nodded. "So I've heard."

Sharita scoffed. "I doubt it, boo. The Romanos don't have shit on the Reel family. Who do you think helps move our product? Do you really think we'd get away with this shit without the police department?"

I just looked at her. It finally dawned on me why Pops wanted me to be part of the team so badly: to monitor the movement of the drugs that my new friends were moving.

Sharita looked at her watch. "Look, it's Valentine's Day, and I'm about to be depressed as fuck after this funeral. I'm planning to get dicked down tonight. I'll make sure Klarissa shows up to the restaurant around nine, and I'll make sure she has Taylor Swift tied up at the hospital for a while. That'll give you some time to talk to Mandy and enough time for Meelah to have an hour to grieve with Dinero. I think their reservation is for a table in the last room in the restaurant. You make sure you're nowhere in sight. As a matter of fact, I'll hit you up in a few to let you know what time their reservation is for. Dinero is always on time. Wait for my text to let you know that Meelah and Dinero are seated before you take your ass in that restaurant. You should know by now that the CMC is looking for you. The only reason why they haven't fucked with Claudius is because of his aunt. I don't want you to fuck this up. You need to talk to her, and she needs to talk to you."

I nodded and watched Sharita rip the invitation to shreds before tossing it at me.

"Next time ya bitch tries to hurt my girl's feelings, I'ma cut her tongue out and feed it to her," Sharita told me before turning around to walk away.

I peeped Claudius looking at Sharita before glaring back at me.

"I said I wanted medium well, and clearly this shit is well-done." Mandy rolled her big blue eyes as she tossed her steak around on the plate. "Where is that waitress? If she wants this five-dollar tip, then she better get this shit right."

I shook my head at Mandy. "We ordered appetizers, an entree, and a dessert. Not to mention I drank three beers because, luckily, they didn't card me. This shit is gonna cost us at least one hundred and fifty dollars, and you're talking about leaving homegirl five dollars? That's not even five percent, shawty!"

Mandy rolled her eyes. "So?" Mandy was rich as fuck, yet she was the cheapest muthafucka I knew.

I sat there, pushing my food around on the plate, not really paying much attention to Mandy. We sat in a far corner in one of the dining rooms of Soul Fusion that night. Thirty minutes prior to that moment, Sharita had texted me to let me know that Meelah and Dinero had arrived. They were in VIP. Dinero's mother's death was on the news. His father showed up to the service, acknowledging Dinero as his son for the first time to the public. Claudius texted me as soon as that shit went live. Sharita also let me know that Meelah was an emotional wreck and would eventually head to the bathroom to get herself together. So, I sat and waited to get a glimpse of Meelah making her way down the hallway toward the bathroom.

"Do you really need all that?" Mandy scoffed, eying my plate.

I frowned. "Need all what?"

"That bullshit you're eating." Mandy was referring to the fried chicken, collard greens, baked macaroni and cheese, cornbread, and sweet potatoes on my plate.

Bitch, do I really need you? The fuck? was what the fuck I wanted to say, but instead, I just put more hot sauce on my chicken.

"Bostyn, that's enough hot sauce!" Mandy was really irritated.

"Man, whatever. How about you worry about your plate, shawty?" I told her.

Mandy rolled her eyes before spotting the waitress. With her prissy attitude, Mandy smacked her lips, flipped her blond curls, then signaled the waitress to come over.

The waitress reluctantly came over, already knowing that Mandy was with that fuck shit. “Is everything okay?” the cute dark-skinned waitress asked as she approached the table.

“No, it is not okay.” Mandy popped her lips at the waitress. “This is not how I wanted my steak. If I wanted to eat some shit this tough, I would’ve asked my husband here to just take off his belt and put it on my plate!” Mandy slammed her fork and knife on the table. “I don’t even want to talk to you, Shanaynay. Where is your manager?”

“First of all, my name isn’t Shanaynay,” the waitress snapped at Mandy before turning around to stomp away toward the host stand where the manager stood and watched Mandy make a fool of herself.

“Mandy?” I frowned.

“What, Bostyn?” Mandy snapped.

“You need to chill the fuck out. Pregnancy doesn’t give you an excuse for mistreating someone who needs this job. One complaint to corporate could have shawty fired. It’s hard out here enough for a pimp, and you’re trying to get shawty fired over a steak that might be a little overcooked?” I scoffed.

Mandy tossed the steak over on my plate. It was a little skimpy, but it wasn’t burnt. “You eat this shit then, Bostyn! You’re always taking up for these black muthafuckas!”

Mandy was causing a scene.

I clenched my jaw. “Mandy, say one more thing, and you’ll be picking your teeth up off that floor.”

The manager walked over, trying to keep her cool. “Hello, Mr. and Mrs. Reel. Is everything to your liking?”

Mandy started to say something, but I cut her off.

"Everything is perfect. My wife"—I could barely say the title without choking—"is just hormonal. She's eating for three, as you can see by the amount of food on the table. Your staff has done a good job taking care of her. The steak is just a little overcooked, so can you remake it, please? With a little more pink in it?" I took the steak that Mandy had tossed onto my plate, put it back on her plate, then handed the plate to the manager. "And I'll have another Corona. Thanks."

The manager nodded. "Yes, sir."

Mandy glared at me, her blue eyes peering into my face. "Amy's brother said that you let some fat-ass black bitch grind on your dick last night at your bachelor party."

I laughed out loud. "The term isn't fat, ma, it's thick. Super thick. And it was a bachelor party. That's what muthafuckas do at a bachelor party. You don't hear me saying shit about the Puerto Rican muthafucka who Roxyn's girl told him had his dick swinging in your face."

Mandy sat back in her seat and rolled her eyes. "I don't want to argue with you on our wedding day. We're supposed to be somewhere with your dick down my throat. I'd rather be eating that than this steak. It's much juicier."

I looked at her, watching her lick her sneaky-ass lips. Then I looked over her shoulder to see Klarissa come through the front door and approach the host stand. "Yo, ain't that your cousin, Klarissa?"

Mandy looked over her shoulder as her cousin approached us. "Hey, Klar. What's going on?"

Klarissa glanced at me before looking back at her cousin. "Hey, Mandy, ummm, we have to get you to the hospital. I was in the lab, and they were going over your blood work. You might need to get to the hospital. You had elevated levels of protein in your urine. Are you having any headaches? Blurred vision? When is the last time you peed?"

Mandy frowned in confusion. "I feel fine. I had an appointment yesterday, and they didn't say anything then."

"They were backed up yesterday and didn't have the chance to run the lab work. Come on, hon. We need to take you to the ER. Right, Bostyn?" Klarissa looked at me, smiling nervously.

"Oh, yeah. Your cousin knows what she's talking about. I'll meet you back at the hotel. I'll wait on your steak," I told Mandy as she grabbed her purse and got up from the table.

Mandy came over and kissed my cheek before leaving with her cousin.

I let out a long sigh of relief as I watched that crazy bitch walk out the front door with her cousin. Just as I leaned back in the seat, I noticed Meelah walking toward the bathroom down the hallway across the dining room.

The waitress came back over to the table with a Corona and looked at Mandy's empty seat. She rolled her eyes like she was glad that Mandy was gone. "Sir, your food will be right out. The manager said the steak dinner will be comped."

I nodded. "Thanks. Ummm, could y'all box it up for me? I'll be right back. Those beers I drank ran right through me." I got up from the table and walked toward the bathroom.

I rehearsed my lines a thousand times, but I knew when I was face-to-face with Meelah the words wouldn't come out right. There wasn't anything that I could say to her that would make her believe that I was sorry about the way that things had turned out. I was all packed and ready to head out that weekend with Mandy to Myrtle Beach. I hadn't seen Meelah since her birthday on New

Year's, but I thought about her damn near every minute. I was in love with her. My heart was hers, but I was sure the ring on my finger was going to make her feel differently.

I managed to catch a glimpse of Dinero leaving the restaurant like he was in a hurry. Sharita came through for ya boy. I made my way down the hallway toward the bathroom. At that point, I couldn't care less if anyone was in the bathroom with Meelah. I just had to see her. I already knew that she was going to be angry with me, and I was prepared for whatever she had to say. But what I wasn't prepared for was to walk in and see her already crying.

Meelah gasped at the sight of me and reached for some Kleenex from the countertop to dry her face. "What are you doing here?"

Meelah was so pretty standing there in a pretty, tight black dress, something she probably wore to the funeral. Her hair was pulled back into a sleek ponytail. Other than the tinted tears that slid down her face, her makeup was flawless. And those heels made her legs look like they went on for days.

"Seriously, what are you doing in here, Easy-B?" Meelah called me by the nickname that she'd given me, which let me know that Sharita was right. Meelah was more hurt than angry. "Aren't you and your bitch supposed to be fuckin' on a beach somewhere?" Meelah snapped. Yup, she was hurt.

I walked up to her at the mirror. "Where's old boy going?"

Meelah looked up at me as I took the Kleenex from her hands and started to dry her face. "The CMC needs him. His mama just died, and he's out there running the streets as usual. My father's driver is supposed to come pick me up." Meelah's lips trembled. She wanted to grab the tissue from me, but she was too hurt. Too upset with me and the entire situation. "I'm not supposed to be talking to you, Easy," she whispered and placed her hand over mine as I dried her face. "He'd kill me right in front of you."

"You'd marry a nigga like that?" I frowned down into her face.

"I don't have a choice. My father is making me do this. He thinks he's saving me, but there is no saving me." Meelah continued to cry.

"Dinero doesn't love you," I told her.

"You don't love me!" Meelah cried. "I've known Dinero all my life. Why not do this?"

"I wouldn't say he doesn't like you. Like is as far as it goes with that muthafucka. He left you to die!" I had to remind her. "There's a difference between a boy who likes you enough to show you off to his friends, and a man who needs your soul next to his."

"Do you love me?" Meelah whispered.

I nodded. "I wish I could love you more, if that's even possible." I touched her hand.

"Me and Dinero are getting married on graduation day. I don't want this ring. I don't want this life. I just want—"

"Me?" I asked her.

Meelah shoved me in my chest before snatching the tissue from me. "How could you not mention the fact that you're marrying that bitch? Bostyn, you fucked the shit out of me in that hotel! You didn't fuck me like you were about to start a family with her! You fucked me like you were about to start a family with me!" She shoved me again.

"I don't want her, Meelah," I let her know. "My parents made me marry her to please her parents."

"So, you don't love her?" Meelah asked.

I shook my head. "Nah. It's just a piece of paper. It's just a business plan. I leave for college this summer, and then I go work for her father."

I couldn't tell Meelah that I was a cop's adopted son or that I was joining a task force to bring her father down. She hated me enough as it was. She had no idea that my father might have been responsible for killing her mother, and I planned to keep it that way.

Meelah dried the rest of her tears. "Dinero's mother died, and I know he'll want to meet up with me after he gets back from taking care of business. I have to help him box up his mother's stuff."

"I'm going out of town for a few days to South Carolina. When I get back—"

Meelah cut me off. "You're going on your honeymoon, right?"

I shrugged. "If that's what you wanna call it."

"I'll be packing up Dinero's mom's apartment all weekend, so if you're trying to kick it with me, you gotta do it now," Meelah told me.

I laughed a little, not expecting her to want to be around me. I thought I'd have to talk her into it. "Oh, word?"

"Your shit is already packed, right? You're not leaving until tomorrow, right?" Meelah asked.

I nodded. "Yeah. Homeschool is a little more flexible than public school. I won't be missing shit but you."

Meelah looked into my face like she wanted to tell me something but was too afraid to say it. "We need to talk. We can't do it here." Meelah looked at me for an answer as to where we could talk.

"My father owns a penthouse suite on Pennsylvania Avenue. He doesn't know that I know the entrance code.

I can take you there for a little while, until your fuck-boy wants you back," I scoffed.

"Pull the car around then, smart ass, before your bitch starts blowing up your phone." Meelah rolled her dampened eyes.

Chapter Ten

Meelah

I jumped in Bostyn's ride that night. As much as I liked the name Bostyn, I decided to just keep calling him Easy, because that was the exact opposite of the situation that we were in.

Easy looked upset at the entire situation as he sped down the highway in his new Mercedes-Benz, probably a wedding gift from his bitch's parents. I was so mad at him, and I shouldn't have gotten in that car with him, but he had me so addicted that I couldn't even tell him no. I hadn't seen him since my birthday—a little over a month and a half ago—but I still felt him inside of me.

I leaned back in my seat, eying Easy's profile, not exactly sure what to say to him. I had just dodged Arcen who was about to pull up in front of Soul Fusion to pick me up. Before leaving the restaurant, I made sure to turn my phone off. My father tracked my every location with that phone. I wasn't sure how long Dinero would be with his crew, but normally he came back just before sunrise.

I wasn't stupid. I knew that Sharita told Easy where we'd be eating that night. She had mixed emotions about Easy. Her mother knew all about Easy and his adopted family but only told Sharita bits and pieces. Sharita wanted me to spend as much time as I could with Easy before my aunt sent me off to California.

I still wasn't 100 percent sure what I wanted to do about my baby. Our baby. Dinero would rip my baby out and kill it in front of me if he thought Easy was the baby's father. I was crazy for riding in that car that night with Easy. If we were caught, I was dead. And just when I started to tell Easy to turn back around, he gripped my thigh with his right hand, his other hand gripping the steering wheel.

"You cold?" Easy asked and turned the heat up a little without giving me the chance to respond.

"Uh-huh," I stuttered and placed my hand over his.

Oh, my goodness, y'all. I was trying my best to be angry at that sexy muthafucka. I had my lines rehearsed. I was supposed to curse him the fuck out when I saw him and ask him how he could not tell me that ho was pregnant. The way her belly was so rounded out, she had to be at least five or six months pregnant, so there was no way that he was just finding out. I was supposed to ask him how he could make love to me like he loved me, then go back to her. The muthafucka hit my clit with the suck and swirl, then went back to kissing her. I wanted to ask him if he really loved me or if I was just his last chance to dip his dick in chocolate before Snow Pale-as-Hell chained him down. But when he stepped to me in that bathroom, looking so good, dressed in all black, looking like breakfast, lunch, dinner, and a snack, I was speechless. I just wanted him to take me home.

"I have got to be out of my mind." I laughed to myself as my eyes traced his profile. I glanced at the wedding band on his finger. "Mr. and Mrs. Reel. Or should I say Gonzales-Romano?"

Easy glanced at me.

"You are probably going to have the prettiest baby with this bitch. Oh, my goodness." I wanted to cry again.

When Easy caught me crying in the bathroom, I was thinking about Dinero. I had known that boy my entire life, yet I felt more connected to Easy. If Dinero could kill a woman who was supposed to be having his baby without any problem, what did I think he would do to me if he found out that I was pregnant with another man's child?

"I didn't mean to hurt you. I tried to tell you. I tried to call. Your aunt threatened to put a restraining order on me," Easy scoffed. "After that shit that happened with that dude I shot, it was best that I lie low. Muthafuckas were trying to jump my dawg Ace for that shit."

"Your nigga Ace is fuckin' with my cousin and your cousin," I told him.

Easy glanced at me.

"He better quit while he's ahead. My cousin is in love, and you know how thin the line between love and hate is," I told him. "Your cousin—my bestie—is just in it for the dick. You better talk to her."

Easy made a face. "That's their problem. We have our own. Pops is trying to hurry up and get me the fuck outta here. I have some of my crew posted up everywhere. CMC been lookin' for me all month. The coach ended up kicking Claudius off the team. You know he's heated and blaming me for all of this. Ya boy Dinero is fuckin' up his brother's life because of what me and you had going on."

"I told him nothing happened."

Easy looked at me like I knew better than to believe that Dinero didn't think he smashed. "Oh, word? You really think he believes that bullshit? I took a bullet for you, ma."

"How is that healing?" I asked.

Easy nodded. "It's a'ight. My aunt dug the bullet out that night when I got home."

"Did the police question you?" I asked.

Easy glanced at me. “Of course. But it was self-defense, so I’m straight. The fact that the dude ran with The Chain helped a little. They asked me who I was with when I shot him, though. I didn’t tell them I was with you, but surveillance footage told on us. Said they saw me going into a room with you. That the dude who shot me was Arcen’s son. Arcen is your father’s bodyguard, right?”

I nodded. “Yes. Supposedly, he’s mine too.”

“Well, they figured the muthafucka was shooting at me because I was with you, someone he’s supposed to be protecting. When my parents found out, they made me stay away from you. They pressured me to marry Mandy because of certain ties her father has with mine. I’ll be leaving for a while soon,” Easy told me.

I looked at him. “What?”

Easy nodded. “Yeah. I’ll be finished with all my courses in about two weeks. I graduate early from homeschool. My family couldn’t care less about me walking across that stage in May. They just want to see me walk across the stage in college.”

“Where will you be going to college?” I asked.

“In Texas.”

“Wow.” I shrank back in my seat. “So, that’s why your parents wanted you to marry Britney Spears so soon?”

Easy laughed a little and squeezed my thigh. “Yeah. Shawty wanted my last name before I left. I’m not feeling her, ma, I promise you. If you have a child in our family out of wedlock, they make you marry the girl. That’s pretty much why my family made us homeschool, so they could control the people in our circle. If Mandy were poor, they’d pay for her abortion. But since she’s rich, marrying into her family helps them just as much as it helps me, so they think. I’m not ready for this shit.”

“I don’t want to marry Dinero, Easy.” I wanted to tell him about the baby, but I just couldn’t yet.

Easy looked at me. "That makes two of us."

We were both quiet for a few seconds, but his thoughts were just as loud as mine. I missed him. I missed him so much. Who knew that you could love so much someone you just met?

"I missed the fuck out of you." Easy's thoughts agreed with mine.

"You did?" I asked.

"I'm about to show you how much in a few minutes." Easy gripped my thigh.

"So, you think that you're just going to fuck me on your wedding day?" I laughed a little.

Easy frowned. "I'm about to fuck you like it's *our* wedding day, Meelah. Fuck you mean? You scared?"

"Hell nah, I ain't scared." I rolled my eyes.

"Cuz if you're scared that your dude will come through, I can drop you back off with your punk-ass fiancé. Would you rather be in bed with him?" Easy frowned at me.

I shook my head. "I haven't been in bed with him since before I met you, Easy. Nothing feels the same since I've been with you. I don't want anything to do with Dinero."

Easy glanced at me before looking back at the road. "Stop playin' with me."

I shook my head. "I'm not playing." I glanced at his left hand gripping the steering wheel, his wedding band glistening on his ring finger. Then I glanced at the engagement ring on my finger.

"That's an ugly-ass ring," Easy commented. "The muthafucka didn't go to Jared—he went to Walmart. Shit looks fake as fuck."

"Your pale-ass wife looks fake as fuck, nigga." I rolled my eyes.

Easy laughed a little. "I'm just saying he could've picked something a little better for someone he plans to spend his life with. The muthafucka makes plenty of bread. He could've put a Ferrari on your finger instead of putting on a Ford Focus. He probably only gave you the ring to get in good with your pops. Marrying you means marrying your money."

"And what does marrying Kendall Jenner mean?" I snapped.

"Means I'm saving my kids from a woman who'd hurt them to hurt me," Easy told me. "I don't want to be with her. There was never shit between me and that girl, ever, and she hated that. She set me up, saving sperm and shit. I tried to tell my parents, but no one wanted to hear me. They just saw it as an opportunity to secure my future and theirs too. When my chance comes to escape this shit, I'm taking that chance. Until then, I gotta play my role. And I don't think that's what you're doing. I think you feel guilty for leaving Dinero. I don't think it has shit to do with what your father wants."

I exhaled deeply. I wanted to tell him about the baby, but I held it in. At least until we got to his father's spot in DC. Whatever his father was into, that nigga had a bankroll out of this world. My eyes were as big as saucers as I stepped through the front door of his father's condo. That spot was a bachelor's dream. The studio entrance was a long hallway that opened into an extremely large multipurpose room that served as a bedroom, kitchen, and living room. The bathroom was up a winding flight of stairs. The walls of the bathroom were made of glass, so you could see the enormous Jacuzzi tub and separate marble shower. The easy-clean-up kitchen was filled with natural light, which beamed in through a window in the roof. The latest electronics were scattered about the living area. There was a stone fireplace with a faux flame crackling. I felt like I was right in the middle of a white man's dream, because I was.

I sighed as Easy slipped my jacket from my arms and kissed my neck. "This is your father's place?" I asked, looking around and taking in the warm air.

"It's my place tonight." Easy took my jacket and hung it on a coat tree that stood at the end of the hallway entrance.

I watched him remove his jacket and toss his keys on a bookshelf. "Easy?" I called. "I kinda have something that I need to tell you."

Easy looked at me as he took off his wedding band and tossed it on the bookshelf alongside his keys.

I laughed a little. "Taking off that ring doesn't mean that you're not married, Easy-B."

"Tonight it does." Easy frowned. He started unbuttoning his shirt and kicking off his shoes.

"It doesn't work like that," I said as I stepped out of my heels.

"It kinda does, sweetheart." Easy walked through the house. "You want a drink, baby girl?"

"I can't drink, Easy. I'm pregnant," I bluntly told him and watched him stop in his tracks.

My heart was beating so hard. I wanted to cry, but I was waiting for his response.

Easy stood in the center of the living area. He didn't turn around and face me at first. He stood there, anxiously running his hands through his hair.

"Fuck!" he yelled out.

"You want me to get rid of it?" I started to cry then.

Easy turned around to face me as I walked up to him. He shook his head, his light eyes full of tears. "Hell nah. Why would you say that?"

"Because of that response you just gave me! Because you're married! And your wife is pregnant too!" I cried as Easy pulled me close. "And Dinero is going to kill me if he finds out!"

Easy's light eyes searched my face as he deeply exhaled. "You haven't slept with him, so he knows it wouldn't be his. Who else knows about this?"

"Sharita, my cousin Zara, all my aunts that you met, and Daddy. When I told my father, he straight up told me to get rid of it! My aunt is threatening to send me to LA! I can't have your baby, Easy!" I fell against his chest and sobbed.

"What do you want to name him?" Easy asked me. "I think it's a boy."

I looked up into Easy's face, watching him looking back at me. "What? What are you talking about? We can't give this baby a name!"

"I like Magic." Easy kissed my forehead.

"Magic?" My heart calmed down a little.

"Because that's what we made that night," Easy whispered. "That's corny, right? I just said some white shit, huh?"

The fact that he was making light of the situation when he was just as scared as I was made me cry even harder.

"No, that's not corny. That's beautiful. I'm scared. Everyone is going to find out!" I cried. "I haven't slept with Dinero! My father is saying to bust it open for the nigga so I can play the baby off as his! But the thing is, I don't even want to sleep with Dinero anymore! Ever since I had you, you're all I want. All I need. And then you got that ho pregnant!" I pushed him off me. "How the fuck could you not tell me that she's pregnant? How long have you known?"

Easy exhaled sharply. "Since the homecoming."

"Since the day we met? You knew that Malibu Barbie was pregnant since the day we met?" I shoved him again. "Why didn't you tell me?"

"Because I didn't want to think about it!" Easy answered. "I don't give a fuck about her! I only did this shit to please my mother, who's always had my back. She took care of me, knowing that I'm the son of her husband's mistress! When she found out that I had Mandy pregnant, she wanted me to do the right thing! My father only wanted me to marry Mandy to get in good with his business partner. Mandy was threatening to tell her father that I raped her! Her family would throw a muthafucka under the jail. I did this shit so that I can take these kids from her when I get the chance."

"Wait, what? Kids, Easy? This is the second time you said you want to save your 'kids.' Like you have more than one child with the bitch!" My heart slammed in my chest.

"Twins." Easy sounded as if he hated to say it. "She's not the type of woman I'd want to have my babies. I didn't tell you because she doesn't matter to me."

"I'm black. You're white. Your real father is my father's business partner. And I don't even know who your adoptive father is, but I can tell by the way this place is decked out that he has to play a major part in how shit is run around this muthafucka! Our mothers died on the same day! I don't know you. You don't know me! And we're having a child together!" I cried. "What if—"

Easy grabbed me back to him, pressing his lips against mine to shut me up. "We'll figure this out, just not tonight. A'ight? You gonna take this dress off, or am I gonna have to rip this shit off?"

I sighed in his mouth as he kissed me, and then I reached behind my neck to show Easy where to unzip my dress. "Easy, we have to talk about this."

"We're just gonna fuck 'til we get it right, ma. That's pretty much all we can do tonight. I haven't seen you all month. Yeah, I wanna talk, but I can talk while I'm inside you. I wanna bust it down. Fuck all this other shit," Easy told me.

I shook my head. "We can't just avoid the subject. I'm having your baby, and so is she!"

Easy aggressively unzipped my dress, pulling the zipper down forcefully. He watched my chest heaving in and out as he pulled my dress down over my body. "Well, tonight you're the only one I'm worried about. Don't nobody know I'm here. Don't nobody know you're here."

"This may be our last time together. Ever," I had to remind him.

"So, are we gonna cry about it tonight, or are we gonna make the most of it?" Easy looked as if he was trying to convince himself that one night together would be enough.

But he was right. I was there with him, a moment I'd wanted to relive ever since the night of my birthday. I needed to just cherish the moment.

"Step out of this dress, baby girl. Let me see you. All of you," Easy whispered.

There was really no time to waste.

Easy grabbed my hand and removed my engagement ring from my finger. He tossed that shit over onto the crystal end table like it wasn't shit. "Tonight you're my wife. I'm not with Mandy. You're not with Dinero. Your father's not working for my biological father, and my mother didn't leave me to be raised by the woman whose husband she was still fuckin'. While we're here in this condo, it's just you and me. No one else. No tears. No fears. Just kissin', touchin', and fuckin'. Does that sound good to you?"

I nodded, drying my tears as Easy started to unhook my bra. "But the rain, Easy—this storm is gonna be a rough one."

"No relationship is always sunny days and sunrays, baby, but we can share an umbrella and survive this storm together," Easy tried to convince us both.

"How long?" I had to ask him as I helped him pull off his clothes. "How long is this storm going to be?"

Easy shrugged. "Maybe forever. But I'm willing to fight through it if you are." He pulled his shirt over his head as I helped unbuckle his pants. "I missed you." Easy kissed my lips, bringing my body closer to his as he kicked his pants off and picked me up like I was light as a feather.

I nuzzled his neck as he carried me over to the bedroom area. "Oh, you smell so fuckin' good," I told him and bit his neck.

"How the fuck did Dinero keep his hands off you all this time? Ain't no way in fuckin' hell."

Easy held me tight. I knew he wanted to throw my ass on the bed and fuck me into the next morning, but he didn't. He hovered over me, kissing me before pulling down my panties and removing his boxers. I looked into Easy's face as I grabbed that dick I missed so much. I put it inside of me, my breath hitching as Easy moaned a little. The intro to round one was going to be sweet and sensual. We hadn't seen each other in a little while, and I was sure we had a lot to say, but we didn't have much time. So we let our bodies do the talking. The first conversation was sweet, but that second conversation, boy, we both seemed to let all our anger out. I don't even know how we even managed to make it to the bedroom that night.

My body was screaming at him for letting that bitch carry his last name. Easy's body tried to convince me that he had everything under control.

"I saved this pussy for you, Easy, and you're just gonna marry that bitch?" I bent over and arched my back, ass in the air.

Easy smacked my ass before gripping it in his warm hands. He moaned deeply as I grabbed his dick and guided it inside of me. "Fuck her. Don't worry about her. I'm just worried about you."

"Did you miss this pussy, Easy-B?" I sighed and started to throw it back, squealing as he smacked my ass and made it jiggle.

"Hell the fuck yeah, I missed this pussy. Don't nothing feel better than this pussy. Pussy feels like chocolate pudding. Watch me dig my spoon all the way up in it, baby." Easy moaned as he pumped into me and I pumped back.

"Easy, we have to talk about this!" I deepened my arch, resting my breasts on the satin sheets. I started to stretch my arms out in front of me. Instead, Easy grabbed my arms, bending them at the elbows and pinning them behind my back. I bit down on the pillow, bracing my cervix for impact. "Shittttt," I moaned as he pumped. "I wish we could be together, Easy!"

"Me too, baby," Easy growled at me as I looked back at him, watching him watch his dick going in and out of me.

I held my arch as Easy beat the pussy like a bass drum.

"I'd date the shit outta your ass. We'd get married and raise the fuck out of our muthafuckin' kids together. I'd give you all the muthafuckin' love, stability, and support you need, li'l baby," Easy told me.

I didn't know what we were doing or why we weren't thinking about the consequences when we were doing it. Easy had just gotten married, and I let Dinero put that ring on my finger to please my father, who never really acted like a father. My mind was going in all sorts of directions, and just when I thought Easy's stroke game couldn't get any better, he slid his hands around my neck. His warm hands felt so good gripping my neck. At that point, he could choke me sexually or fatally. I really didn't give a fuck. That shit felt dangerously amazing. It calmed my soul. He applied the perfect amount of pressure, not just to my neck, but to my cervix as the tip of his dick tapped rhythmically against it.

I arched my back deeper, moaning as Easy dug deeper inside of me. I swore that dick felt like it was busting a hole in my soul. Man, that dick felt like morphine. I wanted him to knock my uterus off the hinges, but I needed to taste it in my mouth.

"Easy, wait." I sighed as I felt his dick stiffen inside of me.

Easy loosened his grip on my neck as I gasped for air. He slowed but deepened his stroke, sinking into me farther, my pussy dripping wet.

"I want to suck it. Please. Put it in my mouth," I told him.

Easy gripped my waist, moaning, giving my pussy a few more strokes before slipping out of me and watching me turn around to face him. I was already salivating at the thought of his dick in my mouth. Moments earlier, I was angry that I'd never get to spend my life with Easy. But at the moment Easy slipped his dick through my lips, I felt like we had a lifetime to get everything right. It's funny how the sensations of sex can change your entire mindset.

I licked my lips before gently and softly kissing the head of his penis. Then I licked around the tip before slowly taking it into my mouth. I slowly eased my way down his dick, making a circular motion from the tip to the base, breathing slowly along the way and relaxing my throat.

"Hell yeah, open up that throat," Easy moaned as he pushed my hair back from my face with both hands, holding my hair back in a ponytail. "Let me give you a hand, li'l baby," he whispered as I licked my way back from the base to the tip.

I lightly grabbed his dick with one hand and started massaging it, all while keeping the tip in my mouth. With my other hand, I gently cupped his balls and squeezed them a little, rubbing my fingers around them. I took him all the way into my mouth, wrapping my lips around his dick so no air could escape or get in. I started to gently suck, making my lips and cheeks close in around his entire penis. Then I slowly moved my head up and down, maintaining my gentle suction.

Easy was gripping the shit out of my hair, careful though as to not pull my hair from the roots. He hissed and moaned, pumping in and out of my mouth a little, his thrusts matching my rhythm. "Shit, goddamn, fuck. When you said you wanted to suck it, I didn't know you really meant that shit! I didn't know you was gonna suck it suck it! Goddamn! Shhhittt, she's suckin' that dick. Fuckkkkkk," Easy moaned heavily.

I felt his dick stiffen in my mouth as I slid my lips and tongue up and down it. I slid my lips down to the very base of his dick, my tongue sliding down between his testicles. By then, my saliva was swirling around his dick, dripping down my chin and onto his thighs.

As Easy climaxed, and I felt his body jerk, I slowed everything down to the pace of a snail. He gripped my hair in his hands and skeeted down my throat, dick brushing across my tonsils as I softly licked, sucked, and caressed his dick with my mouth, lips, and tongue. And even as powerful as that orgasm was, the muthafucka was still hard.

I looked up at Easy, and he looked down at me as I loosened my lips from around him, and he pulled out of my mouth. He was still gripping my hair in his hands as I rose up to look at him face-to-face. Tears slid down my cheeks as he released my hair and slid his hands around my neck.

"Why the fuck are you so nasty?" Easy asked, chest heaving in and out.

I sighed, loving the pressure and the warmth of his hands around my neck. "Just fuck me, okay?" I begged him.

And fuck me he did. That dude made love to me so deep that I felt him under my skin. We had that hard, "I hate you for fuckin' with that muthafucka but I love you and wish we could be together" kind of sex. I swear, he fucked me to sleep that night. He was supposed to be on his honeymoon, and I was supposed to be at home waiting for Dinero, but there we were, me on top of him, him on top of me. Naked.

Waking up next to him was unbelievable. That sleepy, confused look on Easy's face was everything. I couldn't believe that I'd survived my life so long without him. What I wouldn't give to get the chance never to miss a moment to hear him breathe. I was in love, and we were in trouble.

As soon as Easy opened his eyes and saw me already looking into his face, he pulled my body into his. I barely got any sleep. At one point, he was asleep on top of me, face nuzzled in my neck. At another point, I was on top of him, his arms wrapped tightly around me. At another, we were spooning. At another, I tried to get up from the bed to use the bathroom, but he pulled me back to him. As the night went by, I was just like, *fuck it, might as well just stay up*. It was 3:00 in the morning, and I was wide awake as if the sun had come up.

"Bae." Easy's throat was scratchy. "The fuck you doing up just staring at a muthafucka and shit, huh?" He kissed my forehead.

"Just waiting for something bad to happen," I told him.

"Man, we had sex so good I feel like I'm supposed to be tippin' you. We ain't got shit to worry about. Nobody knows where the fuck my father's spot is," Easy tried to tell me.

I laughed a little, then pushed away from him and got up from the bed. "I doubt that. I'm sure he's brought someone here before. We both know that just because a muthafucka doesn't tell his wife and family things doesn't mean he doesn't tell his side bitch or his homeboys. Someone knows about this place. I think we should go."

Easy sat up on the bed, watching me scramble to throw my hair in a bun. "You're scared."

I nodded frantically. "Hell yeah! Do you remember anything about tonight besides fuckin'? I told you that I was pregnant, Easy! What are we gonna do?"

Easy ran his hands through his short hair, exhaling deeply and sharply. "Meelah, do you want to have my baby?"

I looked at him. "What is that supposed to mean?"

Easy looked at me. "Do you want my son or my daughter? Do you want a piece of me? A piece of us?"

I stuttered, "All I want is us, boo."

Easy nodded. "Me too."

I shook my head. "But it's not gonna work out like that. The only way through this is to make Dinero believe this baby is his. My dad's right about that much."

The look on Easy's face changed when I implied that I was going to have to fuck the shit out of Dinero to play the baby off as his. "The fuck, Meelah?"

"So you mean to tell me that you are never going to fuck your wife, Easy?" I scoffed, leaving the bedroom. How we ended up in the bed that night, I couldn't even remember. I didn't remember even walking up that winding flight of stairs. I was pretty sure Easy carried me.

"Hell nah, I ain't fuckin' that bitch after what she did to me!" Easy got up from the bed, then followed me down the stairs to the lower level of the condo. "And where the fuck you going, Meelah?"

I walked through the living room, grabbing my panties, which were lying across the arm of the sofa. "Home."

"Meelah—"

I interrupted him. "This can't happen, Easy!" I slipped into my panties.

"It already happened, baby girl," Easy reminded me.

I really didn't want to start crying. "Easy, just call Sharita and tell her where I am." I sighed as I watched Easy grab his boxers and slide into them.

"Why did you come here if you were just trying to leave me?" Easy asked.

I looked into his face as he approached me.

"You're scared, I get that." Easy cut me off before I could say anything. "We can make this work, Meelah. You just gotta trust me. I can get you out of there. I can get us away from here. Don't go."

I shook my head. "Easy, I have to."

Easy frowned at me, looking down into my face. "You don't wanna be with him, so don't. My homeboy Keith has a cousin in Jersey. We can go stay with them for a few weeks until we figure out where we want to go. Go back to your aunt's place, pack ya shit, and meet me back here tonight at seven."

I shook my head as he grabbed my shoulders. "Easy, we can't—"

"That baby inside of you is going to come out white as fuck. How you gonna explain that to Dinero without him trying to hurt you?" Easy looked into my face. "You gotta leave him. This is the only way."

"Y'all muthafuckas is crazy!" Sharita watched me pack my bag that evening at around 5:00. "Dinero has been calling my phone since he left you at that restaurant! Arcen was supposed to pick you up, remember?"

"Yeah, I remember," I muttered. "You're the one who told Easy where I was going to be eating last night, remember?"

"I told him to go talk to you, not kidnap you and then make plans to run off with you!" Sharita exclaimed. "Arcen's been blowing up my phone. He told your father that you were with me last night when Arcen knows that shit wasn't true. He was just trying to cover for you, and he didn't even wanna do that after what happened to his son. Dinero's been looking for you all day! I had to tell him that your aunt caught us smoking and joyriding in her car last night and had your ass on lockdown. He knows something is up. He's not stupid!"

I glanced over at Tajha, who was eying the chipped gel polish on her fingernails. Aunt Troy was out shopping with Zara. Tajha wasn't even supposed to be at my aunt's place. My aunt had hated her ever since Tajha talked me and Zara into throwing a pool party at my aunt's house in the ninth grade when my aunt was out of town. Aunt Troy came home to a houseful of niggas and a knocked-over mailbox. Aunt Troy called all her sisters up that night, and they all took turns whoopin' the shit out of me and Zara.

"Easy knows better than this. Hiding you out in Jersey isn't going to solve anything! What are we gonna tell your pops? That we don't know where the fuck you are? He's gonna have every cop in every city looking for you!" Sharita panicked.

Tajha looked at Sharita. "Man, fuck the police. Them white muthafuckas in Easy's bitch's family are gonna hunt her down. You think his bitch doesn't know about you and Easy by now? I hope you're ready when that ho runs up. She looks like she can fight." Tajha rolled her eyes and popped her lips.

Sharita resented that. "Tajha, you must be smokin' dick. Run up on who with what? With me around? You got me fucked up. You hear ya girl, Meelah?"

"You're not gonna be around, boo-boo. Easy is taking this girl to Jersey, and you're planning to drop her off. And why the fuck are y'all on the run to Jersey? Didn't the muthafucka just get married yesterday? I heard the muthafucka's father is a cop." Tajha spilled tea as usual.

I looked at her. "A cop?"

Tajha nodded. "Umm-hmm. I heard that your father works for the cop, too. And—"

Sharita cut Tajha off. "You always hearing shit, damn. I wish you'd hear how to shut the fuck up."

"Seriously, though, what would make a married nigga want to run off with his side chick? It's like he's trying to protect you from something. Or someone." Tajha looked at us both, watching me pause from packing my bag. Sharita turned her head the other way like she wasn't saying shit. Tajha's eyes widened. "You're pregnant, huh? That's what it is! You're pregnant!"

Sharita tossed my pillow at Tajha. "Shut the fuck up, Tajha, damn! We're not even supposed to be talking about this!"

Tajha looked over from Sharita to me as I zipped up my bag. "Dinero is going to cut your uterus out, bitch. That is if your daddy doesn't do it first."

I looked at her.

Tajha exhaled deeply. "Your dad must already know. I'm sure he told your black ass to stay away from Easy. Easy is going to get you both killed! You are a member of The Chain! Ya nigga is HNIC of the CMC! And I don't give a fuck what y'all say. Easy's family isn't far behind these muthafuckas. They're just as dirty as your family, with more connections than your family. You're playing a dangerous game. Sable would kill you to save himself, and you're fuckin' with his boss's son. Crazy bitch."

"Yeah, I've been meaning to talk to you about that shit you told Sable," Sharita interjected, cutting me off before I could question her. "What gives you the audacity to talk to the nigga about Easy's biological father? You need to mind your fuckin' business, bitch! You need to be worrying about what happens when Claudius and Keith find out they're fuckin' the same girl. You ain't even supposed to be fuckin' with the Guerillas anyway, *punta*."

Tajha rolled her eyes. "Whatever. Ain't you fuckin' with a nigga from Easy's crew too? What's up with you and Ace?"

Sharita exhaled deeply, trying her best to bite her tongue.

"That's what I thought. Y'all left it up to me to find out about Easy's family," Tajha replied. "That story you told Dinero and them actually was true. That white muthafucka is your cousin. His mother was your mother's twin. Your mama and Easy's mama had a son by the same muthafucka, Stef. Cristobal's father. Cris would love to hear about this. I'm sure he'd like to hear from his long-lost brother."

Sharita was about to jump up from the bed and strangle Tajha.

I grabbed Sharita. "Okay, kids, calm the fuck down."

Tajha giggled as Sharita pulled from me and went over to the corner of the room to calm down. "Sharita, when you gonna tell the boss about his son?"

I looked at Tajha. The only reason she was even with us was that she'd just bought a new car that my father's crew hadn't put a LoJack on. I didn't like her any more than Sharita did. Tajha was real close to Whitley. Tajha didn't talk about Whitley's death, but I knew she resented me for it.

Before I could even respond, the doorbell sounded downstairs.

Sharita and I looked at each other before Sharita stood by my window, peeping through the blinds to see who was downstairs. Her eyes widened before she looked back at me.

"It's Dinero with a bunch of niggas!" she whispered loudly.

My heart thumped in my chest.

Tajha got up from the bed, indifferent to the situation, when Sharita and I were about to shit on ourselves.

I looked at her, watching her check her cell phone for missed calls. "You told him where I was, didn't you?"

Tajha looked at me. "Now why would I do that?"

"She didn't have to. Our phones have tracking on them. I told that bitch to turn her phone the fuck off when we went to pick you up!" Sharita muttered, still peeping out the blinds from the side of the window.

"You need to worry about that nigga downstairs who probably already has a key to this muthafucka." Tajha slyly grinned.

She wasn't lying. Within seconds, the front door opened, and it sounded like a herd of buffalo stampeded through my aunt's living room.

"Ay, shawty, bring ya ass downstairs!" Dinero's voice boomed through the house.

"If you don't go down, he's coming up," Tajha reminded me.

There was really no time to go off on Tajha. I knew she was the one who told Dinero where I was, or at least she led him to me. It didn't surprise me to see Dinero standing in the living room looking like he was ready to fight a muthafucka. But I was surprised to see my father sitting on the couch like he was just there to observe. My father leaned back in my aunt's oversized chair, eying me and Sharita standing in the center of the living room. Tajha knew better than to get between my and Dinero's confrontation. Sharita was always that protective friend. She'd never let me go into a fight alone.

Dinero peeped Tajha stepping her ass out the front door before he looked at Sharita, who was standing next to me. "Don't you think you oughta go out there with your friend?" he snarled at Sharita.

Sharita stood in front of me. "The fuck are you doing here, Dinero?"

"What the fuck was she doing with the muthafucka who killed Evan?" Dinero talked to Sharita while still looking me in the face.

"He didn't kill Evan. Evan killed himself while walking up on a muthafucka who would protect Meelah with his life! Something you never did for her! And she wasn't with the muthafucka last night, nigga!" Sharita shouted as Dinero pushed her out of the way to get to me.

One of Dinero's homeboys grabbed Sharita.

Dinero grabbed my hand and placed the engagement ring that he'd given me in it. The ring that Easy had taken off my finger and tossed to the side. Dinero frowned down at me as I looked up into his face. I should have been afraid for my life at that moment, but I wasn't. I was afraid for Easy's because if Dinero had that ring, that meant that he went into Easy's father's apartment.

"Where is Easy?" I asked.

Dinero shook his head at me in disgust. "You made the toughest nigga on the block fall in love, ma. After all I did for you, you'd fuck around on me with a cop's son?"

"Where is he?" I asked again.

"Did you know that the man who adopted that nigga is the same cop who killed your mother?" Dinero refused to answer my question and dug into my wounds instead.

I just looked into his face. I didn't believe him. Easy would have mentioned it to me. "You're lying," I told him.

"You're fuckin' this nigga with my ring on your finger, ma?" Dinero shoved me.

Dinero's homeboy Rue peeped the display on his cell phone as it chimed. He swiped the screen, shaking his head before looking at me. "Well, nigga, that ain't shit. You were putting a ring on old girl's finger not knowing she's pregnant by the white muthafucka. Tajha just texted me."

Sharita tried to race toward the door to get to Tajha, who was outside the house, but Rue slung her into the wall, pinning her against it.

"That bitch!" Sharita screamed. "When I get to her, I'ma kill that bitch! Get the fuck off me!"

I looked into Dinero's face and watched him remove his jacket before flinging it over on the arm of the chair where my father was sitting. I glanced at my father, who just looked at me sternly, not busting any sort of move. He knew what was about to happen, and he was going to let the shit happen. I looked back at Dinero.

"Shawty, is that true? You're pregnant with that muthafucka's baby?" Dinero got in my face as close as he could get.

I looked up at him. "No," I lied to his face.

Dinero's temples twitched as he unbuckled his pants then pulled the belt from the belt loops. "Strip," he snarled at me.

I glanced at my father. The same father who stood by and laughed as he watched my friends get raped into the CMC when I was a sophomore. He killed muthafuckas on a daily basis and didn't even break a sweat. He didn't cry at my mother's funeral. Though he never spanked me as a child, he would let his crew from The Chain whup my ass. They'd make me strip butt-ass fuckin' naked, and that was what he was going to let Dinero do in front of everyone.

"No!" Sharita screamed. "Don't do this to her. She doesn't deserve this shit! Just let her go!"

"Get her out of here!" my father yelled at Dinero's boys at the top of his lungs.

"How could you let this muthafucka beat your daughter?" Sharita screamed and tried to fight her way out of Dinero's boys' grasp as they practically had to drag her out of the house. "You're no fuckin' father! You're supposed to protect her! Don't let him do this!"

I looked into Dinero's face, trying my best to be strong and not shed a tear. It was hard to watch Sharita being dragged out of the house. I was sure one of the neighbors had seen her going the fuck off outside. My aunt lived in the whitest neighborhood on earth. They'd call the police, but knowing my father, the police already knew the deal. If they could hide the fact that I was raped and left for dead by Stef's son, then surely they'd cover up the fact that Dinero beat Stef's other son's baby out of me.

Dinero looked at me. "You gonna just stand there, or are you gonna take them fuckin' clothes off?"

"Daddy, you're gonna let him do this to me?" I looked over at my father, who at that point went over and looked out the window on the opposite side of the living room with his back facing me.

My father couldn't watch. It was the first sign of emotion that he'd shown me in years. His pride was hurt because I disobeyed him by going back around Easy. He told me to stay the fuck away from him, and I didn't. So, he was going to make me pay one way or another, even if that meant letting my boyfriend beat the shit out of me in front of him. My father didn't care who you were—he was not going to let you disrespect him. I'd seen him kill family members for less than what I'd done. I was no exception.

"So, you like fuckin' white muhfuckas, huh?" Dinero's homeboy Grease chuckled.

I glared over at Grease. "No, nigga, I don't."

"That ain't what Cristobal told a nigga. He let all his crew hit that night. Seems like you ain't been the same since." Grease had to push Dinero's crazy buttons. "Maybe she forgot what a real nigga's dick feels like, Dinero. I say you let us show her."

At that point, my father exhaled sharply. When he turned back around to walk toward me, I thought he was going to put an end to the madness. But, instead, he walked past me and toward the door.

"Don't kill my daughter, Dinero. Whatever you do, don't kill her," my father said before walking out the door.

Before Dinero could even say anything to my father, I spit in his face.

At that point, Dinero laughed at me. It was a hurt yet "I'ma kill this bitch" laugh.

"Ay, crew, take her clothes off. Let's do this," Dinero growled.

Chapter Eleven

Easy

After Meelah left that night, I drove back home to hit up my crew and to get a few things to take with me. Mandy had been blowing up my phone that night. Bitch left about twenty voicemails on my phone. Her cousin Klarissa told her about Sharita bribing her into getting her away from that restaurant the night before. Mandy was a lot of things, but she wasn't stupid. I got back home around 4:15 that morning, and Mandy was waiting in the foyer for me, tapping her Prada heels against the ground.

I huffed and walked past her, not really in the mood to talk with her. It was early as fuck, and I already knew what was going to come out of her mouth. "Yo, shawty, it's too early. It's been a long night."

Mandy scoffed as she walked behind me. "Oh, I bet! Where have you been?"

"Out," I told her while walking through the house toward the living area and taking off my jacket.

"My cousin said that Sharita bribed her into getting me to go to the hospital last night for testing! I waited in the ER for four hours last night! When I went to the bathroom, I caught my cousin in there snorting that Rox powder up her nose! I already knew where she'd gotten it from!" Mandy followed me over to the couch and stood in front of me.

I looked up at her while loosening the button on my shirt. "Sharita isn't my cousin."

Mandy nodded frantically. "Yes, she is! I know all about your family, Bostyn, or should I say Emilio? I bribed your maid to tell me everything!"

I glared up at her. "You what?"

"I told her that my family would deport her fat ass back to Guatemala or Panama—wherever the fuck your people are from—if she didn't tell me who you were!" Mandy shouted.

I stood from the couch and grabbed her by her shoulders. "That's my aunt, Mandy!"

"She's your fuckin' maid!"

"She saved my life!"

Mandy pushed my hands from her shoulders. "Yes, at your mother's expense! Your father wanted your mother dead, so she couldn't tell your adopted mother the shit that he's still caught up in! I know everything about your family! My father has your father by the fuckin' balls, muthafucka! Your father is looking at prison time if he doesn't share the wealth with my father! That's what this is—a business deal! Do I love you? Yes. Do I hate you for loving Meelah? Yes!" Mandy pushed me in the chest. "But my father's connections are going to keep you alive as long as you stay the fuck away from Meelah! Meelah's mother wanted out of the life that her father had them in. Meelah's mother went to the police to get out of this, and once Meelah's father found out, he had them kill her mother."

My chest heaved in and out as I looked into Mandy's face. It didn't surprise me that she knew everything. What shook me was that Aunt Donna had told her everything despite the fact that they made her wear a wire every fuckin' day.

"Where is my aunt?" I asked.

Mandy laughed a little. "Where were you? Were you with Meelah?"

I just looked at her, not saying shit, but she heard me loud and clear.

"Bostyn, we just got married yesterday!" Mandy cried.

"This is just business, right?" I reminded her.

Mandy shook her head at me. "I'm having your babies, Bostyn!"

"Yeah? Well, so is she," I told Mandy, really not giving a fuck about anything at that point.

Mandy looked at me as if her heart stopped. Her skin immediately turned pale as if I'd scared the life out of her. She flopped down on the couch, looking up at me like I'd just told her that someone had died. She sure wasn't the first person I wanted to tell, but I had to tell someone. Someone had to know how seriously I felt about Meelah. It was probably the dumbest muthafuckin' move I could've made, but I was 17 and in love. All I could think about was protecting Meelah.

"I'm leaving town with her tonight," I told Mandy. "I gotta get her out of here. I gotta save her."

Mandy's mouth dropped open, but no words came out. She was speechless for the first time since I'd known her. Tears slid down her cheeks. There was really nothing that she could say to change the situation. She'd tricked me into giving her children, and her father blackmailed my father into giving their family anything they wanted. Including my life. Including my freedom.

Mandy's father wanted to use me to infiltrate The Chain, and fuckin' with Meelah wasn't in their plans. I was fuckin' up their whole operation. The plan was to send me to the undercover police academy so I could go undercover and figure out where their money was going. The profits that The Chain wasn't sharing with the police department. And there was no way that The Chain was going to invite me in once they knew who the fuck I was. Rumors were already going around about me being related to Sharita, and it wouldn't surprise me if they knew about me being a cop's adoptive son. The only option that I had was to get Meelah out of harm's way.

"Do . . . do you love her?" Mandy finally regained her ability to talk.

"What?" I asked her.

"She's pregnant with your child, and since you're telling me you're taking her to safety, I'm assuming you just found out. On our wedding day. We're supposed to be going on our honeymoon, but instead, you're helping your black bitch escape to freedom." Mandy started to laugh to herself in disbelief.

"Call her another bitch, Mandy, if you want to." I started to walk off before I hit her, but she grabbed me as she stood from the couch. "We both know that this thing between me and you was a fuckin' setup! I'm not about to play house with you while her house is falling apart because of our families! Damn right I love that girl! I can still taste her chocolate orgasm in my mouth right now. How's that for honesty, huh?"

Mandy gasped at my boldness. She didn't think I could be as cold as her. She shook off her pain, though, and kept hitting me with shit I didn't want to hear.

"You're going to not only get her killed, but you're going to get yourself killed, Bostyn! She's a mobster's daughter, and his boss is supposed to be your father! The father who doesn't even know that you're his son! Leave this girl alone!" Mandy warned me.

I shook my head. "I can't."

Mandy shook her head at me. "Do you think they're going to let her leave with you? You should have stayed with her at your father's place."

I struggled to maintain my composure. I couldn't figure out for the life of me how the fuck she knew I was at my father's house, and better yet, how the fuck did she even know it was my father's house?

"Yo." I laughed to keep from grabbing her by her neck. "Who the fuck told you where I was?

Mandy grinned. "The tracking device on your car."

"And how did you know I was at my father's place?" I had to ask.

Mandy held a sinister grin on her face. "Because I've been there before."

It took everything in me not to strangle her that morning. Meelah was right. I damn sure wasn't the only one who knew where my father's secret hideout was. That crazy-bitch grin on Mandy's face let me know there was more to the story that I didn't want to know, so I didn't even bother to ask.

"Mandy, you need to just get the fuck outta my face," I told her. "Where is Pops?"

"You got that Slim Shady look in your eyes," Claudius teased me that afternoon as he watched me pace the floor.

I hadn't heard from my father, and it was about three in the afternoon. He didn't come home that night, and my mom was worried like a muthafucka. My aunt Donna wasn't home either, and I was starting to worry. I didn't expect Meelah to call when she turned her phone off to keep her father from tracking her down, but I knew something wasn't right.

"Have I ever told you about my father's condo out in DC?" I asked as I continued to pace across the carpet.

Claudius shrugged. "I don't know, man, maybe. Why?"

"Because I thought I was the only one who knew about that property," I told him.

"Man, ya father gambles and likes to party. I'm sure his poker crew and his side bitches know about that spot,"

Claudius joked before tossing his set of keys into the air and catching them.

"That's what Meelah said too." I stopped in my tracks and turned around to face him.

Claudius made a face. "What's this about?"

"Mandy knew where the fuck I've been all night. The bitch questioned me about it this morning," I responded.

Claudius laughed a little. "Wouldn't surprise me. The bitch is part bloodhound. She probably smelled y'all two fuckin' from forty-five miles away!"

I wasn't in the mood for jokes. "Muthafucka, I'm serious, damn. The bitch isn't supposed to know where my father's bachelor crib is unless she's been there!"

Claudius looked at me like I was crazy. "You think your father was fuckin' your girl?"

"She's not my fuckin' girl!" I corrected him. "And I wouldn't put it past him. He always did like them young and fuckin' dumb. He pushed me to marry that girl to probably hide what he did from her father, who is a major funding source for the police department."

"You're jumping to conclusions based off what? That Mandy found out where your father takes his bitches? Man, she probably tracked your car over there and looked up the property, man." Claudius watched me start pacing the floor again. "Stop looking for reasons not to take this girl on your honeymoon. You got your shit all packed up to go spend time with her, and then you wanna try to renege, my nigga."

"I didn't pack all my shit up to go on that honeymoon this weekend. I packed it because I'm meeting up with Keith's cousin in an hour. I'm headed to Jersey," I responded.

Claudius looked at me. "You and Mandy going to Jersey?"

I shook my head. "Nah, me and Meelah are going to Jersey."

Claudius jumped up from my bed like I had bed bugs or some shit and they were biting his ass.

"The fuck wrong with you, Jody-Joe?" I asked.

"Meelah? You're taking my brother's girl to Jersey? Why the fuck does she need to go to Jersey? What you helping her escape from?" Claudius exclaimed.

"Muthafucka, don't question me," I told his ass. "My aunt Donna was being threatened not to tell me shit about my life, and the moment she opens her mouth to Mandy about my past, her ass is MIA! Mandy's bitch ass is probably pregnant by a muthafucka who cares even less about her than I do! And I found out last night that Meelah is pregnant."

Claudius scoffed. "And? That's Dinero's problem."

I shook my head. "No, it's mine."

"How the fuck is Dinero's baby your problem?" Claudius asked.

"Because the baby is mine." I hated to tell him, but he was going to find the fuck out anyway.

Claudius didn't want to hear that shit. "Nigga!" he laughed and yelled at the same time. "We leave for this secret security shit in just a few days. Your family ain't just gonna let you leave with this girl. You signed that contract to be shipped off. Ain't no backing out of this shit! The best thing you can do now is to join this under-cover shit and help old girl out of this situation the right way. She has money to handle this shit, cuz."

I watched him adjust the gold Rolex on his wrist. "'Handle'? The fuck you mean by 'handle'?"

"Get rid of that muthafucka," Claudius said with no hesitation and looked at me like I was supposed to agree with him.

I looked up at the muthafucka who I thought was my friend. "You know how I feel about her, muthafucka!" I pushed him. "You didn't even say this shit when I told your ass that Mandy was pregnant! Now that Meelah is having my baby, you feel some type of heat?"

Claudius released his usual hatin'-ass laugh. "You get everything you want, nigga. You got our style, our swag, our dance moves, our sports skills, and you can even freestyle when you feel like it. Now you're getting our bitches too? And not any bitch but my brother's bitch?"

"A'ight, man, y'all muthafuckas are too comfortable with calling Meelah a bitch in front of me. I'm white as fuck, but you know better than anyone that I can get dark as fuck real quick. You just said so yourself, so why you testing that water?" I asked.

Claudius's laughter subsided. "You know better than this, dawg, that's all I'm sayin'. If I'm feeling any type of way, it's because I've been through too much already over this shit between you, this girl, and my brother. Me and that nigga have enough beef. I'm trying to squash it. If you really love her, then you need to go with her to get rid of this baby. Nigga, they will kill her! Is that what you want?"

I exhaled deeply. I wouldn't back down when I should have.

"You gonna drop me off at Keith's crib or what, bruh?" I asked.

Claudius shook his head. "Nah. But good luck on this suicide mission." Claudius walked past me and bumped his shoulder against mine.

Claudius didn't take me to meet up with Keith that afternoon, so I met up with Ace at his crib around 5:00. I was supposed to meet up with Meelah by 7:00 back at my father's place. As soon as I stepped foot in his basement that afternoon, it looked like them muthafuckas were getting ready for war fa real. Street artillery everywhere. Machine guns of every sort. My kinda scene. There was just something about the sound of guns that got my adrenaline pumping like a muthafucka.

"Fuck is y'all getting ready to start? World War III?" I joked, but I was serious as fuck.

"Man, shit is about to get real. I don't think you need to be rollin' over to Keith's crib to do shit. The nigga been feeding information about us to Tajha," Ace told me as our homie Boosie assembled a Street Sweeper.

I looked back at Ace. He knew just like I did that Claudius was fuckin' with Tajha too. Claudius was the main one talking about there was a snitch in every crew, and there he was caught up with a snitch.

"You sure it was Keith who was running his mouth?" I asked.

Ace frowned and changed the subject. "Where you been, man?"

"Chillin'," I responded.

"With Meelah?" Ace asked.

I didn't respond.

"Thought so." Ace shook his head at me. "Dinero been sweeping the streets for you, nigga. You need to be lying low."

"That's what I'm trying to do, bruh. I'm supposed to meet Keith so he can take me to his cousin's house in Jersey, but by the looks of things, that doesn't seem like the best idea," I responded.

My phone chimed in my pocket. I pulled it out of my gray sweatpants and peeped the display. It was Pops. I didn't want to answer that shit, but knowing him, he'd track my location and pop the fuck up over at Ace's crib. The last thing they needed was heat when they had all those unregistered guns and shit over there.

"What's good, Pops?" I reluctantly answered the phone.

"You need to meet me at my place in DC, now," Pops demanded before hanging up.

Claudius's punk ass. I should've known. But I couldn't even blame him for the shit that went down. Meelah was right.

As soon as I pulled up to the spot with Ace and a few of our homeboys, the place was flooded with cops. My heart thumped in my chest as I walked through my father's house. It looked like a tornado, earthquake, hurricane, and sandstorm had hit that bitch all at one time. We didn't even have to open the door to walk in. Whoever broke in that bitch took the door off the hinges. Every window was shattered. Every electronic device was gone. The muthafuckas took Pops's entire safe, which had some of his guns from the police department in it, not to mention some important documents. The look on my father's face when I showed up to his place with my homies, man. If looks could kill, we would've been some shot-up muthafuckas.

"Tell ya homeboys to beat it, Bostyn." Zel—the same muthafucka who interrogated me at the hospital after Meelah was beat up last year—approached us.

"Nah, they're straight. They're with me," I told him.

Zel shook his head. "Your father is trying to figure out how the fuck you know about this place."

I just looked at Zel as he held up my wedding band. I couldn't deny that I was there, especially since I rolled up on them without even needing directions. I didn't want to tell them that Aunt Donna told me about the hideaway. Pops used to take young girls there, according to her. He'd promise American citizenship to young girls in exchange for sex with not just him but half the police department, including the muthafucka who was in my face, thinking I was about to let him grill the fuck outta me.

"Man, fuck all that," Ace spoke up. "Y'all need to be trying to figure out who the fuck did this. Jimmie is rich.

The muthafuckas who broke in may have gotten the cameras, but knowing Jimmie, he has to have the footage backed up at another location. Insurance for whatever goes down at his poker games and shit, or whatever else y'all muthafuckas do in this muthafucka with them underaged females y'all drag down here."

Zel looked at Ace like he didn't think about that. He cleared his throat before handing me the ring. "They didn't leave a trace of tire marks, footprints, or fingerprints anywhere, but one of them cut themselves on the glass window over there. If all else fails, we have that. But judging by the fact that your wedding ring was found here, I think you and I both know who did this."

At that point, a million thoughts ran through my mind. Mandy knew where the fuck I was, and so did Claudius. Neither of them were fans of Meelah. Either one of them could've tipped off Dinero. I didn't put shit past anyone anymore. Claudius resented me for fuckin' up his chances at a football career. As close as me and him were, he'd always hated on me because he claimed I was always winning. He was just as privileged as I was, but the fact that I was white always seemed to bother him. The fact that I was white but never fit in with what he called "my own kind" always fucked with his head.

My family and Mandy always said I was too black to be white, but Claudius always said I was too white to be black. The only place where I fit in was with Meelah, but the way things were looking, that was never going to happen. I tried to accept it, but how do you accept something like that? How do you accept the fact that you love someone, and that person loves you, but the world doesn't want you to be together? There were only two of us and millions of them. What were we going to do? Eventually, we'd get tired of fighting the world and start fighting each other. I couldn't have that.

Looking around the room while Zel was talking to me about my choices, all I could see was my future. Could I really save Meelah?

"Bostyn, are you listening?" Zel shoved me in my shoulder.

"Nah, bruh, keep yo' muhfuckin' hands to yourself, homie." Ace stepped up to Zel.

I stood between the two. "Chill, dawg."

"Bostyn, I asked you a question. Are you even listening to me?" Zel exclaimed. "How long were you here with Meelah Summers?"

"How the fuck do you figure that I was here with her?" I asked.

"Your father found an earring in the bedroom," Zel responded.

I scoffed. "Did you ask him if he was sure it wasn't Mandy's?"

My boys looked at me before looking at the confused expression on Zel's face.

I shook my head at Zel in disgust before looking at my father, who was signaling me to come over and talk to him before he went upstairs to his room. I made my way through the glass and tattered furniture toward my father's room. When I got to my father's room, he was standing in the center of the room, looking around at the mess that my life had made. Or, should I say, that his life had made.

"Pops?" I called his name to get his attention.

Pops looked back at me before turning around to face me. His face was flushed, and his eyes were red as hell. He was mad, fired up, drunk, and pissed the fuck off.

"Why the fuck would you bring that girl here?" Pops growled at me.

I clenched my teeth, trying to restrain myself from asking about what had gone down between him and Mandy.

"No one gives a fuck about Meelah but me," I responded.

My father glared at me. "You keep thinking that stupid shit, son."

"Oh, I'm not right? At the hospital, the night that I got Meelah some medical help last year, you told the doctor to hide the evidence that my brother raped her. You said that if Emmanuel Summers knew that Cristobal raped her, there would be an all-out war. You don't think that muthafucka found out by now that his daughter was raped by his boss's son? Them muthafuckas are still chasing money! First, I heard that them muthafuckas supply your crew with drugs and money! Then I heard that y'all muthafuckas are the real suppliers. That my biological father gets his shit from your department!" I cursed my father out as he approached me.

Pops laughed a little as he stood before me. He knew where I'd heard that shit from. On the way over, Ace gave me the rundown on some stuff he'd found out about not just my birth father but my adopted father as well. To keep the peace in the streets, those two were actually working together. Working together meant that my father could distract my birth father from finding out that I was still alive. And I was starting to believe that the reason my father killed Meelah's mother was that she found out about me and was trying to warn my real father. She probably wanted out, and she was taken out to shut her up.

"You need to stay in your place," Pops warned me.

"I am in my muthafuckin' place!" I yelled. "I signed a contract to work with y'all muthafuckas for five years of my life. Y'all got me into this shit to save your own ass! Talking about y'all sending me undercover to help bring down the crew who actually works for you! You gave the streets to these dudes, man. They're not gonna give it back! I didn't sign up for this shit!"

My father disagreed. "Yes, you did. You signed up for this shit when you decided to fuck with Sable's daughter! I told you to stay the fuck away from her! Who do you think came in my place and fucked my shit up? I told you that you needed to be careful with the company you keep, and when I say that, I'm talking about your friend Claudius. You keep thinking that he's not cool with anyone in the Clean Money Crew."

I exhaled sharply as I looked into his face.

"He's seeing one of Meelah's friends. A friend who would do anything to take Meelah and her family down. Claudius blames you for fuckin' up his chances at a football career, Bostyn. He might hate his brother, but he's about to hate you even more for choosing a bitch over him," Pops snarled and shoved me in my chest. "You're about to leave to train for the Street Security Squadron while your boy is going to train for my unit, the undercover affairs department. They plan to make you captain of my unit because they believe in you, son. They know that with your and Claudius's help, we'll take back the streets."

"From what I heard, y'all already run that shit. Y'all don't need me or Claudius's snitchin' ass to take over this shit. I already know that if I don't train for this shit, I'll get federal time. I took an oath to join this shit, but I didn't take an oath to marry a bitch who's fuckin' my so-called father," I had to tell him.

Pops's eyebrows lowered. "What did you just say?"

"How the fuck does Mandy know where the fuck this place is?" I asked.

"How the fuck do you know, you ungrateful bastard?" Father questioned me.

I laughed a little. "Don't worry about that. Ungrateful? What the fuck do I even have to be grateful for? Tell me that! You ruined my fuckin' life! Tell me, are these children Mandy is pregnant with mine or yours?"

Pop's exhaled sharply. "I don't know," he admitted.

I could have cracked his head with the lamp that was next to us. It took everything I had to not knock that muthafucka out at that moment. "You don't fuckin' know? I just married Mandy yesterday because that bitch had everyone thinking that she's pregnant with my twins! And you're telling me right now that you don't know if those babies are mine?"

"She's seventeen, Bostyn. I'm thirty-eight years old," Pops admitted despite the fact that I was cracking my knuckles. "She followed me here one night after a poker game at her house. I was drunk, and I was about to invite a few girls over. When she showed up, crying about you, I was just trying to get her to stop crying. Next thing I know, I wake up naked on the couch, and she was on top of me. I drove her home and went back home. A few weeks later, Mandy comes to me crying, telling me that she's pregnant, and that if I didn't convince you to be with her, she'd tell your mother everything and tell her father what happened. She refused to have an abortion. She wanted to use her pregnancy as collateral to get me to do what she wanted me to do. She doesn't want these children, and neither do I."

"And, muthafucka, you think that I do?" I yelled. "I got my own problems! I ain't got shit to do with the fact that Mandy has daddy issues and you're a pedophile! Meelah is pregnant!"

Pop's frowned at me. "What the fuck, Bostyn?"

"She hit me with the news last night. I planned to take her away from here to get her away from all this chaos around us." I pointed at the broken shit in his room. "Meelah doesn't deserve this shit, Pops! Those babies Mandy is having don't deserve this! So, I'm just supposed to raise your children? You're paying me back for some shit that my mother did to you, huh? Is that it?"

Pops shook his head. "No, that's not what my intentions were. This would kill your mother and your brothers. I've done enough. Your mother never forgave me for raising another woman's son or for allowing that woman's aunt to work for us. I mixed my entire family up in a dangerous situation, but in the end, it will pay off, trust me. I'm just going to need your help."

"You want my help? Get me out of this marriage so I can be with Meelah, Pops! Today!" I told him.

Pops continued to shake his head. "I can't do that, son. And you can't be with that girl. Do you see this place? If you think this place looks bad, I promise you that Meelah looks even worse."

My heart stopped for a second before it slowly started to beat again. There I was, being distracted again. I was so hung up on finding out the truth that I didn't take a second to step back and think about where Meelah was. Dinero probably went straight to Meelah's aunt's house.

I turned around, about to head back downstairs, but Pops grabbed me.

"Bostyn, the only way to save that girl is to bring her father down. Not just her father, but your father too," Pops told me.

I snatched away from him. "Get the fuck off me! Which father are you talking about? You or Stefano?"

Pops laughed a little. "You don't want to play this game with me, little boy. Just stay the fuck away from her! I already warned you about her, Bostyn!" Pops called after me as I left the room to get my boys to go after Meelah.

Ace was always down to ride. He got as many Guerillas as he could find to have them post up around Troy's neighborhood that day. We thought we were going to run into the worst, but instead, when we got to Troy's house, the only thing we ran up on was an empty parking space. No one was there, and the neighborhood was quiet, but what I did notice were neighbors peeping out their windows. An old lady was in her garden, trying her best not to look our way. Of course, Ace wanted to confront her, but I knew his tattoos and the gun at his waist would probably give the old white woman a heart attack. I was sure she'd seen enough shit that day.

I walked over to her as she stood from the ground, removing her gardening gloves. "Good afternoon, ma'am."

The woman looked me over a little before looking over my shoulders at Ace and his crew, who looked like they were about to shoot up the block. She looked back at me. "Hello, Mr.—"

I held out my hand to shake hers. "Easy."

The woman laughed. "Easy? Okay, Easy, I would ask how I can help you, but it looks like you and your friends already have everything under control. What are you doing at Mrs. Heinz's place?"

"I'm looking for her niece, Meelah," I told her, then watched her turn around and put her gloves back on before pretending to look over her rosebush.

"Some other men came by looking for her today," the woman told me as she looked back at me over her shoulder.

"Did they take her with them?" I asked.

She frantically shook her friend. "They took her Hispanic friend with them. They left her in the house. You just missed Troy and her daughter. Oh, and the ambulance."

"Ambulance?" I stood behind her. "In a bag or on a stretcher, Miss—"

The woman hesitated. "Ms. Yula. The paramedics carried her out of here on a stretcher. She's alive but barely. I take it what happened to her has something to do with you. The Hispanic girl was screaming, 'Wait until Easy finds out about this,' when one of the men shoved her into the back seat of a black Mercedes. And if you're thinking about going to the hospital, I'm sure the men who did this are waiting for you."

My blood was already boiling. There was no turning back at that point. It was my fault that she was in the hospital, and I had to get her out of there. I turned around to walk toward my crew, who peeped the look on my face and jumped back in our ride.

"Easy," the old woman called out to me, "they don't fit in our world any more than we fit into theirs. The girl's own father walked out of that house knowing what they were doing to her."

I stopped in my tracks.

"His hate for who you represent caused him to hurt his only child. He let those men do this to her to draw you closer. It's a trap," Ms. Yula warned me.

But I didn't care. We pulled up to the hospital that evening, and just like Ms. Yula said, them muthafuckas were waiting for us at the doors with no police in sight. At the head of the crew was Dinero, his gun already drawn on me as I stepped out of Ace's ride and walked down the sidewalk toward him.

"You might as well put that shit down, muthafucka," I told him with the crew following me with their dual-wielding full-auto Glock 18s with hundred-round magazines. Dinero's crew had heat but not like ours. We'd put a hundred bullets in their ass before they even had a chance to fire a shot.

Dinero wasn't backing down. "Turn the fuck around and walk away. This shit doesn't have anything to do with you."

"You know it does," I said, walking right up to him.

"Nigga, I know who you are, and I really don't give a fuck. Stay the fuck away from Meelah. This shit happened because of you." Dinero's finger was over the trigger.

"The fuck did you do to her?" I was ready to fight the nigga, gun at my chest or not.

"The fuck did you do to her?" Dinero growled back.

"All right, gentlemen, calm it down."

I heard a voice to my left that I hadn't heard before. A tall white man with dark hair and a dark Italian suit to match walked toward us with men wearing matching suits. Them muthafuckas looked like the cast of *The Godfather* or some shit. As soon as they approached us, Dinero's crew stood down and lowered their guns. My crew couldn't care less. They kept their guns aimed on everyone at that point.

The man leading the crew walked up to me with a younger version of himself to the right of him. The two of them looked me over for a few seconds before Dinero backed away from me.

"So, you're the one causing problems, huh?" The man laughed.

I frowned at him, giving zero fucks about him or the crew he came with. "Nah, but I'm about to," I told him.

The man laughed, and his crew chuckled behind him. The muthafucka alongside him looked at me like he didn't like me for whatever he had heard about me.

"You need to turn around and never look back." The man looked my face over. "This young woman got herself in a situation that she can't get out of. She violated the code of conduct—she disobeyed her father's orders. Her father is the leader of one of the biggest crime mobs in the country. When he says don't do something, that means don't fuckin' do it. She overstepped her boundaries, and so did you."

"Let her come with me." I could barely get the words out before the man started laughing.

"And who the fuck are you? What's your name?" he asked.

"My crew calls me Easy," I told him.

"Word on the street is that your father is a police officer." He watched me shake my head.

"Nah, bruh," I told him. "I don't know my father."

"What about your mother?" he asked.

"I don't know her, but she was killed in front of me."

"What was her name?"

"Maria Alejandra Gonzalez." I peeped the look on the muthafucka's face next to the man who was in my face before I looked at the man who was looking at me like he was looking into a mirror. "The fuck are you looking at me like that for? You got all these questions for me, but you still haven't told me your name."

"Stefano Romano," the man said with nostrils flaring.

I just looked into his face for a few seconds before looking at the man next to him, who had to be Cristobal. The muthafucka who raped and beat the fuck out of Meelah. I wanted to pull my gun out of my pants and shoot him right in his face, fuck the consequences, but I was going to get to him in due time. Pops was making sure of that.

I looked back at Stefano.

"You don't know your father?" he questioned me.

"Nah. I don't want to know the muthafucka either. I ain't got shit. No one. Just me and my crew. And that girl in there," I told him and watched him shake his head.

"Your mother, Maria Alejandra, is the daughter of one of the biggest drug traffickers in Guatemala. Not to mention her mother is the daughter of a drug trafficker who worked for the Panamanian government. The Gonzales family from Guatemala and the Ruiz family from Panama gave us power beyond measure. Both families made deals with congressmen, government agents, federal agents, and police departments. Her family appeared to be poor, but they had access to more money than we could ever imagine. The Gulf of Mexico and Atlantic Ocean are ours because of that family. Her family is responsible for the war on drugs. There is no stopping us because our Chain runs this country. I'm standing out in front of this hospital, and the children of some of my best men are out here. They could kill you and your boys and could get away with it." Stefano laughed at me.

"Maria's only son is dead," Cristobal spoke up.

I looked from Stefano over to him. "Nah, muthafucka, I'm standing right here. Aunt Jimena's son is about to be dead though, if he doesn't get the fuck out of my face."

Cristobal started to step to me when Stefano told him to get the fuck back.

"Cousins, huh?" Stefano chuckled a little.

"I heard we had the same daddy, so that makes us brothers, too, muthafucka," I said and watched the smile wipe clean off his face.

"He didn't kill you because you're my son." Stefano spoke so only I could hear what he was saying. "Leave." Stefano spoke loud enough for everyone to hear. "Leave her."

I shook my head. "She wouldn't leave me."

"This isn't the way to save her," Stefano told me.

"Why the fuck should I listen to you?" I growled. "You ordered a hit on my mother! You told Sable to kill my mother if she didn't kill me! But Sable killed her so she wouldn't kill me."

Stefano made a face. "What are you talking about? They told you that Sable killed your mother to save her from killing you?" Stefano laughed a little. "You have a lot of truth to learn, but not today. I know I was labeled the bad guy, but I'm not. Get out of here before the police department shows their faces. We don't need the attention. Take your crew and go, Easy, now."

I shook my head. "I can't leave her."

Stefano looked me in my face. "They will kill her to kill you, son."

"Don't call me son. I don't have a father," I told him as Ace pulled on my arm, dragging me away from Stefano.

"Man, let's roll out," Ace told me. "We'll come back for her. These niggas will leave. They won't be here all night."

Ace was right. They weren't standing in front of the hospital all night. By the time we came back, they were gone, and so was Meelah. I needed answers. I found out who Meelah's doctor was and followed that muthafucka home. The doctor said that Meelah's aunt had her flown to a hospital in California. Meelah wasn't coming back. As soon as I made it back to my crib, thinking I was going to confront Pops, officials from the Secret Security Squadron were there to escort me to Texas where I'd be spending the next five months training to work for Mandy's father's undercover agents.

When I tell you them muthafuckas had to fight me to leave, I mean that shit. I wasn't trying to leave without finding out if Meelah was okay, or at least fuckin' up Dinero's entire crew. My half brother included. Stefano talked to me out in the open when he could've just killed me. I could've been lying. For all he knew, I was Jimmie's son, but the way he talked to me let me know that maybe he wasn't the bad guy. Maybe the man whose roof I'd been living under all my life was the one I needed to look out for.

Chapter Twelve

Easy

Five Months Later

"I'm so proud of you, honey!" Moms hugged me the night of graduation: July 30, 2013.

I'd graduated with honors from the SSS, and my people came to see me march across the field of the Undercover Agent Association. I wasn't feeling the situation whatsoever, but I knew that I had to do what I had to do to get back to Meelah. My only contact with Meelah was through Zara. She'd kept in touch with Ace, letting him know about Meelah and how she was doing. She'd let Ace know that Meelah had been beaten up by Dinero while he let his goons run through her. And her own father knew about the shit.

Aunt Troy took Meelah to the hospital. Meelah was too out of it to say who hurt her, but Zara said that their neighbor—the woman who talked to me—told them that her father had come to the house with a group of young boys. Zara said that Aunt Troy filed charges against Dinero and Sable, only to have the charges dropped because Meelah refused to testify once the court date came around. She didn't want to step foot back in Maryland where the charges were filed. She just wanted to get on with her life in Los Angeles. Zara also told Ace that Meelah found out that my adopted father killed her mother, and that I knew about it and didn't tell her. Yeah, shawty was pissed than a muthafucka at me, and I couldn't even blame her.

"Congrats, little bro!" Jaxson hugged me tight. "How does it feel to know that you're about to do something with your life for once?"

I gave him the side-eye as my two brothers cracked up at me. "Feels like I'm about to use some of the martial arts that they taught a muthafucka on y'all asses."

Roxyn playfully punched me in my arm. "Man, you and Claudius are gonna be unstoppable. Have you heard from him?"

I nodded. "Yeah, he graduated yesterday. His flight comes in this afternoon. He's just gonna meet up with me at the hospital. I have to complete my physical before we're shipped off to Morocco, man. They got us going undercover to find out what's going on in this drug and human trafficking ring in Africa. There's no telling when I'm coming back home."

I peeped the tears sliding down Aunt Donna's cheeks. She ended up going back home to be with her sick brother in Guatemala. My grandfather. Donna smiled through her tears. Though she was sad to see me go, I was sure she wanted to get me away from the chaos going on back home. She knew herself that once I got my hands on Cristobal, he was dead. My crew back home was ready to run down on The Chain, but I knew better. My father didn't even come to my graduation. He kept an eye on the activity going on back home.

Though me and Mandy had our own house, Mandy spent a lot of time with Moms. She gave birth to twins, a boy and a girl who she named Boss and Majesty. I was at training when she gave birth back in June, but Donna was there to capture it all via FaceTime. They were delivered by C-section on June 7 at 3:30 a.m. Those babies were two of the most beautiful babies I'd ever seen, mine or not. Pops didn't acknowledge them as his, and just days after they were born, Mandy was back to doing what she did best—shopping and hanging with her friends. Mandy hired her maid to watch over them, but once Donna touched back down in Maryland, she took over full-time as their nanny.

"*Felicitaciones, niño!*" Donna pushed my brothers off me to hug me tight and congratulate me. "Let me take you out to dinner!"

"Donna, we're here all week. We have plenty of time for that." Moms rained on Donna's parade as usual. She never cared too much for my aunt, resenting her for the fact that she was related to my birth mother by blood. Though Moms knew Donna was my family, she refused to acknowledge her as my aunt and only the housekeeper. "I'm sure Bostyn will be spending time with his classmates after he leaves the hospital. We already have dinner plans with Bostyn tomorrow. The reservations are only for four," Moms let Donna know.

Jaxon and Roxyn looked at me before looking at my aunt for a reaction.

Donna laughed a little before looking at me. "Congratulations again. You look so handsome. Your mother would have been proud." Donna peeped the irritated expression on my mother's face before looking back at me with a mischievous grin. "This uniform looks great on you, but the uniform should have been blue instead of green."

I looked into my aunt's face before she stood on her tiptoes to give me a kiss.

Aunt Donna winked at me before making her way through the crowd of family members and probably back to one of the rentals that my family had.

Code blue was something my aunt would always refer to when she had something important to tell me. Code green was telling me to call her when I was free. Over the past few years, everything my aunt said to me was in codes, and it was up to me to try to figure everything out. I was sure she'd removed the wire that my father made her wear. I'd found out just about everything about my family that I needed to let me know that Jimmie Reel was just as dirty as the people he tried to put away or that he was working with.

As soon as I got away from Moms and my brothers that afternoon, I made my way to University Hospital, where my unit was completing my physical. I didn't get to finish my physical a few days earlier because I got into a fight with one of the muthafuckas in my dorm who thought it was cool to borrow a few of my white T-shirts because his weren't clean. I spent most of my time at that school defending my color and my family name, both of them. They'd all heard who both my adopted father and who my biological father were.

Josh Wineyard—Mandy's father—caught wind of the heat that I was getting from everyone about being a Reel and a Romano. There was no doubt in my mind that he already knew about my lineage, but he pretended not to know when he was questioned by the board members as to why he was going to send me to go undercover back home in Maryland. That was the reason he decided to send me to Morocco for a few years until the rumors died down. Claudius would handle things back home. Claudius still had Tajha playing both sides. She'd get him in good with Dinero as long as Dinero believed that Claudius and I weren't speaking anymore.

As the Uber driver let me off in front of the hospital, I spotted my aunt standing out front. Imagine my surprise when I saw her standing there with Sharita. I got out of the car, straightening out my uniform and trying to remain as cool as I could, but my ass was nervous as fuck. What was Sharita doing there?

I approached the two of them, watching Sharita standing there with dark tears sliding down her face. Before I could even say so much as a hello to shawty, she started going off on me.

"You let them take my best friend away from me!" Sharita pushed me in my chest.

I shook my head. "I didn't let a muthafucka do shit."

Sharita exhaled deeply. She didn't know who to blame. She knew like I did that there wasn't much that I could do to stop what happened to Meelah other than to not fuck with her in the first place. But Sharita also knew like I did that Meelah was trapped in a world where she had to do what muthafuckas wanted if she wanted to survive.

"You don't know shit about who you are, and it's about time that you do," Sharita told me. "Our grandfather has access to some of the purest forms of cocaine out on the market. Our mothers were drug mules for our family. They smuggled drugs into the country for our grandfather, which is how they met not just Stefano, but Jimmie, too."

"But your mother said that our family in Guatemala was poor," I responded.

Donna shook her head. "No, that's just . . . how do you say, Sharita?"

"A cover," Sharita answered our aunt. "Our families back in Panama and Guatemala have most of their money tied into the government, both foreign and domestic. Jimmie ran with The Chain when he first started working for the police department. Your mother couldn't care less about him and only used him because of his status. Your family gives our family immunity, which was the only use we had for them. Your mother went back to Guatemala to get away from your adoptive father. She ended up being Stefano's first wife, though. I know you probably heard that your mother was kidnapped. She wasn't sent to kill you, Easy—she was sent to get you back."

I shook my head. "I really don't want to hear this shit, Sharita. It's the past. I moved the fuck on."

Sharita looked at me. "Your adoptive father received a tip that she was coming back to get you. The tip was from Emmanuel Summers, ya know, Sable—Meelah's father. He'd rather work alongside someone than for someone, and whose side better to be on than a cop's side? Her father killed your mother because your father asked him to. He wanted her, and all she wanted was you. Stefano was going to let her move to Panama with her mother's side of the family. She just wanted a normal life with her son, and Jimmie wasn't having that. Meelah's mother, well, she got caught in the crossfire too."

"Why the fuck are you telling me all of this? You had to fly all the way here to tell me this shit?" I looked Sharita in her face.

"A few days ago, Meelah went to her checkup. Turns out her baby is dead. Your baby is dead, Easy." Sharita watched me remove my hat from my head. "Meelah is here, cousin."

"Wait, what?" I could barely talk. I didn't even wait for her to respond. I just made my way toward the entrance of the hospital.

Donna and Sharita followed me.

"She called me up and told me that they wanted to check her into the hospital to, you know, get rid of the baby, but she wanted to do this with you. Easy, she's so mad at you!" Sharita let me know as we entered the hospital.

"What room is she in?" I asked.

"She's in labor and delivery. Just go to the nurses' station and ask for her room. I'll wait in the lobby with Donna. Easy," Sharita grabbed my arm. "Cousin, I'm so sorry."

There was nothing I could say at that moment. I could feel Meelah's pain the moment Sharita said our baby was dead inside of her. I made my way into the hospital, and my heart slammed against my rib cage as I made my way toward Meelah's room. I had completely forgotten about the fact that Claudius was already supposed to be in the hospital waiting for me, and I ran into him as soon as I stepped onto the elevator. Claudius was happy to see me until he saw the terrified look on my face.

"What's up, Easy?" Claudius's excited expression turned to one of concern. "You a'ight?"

"Nah." I looked straight ahead as the elevator door closed, and I pressed the button for the labor and delivery floor.

"Why the fuck are we going to the labor and delivery floor? I thought you said we were supposed to go to your doctor's office. I thought he had to work here today instead of at the clinic, and we were going to his office to get the blood work and then roll out. You got some bitch pregnant in training, nigga?" Claudius joked.

"Meelah is here," I told him.

"Meelah?" I felt Claudius's confused glare burning a hole in my profile.

I looked at him. "Yeah. Sharita's here too."

"What the fuck for?" Claudius frowned at me. "You invited them to this shit? You're not even supposed to be around either of them. Shit, I ain't even supposed to be around you right now! But I came to show my support since I know your father couldn't come to see you."

"Yeah, which one?" I huffed.

"Anyway, what's Meelah doing here all the way from LA?" Claudius asked.

"She went to a checkup the other day. Sharita said they told her that my baby's dead." I could barely say it. "She came here so I could be with her when they removed my baby. Shit is fucked up, man."

Claudius was stunned to silence for a few seconds before saying, "Damn."

I knew he wanted to say some shit like maybe what happened to our child was for the best, but he saw me fighting off the urge to cry, so he didn't say anything else. He just went with me to the nurse's station to ask for Meelah's room. After the nurse let me know that she was waiting for me, Claudius went to the lobby. I made my way to Meelah's room and tapped on the door before pushing it open. When I walked into the room, Meelah was lying on her side, sobbing, while a nurse rubbed her lower back.

The door shut behind me as the nurse looked up at me. She patted Meelah's back before getting up from the bed to walk up to me.

She looked back at Meelah before looking me in my face. "This girl traveled a long way so you could be here with her tonight for this," the nurse let me know.

I looked at the nurse before looking over her shoulder at Meelah. It hurt me to see her hurting. Meelah was everything to me. She was the only person I'd ever met who made me forget that there was a world around us that existed too. She was all that mattered to me.

I looked back at the nurse. "So, when does she . . ." I couldn't even get myself to say what was about to happen.

"We started her Pitocin drip when she got here about two hours ago. She was in labor when she got off that flight. We gave her the drip to help her along. I'm Nurse Erin. I'll be here to help her through this. It'll be a long night, so if you have anything else you need to do—"

I cut her off. “It can wait until tomorrow. I’m not shipping out until this weekend.”

“Okay, well, I’ll let you get comfortable.” The nurse started to walk around me to leave the room when I grabbed her arm.

“Why . . . why did this happen?” I had to ask.

The nurse shrugged and looked over my shoulder at Meelah before looking back at me. “Stress, I’m sure. It’s a wonder the baby lasted this long. My guess is that the baby has been dead for a few weeks. She was attacked at a mall and kicked in the stomach during a robbery. It was local news in Los Angeles. The only reason I know is that my cousin, who’s a nurse, lived there. They checked her then, and the baby was fine, so they thought anyway.”

I looked back at Meelah as I took my jacket off.

“I’ll see you two in a little while.” Nurse Erin patted me on the shoulder before leaving the room.

“If you have somewhere else you’d rather be, Easy, then go,” Meelah told me as I walked up to her, removing my tie and unbuttoning my shirt a little. She looked up at me before burying her face in her pillow.

“Nah, I’m right where I need to be,” I told her as I laid my jacket and tie on the chair across from her bed. I pulled the chair closer to her bed and sat down, facing her.

“You have a life without me.” Meelah looked up at me as tears slid across her nose. “I came here because no one else cares about me, but I see now that you’re doing just fine without me too. Better even.”

I shook my head. “Hell nah, I’m not doing better, Meelah!”

Meelah laughed a little. “You graduated from so-called college today, huh? What kinda college graduates in five months?”

“I wasn’t supposed to talk about it, shawty,” I told her.

"I guess you weren't supposed to talk about the fact that your adoptive father works for the police department that killed my mother, huh?" Meelah snapped.

I exhaled sharply. "I'm doing this shit to save us, Meelah. I'm planning to take down this entire police department while Claudius takes your father's crew out."

Meelah laughed a little. "This is bigger than us, Easy. Go live your life. Forget about us."

"Meelah, I didn't want to leave you in the first place. When we separate, the worst shit happens! Had I not been shipped off to training, I would've ended all this shit! Cristobal, Dinero, Stefano, yo' father, Pops, all that shit would've been over!" I tried to tell her, but she wouldn't listen. "I'm sorry they hurt you."

Meelah laughed and cried at the same time. "You can't save me."

"Let me get you out of here! I'm not going to just stand around and watch you hurt, Meelah!" I said.

Meelah agreed with me. "You're right, you're not. Where're you shipping off to this weekend? And how long are you going to be gone?"

"I'm going to Morocco. Five years." I hated to tell her, but I had to.

Meelah cried and laughed again. "Get out, Easy. It's too late for us. It's going to be a long time before your family sees you again. Go be with your family."

"You are my family," I told her and grabbed her hand.

Meelah held my hand tight. "It's been a mean world without you, Easy," she whispered.

I nodded. "I know."

"Aunt Troy is sending me to school in Canada. A school I haven't told anyone about. She told me to pick one and not tell anyone where I am, not even her! She wants me where my father can't find me." Meelah sighed as I pushed her hair from her face. Beads of sweat had formed on her hairline. "How is she?"

I looked into her face as she cringed in pain. "How is who?"

"The bitch with your babies. Who else?" Meelah groaned in pain and squeezed my hand.

I laughed a little. "You don't give a fuck about her."

Meelah agreed, looking into my face as her deep brown eyes sparkled. "You're right. I don't give a fuck about Miley Cyrus, but she had a part of you, so I thought I'd ask. Are the babies okay? Do you have a picture?"

I just looked her face over for a few seconds. Right then, there was nothing I wouldn't do for her. She was about to give birth to our dead baby. Meelah had been through the worst that year, and there she was, asking about the babies she thought I had with a bitch she gave zero fucks about. I didn't bother to get a DNA test done. There was no point. When the kids got old enough to understand, I'd tell them what a bitch their mother was and what a fuck muthafucka my adoptive father was. But, at that point, I didn't think Meelah needed to hear that they weren't mine. She just needed to hear something happy for a change.

I nodded. "They're doing good, li'l baby."

Tears slid down Meelah's sweet face. "What are their names?" she cried.

"Boss and Majesty."

I pulled out my phone with the hand she wasn't holding and showed her a picture of them.

Meelah released a scream before saying, "They don't really look like you."

I grinned a little. She already knew the deal. That was why I loved her. I kissed her on her nose.

"My aunt doesn't know I'm here. She's going to kill me, but I feel like I'm already dead," Meelah told me.

"I know, baby, I know," I whispered.

"We're never going to be together, are we?" Meelah asked.

"My aunt Donna told ya boy to never say never," I told her, even though the odds were all the way the fuck against us.

Meelah looked up into my face. "All this time, I thought it was the Baltimore City Police Department who killed my mother. Turns out, it was the Anne Arundel Police Department responsible for killing her. Your adoptive father is the one they say killed my mom. Did you know that?"

I nodded. "Yeah. Bits and pieces."

"They lied to us," Meelah whispered.

I agreed. "Yeah, baby, I know."

"Easy-B?" Meelah sobbed.

"Yeah, bae?" I answered.

"My water broke," Meelah choked. "He's coming."

I exhaled deeply and grabbed the controller on the bed to press the call button for the nurse.

Imagine holding hands with the girl you love while she's giving birth to your dead baby. Imagine crying with her as she pushes that dead baby into your hands. Imagine cutting the umbilical cord. Imagine that the baby who doctors said died in the womb takes a deep breath and opens his eyes, looking into yours. And just when your heart starts to pound with excitement in your chest at the sight of your baby breathing, you find out that breath is the baby's first and last breath. Imagine holding that beautiful baby boy in your hands for a few seconds before the doctors take him from you and place the baby on the stomach of the love of your life. Imagine watching her scream and wail as they take that baby from her and wrap the baby in a blanket. I'd never felt pain so deep.

What was supposed to be a beautiful moment turned ugly real quick. Meelah damn near had a heart attack in front of me. The doctors made me leave the room. When I went out to the lobby, Claudius was waiting there for me. I was too angry to cry at first. I started slinging shit across the lobby, even cracking a vase against the wall before trying to punch a hole through it.

Claudius grabbed me before hospital security could get to me. I cried and screamed in his arms. I swear I'd never felt a pain so intense. I cried because it was the only way my heart knew how to speak when my lips didn't know how to describe how much pain I was in. All I could do was cry and scream out for my babies, both of them—Meelah and Magic.

Chapter Thirteen

Meelah

Five Years Later: Present Day

"I don't know what happened, got people steady askin' how you go to sleep mad one day, the next wake up so happy." I sang softly with my favorite song by Nivea playing on SXM radio. It felt like a normal, cloudy October day in Toronto. What was depressing about that day was that it was the anniversary of my senior year homecoming dance. The dance where I first met Easy. I hadn't seen that boy in five years. He was doing undercover work in Morocco, risking his life for the freedom and safety of kidnapped citizens of Morocco who were forced into sex and drug trafficking. I was worried about him, but at least I knew he was alive. Sharita would've gotten word if something had happened to him.

Sharita was the only one back home who I'd kept in contact with. I'd call her from a coworker's phone or inbox her from a fake social media account. I even lost contact with my aunt and my cousin. Sharita told me that she saw Aunt Troy having dinner with my father a few times. I didn't feel comfortable with that situation, especially since my aunt claimed to hate my father. Especially how everything went the way it did.

Aunt Troy knew that it was my father's doing to have me attacked while I was pregnant with Magic. She knew that he wanted to destroy my life for disobeying him. There was no way she should've been anywhere near him, especially when her niece was still trying to overcome everything that had happened to her over the past few years.

I graduated with honors from the University of Toronto, majoring in journalism. I landed a job at a major reporting firm, Tea of Toronto. I wanted to be a lead reporter, but that would put me in the spotlight, somewhere I didn't want to be. So, I made a decent living off being a lead social media specialist. I was pretty much the PR rep for the firm, but I barely showed my face in public. Our headquarters was located in DC, the political capital of the world. There was so much tea when it came to the personal lives of politicians.

I can't tell you how much drama was happening in the lives of Claudius's and Dinero's family members. I tried not to lurk too much, but I couldn't help it. My mind often wandered back home, even when I didn't want it to.

Though life in Toronto was peaceful, I was lonely. I didn't make any friends for fear that they'd find out who I was. My father's name stayed in the news. Not for his illegal activity but for the new businesses that he and Dinero had invested in. They opened a casino and several funeral homes. The more legit money my father made, the more dirty money he could clean. I didn't want shit to do with that family anymore. Luckily, no one associated my last name with my father's since Summers was a pretty common name. I was the only black woman in my department. I think they were afraid to approach me about my last name with the way my attitude was set up. They knew my response would be, "Oh, so you think all niggas look alike?"

I missed my crew like a muthafucka. I missed Sharita getting chased by the niggas. Never had I ever seen her date a Hispanic guy. Her soul craved dark meat. I'm talking Southern-fried dark meat. The darker the better to her. She was probably somewhere riding dick or being eaten like the Last Supper. Some people used drugs as an escape. Sharita used sex. Seemed like it had gotten worse after what my father let Dinero do to me that day he found out I was carrying Easy's baby.

Sharita felt like she lost me that day. She knew they'd either kill me or my aunt would send me away. She knew like everyone else that Dinero would get away with hurting me. She knew like everyone else that my father's crew got away with worse each and every day. After Dinero humiliated me in front of our crew, I was rushed to the hospital. It was a miracle that my baby survived the first beating.

Dinero had poured a gallon of bleach down my throat while another crew member sodomized me with a dustpan handle. I begged God to make Dinero kill me. Instead, God allowed my body to go numb before going unconscious that day. When I woke up, I was in the hospital in Los Angeles, staring into the face of a doctor who was astounded by the fact that both I and my baby had survived that first beating. Unfortunately, little Magic didn't survive the second one. I didn't think I would make it after he died, but I did. Barely.

"We're taking a trip to headquarters tomorrow, Meelah!" My secretary, Mora, followed me as I walked into work that dreary morning. "I've never been to Washington, DC!"

I exhaled deeply as we moved through the busy office. The talk of the office was election time. Turned out Dinero's father was running for mayor of DC. Last I heard, Dinero had reunited with his father. Pictures were all over the news of the two together. Every time I saw his face or someone mentioned anything about the corrupt government, I'd get flashbacks of the life that I lived back home. I was once a naive girl who did whatever my father and my then-boyfriend asked me to do. I had no idea that some of the kids who I supplied drugs to were children of local government officials. I had no idea that some of the children of those government officials helped us distribute drugs among their parents' peers. I helped to host parties for these officials, not realizing that I was helping my father pimp the women who worked for him. Not realizing that my own father was pretty much pimping me too.

"Are you going with us, boss lady?" Mora asked me, her bright gray eyes peering into my face as I stood at the coffee maker, grabbing the cup of coffee that was waiting for me.

I shook my head and took a sip.

Mora frowned. "Why not? You never go home for the holidays. You've been here five years, and no one has even come to visit you. It's like you're hiding here in Canada, away from people who I'm sure care about you. Your family, your friends. I know you had a boyfriend."

Easy's grin flashed through my mind the instant she said boyfriend. Sharita's laugh echoed through my mind. Tajha's eye roll and hate for me brought me back to reality before thoughts of Dinero whipping me with his belt brought back anxiety. I exhaled deeply, getting my emotions in check.

"I needed a do-over," I explained. "Y'all go have fun. Interview the politicians. Bring back some tea. I can monitor what's trending on social media from here, boo. I've seen the White House. I've partied with the local government and their spoiled offspring. There's nothing for me in the DMV but painful memories. And it's homecoming weekend. The streets are going to be lit up with teenagers going out to party after the game and do last-minute shopping for the dance. I'm good where I'm at."

"Listen up, everyone." My boss, Darla, walked into the room, getting everyone's attention that morning. She wore a tight blouse and fitted slacks, looking more like a model for *Glamour* magazine than a director and CEO of a journalism company. "Breaking news in DC. I just got word that there was a mass shooting at one of the senator's offices in Maryland."

My eyes widened a little as I sipped from my coffee cup.

"How many people were killed?" one of the reporters asked.

Darla shrugged her narrow shoulders. "There hasn't been a body count given as of yet, but I already have a few reporters headed there right now. Seems that some sort of business deal was going down. I do know that among some of the dead bodies found was one of the biggest drug distributors on the East Coast. Emmanuel Summers, known on the street as Sable."

Darla barely got the words out before I dropped my cup of coffee. I'd deactivated my fake social media accounts that week, knowing that Sharita was about to be blowing my phone up about the college homecomings. I didn't want to think about Easy or our first dance. I just wanted to concentrate on work and the promotion that I was shooting for. Who would have ever thought that the week I decided to deactivate my shit was the week my father would be killed? I should've been hurt, right? But I wasn't. I was scared as fuck because I knew it wouldn't be long before family members reached out to me to not only come to his funeral but take over the family businesses.

"Boss lady, you good?" Mora asked me as everyone watched me standing there shaking in my heels.

"Who else did they find?" I stuttered, my heart stuttering in my chest as well.

Darla shrugged again. “Some of his men were shot up as well, honey, I’m not sure. They were interviewing Dinero Rodriguez a few minutes ago on Fox News. Apparently, he wasn’t there during the shooting. He—”

I didn’t hear a word after she mentioned Dinero’s name. The fact that he wasn’t at that office that day right along with my father told me that either Dinero had arranged that shit or he at least knew that it was going down. Last I heard, Dinero was my father’s right-hand man. Everywhere my father was, that nigga was right there. I really wasn’t trying to go back to that life, but I found myself packing that night before boarding a flight with my boss, secretary, and about five reporters from our department.

“You okay, Summers?” Darla peeped my leg shaking anxiously as she sat down behind me on our business class flight on WestJet Airlines to DC.

I exhaled nervously and looked over my shoulder at Darla as the stewardess greeted her with a smile. I hadn’t been home in five years, shit, if you even called it home. It had taken me nearly three years to put my past behind me. I still broke out in cold sweats at night from the nightmares of losing my son. Easy was lucky that his family had forced him to join the police academy. Of course, I didn’t want him to leave me, but leaving meant that he could leave the country and forget his problems for a while. I, on the other hand, couldn’t seem to escape my life. I moved to another country and still managed to work for a company that was fascinated with politicians and the crooked muthafuckas the politicians ran with.

“Yeah, I’m good. Where is the champagne, shit?” I muttered, sitting uncomfortably in my seat.

Everyone around me was so excited to be going to DC. They didn’t often get a break from Toronto. They couldn’t wait to get to DC and see all the street celebrities riding around in their "what the fuck is thats." They were going to DC to get a story. I was going there for a funeral. I tried to leave my life behind, and my boss unknowingly was taking me back to it.

"I know you mainly deal with the social media aspect of this company, but this week, I'm going to need you to help out the reporters," Darla let me know.

I looked back at her, heart thumping in my chest. I had to just tell her that the entire situation was too close to home. "I don't know if I should," I stuttered. "I have to contact my family as soon as I touch down in DC. I haven't seen my family in five years. Not that I'm in a hurry to meet up with them, but I think I'll have to help my aunt with funeral arrangements."

Darla's eyebrows frowned in confusion.

"Sable is my father," I mouthed.

Darla sat up in her chair, her bright brown eyes widening. "What?" she mouthed. "You mean to tell me that Sable Summers is your father, and you didn't say anything?"

I shrugged. "I don't want to draw attention to me being associated with a kingpin. My family is ruthless, and now with politics on my family's side, there's really no stopping them."

Darla's surprised expression changed to certainty. "You mean 'us' now. There's no stopping 'us' now. That's your family. There's no running from them. There's no running from us."

I looked at her.

Darla shook her head, removing her glasses from her face. "My maiden name is Rodriguez. Miguel is my older brother."

I turned around in my seat to face her. I wondered why I felt so close to my boss. I felt like I knew her, and I did in a way. I had known her nephew all my life. "You . . . you knew who I was this whole time?"

Darla hated to admit it. "Dinero paid me to hire you. I promise you, I'm nothing like them, Meelah." Darla grabbed my shoulder before I turned around in my chair. "I'm looking out for you. I got you a job, I kept you at work instead of hanging out with your coworkers, I made sure you graduated with honors, and I got you a job before you even graduated. I pay you more than I pay any of the other workers who have been there for years!"

"So, he knew where I was all this time?" I asked.

Darla shook her head. "No. He thinks I own a company in Quebec. I don't want to be associated with the Rodriguez family just as much as you don't want to be a Summers. Politics is in my blood, which is why my firm concentrates on the political tea. I try not to put my family on Front Street, which is why you don't see any of the gossip about the Rodriguez family on our sites, magazines, or newspaper. But this story is big. My brother is involved in this just as much as my nephew is. I apologize for your father's loss, but we both know this is a game of power, and I'm sure your father was gaining too much of it. You already know that once you touch down in Maryland, you will become a target. A target for some people you may have known all your life. You're a smart girl, honey. If I were in your shoes, I'd go straight to the top for protection."

I looked at her for a few seconds before turning around in my seat. Was I supposed to trust Darla? I was an intern for her for two years before landing a permanent job at the company. She knew who I was. In fact, homegirl sought me out in a crowd at a job fair at school during sophomore year. I got the intern position at her firm out of hundreds of girls at the university, girls who had way more journalism experience.

My internship was paid when most interned without pay. I already had four raises. My car and apartment were paid for by the company. My cable and cell phone bill were paid for. Shit, I barely had to pay for clothes. Companies that we advertised in our paper and on our sites sent us free clothes on the regular. I'm talking Gucci, Fendi, Prada, Dolce & Gabbana, Christian Louboutin, Christian Dior. Darla lured me into the company because it was drama free and paid me well. I didn't stop to think about the fact that there was no way she never questioned me about my last name. She knew all the dirt on every politician and the muthafuckas they ran with, which meant she knew all about my father, including the fact that I was his daughter.

I didn't question Darla anymore. My main concern was getting away from the bitch and the rest of the crew once we touched down in DC. The airport terminal was crowded with press, so slipping away wouldn't be a problem, or at least it shouldn't have been a problem. But as soon as I stepped foot into the terminal, I was confronted by men who I recognized as Stef's bodyguards. Darla wasn't paying me much attention, as she was trying to get through the crowd of people to wait for her luggage.

Stef's bodyguards blocked me from making a getaway.

"What do you want, Diablo?" I huffed.

Diablo stood six feet four inches before me, dark brown eyes looking down into my face. "We are very sorry for your loss," he let me know.

I rolled my eyes, trying to mask the pain that I refused to allow myself to feel after the pain my father allowed me to endure. "What loss?" I muttered.

"The boss would like to talk to you," Diablo responded.

"Well, what if I don't want to talk to him?" I asked.

"It would be in your best interest to talk to Stefano unless you'd like to talk to Dinero, the man who'd love to take over your father's businesses." Diablo huffed. "The car is waiting outside for you, young lady."

"What about my luggage?" I asked. "I only have one suitcase. The same burgundy plaid suitcase I've been using since high school."

"One of us will get it for you." Diablo signaled one of the bodyguards to get my suitcase.

I should've felt uncomfortable riding with those bodyguards, but I didn't. Life as I knew it had changed years ago. There wasn't anything worse that I could go through than what I'd already been through. Stef's bodyguards took me to Ciao Baby, a cafe in DC owned by Stef. It was the place where Stef often conducted his card games and did most of his meet and greets. My mother loved that restaurant and had hosted there a few times.

As soon as I walked into the lobby of the cafe, I was confronted by a portrait of my mother and a woman who looked like Sharita's mother. I froze in my tracks, staring at the stunning portrait.

"Your mother was beautiful." Stef's voice echoed throughout the empty cafe.

I glanced at him, watching him walk toward me and signal his bodyguards to get lost. "Yeah? Well, she lived an ugly life." I looked back at the oil painting.

"We all do," Stef reminded me. "My condolences for your loss."

I turned to Stef and watched him look me over a little before looking into my face. "Did you kill him?"

Stef made a face. "Why would you ask me some shit like that? After all I did to protect your father's business over the years, you think I'd kill him? Even though your father teamed up with an old friend of mine, I never turned my back on him. Your father was like a brother to me!"

"Then where were you when he died?" I snapped back.

Stef exhaled slowly and deeply. "Attending my own son's funeral."

I looked him over. He was dressed in a crisp shirt and slacks as if he'd come from a very special occasion. I looked back into his face. "Your son's funeral?"

"Cristobal." Stef watched my eyes widen. He tried to hide from his face every emotion I was sure he was feeling. "He along with about twenty members from his crew had been missing for about two weeks. Turns out he was in Morocco."

My heart was going crazy in my chest. I cleared my throat. "Ummm, how do you know he was in Morocco?"

Stef looked at me and frowned at the nervous expression on my face. "Because whoever killed him and his crew sent pieces of their body parts back to me and our family members. The postage and meter stamps were from Morocco."

I swallowed hard. I already knew who had put an end to Cristobal. Easy must have lured him there some way. I wanted to find out more, but I wasn't sure exactly what Stef knew about Easy's whereabouts, so I didn't ask any more questions.

All I could say was, "Well, I would say that I apologize for your loss, but I don't. Karma is a cold bitch."

Stef looked at me before adjusting the collar on his shirt. "Your father's funeral arrangements are being handled by your aunt Troy, or should I say, stepmom Troy."

I looked into his face. "What are you talking about?"

Stef grinned a little. "Oh, you've been gone a long time. You had no idea that your aunt married into the family business. I'm sorry."

I shook my head frantically. "No, I didn't know! When? When did they get married?"

Stef pretended like he was thinking about how long it had been since they'd gotten married. "About two weeks ago."

I cringed. That was about the time I'd stopped contacting Sharita so I could get some work done.

"There was really no point of me coming home. She's got everything settled, from his funeral arrangements to his fuckin' businesses," I responded.

Stef shook his head. "I don't do business with your aunt, which is another reason your father decided to work with Jimmie instead of me. I don't like the way she works. No one had any idea that those two were working together all these years, but I did. He'd been sleeping with your aunt since your mother was alive. Not only was your aunt sleeping with your father, but I found out that she was also connected with Jimmie, Easy's father. She was sleeping with your father around the time your mother was killed."

My heart nearly stopped in my chest as I backed up into the host stand, hand over my heart.

"You know a woman would go to any lengths to be with a man she loves. Your mother—"

I held up my hand to stop him from saying any more.

"Meelah, everything your father owns belongs to you, not her."

I shook my head, trying to catch my breath. "I don't want any of this shit!" I breathed heavily between my words. "That bitch helped raise me! She's hated my father all of these years!"

Stef shrugged. "Well, you know what they say—it's a thin line between love and hate."

I looked at Stef, struggling to catch my breath. It dawned on me that Easy's aunt and mother were both in love with Stef. It wouldn't have surprised me if Sharita's mother, Jimena—Easy's aunt—paid my father to kill Maria, Easy's mother. The lengths a woman would go through to be with a man.

"Jimena, she killed Easy's mother, didn't she?" I watched Stef nod. "She had her own sister killed!"

Stef looked at me like he didn't want to even have the discussion. "There's a lot to explain. A lot that you wouldn't understand. Everything is about power. I knew Easy was alive. He was safer with the Reel family than he was with my family. I stayed away from him to protect him. I didn't acknowledge him to keep him alive. As long as I didn't acknowledge him, Jimena didn't either. She was determined to have him killed the moment that she found out Maria's son was mine. Jimena paid your father millions to kill Maria. Your aunt Troy got word that Sable was seen outside the house of a woman he was sleeping with. The woman lived across the street from Jimmie's house. Not knowing that Sable was at that woman's house to get a better visual of Maria to shoot her, Troy had your mother killed in revenge. To hurt your father."

"To hurt me too." I held back the tears.

"Your mother was tired of this life and wanted out. She went to talk to Jimmie not knowing that her sister had already talked him into having his men kill her while in custody after being pulled over that night. I'm sure you don't want to hear any more." Stef already knew my emotions were swarming through my soul.

"So, Aunt Troy stepped into my mother's shoes, huh?" I laughed off the pain. "The bitch was so obsessed with hating my father. I should've known. He let her get away with so much out of guilt."

"Your father's assets are yours, young lady. Do you really want your aunt to win? Your father left everything to you, little does she know. I know because we have the same lawyer and the same investment banker, Meelah. Don't walk away from this," Stef urged.

I shook my head. "I lost so much already, your grandson included." I felt Stef's stunned expression burning a hole in my profile before I looked at him. "His name was

Magic. Dinero had his goons beat him to death while I was pregnant with him. I pushed that baby into Easy's hands, Stef."

Stef frowned, his dark eyebrows connecting.

"I don't want to lose any more," I whispered.

"Where is my son?" Stef demanded.

"Last I heard, he was in Morocco," I told him, wanting him to know that Easy wasn't to be played with.

Stef laughed in disbelief before just looking at me and hoping my serious expression would change. When he saw that I was serious, he ran his fingers through his thick, dark hair.

"So, Jimmie has him doing his dirty work, huh?"

I laughed out loud. "Jimmie didn't have Easy kill Cristobal! Easy did that for me! For what your son did to me! Did you forget about that shit? I was in a coma after your son left me for dead!"

"Cristobal was wrong, yes, and I know my apologies won't take away the memories. But Cristobal is a big asset to the Gonzales family. His crew helped to move drugs worldwide, Meelah. There's no way I'll get access to that shit! Jimena is a woman—her family only does business with men." Stef looked over my shoulder, signaling his men who were standing outside of the cafe to come in.

I looked into Stef's face. "So, those territories that Cristobal's crew ran—"

"Now belong to Easy, or should I say Bostyn, or should I say Emilio?" Stef looked back into my face.

I shook my head. "Easy is a cop! He'll never agree to this!"

Stef scoffed. "You obviously don't know cops."

"He's one of the good ones," I let him know. "And even if he weren't, you actually think he'd want anything to do with you? I'm not about to let you use him. You don't want to get to know your son. You just want him to keep your money going. Easy got away from this bullshit. He has a family to provide for, so just leave him alone."

"He's involved with this shit more than you know. What do you think his father has him doing out there? Every large organization is funded by drug smugglers. Easy is going to be used either way you look at it. People follow him. He's a natural-born leader. He belongs with The Chain." Stef watched me shake my head.

"I hope he doesn't come back here. I hope he stays where he is. He's safer out there than he is here." I prayed to God in my head to keep Easy safe and away from both Stef and Jimmie. I didn't trust either of them.

Stef's temples shook as he frowned into my face. "I'm sick and fuckin' tired of Jimmie winning, Miss Summers. I want my shit back. Jimmie's organization grows stronger each day because of the undercover work he has his crew doing. Easy doesn't know what he's involved in. He's only helping his father gain more power. The police pretend to be fighting the war on drugs. Little does the public know the police are behind the entire thing. Trust me, he's on his way home. You want to save my son, you bring him to me."

Boy, you a deal wid di realest
And when me a cum, you gon' feel it.

Sharita danced to Cardi B vibrating through the speakers in my father's casino. She was twerking so hard in her short-ass leather skirt that she didn't even see me walk up on her.

"'Dat pussy tight, so ya cum faster! And when me done with you, you a gon need water!'"

"Yo ass is always talking about fuckin', dang. You're such a fuckin' ho. I love it!" I laughed, walking up on her.

Sharita damn near jumped out of her skin at the sound of my voice. She turned around, eyes big as hell. Sharita looked just as excited as she looked scared. She ran up to me, hugging me tightly in her arms before grabbing my arm and pulling me off to talk in private before anyone recognized me. Security wasn't really tight that night. A security guard I didn't recognize frisked me down as I entered the club. I didn't even recognize the people at the door who checked everyone's ID as we entered the casino, which was more like a club.

Summer Session was the name of the casino. The place was hot. The girls who worked the place looked like my cousin Zara personally picked out their outfits, the outfit Sharita wore included.

"Girl, what the fuck?" I exclaimed as soon as Sharita pulled me into a bathroom and locked the door behind us. "When were you going to tell me that my father was killed? When were you going to tell me that my aunt married my father?"

Sharita sighed deeply, smoothing down her edges as she looked into my frustrated expression. "I don't have your number, and not to mention your social media accounts were deactivated! How the fuck was I supposed to contact ya ass? I figured you'd see the news eventually. I told you that I saw that bitch eating dinner with your father. I don't think your father wanted to marry that bitch. I think he just knew some shit was about to go down. I think he knew that if he married her, that would make you come back home to take over all this shit before Dinero and the police department got access to all of this shit. Claudius is working with his brother now."

I looked at her. "Claudius?"

Sharita nodded. "The nigga is a cop. He worked undercover for a while in Virginia, and now he's out here working the streets with his brother. Tajha is the one who told me that he was a cop. I don't trust him because as soon as we do some shit he doesn't like, he's turning us in. I think he was sent to work with us to get access to your father's Rox labs. Supposedly, Claudius was the one who killed your father, Meelah. The head of the police department, Jimmie Reel, wanted him dead. Something about leaving all of his assets to you instead of turning them over to the police."

"Reel? Easy's last name is Reel."

Sharita nodded. "His father runs the Anne Arundel County Police Department. You know, the department that—"

"Killed my mother," I finished her sentence.

Sharita laughed nervously. "I know what you're thinking. Easy is in enough trouble as it is. He fucked up the distribution route in Casablanca, Morocco."

"So, that's what Cristobal was doing there," I said to myself.

"You know about Cristobal?"

I nodded. "Yeah. I know his body parts came back here in pieces."

Sharita looked at me with a funny expression on her face. "Yeah, well, we acquired a new territory there a few weeks ago. Whatever happened there went wrong. Easy shouldn't have even known that he was there. Stef just came back from a funeral today. That's why the house security isn't here. They're standing guard outside of most of our houses, not sure when we will be hit as well."

I shook my head. "We both know what happened. Everyone else is safe, for now, unless Dinero makes a trip to Morocco. He's probably next on Easy's list."

Sharita shook her head. "Dinero and Claudius work together. Easy doesn't know about this shit. As far as he knows, Claudius is supposed to be undercover to take down the crew over in Chesapeake. He doesn't know that his boy and Dinero linked up. The same nigga who damn near broke you in pieces five years ago. Easy wouldn't like this shit, and you know it."

"How is Easy?" I changed the subject.

Sharita shrugged. "Alive."

"How are you? How's your mother?" I hated to ask.

Sharita frowned. "Mom's taking it hard. Cristobal was her heart and soul. Her only tie to Stef. With him gone, Stef really has no need for her. He hasn't once told her that he was sorry for her loss. He hasn't even called her. His only concern is who is taking over Sable's spot. Stef couldn't care less about Dinero, who's in too deep with the police department. I think Stef wants to bring the police department to an end. The streets are crazy right now. It's hard to tell who the real gangs are—the street crews or the police."

"I didn't plan to come back here, Sharita, but my boss brought me back here. I work for a journalist firm," I told her. "Turns out my boss is Miguel's sister. I just can't catch a fuckin' break. The bitch has been keeping an eye on me for years, and I'm sure Dinero put her up to it."

Sharita folded her arms. "So, you're about to put our families on blast? Is that why you're back?"

"No, I'm not. I didn't want to come back here, and you know it. I'm only back here on business. I couldn't care less about a funeral."

Sharita scoffed. "So, you weren't worried about me? You just started a new life without me?"

I shook my head. "I couldn't come back after everything that's happened. No one knew where I was. After I lost Easy's baby, I felt like I lost a piece of myself. He was sent off to Africa, and I left the country to try to forget the pain I've endured. I lost everything."

Sharita's bright brown eyes watered. "I lost everything too! You were my everything, Meelah!"

"You can come back with me!" I told her and watched her shake her head. "Why not? You actually want to be here?"

"I'm stuck, Meelah. They'll find me anywhere that I go. They even managed to find you. You just said you've been working for Dinero's aunt all these years. They've got us trapped!" Sharita told me.

"How the fuck did you end up working here for my father?" I asked.

"I'd rather work for him than against him!" Sharita exclaimed. "My life has been hell since you've been gone! You don't want to know what Dinero had us bitches doing! Everything from smuggling drugs to selling pussy and throat! I took this job here at the casino because at least the men they have me fuckin' are real ballers! Some of these niggas are old as fuck and can't even get it up. All I gotta do is pop one of these pierced nipples out or twerk for their ass! They got Tajha smuggling Rox in her ass to different countries. I tried going to my mom's family for protection, but they won't get involved. All they care about are the men in this family. Women are a liability to the Gonzales family. And Keith is dead!"

I gasped. "Easy's homeboy?"

Sharita nodded as tears started to line the bottom row of her lashes. "Yeah. I heard Claudius got 'im, girl. Had his ass set up to be robbed and killed. Easy is gonna flip when he finds out. Tajha isn't worth two condoms busted, but you can't tell Claudius that. The only reason Dinero is even fuckin' with Claudius is that Miguel started back fuckin' with Claudius's mom. Claudius got Miguel to help distribute the drugs throughout his political party. Dinero needed the business. Don't get it twisted. Dinero doesn't trust Claudius. Claudius is trading out his own people, and no one trusts a traitor."

"Damn." I was getting a headache.

“The gang is getting together after the Howard homecoming game. Tajha’s cousin played last night and brought his team to victory. There’s a post-game party at Club Stoner.”

I shook my head. Club Stoner was a nightclub owned by my father.

Sharita sighed at the irritated expression on my face. “I know you’re not trying to go to your father’s club, but you need to go. It’s the perfect time to get up with your cousin Zara. I’m sure she’s at Ace’s place getting ready for the party right now. Your aunt has been lying low since your father was killed. The only way to see her is through ya cousin.”

I frowned. “I’m here to work. I’m sure my aunt will get up with me to plan this funeral.”

“I’m sorry about all this.” Sharita gave me a sympathetic look.

She knew better than anyone how much I loved my father, and she knew that I always hid pain behind anger. Sharita knew like I did that I was going to lose it as soon as I saw my father’s dead body.

I shook my head. “I’m good, boo.” I tried to laugh off my pain.

Sharita shook her head. “That’s your father. You’re not fine. As much as I hated my brother, you don’t think it hurt when I found out he was dead?”

“I’m here on business.” I changed the subject. “That’s it. Everything else doesn’t even matter. Stef says I need to be hooking up with my father’s lawyer, Archie Lanes. I need to find him before Aunt Troy gets to him. Fuck that party. Where is this bitch anyway? I know you know, Sharita. You work for her.”

Sharita shook her head. “Man, let me take you to Zara first. And I don’t work for that boujee bitch. I work for you. Everyone knows this place is yours. Well, half yours.

Dinero is your father's business partner. Not to mention your father has several police officers working as security guards here. And Archie Lanes isn't your family lawyer anymore."

I looked at Sharita as she nervously bit her lip, the way she always did when some bullshit was about to happen. "Sharita, who's my father's lawyer?" I was afraid to ask.

"Leanne Crosby," Sharita hated to tell me.

My eyes widened. Leanne Crosby was Claudius's mother. Why or how she ended up working for my father, I had no idea. Her connections with my father let me know that her son couldn't be trusted. I was sure Easy had no idea that his homeboy was connected to my father's bullshit. The undercover police work that he was supposed to be involved in was a cover. Shit, the way the law was so corrupt, Leanne probably wasn't working for my father. He was probably working for her.

"Welcome home!" Zara threw her arms around me the night that I showed up at Ace's front door.

Sharita got someone to cover her shift at the casino and took me straight to find my cousin. Everyone was getting ready for the homecoming game after-party in the midst of my father's death. No one seemed bothered. Life went on as normal. I hadn't too long left Arcen, who was conducting business at the lab as usual. He wouldn't talk about what went down or why he wasn't there with my father. All he could tell me was that shit had changed. That The Chain had a few missing links. That we no longer worked with Stef, and that we worked alongside the police department and the local government.

"Where's your mother?" I pushed her arms off me and walked through the houseful of people. I recognized a few of Ace's people from a few years ago and remembered their perverted faces from the bleachers during a few football games.

Zara rolled her eyes at Sharita as she followed the two of us into her so-called boyfriend's place. "She's out handling funeral arrangements. She'll be at the club tonight. I think she's meeting up with the lawyer at the Big House."

I exhaled deeply, stopping in my tracks in the center of the living room.

Sharita grabbed my arm, knowing I wanted to go the fuck off.

The Big House was the name we called my mother's mansion in Upper Marlboro. Only family members were welcome at that house. I should've known that my aunt was fuckin' around with my father. I'd see things of hers at the house when I was younger. Anything from earrings to coats to shoes. Shit, sometimes panties. I didn't think anything of it because my mother was always borrowing Aunt Troy's things or my aunt was always spending the night when she got into it with her ex-boyfriend. But my other aunts had to know about it. They backed Aunt Troy in whatever she did.

My mother was the youngest and the prettiest of the sisters. She had a different father. A rich father, and she was envied because of that. The Big House was left to my mother when her father died, and when my mother died, it was left to me.

Zara walked up to me, peeping the irritated "I'm about to stomp a hole in your mama's face when I see that bitch" expression on my face.

"You missed the wedding." Zara grinned a little.

"Bitch, he's your uncle," I told her.

Zara shook her head. "Well, he's my father now, sis."

"Meelah, boo, chill." Sharita grabbed my arm before I could reach for my cousin. "She's not worth it. You and

Dinero have enough beef. That nigga has got this bitch working right under him."

"I bet." I snatched away from Sharita and got in Zara's face. "You're not even supposed to be around Ace. Our parents told you to stay away from him after what happened with me and Easy."

"Well, Daddy is dead now, so it doesn't matter what he told us not to do, now does it?" Zara snapped. "A lot has changed in five years. Dinero's brother been kickin' it with the crew, so I don't think fuckin' with Ace is a problem, sis."

I shook my head at her. "Dinero doing business with his brother doesn't mean he's cool with you kickin' it with his boys. Dinero wouldn't want you over here! I'm telling you, that nigga is crazy. You work for him!"

"Nah, he works for me, bitch. I'm a Summers now. I changed my name as soon as our parents were married. Well, I got it hyphenated just like your moms did. Heinz-Summers. I run this shit." Zara grinned.

"Your mother had my mother killed. She's been fuckin' my father this entire time! And you're cool with this?" I shouldn't have been surprised.

Zara nodded her head, a tear sliding down her cheek. "She's been fuckin' *our* father, sis. *Our* father. My mama had your mother killed because she was tired of sharing our father with your mother. We're about to bury our father, sis. We're meeting with the lawyer tomorrow to discuss what our father left us. I bet you didn't think you'd have to share your shit with someone else, huh? Remember all the clothes that you left? I've been rockin' the hell outta that shit. You remember that dress that your mom helped you make for prom? I wore that sexy muthafucka to prom. Ace fucked me three times in that dress, bi—"

Zara barely got the word "bitch" out before I punched her dead in her mouth and tackled her to the floor. Sharita backed away from me, and no one in the house stopped the fight. They let us fight right there in the middle of Ace's living room. At that moment, all I could see was red. Anger was all I could feel. At that moment, I hated my father even more.

It was bad enough that Tajha was supposed to be my sister and he never acknowledged her. But then my own aunt's daughter—the girl I grew up believing was my cousin—was actually my sister? And she was actually rubbing the shit in my face? And she actually thought she was going to get what my mother left behind to me? And the bitch was fuckin' in my dress? The last wonderful memory that I had with my mother?

Zara knew the pain I felt when I lost my mother. She knew how much I craved my father's love but never really got it from him. She knew the entire time that her mother was fuckin' my father. My father never acknowledged her as his daughter, or maybe he did, just not around me. Zara always looked up to my father, and I finally found out why.

Yeah, Stef was right. I had to come for my shit. She wasn't about to get it, and neither was that bitch who was supposed to be my aunt. I beat that bitch within an inch of her life. By the time Ace and his boys decided to break us up, I had a fistful of Zara's hair in my hand and Zara's blood all over my shirt. She was alive. Shit, barely. If she didn't know to respect me before, she learned that muthafuckin' day.

Chapter Fourteen

Easy

"Welcome home, bro!" Roxyn hugged the fuck out of me that rainy day in October when I walked out of the BWI Airport to one of my father's cars.

Being back in Maryland after being gone for five years was a culture shock. The shit I saw in Morocco had changed my entire mindset about life. If I wasn't a soldier before I left, I definitely was one when I came back home. I saw kids as young as 2 years old homeless and roaming the streets looking for food to feed their other siblings. I saw prostitutes as young as 6 and 7 years old selling their bodies to feed their entire family. I saw mothers selling their children to pay for drugs or medical bills. I saw mothers killing their own children because they couldn't afford to feed them.

There were kids as young as 5 in their military units, fighting to defend their communities from tribal wars. Our mission was supposed to be to stop the slave trafficking that was going on in Casablanca. Turned out, our unit was there to take over the drug territories, and that was how I caught wind of Cristobal's connect.

After I went to war with Cristobal on his own drug territory and won, my unit sent me back stateside. I was a target. Not just me, but the men who followed me that day to attack Cristobal and his crew. The team I had in place followed ya boy everywhere. They trusted me. They knew going in that some of us wouldn't make it back. Most of the men who followed me didn't have a family because their family was either murdered or they didn't know their family members because they were in the foster system.

You'd think that my commander wouldn't send me back to Maryland knowing that my biological father, whose son I had just killed, would be ready to run down on me and my crew. But the unit commander sent me right back home, right in the middle of chaos. The police department was just as corrupt as the muthafuckas they claimed to be trying to take down. It was all about money. They let the whole hood sit at the table, and everything was out of control. The police didn't know where to break the door in, shit, at their own house or in the hood.

On the flight over, I received word that Emmanuel Summers was killed. I should've known I was sent to Africa for a reason. Emmanuel was the muthafucka who profited off the money made in Morocco. The men who we ambushed were responsible for most of the money made at the casinos, restaurants, department stores, and banks owned by the Summers family. Some of these people we killed were Emmanuel's family members.

Once I found out where the headquarters was, I had one of the village people contact Cristobal and tell him the product was ready for delivery. I didn't care what I had to do to get to that muthafucka. I promised American citizenship and a job to whoever would help me get that muthafucka and whoever came with him. By the time we were done with Cristobal and his crew, the only identifiable pieces left were their teeth and a few fingers. Everything Cristobal did to Meelah, I made sure that shit was done to him. The last thing that muthafucka saw before he took his last breath was me drilling holes into his chest. The only thing that would've felt better than killing Cristobal was if I got to kill Dinero too. The muthafucka was lucky he wasn't with Dinero, or I would've killed two birds with one muthafuckin' stone.

When my unit commander (Colonel Russ) decided to send me back home to Maryland, I should have known that he had a plan in place to get rid of any problems that I would encounter back home. I wasn't stupid. I knew Emmanuel's death was no accident. I already knew going home was a setup, but I went home anyway. I needed to see the kids I FaceTimed every night who knew me as their father, and I needed to make sure Aunt Donna was safe. And I was hoping Emmanuel's death would bring his daughter home. My fathers—both biological and adoptive—knew that killing Emmanuel would bring his daughter to the forefront. And they knew that with Meelah in town, I was going to do whatever I had to do to protect her.

I could barely greet my brother that morning as my two blond children came running into me and damn near knocked me over. I wasn't there for their birth. I wasn't there when they took their first step. I wasn't there for any of their birthdays. I wasn't there on their first day of kindergarten. I never even got to hold them in my arms. I had missed five years of their lives, but at that moment, you would've thought I'd been there from day one. Majesty and Boss hugged on me like they never wanted to let me go. I knelt down and surrounded them in my arms.

"Daddy!" they cried out on my shoulder, gripping my jacket in their hands.

"Boss, Majesty, what's up? Damn, y'all got big! I see my aunt has been making sure y'all eat!" I laughed, hugging them tightly before letting them go to look into their angelic faces.

"We missed you, Daddy!" They both laughed at the same time, looking into my face as if I was the answer to all their prayers.

"I missed the both of you too. You been doin' a'ight?" I asked them, and they nodded their heads. "How is school? I know my babies are the smartest kids in class, huh?"

I heard the irritating sound of a woman clearing her throat and looked up to see Mandy standing there, hands on her hips, Fashion Nova beige leather dress painted over her curves. I'm not gonna lie, she'd gotten thick as a muthafucka over the years, probably from all the back shots she'd been getting from all the muthafuckas we knew. A fine-ass demon in a dress was what she was. She strolled over to me, face full of makeup, honey-beige skin glistening, Burberry umbrella in her hands.

The kids let go of me and looked over their shoulder at their mother as she approached us. They backed away from me a little as if they knew their mother was going to call them out for whatever petty shit she was mad at them about while I was away.

"This bitch," my brother huffed, then went over to get my bags and put them in the car.

Mandy rolled her eyes at the kids and my brother before looking into my face as I stood up from hugging my kids. She watched me take a sip from the bottle of water that I had in my hand. I guessed she figured that I was going to greet her with a friendly hello. She peeped the fact that I wasn't wearing my wedding ring, and I peeped the fact that she was wearing hers proudly.

Mandy looked hurt and disgusted at the same time, but she shook her feelings off for the moment. "BJ, tell your father what happened at school today." She shoved our son forward a little to speak up.

Boss frowned at Mandy before looking at me. "The holidays are coming up, and Miss Linda tried to tell me there's a such thing as Santa Claus, and I told her there wasn't one."

I shrugged. "And?"

"Tell him exactly what you said, now!" Mandy hissed.

Boss hesitated.

Mandy didn't have time for Boss taking his time to tell me what happened. "He told the teacher, in these exact words, 'My daddy said there ain't no goddamn Santa Claus! He said he buys everything in our muthafuckin' house. Ain't no fat muthafucka sliding down our chimney and eating up all our milk and cookies! Da fuck you thought, bruh?'"

I damn near spit my water out. I hadn't had a laugh like that in a minute. When he was about 4, I had told my son those exact words. Since I couldn't mail things from my location, for obvious reasons, I had my aunt Donna buy him the four-wheeler he wanted. He told me that he was going to write a letter to Santa to thank him for the present. I set him straight, letting him know ain't no muthafuckin' Santa Claus out this muthafucka. He was just letting his teacher know that she could save the fairy tales and shit.

"You think Boss using profanity in front of his teacher is funny, Bostyn?" Mandy snapped at me, weight shifting to one leg.

I shrugged and grabbed my kids back to me, getting them out of the rain and underneath the overhang. "It's over and done, Mandy. What do you want me to do? Maybe if you spent more time with your kids than with your homegirls, he would know what's appropriate to say at school and what's not."

Mandy huffed. "What? I need to spend more time with my kids? What do you think I've been doing the past five years while you've been doing God knows what in Africa?"

"Shopping. Clubbing. Spending money on surgeries and implants. Making new friends. Doing whatever you were doing with my son's soccer coach." I let her know that my mother had told me the shit she was into while I was away. I didn't get to call home much, but when I did, either Moms or Aunt Donna would tell me about the things that Mandy was doing. And the bitch was doing everything but raising our kids.

Mandy rolled her eyes and cleared her throat a little. "You have enough shit to be worrying about. Your father isn't happy with you." Mandy peeped Roxyn getting into the driver's seat of his car. She looked back at me. "I heard him talking to my father last night. They didn't even think it was a good idea for you to be back here in the midst of everything that's going on. You know Sable Summers is dead, right?"

I nodded, peeping at Mandy's driver getting out of the car and signaling the kids to come back to the car.

"Go on, kids. Daddy will see you back at home, okay?" Mandy told the kids and watched them scurry back to the car. Mandy looked back at my face. "They really miss you, even if they barely know you."

I watched the kids look at me one last time before getting back into the car. I looked back at Mandy, watching her look me over like she wanted to suck the meat off my bones. "Have they gotten to know my father at all, Mandy?" I asked, ignoring her sultry gaze.

Mandy looked at me like she didn't expect me to bring up the fact that I was going to help her raise kids who I knew were my adoptive father's. She hesitated. "He doesn't want to know them. As far as he's concerned, they're your kids. I'm doing what's best for them. And like I said, Sable's dead."

I nodded. "Yeah, I know."

Mandy shook her head at me. "They're going to be aiming at you next."

"Who?" I asked.

"Everyone you think you can trust," Mandy let me know.

"Bostyn, come on, man, we gotta go," Roxyn called out to me through the driver's side window.

I peeped the irritated expression on Roxyn's reflection in his sideview mirror. I looked back at Mandy. "I'm not coming home, Mandy. You know that, right? I don't give a fuck what your father has going on. I don't give a fuck what Pops has going on. Shit, I don't even give a fuck if you tell your father that my father fucked you while we were in high school and the twins are my father's kids. I just want my life back."

Mandy frowned. "So, you don't give a fuck about your kids?"

I shook my head. "That's not what I said."

"No, that is what you're saying. If you don't come home tonight, I won't let you see them again, I promise you. Your family doesn't want to deal with me in court, Bostyn," Mandy warned me. "I will take you and your father for every penny that you have!" Mandy shoved me. "Bring ya ass home tonight, Bostyn."

I watched Mandy walk away before I walked over to the passenger's side of my brother's car. I opened the door and slid into the seat, leaning my seat all the way back so I could rest my fuckin' brain. I ran my hand across my close-cut hair. I knew being at home was going to be frustrating as fuck, but I wasn't prepared to have to fight with everyone in my fuckin' life.

"Not the welcome home you expected, huh?" Roxyn scoffed.

I shook my head to myself, looking at my brother as he drove off from the curb. "Hell nah. I at least expected to see my aunt bring the kids. I thought Mandy would be off spending my money or some shit. I have enough shit on my mind, and she's talking about not letting me see the kids if I don't come home."

"Bro, go do whatever it is you wanna do tonight, then go back home to the bitch. We were going to the homecoming after-party tonight, but I think you need to stay home," Roxyn told me, knowing I was going to ask questions about the party.

"Party? Y'all still go to that homecoming shit?" I asked.

Roxyn nodded. "That shit be lit like a muthafucka. I'm sure your crew from Morocco would love to meet your crew out here. How many of them did you fly back here?"

"About twenty. Shit, the Guerillas need to get as deep as possible. With Dinero running these streets and Sable out of the way, shit is going to get hectic," I told my brother.

Roxyn glanced at me as he drove down the ramp to get onto the highway. "Yeah, I heard about your biological brother, Cristobal. I heard he was killed."

"Oh, word?" I tried my best not to grin before looking out the window.

"Yeah." Roxyn laughed a little. "Yeah, I heard his body parts were sent back stateside from Morocco. What was left of his body parts anyway. The only way the authorities identified that muthafucka was from his fingerprints and a few of his teeth. I think Pops mentioned that someone sent the muthafucka's heart to Jimena Gonzales, the muthafucka's mother!"

"Oh, is that right?" I mocked the situation.

"That muthafucka is your brother!" Roxyn exclaimed.

"*Was* my brother, Roxyn—past tense, was," I reminded him. "History. Dead. The maggots are nibbling on what was left of the muthafucka right now." I chuckled a little.

"This shit is funny to you?" Roxyn questioned.

I looked at him, watching him frown. "It was funny to him when he was beating the fuck out of someone who didn't deserve what they put her through. Whoever put a stop to his life made sure he'd never put his hands on another woman again."

"You're letting this black shit fuck with your head, bro." Roxyn huffed.

I looked at him. "What black shit? What does being black have to do with the death of a muthafucka who is lucky I let him go on breathing as long as he did?"

"I don't give a fuck how many black people you saved from Morocco. You're not black. Them muthafuckas don't give a fuck about you," Roxyn tried to tell me.

"Say what you want. I love being black. Shit kinda dangerous, but it's lit as fuck," I joked.

Roxyn looked at me and shook his head. "You're wild as fuck, bro. I'm trying to tell you that when it all comes down to it, they are going to choose each other over you. And when it comes to our family, they're going to choose money over your safety. You're back home, after they know it was you who's responsible for fuckin' up their connect in Morocco."

I looked at Roxyn, watching him make a face like he knew he'd said too much. "What?" I questioned him.

"Shit!" Roxyn muttered to himself.

"Nah, what was that you said? 'Their connect'? Those labs in Morocco, that shit was run by some of Sable's family members. Cristobal was coming to collect the drugs and the money. Pops was in on that too?" I asked my brother.

Roxyn hesitated to nod. "With Sable dead, Dinero is in charge of everything that he ran. His father, the senator, is in on it too. I have seen ya boy, Claudius, hanging around his brother, even though he told Mandy's father that he couldn't get close enough to Dinero to take him down. I'm pretty sure Pops is the one who ordered the hit on Sable. Dad is into some dirty shit, Bostyn. I don't know everything, but I know enough to know that Dad brought you home so you can go get his money."

"I ain't getting to shit but Meelah," I told my brother.

Roxyn laughed a little. "That's what they were betting on, stupid."

"Welcome home, son!" Pop greeted me with open arms when I walked into the undercover affairs unit that night.

I walked through the station, eying everyone watching the news. No matter the station they were watching, the reports were the same. The latest buzz was Emmanuel's death. Politicians were getting involved in getting justice for Emmanuel's death. The same people who were sitting there watching the news were the ones who played a part in killing him.

Claudius stood by my father's side, grinning at me as I walked through the office of people. I didn't show up to the station alone. I made sure to invite my recruits from Casablanca. They stood in the lobby of the station waiting for me. I wasn't sure who I could trust back home. A few of the men who were on my crew in Morocco seemed to sing a different tune once we touched down back in Maryland. It almost seemed as if they jumped ship. None of my homies back home were answering my calls, not even Ace.

"What's good?" I pounded Claudius before looking my father in the face. "Pops? What's the word? Why did you have me meet you here?"

Pops grinned and sat on top of his desk, facing me, fingers interlocked. "The commander said great things about you in Morocco. He said you banded together a group of about two dozen locals who would follow you to the ends of the earth and back."

I nodded. "Me and my unit helped to free several of their sisters, mothers, and wives from captivity. Some came back stateside while others sought citizenship in France. I already got them American citizenship. I thought we could give them employment here at the station. They can train. They're soldiers. They'll defend this unit with their life."

My father nodded. "All right."

I made a face, not expecting it to be that easy. "'All right'? You're in a good mood. Mom finally did it with no hands, huh?"

The unit chuckled.

Pops laughed mockingly. "You can do whatever you want with your soldiers. Camp is yours."

I just looked at him, not really registering what the fuck he was saying. "Say what?"

"He said welcome home, Captain." Claudius nudged me in my shoulder.

I just looked into my father's face. "Captain? Pops, this is—"

Pops interrupted me. "I'm stepping down and taking an office position at headquarters. We're family. It would be a conflict of interest to work in the same department."

"Five years abroad, and I come back stateside as captain of the UAD? I don't know anything about running a police department, Pops, and you know it," I told my father.

Pops disagreed. "You took over the unit in Casablanca. Your superior officers didn't know what to do in situations that they had been used to for years. You came to that city in a country where you'd never been and turned everything around. You helped bring clothes, food, and supplies to cities that were gang infested and corrupted by the local government. You helped lead rescues that brought thousands of citizens home to their families. You—"

"Led hundreds of people into a fight that could've gotten us all killed," I reminded Pops.

"But they followed you anyway, son." Pops seemed like he hated to admit it. "If they didn't believe in you, they would have let you go into that fight alone."

"Bruh, we got you," Claudius assured me. "We know the procedures, we know the paperwork, and we know the streets. You lead and we'll follow."

I heard Claudius, but I was looking my father in his face, watching him spark up a cigar as the others in the room began to pour shots of cognac.

"This is supposed to be an undercover unit, and our cover was blown. Not just by what went down in Morocco, but in this unit, too. Everyone knows we're cops," I told my father.

"And right now, that gives us leverage. Both in politics and out there on the streets. Now we're untouchable whether they trust us or not. They either work with us or end up like Cristobal. You helped us get our point across," Pops boasted.

I shook my head. "Innocent people died out there in Morocco, and the way things are going here, more innocent people are going to die."

"It's what we signed up for, sir." Claudius grinned at me, holding up his glass. "Welcome home, Captain—it's been five long years without you, bruh."

"Welcome home, Captain!" Everyone cheered me on.

"Captain Reel?" Officer Zel called out to my father. "The press is here. Darla from that journalist firm in Canada is here, said she wanted to interview you."

Pops nodded at Zel before looking back at me. "Congratulations again, son."

I wasn't feeling the situation. Over the phone the day before, Pops was pissed. I was pretty sure it wasn't his idea to step down. I fucked up when I fucked up his connect, and I was sure his fellow associates made him pay for my mistakes. Before leaving the station that evening, I approached Pops in his office. I waited until the camp was mostly clear before approaching him.

Claudius waited for me outside. We were supposed to go over to his spot that night to change and get ready for the party. I wasn't trying to party. My main concern was trying to see whether Meelah was in town, and if so, if she was okay. Her father had just died, and muthafuckas were trying to celebrate.

"Pops?" I approached Pops at his office as he got his things ready to go home.

Pops turned to me and placed his glass of Hennessy down on his desk. A drunken smirk swept across his face. "Headed to the party, son?"

I shook my head at him. "You have a ride home, Pops? You don't need to be driving drunk."

"Officer Kelly is going to drive me home, son," Pops let me know.

I laughed a little, shaking my head. "Married Officer Terra Kelly?" Yeah, that's why pops was in such a good mood. He was back to fuckin' his old partner. At one point, they were accused of having an affair, so the unit placed them at separate precincts. "You still fuckin' with Officer Kelly after you almost lost your job? After Moms almost divorced you and took everything you own, including the air you breathe? Moms is tired of these bitches. You can't keep getting away with the shit that you do. It's going to catch up to you sooner or later, Pops."

Pops grinned, taking another sip from his glass. "Is there something I can help you with?" he asked, eyebrows lowering.

"Why did you let Mandy's father put me in charge of this unit? I thought you once told me that you were trying to protect me, that you were trying to make sure I didn't have to do the same shit that you had to do, and that me and the family you forced me into were going to be safe. Why did I just watch this whole unit salute me? Why did Mandy's father just pin on my brass? Why am I promoted to captain after only being on this muthafuckin' job for five years? It took you, what, twenty years to be captain of this bullshit? How the fuck did I get this shit in five years?" I exclaimed in my father's face as he stood before me. "I see you have Claudius doing your dirty work for you. Why didn't you give the unit to him? He's finally getting to know the father he never knew. I'm sure he's got the entire senate on your side at this point. Claudius has always been more of a son to you than I've ever been. His name should've been Tom."

The grin gradually disappeared from my father's face as he set his glass back down. "You deserved this unit, son, and that's why we gave it to you."

I shook my head. "Nah, there's more to it than that. Meelah's father is dead."

Pops chuckled. "I'm well aware of that."

"You worked with the muthafucka, Pops. You're well aware of a lot," I reminded him. "Claudius told Mandy's pops that he couldn't get to Dinero, but you and I both know that Claudius is working with his brother. Shit, you're workin' with his brother too."

Pops's dark eyebrows formed into a frown. "Sable owns several buildings, warehouses, banks, and communities up and down the East Coast. We had an agreement that whatever illegal activity he was involved in, we had to know about it."

"You mean that you wanted a cut of the deal?" I asked.

Pops scoffed. "The deal was that my unit supplied the drugs and Sable had his men distribute them. Sable took the money that he made from our drugs and invested in his own labs. Started selling his own product even though he claimed that it was Stef and his crew who were the ones controlling the Rox labs. Sable did business with other drug distributors and invested into legal businesses. He stopped paying us because we'd already given him immunity. He already had investors. He already had half of my men working for him, killing muthafuckas out there for him at the drop of a hat. What use for us did he have?

"So, you had him killed?" I asked.

Pops didn't directly respond to the question. "This police department is a key asset to this community. We control a heavy influx of drugs coming in and out of this community. That's no secret."

I looked at him, hearing my father openly admit for the first time his involvement with the drug distribution ring.

"Sable worked with Stefano to get the connections that he needed, and then he worked with us—the police department and the local government—to get the protection that he needed. Once he got everything he needed from my team, he tried to branch off on his own. Make money that we didn't know about. Do things that were outside of the terms that we agreed to," Pops let me know. "Even after he swore on his life that he was no longer working with Stefano, turns out he was still doing business with Cristobal. Cristobal did business with some of his own father's competition. Once I found out about Sable's connect in Morocco, I met up with Cristobal and told him that I wanted in. Do you know how much of the police department's money I put into that shit?"

I looked into my father's face, realizing then that shit was about to get real, and real fast. That I was more involved than I realized.

"This is your unit now. You get to clean this shit up. You get the privilege of making our money back. I don't give a fuck how you do it as long as you do it and do that shit fast. Troy is meeting up with the funeral director at the Summers Funeral Home tomorrow to plan Sable's funeral," Pops started to explain when I cut him off.

"Why isn't his right-hand man, Dinero, handling that shit? Why the fuck is she planning his funeral? She never gave a fuck about that muthafucka." I watched Pops scoff.

"Sable and Troy were married a few weeks ago."

I stared at him in confusion.

"I'm pretty sure your little girlfriend looked the same way when she found out. Sable has been fuckin' Troy since before Meelah was born, Bostyn. Troy invested into our police department too and thought she owned us," my father told me.

"She's the one who had Meelah's mother killed. You helped that bitch kill her own sister." I looked into my father's face as he picked up his glass and put it to his lips to take the last sip.

Pops looked at me like I was crazy as I snatched the glass from his hands and threw that muthafucka against the wall. Pops sat down on the top of his desk, facing me, trying to keep his drunken composure. "That bitch you love so much is heir to businesses that she has no idea that her father invested into. If she's smart, she won't let her aunt—or should I say stepmom—have what was meant for her mother. She's not about to let her aunt continue to do business with us. Meelah is going to do whatever she can to fuck up her aunt's ties with us. Meelah will probably go to Stef for help. If Meelah decides to go after her father's businesses, Meelah is about to be our biggest competition. Her father's people in Morocco will be reaching out to her. And something tells me that Stef will be reaching out to you to take over his son's territories. Take Meelah out so we can take over. You fucked up my plans for the drug channels in Morocco. You owe me this shit!"

"How the fuck was I supposed to know that was your shipment that I was fuckin' up? How was I supposed to know that the entire reason you put my life in fuckin' danger out there was for money?" I yelled.

Pops stood from the desk and pushed me. "It's always about the fuckin' money! I guarantee you that Stef is about to work overtime to get you on his side."

"After I sent his son's heart back to him full of holes?" I scoffed. "I doubt it."

"Stef wants his empire back. That's all that matters to him. He knew his son's days were numbered. Stef is more interested in getting his hands on Sable's connections than avenging Cristobal. His only concern right now is avenging the loss of you, Bostyn," Pops told me.

"The fuck are you talking about?" I questioned. "He doesn't give a fuck about me. He had years to find me, and he left me with you, knowing you're the reason my mother is dead." I looked into Pops's face, letting him know that I blamed him for everything that went wrong in my life.

"It's because of me that you're even still alive," Pops growled. "I protected you from the life that the girl you love so much had to live! These muthafuckas kill their own children to survive! Look what Sable let happen to his own daughter!"

"And look what you let happen to me!" I pushed my father back into his desk, fighting the urge to pull out the gun I had at my waist. "Your beef with Stefano is the reason my mother is dead! You had your wife raising your side-chick's son! And now you got me raising your side-chick's kids, too! I don't want any parts of this shit!"

"You should have thought about it when you decided to kill a major link in The Chain, Bostyn. I'm trying to protect you from people in this unit who didn't even want you to get back home in one piece!" Pops shouted at the top of his lungs. "I had Sable killed so that you could make it home with no one at your head. Everyone would be too distracted with his funeral to think about you coming back here. The funeral is happening this weekend. That gives you until Monday to make things right."

"What is it that you think I'm about to do to help you?" I asked.

"It's about helping Meelah. You see, if you don't jump on board with this squadron and take over The Chain's operation, I'll make sure she ends up lying in a hole right next to her father. I don't give a fuck what you have to do to get my millions back, but you have three days to do that shit. If you think I won't kill your girlfriend the day she buries her father, try me," Pops warned.

"The unit is hookin' you up like a muthafucka, I see," I commented as I stepped through the door of Claudius's executive suite at the Four Seasons in Baltimore that night.

Claudius grinned, walking through the suite, arms stretched out. "In a few hours, there will be bitches everywhere. I plan on dippin' my dick in at least eight pussies tonight. About to celebrate my nigga being home. I saw a few of them hoes on your unit from Morocco. Them hoes are bad as fuck. Invite 'em up."

"Nah, bruh. They're soldiers, not pussy. And they don't play the games you play. They will fuck you up. Cut ya dick off and eat that bitch in front of you," I warned him. "Stay away from my squad, muthafucka."

"Man, whatever. I'm about to get fucked up before we head out to this party. The drinks at this club cost like eight fuckin' dollars for a shot. Meelah's aunt is fuckin' trippin'," Claudius huffed.

I shook my head and went over to the couch where my outfit for the night lay draped across the chair. Aunt Donna had the birthday present that she'd bought for me that year but never got to send it to me delivered to the hotel. A Fendi outfit. Brown button-down shirt. Dark denim jeans. Dark brown shoes. Jacket and hat to match. My hitta. Aunt Donna knew my taste more than my own parents cared to notice. I wasn't really in the mood to pop out that night, but since I was going out, I had to make sure I stepped out fresh.

"How does it feel being home?" Claudius asked, kicking off his shoes in the middle of the floor.

I eyed the fire crackling in the fireplace before looking around the room at all the liquor, jewelry, and money lying around. "Feels a'ight. Yo, why do you have money and shit lying around? You trust ya crew like that? I know you have ya crew in this muthafucka. And why the hell are you in a hotel?"

"Man," Claudius said, walking over to the bar, "shit has been crazy. I'm not really on good terms with the crew right now. I'ma need you to talk to Ace for me."

I was confused. "Since when haven't you been cool with Ace?"

"Since Keith was killed." Claudius hesitated to look up at me because he knew I was going to pop the fuck off. "Now, before you go jumping to conclusions—"

"You had ya boy killed over a bitch?" I shouted, walking up to him at the bar. "Over Tajha? That ho whose own crew doesn't even trust her?"

Claudius's temples twitched. "Nigga, I ain't do shit. He got killed in a shootout."

"Yeah, a shootout that I'm sure you had something to do with," I snarled at him. "Keith has been ya boy since the first grade! Tajha has been fuckin' every muthafucka on the CMC! I'm sure you brought her around the station, huh? Whatever she hears that goes down at the station, I'm sure she runs back and tells Dinero!"

"Dinero is working with us, muthafucka." Claudius clicked his teeth.

"For how long? Until some shit doesn't go his way?" I shook my head at Claudius's dumb ass. "That muthafucka doesn't fuck with you! The only reason he even tolerates you is that I hear your father finally decided to acknowledge you. The media coverage is that the casino and the other businesses that Dinero ran with Sable needed the senator's appearances to make that shit look completely legit. Politicians on their side makes them more powerful. You're supposed to be reporting everything that goes down with them muthafuckas back to the UAD. Do you do that shit, Claudius? Nah. But I'm sure whatever Tajha sees, she goes back and tells them. They don't trust you, dumb ass!" I shoved Claudius. "They're using you, and you're too blind to see that shit! Keith is your brother!"

"Nah, Dinero is my brother, nigga." Claudius shoved me back.

I laughed to keep from punching that idiot in his face. "After what he did to Meelah, you'd fuck with that muthafucka? You know what that girl means to me! He damn near killed her! He had muthafuckas stomp my baby out of her!"

"You should've never fucked with another nigga's girl," Claudius told me.

"The only reason your brother is alive is that I couldn't get to him! If he had shown his face in Morocco, Cristobal would've had some company on his way down to hell, muthafucka! You better enjoy your time with your brother now, Claudius, I'm warning you. You didn't have to do your boy Keith like that, and you know it!" I yelled.

Claudius shook his head. "Man, fuck Keith. Keith is dead. You're still alive, nigga. Move the fuck on. Take care of your wife and leave the past in the past."

I couldn't believe that muthafucka. Yeah, he'd always been a fuckin' hater. We had the sibling rivalry game on lock. But what he was on, five years later, was some other shit. It was like I didn't even know him.

"I don't know you," I told him. "This shit changed you, bruh."

"Life is supposed to change you, muthafucka." Claudius poured himself a glass of Hennessy.

"Bruh, you have been here stateside, living it up in five-star hotels and shit!" I stretched out my arms, showing him his lavish lifestyle. "I've been overseas living in the villages with people who didn't even have clean water to drink! Who wore the same muthafuckin' outfit until their pants had a hole so big they didn't even have to unzip their pants to piss or take a shit! I've seen mothers blow their own children's heads off because they couldn't afford to feed them or get them the health care they needed! I had to kill fathers who were raping their daughters! I had to kill children who walked into our villages with bombs strapped to them! I had to amputate legs and dig bullets out of muthafuckas! I gouged muthafuckas' eyes out with my bare hands! Half of my squad was murdered in cold blood when they followed me to Cristobal's spot!

"Don't you tell me about life changing a muthafucka, bruh! I'm still me! I ain't switching up for no muthafucka! You can't put a price on peace! The hell that I've been through should've created a fuckin' monster! But my heart still beats the same! I've been knee-deep in hell since birth, and I'm still that same Bostyn Emilio Zachariah Reel I've always been! Easy until the day I leave this muthafucka!"

Claudius scoffed. "Always trying to school a muthafucka. You ain't the only one who's been through hell. I'm trying to get out of this muthafucka. When everything is said and done, after your pops is done using us, what do you think he's gonna do with us, huh? I'm not his son, and technically, neither are you."

I just looked at Claudius, who had a point. But regardless, there was no way I was going to trust a muthafucka who would rape and beat his own girlfriend in front of her father. "Fuck all that. I'm gone for five years and look at you—teaming up with a muthafucka who, at one point, you wouldn't even acknowledge as family. What is he offering you that the unit isn't?"

"Protection," Claudius growled.

"You had that with the Guerillas!" I told him.

Claudius shook his head. "Not anymore. That's why I need you to talk to Ace. He'll listen to you. He won't listen to me or anything that I stand for. He doesn't trust your father. Meelah's cousin Zara even tried to convince the nigga to work with us. He won't budge."

Just then, there was a forceful knock on the door.

Claudius looked at me before walking to the door, drinking his glass of Hennessy down to the last drop. He peeped through the peephole and exhaled deeply before peeping back at me.

I frowned, already knowing who it was by the way he only opened the door slightly instead of just letting the muthafucka in. "Just let the muthafucka in." I already had my gun cocked and in my hands at that point.

Claudius reluctantly let Dinero into the hotel room with about four tall muthafuckas. "A'ight, Easy, chill," Claudius told me, already knowing I was waiting for the chance to get face-to-face with Dinero after five years of wanting to blow his brains out the back of his head.

Dinero chuckled a little. "I ain't got no beef with you, Li'l Pump."

Dinero's hittas laughed with him.

Claudius's dumb ass stood between us.

I looked into Claudius's face, extending my arm, and aiming my Glock 38 at his face. "Muthafucka, you think I won't shoot the muthafucka with you standing between us? I'll shoot a hole through your head and pull the other gun I have in my pants out and shoot ya brother at the same time. I'll send both of y'all asses to hell together! Move, bruh, I'm telling you."

"You seen ya girl since you been in town, Easy? Did you know she was here for the funeral?" Dinero said over Claudius's shoulder.

"Whose funeral? Yours, homie?" I responded.

"Nah, her own, nigga," Dinero replied. "I'm surprised your unit hasn't called you yet. There's a warrant out for her arrest. She put her cousin Zara in the hospital."

I lowered my gun, watching Claudius look back at Dinero before moving out of the way to let us talk face-to-face. "The fuck are you talking about?"

"Meelah went over to Ace's crib to confront Zara. I don't even know what the bitch was doing over there when she was supposed to be helping her moms get everything ready for the party at the club." Dinero looked at me, he and his crew watching the way I gripped my gun in my hand, ready to start popping muthafuckas as soon as they said the wrong thing.

The way I was feeling, I would have at least gotten three or four of them before they even got to their guns to aim at ya boy.

"Meelah must've found out about her and Zara being sisters." Claudius peeped the surprised expression on my face. “Knowing her cousin’s mouth, the words came out reckless.”

“It don’t matter,” Dinero told Claudius. “Zara was supposed to talk Meelah into signing over the casino and a few banks to her. Sable didn’t leave shit to Zara. Never even acknowledged her as his own. As of right now, Meelah owns half of my shit. We got rid of her father, and now it’s time to get rid of Meelah. Arrest that bitch.” Dinero looked back at me, watching my face turn red and my jawline twitch. “Arrest your girl before she gets buried with her father.”

Claudius nodded in agreement.

Man, it’s always the muthafuckas who you fuck with the hardest who show you that you gotta watch who you fuck with. I knew it was only a matter of time before I had to choose between someone I considered my brother and the woman I considered my soul mate. A few hours to be exact.

Chapter Fifteen

Meelah

"How do I look?" I asked Sharita, standing in the mirror and smoothing out my Vera Wang nude minidress.

"Like someone who just beat a bitch's ass." Sharita exhaled deeply, smoothing out my hair and eying the bun on top of my head. "Stop shaking so much."

"You already know someone over at Ace's crib called the police on me," I said, standing in the mirror of the bathroom at the club.

"I told you that we should've just left town, but no, you wanted to come here to confront your aunt. What do you think she's gonna do when she finds out you busted her daughter's face wide the fuck open? You won't even make it to the bail review hearing on Monday! She'll make sure you die while you're in lockup! What if the police come here looking for you? They're probably already here!" Sharita was more nervous than I was. "I can't lose you again, Meelah! You just got home! What were you thinking? Why didn't you just let me get some of the girls at the club who don't like the bitch to fuck her up?"

"Because she's my problem, Sharita," I told her.

Sharita shook her head. "Nah, she's our problem," Sharita told me. "Talk to your aunt in the office, and then I'm taking you to my crib in Columbia. Moms ain't home. She's with family back home, mourning her son. Not even realizing her daughter needs her too." Sharita's bright brown eyes sparkled. "I'm sick of living like this, Meelah. But if I run, they'll kill me. We have no protection. There's no way to know who to trust. Friends have become enemies and enemies have started teaming up. We have to be careful." Sharita peeped over her shoulder as a few girls made their way inside.

It didn't surprise me that Tajha showed her face that day in the bathroom. I tried to hide the fact that I wanted to choke her with that cheap-ass lace front, but my facial expressions didn't have an inside voice.

Sharita grabbed my arm, already knowing what was on my mind. "Meelah, you need to turn down for everything right now!" she muttered through her clenched teeth. "Ya cousin is laid up at the hospital."

Tajha grinned as her crew walked in with her, making their way to the bathroom stalls. "Your mama-auntie is looking for you, boo. She said your sister-cousin is in the hospital. Any idea how she got there?"

"Hell nah," Sharita grunted.

"Hell yeah," I responded as Sharita nudged me in my side.

Tajha shook her head. "You know your cousin has been keeping Dinero's dick wet while you've been gone, just so you know."

I rolled my eyes. "I couldn't care less what the fuck either of the two do with their body parts, Tajha. I'm just here to bury my father and get back everything that would've been my mom's if she were still alive. This club, the casinos, the banks, the houses, the funeral homes, every fuckin' thing. Everything that my father ran belongs to me whether I know what to do with the shit or not. Dinero is going to fuck up my father's entire operation!"

Tajha scoffed. "What do you care? The nigga never cared anything about you or the bitch who's standing next to you."

I peeped the hurt expression on Sharita's face before looking back at Tajha.

"Her name wasn't anywhere on those deeds. She should be getting a portion of her father's legacy too." Tajha smirked at the shocked expression on my face.

"Shut up, Tajha," Sharita growled.

"Did you ask Sharita where she was the day your father was killed? Did Sharita tell you that her mother finally admitted that Sable was her father? Did she tell you she was at that press conference the day your father was killed? Bet she didn't tell you that Claudius got rid of the murder weapon that had her prints, did she?"

It was me grabbing Sharita's arm that time.

"He let his own daughter get raped, and he didn't do shit about it!" Sharita pulled away from me. "Fuck acknowledging me. He never acknowledged her! When Claudius asked me to off that nigga, hell yeah, I didn't hesitate to blend in with the crew who ran up in there to take him out! If no one else was going to take him out for what he did to Meelah, then I sure as hell was! I shot him dead in his face! And I would do that shit again! I know it was a setup for the police department to use it as blackmail, but I didn't care! Meelah has been gone for five fuckin' years because you all pushed her away!"

Tajha shook her head at Sharita. "Well, you killing her father brought Meelah back just so the muthafuckas who told you to kill him could kill her too, dummy."

Sharita's hard exterior softened a little before she let out a heavy sigh. "She's my homegirl, the only one who ever really looked out for me. I'd die for her."

Tajha nodded. "Looks to me like you're about to die with her, boo."

I tugged on Sharita's arm. "Come on, Sharita. We gotta get out of here. Fuck my aunt."

Before we could make it halfway down the hallway, all I saw were my father's henchmen coming my way with who looked like Claudius and probably a few members from his unit. And just when we thought we could turn around and walk the other way, Dinero was coming toward us with members of his crew and my aunt. We were fucked.

Aunt Troy approached me, Prada stiletto heels tapping against my marble floor. Her dark brown eyes glossed over as she glared into my face. "Is there a reason why my daughter is in intensive care? You had no—"

Aunt Troy barely got her words out when I spit in her face. Her henchmen on both sides of us immediately pulled out their guns on me, but my aunt laughed devilishly and put her hand up, signaling them to back down.

"You have every right to be mad at me, but not Zara. It's not her fault that your father got me pregnant then married your mother instead of me. It isn't her fault that he only acknowledged you as his child. And it damn sure wasn't her fault that he was still fuckin' me while he was married to your mother but never left her for me." Aunt Troy wiped her face. "All this shit was supposed to be mine, not your mother's. And not yours."

I glanced at Dinero, whose finger was over the trigger of his gun. "I thought you loved me, and this entire time you just wanted to destroy me. You helped tear me down all these years. I trusted you! After everything my father let happen to me, you'd marry him? And now you're working with Dinero? The same muthafucka who murdered my baby? You wanted me as far away from here as possible so you could get in good with my father and take over my mother's life! You had her killed so you could have my father! It wasn't just you he was fuckin'!

He was fuckin' Whitley's mom! Not to mention Sharita's mother! She's my sister, too!"

Aunt Troy glared at Sharita.

"So, I guess that's why the bitch murdered Sable, huh?" Dinero spoke up. "Because he wouldn't claim her. Because he let Cristobal get away with fuckin' on his little sister all these years."

Sharita stepped in front of me, glaring at my aunt before looking over her shoulder at Dinero. "I didn't kill anyone."

Dinero scoffed. "Your gun was in a dumpster right outside the crime scene. And they got you on camera walking into the building and putting your mask on."

Sharita shook her head. "I have no idea what you're talking about. I wasn't there. I don't know who killed him, but whoever killed him had good aim. I heard the person got the nigga right between his thick-ass eyebrows." Sharita looked at my aunt. "You lied to your niece, bitch."

"And your mother lied to you." Aunt Troy looked Sharita over. "The bitch had children with both sides of the game. She fucked her way into the game. I earned my spot. I stayed loyal to Sable. I was a judge. I kept him out of prison. It's because of my affiliation with this police department that the bastard didn't die in prison years ago! I'm the reason that he had immunity! I'm the reason why this whole operation stayed intact so long!"

"And you're the reason his daughter was raped by the nigga standing behind you and the muthafucka who my mother always loved more than me. You were supposed to take care of your niece, not join the muthafuckas who want her father's spot!" Sharita shouted.

One of Dinero's men took out handcuffs.

I looked over my shoulder at one of Claudius's men juggling handcuffs in his hands as well.

"We meet with the lawyer bright and early tomorrow morning to go over your father's assets. Out of guilt, he left everything to you, Meelah." My aunt looked over Sharita's shoulder at me. "My daughter is hanging on for her life right now. I'm leaving the party in Tajha's hands until I get back from the hospital. Zara is all I have, and you beat the life out of her! Sign over everything your father owns to me, and I might make sure you live while you're in prison."

"Sharita doesn't deserve to be in jail. She was set up!" I told my aunt, pulling Sharita back as the man with the cuffs stepped forward to grab Sharita.

"It's okay, *hermana.*" Sharita chuckled at the situation. "God doesn't like ugly. They'll get what they deserve. Don't give her a muthafuckin' thing!"

I tried to reach for her when I felt a jerk on my arm before my wrists were tightly cuffed. I cringed at the feel of the cold metal on my wrists.

"Take her to the car," Claudius snarled.

I huffed as I was pushed forward by one of the men with Claudius. Claudius and a few of his men followed us while a few led in front and out the back entrance of the club. My heart slammed against my chest as we made our way toward the garage. I didn't trust Claudius. They'd set Sharita up to kill our father so they could put the blame on her. They wanted to take over my father's operation, and they wanted me out of the way so they could do that without any issues.

"Take her back to the station," Claudius told one of his men. "I gotta get back to this party. I didn't get fresh to spend all night at the station doing paperwork. Make sure Jimmie gets to personally talk to the bitch. I'm sure he'd like to meet the woman who has his son's head all fucked up."

Before the agent could even shove me in the car good enough, a few cars came zooming into the garage where they were parked. I gasped as the agent who shoved me into the car slammed the door behind me. I peeped over the headrest at the people getting out of the car. Men and women jumped out of the car, guns already drawn on Claudius and their crew. The crazy part was these people were jumping out of police cars, too.

"The fuck y'all muthafuckas doing here?" Claudius pulled out his gun but was reluctant to extend his arms when one of the women in the crew cocked her pistol, walking up to him, arms stretched out and gun aiming right at his face.

"Captain Reel said to let her go," the woman growled in a foreign accent.

Claudius made a face. "Captain Reel? The same nigga who told me to bring her to the station?" Claudius paused before laughing out loud. "You're not talking about Jimmie. You're talking about Easy's stupid ass. Yo, tell the nigga that we came to do the job that his bitch-ass couldn't—"

He could barely get the words out before she shot the person standing next to him in his head. The men watched his body drop to the floor before aiming their guns at the woman.

The woman didn't back down. "He told me to kill you if I have to, to get her from you. Stand the fuck back and give her to me."

I watched as a few of Dinero's hittas stepped off the garage elevator. Once they peeped the situation, they didn't hesitate to start spraying. And Claudius's men followed suit. I ducked down in the back of the car, covering my ears to block out the deafening sound of bullets flying around the garage. I thought the madness would never cease. I just knew one of those deadly bullets would pierce through the car and put an end to my life. My life was already over anyway. They'd gotten Sharita. They'd set her up for my father's death.

Sharita had waited her entire life to put an end to my father. Our families never really cared about us. We were all we had, and I left her. I should've never left her. I had to get her back. She wouldn't survive in jail. They'd kill her the way they did my mother, and they'd get away with it for sure. Just when I thought I was going to die in the back seat of that police car, the back door flew open and I was snatched out.

I didn't even have time to see who'd snatched me out of the car. I ducked down outside of the car. I looked up to see two beautiful rich-chocolate young women alongside me, firing back at the people firing at us. One of them grabbed me, telling me to stay down as she pulled me off to a black Lexus with limo-tinted windows. She shoved me in the back seat as she and the other girl hopped in behind me and slammed the door behind them. The driver sped out through the garage. We all struggled to catch our breath.

"*Makek?*" The girl up front in the passenger seat asked me.

I looked at her in confusion, trying to figure out what language she was speaking.

"It's Moroccan Arabic," I heard Easy's voice say from the driver's seat. "She's asking if you're okay, li'l baby."

I gasped and sat up in my seat, watching Easy pull his dark hood from over his head. "Easy!" I squealed, and he grinned.

"We have to go back and get Sharita!" I yelled at Easy as one of the women with Easy grabbed me by the handcuffs, pulling me along with them.

I followed them into a huge mansion, which was in a neighborhood not too far from Jimena's place in Columbia.

"Sharita will be fine in custody. I brought back plenty of help from Casablanca. I have some on the force, some as security guards in a few jails and prisons, and even some posing as inmates," Easy told me. "They're using Sharita as bait, hoping one of us would come after her. I pulled you out because they were going to kill you, leaving your aunt with everything."

"Where am I?" I asked Easy as I stopped in the huge corridor, watching a few maids walk by. I noticed family portraits in the halls. "Easy, this is your place! You brought me back to your place?"

Easy signaled a few of his soldiers to give us some privacy. "I brought you to one of my mom's houses. It's the last place anyone would think to look for you. They wouldn't expect me to bring you here."

I looked at the woman who was gripping my wrist in her hands. "Uncuff me," I hissed at her.

The woman glared at me before looking at Easy for clarification.

Easy shook his head. "Nah, Anisah."

"They have my fuckin' sister!" I screamed at Easy.

Easy looked at me, his eyebrows lowering.

"Jimena had children with Stef and my father! Sharita is the one who shot my father! They set her up! They're going to kill her, Easy! Please!" I tried to break my wrists free.

Anisah sighed heavily and stepped to the side as Easy approached me.

Easy backed me up to the wall, even though I was trying my best to break free from the handcuffs. I was fighting so hard to get out of the cuffs that Easy had to pin me against the wall. "Meelah, chill!"

"What happened to me is going to happen to her! No! I won't chill, Easy!" I screamed.

"Meelah, I missed you so much!" Easy yelled at me, eyes tracing my face. His voice was forceful yet embracing at the same time.

My heart was beating so fast that I thought I was going to pass the fuck out. But I didn't. His voice was soothing to my soul. I hadn't seen him in so long. Everything was happening so fast that we didn't even get the chance to embrace the fact that, after five years, we were finally in each other's presence again. But the moment he told me that he missed me, all those feelings that I felt on the dance floor five years earlier came seeping back. And I stopped trying to fight my wrists free.

"I missed your smile. I missed your voice. I missed your hair. I missed your touch. I missed your white-boy jokes. I missed the way you feel. I missed your everything, Meelah!" Easy told me, shoving me back into the wall. "And you got me fucked up if you think I'm about to let you go after Sharita! I just told you that she'd be fine!"

"Your crew just shot up cops!" I reminded him, looking up into his handsome face. He'd changed so much, but damn if he didn't change for the better.

"We're cops too, boo," Easy told me. "This is Sergeant Anisah Abdella. Her crew is already in place at the women's correctional facility in Jessup, waiting for Sharita. I already knew the deal. I overheard Dinero and Claudius talking about having Sharita arrested for killing Sable. They wanted me to have you arrested. They knew I wouldn't do it. Trust me, they were expecting me, but they weren't expecting my crew."

"They're going to come after you," I told him.

Easy scoffed. "Let them come. I'm ready. Been ready."

"Your father, Stefano, wants you on his team. Maybe you oughta join him," I was reluctant to say.

Easy frowned. "You never want me to take these cuffs off, do you?"

I sighed heavily. "He wants you to take over Cristobal's territory in Morocco. You already got a team here to help you out there."

"Yeah, a team who doesn't want to go the fuck back to fuckin' Morocco. Nah, I'm not doing it. He can figure out another way. And you shouldn't come back here!" Easy exclaimed. "I hope you don't think with all of this shit going on that I'm about to let you go to that funeral."

My heart dropped in my chest. "Easy, he was my father," I finally said.

Sharita was right. It did hurt. Even though I'd told her that I was just back for business, a part of me wanted to see his face again. My phone was in the back of the cop car that Easy's soldiers had pulled me out of. I knew Darla was blowing my phone up. I was sure she'd gotten the news of the shootout that went down in that garage. She probably thought I was dead. That she'd be attending not just my father's funeral, but mine too. "Easy, you're really not going to let me see my father?" I asked him again.

Easy just looked down into my face like he wasn't about to entertain my question with a response. That "you got me fucked up" handsome expression on Easy's face had my heart jumping in my chest. I was angry at him yet turned on at the same time.

"Easy, I haven't been home in five years! Maybe if I stayed home, he wouldn't be dead! This is my fault!" I screamed.

"If you had stayed home, you would've been dead five years ago!" Easy had to remind me. "Do you not remember what they did to you? Do you not remember what your father let happen to you? These muthafuckas told me that your father walked the fuck out while he let Dinero do what the fuck he wanted to 'punish' you for having my baby! What happened to you is my fuckin' fault! All of this shit is my fuckin' fault! If I'd just done what my father told me to do, then your boy wouldn't have even been so caught up on taking over your father's shit. Then your father wouldn't have been so caught up on taking over my father's shit! All this shit is happening because two people who weren't supposed to love each other fell in love!"

I looked up into Easy's face, the tears finally coming down.

"I love you, Meelah. I prayed for you, Meelah. I couldn't help that Dinero's girl was the girl I'd been praying for. I needed you, and I just couldn't stay away. And I'm sorry." Easy held my face in his hands, drying my tears.

"Take these cuffs off, please," I cried.

Easy looked my face over a little. "Sergeant, give us some time."

Anisah nodded. "We have crew scattered around the neighborhood. I'll be outside. Take all the time you need. But, sir, we need to get her out of here. You know your wife will be searching high and low until she finds you."

I rolled my eyes as Anisah gave me the side-eye before walking through the corridor and out the door.

Easy took his phone out of his pocket and chuckled at the display. "What?" I asked him.

"Claudius made it through the shootout. The mutha-fucka is blowing up my phone." Easy grinned and put his phone back in his pocket. "We're in a lot of trouble, li'l baby." He grabbed me by the cuffs and led me into the living room.

The living room was lavish and extravagant, like something on an old black-and-white movie. Expensive as Easy's family's taste was, the living room was still inviting and comfortable. Standing there in that living room, I felt like I was standing in the middle of a house in Italy. The wooden end tables and coffee tables were hand carved. The furniture was wrapped in expensive beige Italian leather. Silk cream-colored drapes hung over the windows. The crystal chandelier in the center of the cathedral ceiling captured the light of its candle bulbs perfectly. A Fire Line Automatic fireplace fit right into the recess in the stone wall. A white fluffy silk rug lay in front of the fireplace. The place felt like home because it reminded me of the mansion my aunt was trying to steal from my mother. I had to get out of those cuffs.

Easy was Fendi down that night, looking like he was ready to hit the clubs hard. We all were supposed to attend the homecoming party, but I fucked that up when I fucked up my cousin's face. I stood there in my fitted dress, watching Easy undress down to his boxers. He had more tattoos inked over his skin than I'd remembered. He was trying to hide his war wounds behind the tattoos, but I could still see them. He even had two M&Ms holding hands over his heart.

I laughed a little. "What's with the M&Ms? Is it because everyone's always clowning on you, calling you Eminem?"

Easy shook his head as he walked back up to me, pulling me closer to him by my dress. "Nah. I couldn't put Meelah and Magic on my chest, so I put two—" Easy stopped talking when I began to cry. "I know this is a lot to take in. I'm not taking those cuffs off, Meelah, because I already know you're going to try to run. Your aunt wants everything your name is on, and she'll kill you to get the shit. Her daughter isn't going to make it, baby. Ace hit me up. Said that you cracked that girl's skull."

"She hit a touchy subject. She always did have a mouth on her." I rolled my eyes.

"I'm not one to run from a fight, but I gotta get you out of here. Where you been all these years, ma? I'll take you back there," Easy suggested.

"I can't go back to Canada. Turns out I've been working for Dinero's aunt the whole time. He'll blackmail her to find me at this point." I looked Easy's face over. I missed him so much.

Easy looked my face over too before loosening his grip on my dress a little. "They're going to come after us. We need to change clothes, grab a few guns and extra clips, and roll out. I'm sorry about everything."

I looked down at his hand, noticing there was no ring. I looked back into his face. "You divorced yet?"

Easy grinned. "Nah, but it's coming."

"How are your kids?" I asked.

Easy's grin vanished. "You mean my father's kids?"

My eyes widened. "What are you talking about?"

"Boss and Majesty are Jimmie's kids, not mine. But I love them anyway. I have to because neither of their parents do. Soon as this chaos is over—if it's ever over—I'm taking them with me," Easy told me.

"Where would you take them?" I asked.

"I don't know yet. Same place I'm taking you."

I wanted his hands all over me, but all I could think about was the sound that his keys made when he put his phone and keys down on the coffee table a few seconds earlier. His crew was outside. They weren't going to leave him. How was I going to escape him? How could I get him to take the cuffs off? If saving Sharita meant giving my aunt the keys to my father's kingdom, then I had to give her what she wanted.

"We met this same day five years ago," I told Easy.

Easy looked at me as he sat down on the couch behind him. "Facts. I knew the day I met you that you were the perfect one for me. There wasn't shit anyone could tell me that day that could convince me that you weren't mine. I was in a war that I was running from. You were the peace that I needed to run to."

I laughed a little as Easy bent over to unbuckle the straps of my heels before watching me step out of them. "There is nothing peaceful about being with me, as you can see. I've never dated anyone brave enough to love me until you."

"You're soft but strong, with a good heart. You're honest and unapologetic. You're the type of woman you go to war beside, li'l baby. Dinero is a fool to go against you. We can win this shit, I promise you," Easy tried to tell me.

My heart didn't want him involved in any way.

"I didn't have a heart before you, ma, I promise you, but there was something about the way you touched me that day on that dance floor that had me feeling some type of way. I had this whole life planned out for us in my head. I was going to create heaven for you because you were like an angel." Easy grabbed me by the handcuffs and pulled me onto his lap. He licked his lips as he watched me straddle his waist, my dress hiking up around my hips. "Dinero didn't like that shit. Everything was all fun and games until he saw another muthafucka making his girl smile. He hurt you, and I'm going to heal you. I'm in love with you, Meelah. Five years apart doesn't change that. I ain't been doing nothing but fighting my way back to you for five years."

"These chocolate Playboy Bunnies seem to feel some type of way about you. The bitch was looking at you like you were Tarzan or some shit. Like she wanted to have your babies." I glared into his face and watched him chuckle. "You didn't fuck her? Or anyone else?"

Easy shook his head, his laughter fading. "Nah. I couldn't even think about fuckin' when I was trying to survive. I had to make it back to you. Sharita got in touch with me a few times to let me know you were safe. That's all that mattered to me. A piece of me died that day in Texas when I held our baby in my hands. I wanted to build a family with you. I needed you, and no one wanted that. I knew that being together would be a problem, but I wanted to face that problem with you. I wanted you, all of you. The good, the bad, the in-between. Do you still love me, Meelah?"

I felt my eyes growing misty again. "Take these cuffs off me, Easy. Please."

Easy looked in my face for a few seconds before gripping my hips and scooting to the edge of the couch to grab his keys. He didn't unlock my cuffs just yet. He tossed the keys to the other end of the sofa. I watched him as he slid my dress up and over my head then tossed the dress on the same end of the couch as the keys. I looked into his face as he unhooked my strapless bra and tossed it over with my dress. I lifted my booty a little from his lap, and he slid off his boxers and kicked them off to the floor.

I looked down at his dick, eyes widening at the way it had thickened and stretched over the years. Before I could remind him that his bitch army was waiting outside for him, he gripped my waist, pulled my panties to the side, and eased me down onto his dick. My body opened up around him as he pressed me down until his dick tapped against my cervix before making its way to the pocket behind it. Easy watched the beads of sweat line my hairline as my pussy adjusted snuggly around his dick.

"Fuck!" we both hollered.

And just went I thought Easy was going to lie back and let me wild out on the dick, he pumped back, knocking on my cervix like it owed him rent money. I'm talking like I was three months behind on rent and the sheriff was at my fuckin' door. My heart was going wild, singing like a caged bird. There was no better feeling than when he wrapped me in his arms, my body intertwined with his. But I pushed him off me, hands pressed against his chest as I rode his dick.

"Answer my fuckin' question, Meelah," Easy growled, sitting up and gripping my waist.

I wrapped my arms around his shoulders as my wrists started to ache from the cuffs.

Easy watched my hips. "You know I love it when you slow wind on me, but I haven't had pussy in five years, baby. Fuck this slow shit. Let me drill ya shit."

I gasped as Easy held on tight, turning our bodies around so that we were lying on the couch, my body under his. He pulled out of me, fingers slipping between my thighs to feel the juices flowing between my legs. My pussy was wet like a Slip 'N Slide. The nigga pulled my panties off so fast that he damn near ripped them from my body. I wrapped him in my legs as he slipped back inside of me. It seemed like that dick was throbbing to the beat of my heart.

"Now, this is what it really means to slip into something more comfortable." Easy kissed my lips and sucked on them a little. "I asked you if you fuckin' loved me."

"It hurts to love someone, Easy," I admitted.

"Yeah, but with the right person, love can be beautiful." Easy kissed me and slid his hands over my body. "I can love you hard. I can love you crazy. I can love you for the whole world to see, Meelah. Do you love me? Because I have enough love in me for us both."

I nodded. "You know I love you, Easy."

"That's what I needed to hear. I thought about you every day while I was away. I told myself that if I ever saw you again, I'd never let you go," Easy growled at me.

I hissed and moaned as Easy unwrapped my legs from around him and threw them over his shoulders. My pussy sighed as he started to dig into my soul. He held me tight while he made love to me, making me feel a way I'd never felt before. It had been five long years. He felt better than I remembered. As he moved in more, I could feel every inch of him. I had no choice but to surrender. He went deeper until we melted together into what felt like an explosion.

I held his face to see the madness in his eyes as he went hard. Our bodies merged together, and we came at the same time. Even though we came together, Easy was far from finished. I could feel his dick throbbing inside of me as his juices mixed with mine and slid down my thighs. I moaned close to his ear, and he started stroking me crazy again. He pulled out of me, quickly turning me over. He hiked my booty in the air.

"You better hold on to something, ma, 'cause I'm straight drilling this pussy," he growled in my ear, watching me grip the sofa in my hands. He had a fistful of my hair in one hand and a handful of ass in the other. He showed me who was in control that night as he knocked the Mario coins out of my pussy.

I moaned, cried, and begged him to keep fuckin' me crazy with every stroke. Easy sent my hormones into a frenzy as the strongest orgasm I'd ever had ripped through my soul like the waves hitting the seashore on a stormy night. He wouldn't stop until he had busted at least three times inside of me. He drilled inside of me until he couldn't cum anymore. And even then, he wanted to keep going. By the time we finished, I was lying flat on my stomach, face buried in the armrest of the sofa.

Easy pulled out of me and lifted me up from the sofa by my hips. We were both out of breath. I sat up on the sofa as Easy pushed my hair from my face. My messy hair had come out of the sophisticated bun that Sharita had put it in a few hours earlier. I watched as Easy grabbed his set of keys and finally removed the handcuffs. I looked into his face as he stood from the sofa and grabbed his boxers.

"You wanna get in the tub? Soak some of this pain away for a little while before we pop out to my crib across town?" Easy asked.

I nodded. "Sure. Can I just grab something to drink?"

Easy nodded. "I'll go run the water."

I watched Easy make his way up the stairs, and when he was out of sight, I grabbed my panties and bra, then quickly slipped into them. I threw on my dress and grabbed my heels. It would have been nice to grab my purse and coat, but they were back in Sharita's car, which was parked back at my father's club.

Easy was that one person who I could run to when everyone else was done breaking my heart. I'd gotten him caught up enough as it was with my family. I had to do it. I had to make a sacrifice. Every woman has had to let go of a man she didn't want to let go of. I didn't want to leave him, but I had to fix everything. I had to save Sharita. I had to give everyone what they wanted.

I tiptoed out of the door and bumped straight into Anisah. She cocked her gun at the sight of me.

"Where are you going?" she growled.

"I have to go get my sister back. Please." I held my hands up because I knew that bitch wouldn't hesitate to shoot me.

Easy might have not been thinking about that bitch, but that bitch was definitely thinking about him.

Before Anisah could even respond and aim her gun at my face the way she wanted to, a black Escalade pulled up in the driveway. Easy's people didn't approach the car defensively. One of the women went over and opened the back door of the car, and Stef got out, signaling me to come with him.

I looked back at Anisah, who lowered her weapon to her side. Why didn't it surprise me that those women really worked for Stef? And I was sure Easy had no clue. All that time, Stef really was protecting his son over in Morocco.

"Come on, Miss Summers," Stef demanded, and I looked back at the house.

I eyed the glare on Anisah's face before I hurried and got in the car with Stef.

Stef got in behind me and slammed the door. His driver peeled off out of the driveway and away from Easy's house.

I looked back at the soldiers as they watched us leave. Stef leaned back in his seat smoking a cigar.

"Them bitches work for you, Stef? Does Easy know?" I asked. "That's a dumb question. No, he doesn't know!"

"I hired them to watch Cristobal when he was back in Morocco. He was stealing from me. When Easy helped to free some of their people from bondage, they trusted him. They told me what he did for them, and I told them to protect him with their lives," Stef assured me.

"Where is Sharita?" I asked. "Is she okay?"

Stef was reluctant to say, "I don't know." He watched me huff and lean back in the seat. "But I can find out. I was coming here to get you to take you away from here before the police came searching for you, but it seems like you were already leaving."

"I didn't want Easy involved in this. I just need to get to the funeral home and tell my aunt that she can have it all. I just want to leave town in one piece," I told Stef, and he shook his head. "No?"

"Zara died a few minutes ago," Stef let me know.

My heart sped up.

"You won't survive jail at this point. You have to leave town. I'm talking out of the country," Stef warned me.

I shook my head. "I'm not leaving Sharita. And what will happen to Easy?"

"Easy can take care of himself. Sharita knew better than to kill Sable. She has no immunity. The protection from her family doesn't extend to her. The truth of the matter is that the laws aren't in place to protect people on the bottom. Your father never claimed her as his, and Jimena only cared about protecting herself, which is why she involved herself with both me and Sable. You have to protect yourself," Stef tried to convince me.

"I'm not leaving. At least not until the funeral. I have to see them bury my father. Please. Just take me somewhere safe until then," I begged.

"Okay, but don't say I didn't ask you to leave town before it was too late." Stef puffed smoke from his cigar.

Chapter Sixteen

Easy

Finding out that my soldiers worked for Stef shouldn't have come as a surprise. Most of the drugs that came into town were from Mexico and North and East Africa. My soldiers didn't want to tell me that they worked for my biological father because of my affiliation with my adoptive father, the enemy of their real employer. I felt betrayed even though they assured me that they had my back to the fullest. That they would follow me anywhere because of everything that I did for them.

My father supplied them with weapons and supplies to fight their local government. He brought money into their towns. While he tried to protect them from afar, I was right there fighting with them, which was why they were down with me. I was pissed the fuck off that they let Meelah go with him. I couldn't reach her. I couldn't be there with her. I'd let so much happen to her already. I was dying on the inside. Two days went by with no word from her, and the reality of the situation was starting to sink in.

And to make matters worse, Mandy's bitch ass kept calling me.

"Bostyn, you must've thought I was playing when I asked you to come home the other night!" Mandy's irritating-ass voice oozed through my phone.

"Mandy, I really don't have time for this shit. Did you take my kids to the place I told you to take them to?" I responded. I told her to take the kids to the bus station to meet one of my crew members. Aunt Donna was supposed to meet them to take them out of town for a little while.

"Yes," Mandy huffed. "Did you know your bitch worked for this journalist firm in Canada? Her boss just aired a missing report for her on the news! There's a warrant for her arrest. Are you harboring a fugitive? Claudius said you broke her out of police custody!"

I chuckled to myself. "Man, I ain't do shit."

Mandy was quiet for a few seconds before she questioned me again. "Did you sleep with her?"

"Nah, we didn't go to sleep, shawty." I tried not to laugh.

"Bostyn, you think this shit is funny, don't you?" Mandy hissed.

"It's fuckin' hilarious." I laughed.

"Let's see how hard your ass laughs when your black bitch ends up in police custody with a noose around her neck," Mandy said before hanging the fuck up on me.

"I hate this bitch, homie. I swear to God!" I howled.

"Dawg, we'll figure this shit out. Chill," Ace tried to tell me that day at our man's crib in Brooklyn, a small city right outside of Baltimore. "You got all these bitches from Wakanda up in the crib, man. Why couldn't you tell them to stand the fuck outside?" Ace looked around the room at my crew.

I paced the floor in the living room. "Man, shut up. These women go harder than most of you muthafuckas. I got the men at the station telling me what's going on there. And shit ain't pretty. Have you heard from Claudius?"

Ace looked at me like I had him fucked up. "Man, I told you, I'm through fuckin' with him after what happened to Keith. Now if you need the Guerillas, we're here to protect you and only you, bruh, that's it. Fuck Claudius."

"What about Meelah?" I asked him. "Who's protecting her?"

"Man, ya real pops got her straight. Fuck her. You gotta let her go, bruh," Ace told me.

Now I was looking at him the same way that he looked at me when I asked him about hearing from Claudius. "'Fuck Meelah'? Huh? Is that what you just said?"

Ace backed down a little, knowing I didn't play when it came to her. "She beat her own cousin to death! My homegirl who's a nurse at the hospital just said Zara flatlined!"

"Where the fuck were you when Meelah was beating her cousin? They say you were standing right there! You let her catch that beatdown because she was fuckin' Dinero, right?" I shoved the muthafucka back against the wall that he was standing in front of.

"I let them do their thing because that was their fight, nigga," Ace snarled at me. "Just like this shit right here is Meelah's fight. Your biological father is protecting her. She's safer with that muthafucka than she is with you, and you know it. He can get her out of here before she ends up in prison for involuntary manslaughter. If she survives that muthafucka. Her aunt ain't gonna play with her over her baby, man."

"And I'm not going to play with her aunt over my baby," I told him.

Ace shook his head. "Stef is looking for you, trying to get you on his team. He has your girl to try to pull you closer to him! Then you got Dinero and Claudius working together, when Claudius is supposed to be on your muthafuckin' team! They're hoping your stupid ass shows up to Sable's funeral looking for her. Sharita is sitting in jail for Sable's murder. All the evidence points to her. Whatever protection you had for her in jail is working because she is in there fuckin' bitches up. So, she's good for now and waiting for her court date.

"I heard your girl met up with Claudius's mother to sign over rights to everything her father left to her. She gave all that shit to her aunt. Her aunt is about to run all this shit. Do you think Stef is about to let that happen? He's gonna need you to take this city back. And do you think Jimmie Reel is about to let that happen? You got bigger problems than Meelah, bruh. Your fathers are about to go to war over you at this funeral, bruh."

I nodded. "A'ight, bet. Time to get strapped and suited up. Let me wear one of your black suits, muthafucka."

It wasn't going to be easy getting to Meelah that day, but Ace was right—Meelah was there, front and center at the church, staring at her father's dead body in his casket. Of course, I didn't go in the church. I sent a few of the men in my crew to scope out the scene. Turned out, Stef escorted Meelah to the funeral. Half of the task force was there, including my father. Half of Meelah's father's family was there. Her aunts were there, sitting behind her. Dinero sat a few rows behind Meelah. Dinero even helped carry the casket out of the church. I wanted to be there with Meelah, but I knew I would've started firing shots inside the church.

I didn't make any sudden moves until later that afternoon at the gravesite. I let everyone grieve over Sable's dead body. I even let Meelah get one last glance at her father before they lowered his casket into the ground. As the crowd started to dissipate, my crew decided to make our move. We made our way out of our cars and onto hallowed ground just as my father, Claudius, Dinero, and a few members of the police department made their way back over to Meelah and Stef, who stood around the hole made for Sable's casket. Meelah's aunt Troy strolled over. They weren't surprised to see me walking up with twelve deep.

Meelah gasped a little when she saw me, but she directed her attention to her aunt, who stood alongside Dinero and Claudius. "Aunt Troy, you got what you wanted." Meelah dried her face. "I met with the lawyer to sign my rights over. Everything with my father's name now belongs to you. You can run it how you want."

"For now," Stef made sure he interjected. "Just remember that the casino and the clubs downtown are on streets owned by the Romano family. I'll take this city back one way or another. Meelah signing over her rights to her father's businesses and estates is going to hurt you in the long run. Dinero doesn't know shit about running any legit businesses. All he knows is the street life. You're better off selling to me now while you can."

"Is that a threat, nigga?" Dinero responded in a defensive stance.

Stef chuckled. "It's a prediction, muthafucka. You worked for me, remember? You were all my army at one point in time. No matter what you steal from Meelah, I'll find a way to give it back and then some."

Troy glared at Stef before looking back at Meelah. "Though I deserve it all for everything your father took me through, all the money in the world won't bring my daughter back," Troy snapped. "There's nothing Stefano can do to keep you out of prison for murder, little bitch."

Dinero looked over at me. "You have a lot of nerve showing up here, nigga."

"Watch the way you talk to my son," Stef spoke up.

"I'm not your son," I corrected him.

Pops chuckled a little.

"I'm not yours either, muthafucka." I checked his ass too. "I didn't come here to reminisce. I came here for Meelah, and I'm not leaving without her."

"I brought her here to see her father one last time. She's leaving with us," Stefano let me know. "If she goes with you, she's dead, and you know it."

"She killed her cousin. She's getting jail time," Pops let Stefano know.

Meelah shook her head. "Leanne Crosby told me that if I signed everything over, the charges would be dropped."

"That's not how it works once the state presses charges against you, too," Pops let her know. "Just cooperate, and we won't have to throw you down there in that hole with your father." Pops didn't flinch when he heard my gun cock. Instead, he laughed a little. "Bostyn, you're in enough trouble for helping her escape a few days ago. Your crew from Morocco got her out of police custody and took her."

"Well, we're cops too, bruh, so technically she was still in police custody," I let him know and extended my arm toward Stef. "Let her go. Everyone needs to leave but me and my father. Both these muthafuckas. I got snipers all over this cemetery. Before any of you can even press the trigger on your gun, they will unload on every one of y'all. The cemetery is the perfect place for a war. They don't even have to move us far to bury us, muthafuckas. Everything Meelah just gave up can go with y'all greedy, lying, backstabbing muthafuckas when you meet your Maker."

"Meelah is going to do jail time, Bostyn. She killed her cousin," Pops tried to tell me.

"That muthafucka in the ground let Dinero beat the fuck out of his own daughter! Dinero had his crew assault Meelah, and then he killed my baby! Why the fuck isn't he in jail?" I asked.

"If what you say happened, then why the fuck didn't she report the shit to the police?" Dinero barked.

"Muthafucka, I wasn't talking to your bitch ass." I stepped to Dinero.

Dinero had been waiting for me to step to him so he could try his luck with me. "Nigga, I'm standing right here. What you gonna do?"

Then Claudius pushed me away from his brother and pulled his gun out on me.

I stared down the barrel of the gun before looking up at Claudius's face. "And this whole time, I thought we were brothers."

"Put the gun down, Claudius," Stef told him.

Guns cocked in the distance in all directions, though it was hard to tell from which direction the echoes were coming.

Claudius lowered his weapon because he knew that as soon as he fired on me, a thousand bullets were going to spray in his direction.

"Mrs. Troy Summers, we will make sure Meelah goes to the station. I think it's best you get back home," Pops told Troy.

Troy eyed Meelah one last time before heading toward her car.

Stef looked at Pops. "Did your son have any idea you sent him to Morocco to take over my territories? You put him in danger for five years to try to take over a drug empire that was put in place by my blood, sweat, and tears, not yours! Emilio Zachariah Romano shouldn't have been involved in this shit!"

"I saved his life! He fell in love with a girl he had no business being in love with! I saw him going down the same path we did! The woman I loved betrayed me for a man who was higher on the food chain than I was! And in the end, she still needed me to help her! To save her son from her own family who wanted him dead!" Pops stepped to the front of his squad to face Stef.

"Seems like you want him dead too." Stef glared into Pops's face. "Let these people go, and let's settle this like men. Let my men escort Meelah to safety. Let Bostyn go home to his kids. Let Claudius betray his only friend for a brother who's using him. Let the past stay where the fuck it is so the son you claim you care about can finally live his life. He doesn't want to work for you anymore."

"And I don't want to work for you either, muthafucka!" I turned to Stef. "I want out of all of this shit! I just want a life with her! That's it!"

Stef's light eyes sparkled. "It's not that easy, son."

I walked up to Stef, and his men tightened up around him. I snatched Meelah away from him by her wrist.

"Run toward the black Lexus and don't look back."

I told her to run that way because if anyone aimed their guns that way, that was the signal for my crew to start spraying. "Go!"

Meelah didn't hesitate to run.

"I'm out, Pops," I told the man who raised me. "I already left my badge and service pistol at the station.

Pops shook his head. "You're not walking away from me that easily."

"Claudius, you might want to start walking away too." I placed my hand over the trigger of the gun in my hand, which was my crew's signal to get ready to fire.

Dinero already had his gun drawn.

"Walk away, Dinero," I warned.

Dinero didn't budge. His crew stood behind him, ready for whatever I was about to bring.

I already knew when I turned my back to walk away from the people I once called family, they wouldn't hesitate to stop me from walking away at all costs. And that was when I heard a gun cock behind me. Stef could barely yell out my father's name before I heard a gun go off and a body fall hard to the ground. Everything from that point on was a domino effect. Once the first shot was fired, my crew went in.

I took cover behind one of the huge tombstones and barely got the chance to eye my pop's body lying in a pool of blood on the ground when I felt the cold metal of a gun pressed against the back of my neck.

"Tell your mother I said hello," I heard Claudius's voice snarl over my shoulder before his gun went off.

"So, I've been lying in this hospital bed for how long, homie?" I lay in the hospital bed, rubbing my head in confusion. I didn't remember much about my life at all.

According to the way Claudius told me the story, Meelah's ex-boyfriend was the one who shot me in the head. Bits and pieces were missing from his version of the story. He was lying to me in my face, but I had to ask more questions to prove it.

"A month." Claudius stood before my bed, eying all the presents scattered around the room. "Your kids stayed with your aunt Donna for a little while, until the shit in the street calmed down a little."

"And who killed my father again?" I questioned.

Claudius looked at me. "The man in that picture with Meelah, but we made it look like Dinero is the one who shot him. We got him down at the station for you, sir."

I looked up at Claudius as bits and pieces of my memory burst through my mind like fireworks. I couldn't put my memories together, and it was frustrating the fuck out of me. But from what I could put together from the story Claudius told me, Dinero and Claudius were related in some way.

"He's your brother." I cleared my throat. "Isn't he?"

Claudius hesitated. "You're my brother, and that's all you need to worry about."

"Where's Meelah?" I asked.

"I told you, she killed her cousin, and she's at the correctional facility in Jessup. She's fine from what I've heard. She's got a group of bitches looking out for her in jail. Troy tried to get to her, of course, but your biological father took care of that." Claudius looked like he hated that Meelah was safe. "Remember old girl I was fuckin' with, Tajha? Of course you don't remember. Well, anyway, she got lit up in an alley a few days ago after running her mouth to Dinero and telling him that I was the one who told the unit about the warehouses that got raided."

"Why did y'all frame Dinero for my father's murder?" I asked.

Claudius laughed. "Well, Stefano has immunity. After your father was killed and a few of the soldiers you brought over from Morocco reported our unit to internal affairs, then a couple of Sable's warehouses were raided. Warehouses run by Dinero. He thought I set him up, so he was trying to set me up."

I sat up in the bed. "Soldiers from Morocco?" I changed the subject while I tried to gather my thoughts. "Are those the ones outside guarding the hospital for me?"

Claudius shook his head. "Nah, it's Ace and them. They're waiting on me and the police department to come out. They think they're about to run up on us."

"For what?" I asked.

Claudius frowned at me. "They're saying I tried to kill you. Most of these letters and cards and flowers have messages in them telling you to watch out for a nigga."

"I've known you all my life, right?" I asked.

Claudius nodded. "Hell yeah."

"I've always had your back, right?" I asked him.

Claudius nodded. "No question."

"Then why would you shoot me?" I had to know.

I didn't see the face of the shooter, but for whatever reason, I remember the clanking of jewelry over my shoulder. The same sound that the jewelry around Claudius's neck was making that day in the hospital.

Before I could even reach for the assistance button on my bed, Claudius pulled his .45 out on me.

"We got your crew sent back to Morocco. The ones we could find anyway. Call ya niggas off. I ain't about to go down for shit. You got your father killed. After all he did for you, you would turn your back on him for a bitch you barely knew. Get the fuck up and dial this number," Claudius growled.

"Who the fuck is Ace? You know I don't remember shit, muthafucka. You made sure of that." I sat on the edge of the bed, struggling to get up.

"The nigga's number is 4-4-3—" Claudius barely got through the area code before I heard the sound of a gunshot masked by a silencer.

I just sort of stood there frozen as his body hit the floor. And there stood a familiar face, placing her gun back in her purse. The older Hispanic woman smiled as nurses flew down the hallway for help. She placed her hands in the air, and she was immediately tackled to the ground by security.

"Mr. Reel, are you okay? Sir, do you know this woman?" one of the security guards asked with his knee in the woman's back as he cuffed her.

"Yeah, she's my aunt," I told them. "She just saved my life," I said as my eyes moved to Claudius's lifeless body on the floor.

Epilogue

Easy

Two Years Later

"Daddy, you got me the new iPad?" Boss yelled with excitement that Christmas Day in my two-bedroom apartment in San Antonio, Texas.

I laughed out loud as I watched Majesty and Boss rip open their gifts that morning. It was their first Christmas without their mother, and I was nervous as fuck. I was just getting to know them again after having no memory of them whatsoever. After I was released from the hospital once I woke up from the month-long coma, I told myself that I was going to get my life back on track. That I was going to discover who I really was.

The truth came out about not just my biological parents, but the twins' parents as well. Turned out Jimmie was their father. After his death, I skipped out on the reading of the will. I inherited a few cars, houses, condos, and the money in one of his savings accounts that amounted to a little less than $1 million. I didn't need his money. I had my own. I put the money into an account for the twins. I tried to tell the kids that Jimmie was their father, but they wouldn't accept it. I wasn't sticking around Maryland. And once the twins found out the truth, they wanted to go with me. And you know what? Mandy didn't even fight for them to stay.

“They love their daddy, boy.” Roxyn strolled into the living room, drinking his third Heineken.

I grinned. Getting to know my adoptive brothers again was awkward, but they tried to make it as comfortable as possible. They knew they were all I had. I didn’t want to know Stef despite everything he was doing to try to fix things between us. It was a little too late as far as I was concerned. My aunt Donna didn’t do any time for Claudius’s death. She was defending me. She had been through enough with my family and decided to go back to Panama. Sharita was facing ten years in prison, and Meelah, well, she didn’t want to see me. Believe me, I tried to see her.

“No word from Meelah, huh?” Jaxon chimed in as he came out of the kitchen and over to where I sat on the sofa watching the kids.

I frowned and scratched my head. “Every time I get close to reaching out to her, they move her. She doesn’t want to have shit to do with me.”

“She’s responsible for what happened. You wouldn’t have gotten shot if you hadn’t gone after her, Bostyn.” Roxyn shook his head and sipped from his beer. “And Pops would still be alive.”

I looked from Roxyn over to Jaxon, who scratched his head and cleared his throat. “That’s what y’all think? That all this shit was her fault like I didn’t play a part? Like my father didn’t play a part? Like muthafuckas didn’t lie to us?”

“Hey, don’t shoot the messenger.” Roxyn grinned.

I looked at him. “You went to go see her in jail?”

Roxyn grinned. “She has been out of jail for about, what, six months.”

I jumped up from the couch. “The fuck? Y’all knew about this shit?”

"She needed some time, bro. She was in Panama with your aunt." Roxyn watched the angry expression on my face.

"Where the fuck is she now?" I asked just as the doorbell rang.

I watched my brothers laugh among themselves, and I peeped the kids playing alongside the Christmas tree.

As I made my way toward the door, the blood had already started to rush through my heart valves. I didn't need to look through the peephole to know who it was. When I pulled the door open to see Meelah standing there, I frowned down into her face, watching her bright brown eyes sparkle under my porch light. I wanted to be happy to see her, but I was still angry at her. It had been two years since I'd been shot. My memories still hadn't come back. Every memory I had was from what others fabricated except the memories I had of how I felt about Meelah.

"I was lying in the hospital bed for over a month because a muthafucka who was supposed to be my best friend shot me in the head and in my back, Meelah," I told her.

She nodded. "I know."

"I don't remember anyone but you, and you left me," I told her.

"I just wanted the pain to stop," Meelah whispered.

"Did it stop?" I asked, and she shook her head. "Sometimes the muthafucka who spends most of his time trying to make others happy is the loneliest person, so don't you ever leave that person! The only full memory I have from my past is the day I told you that I wasn't letting you go. I basically told you that I needed you. Do you have any idea how hard that was for me? Telling someone that I needed them? All I wanted was you! All I needed was you, and you left me! I know you went to jail, but as soon as I got out of that hospital, I started trying to see you, and you wouldn't see me! Why?"

"I just needed time to adjust to everything. We'd been through a lot. We lost a lot. We both needed time, Easy. I needed time to forget everything."

"Even me?" I responded.

Meelah hesitated. "I wanted you to take some time to heal too. Get to know your family again. They may not have been your blood, but they were still your family. Your brothers love you. Your mother missed you. Your father died, and they needed your strength to help them get through. I just needed to take time to get over the pain of being a criminal's daughter. And my best friend was doing time for killing my father, who she'd just found out was her father too. It was too much. I left the country after I was released from jail. I was hurting. The truth hurt," Meelah admitted.

"Hurt? That shit almost killed me! I shouldn't even be alive right now, but God isn't finished with me," I told her.

"I'm sorry. I shouldn't have come over," Meelah stuttered, "but your brothers invited me."

"You can stay . . . but your clothes gotta go." My frown turned into a grin as I watched her blush from head to toe.

Meelah shook her head. "Why do you always insist on taking my clothes off? I have a gift for you. I went to stay with your aunt for a while in Panama." Meelah grinned and looked to her left, signaling for someone to get out of the car and come up to my apartment door. She looked into my face as footsteps approached.

I looked at Meelah's face before looking at the woman who approached her side. The woman was my aunt Donna. She stood alongside Meelah, holding a toddler who had to be about 18 months old. The little girl was wrapped in a fur coat. Her light cheeks were bright red. Her eyes were bright brown. Her smile lit up every dark part of my soul. I swear seeing that baby took every amount of pain I had in my heart away.

"Come in. It's cold as fuck." I pulled Meelah in by her coat.

Meelah stepped inside, bringing Aunt Donna with her. Before my aunt could even hand the baby over to me, that little girl was already jumping into my arms. I smiled, heart racing as I held the little girl in my arms.

"Aunt Donna!" The twins raced up to my aunt, running into her legs. "We missed you!"

"Oh, I missed you too!" Aunt Donna cried out, hugging them before looking back at me and Meelah standing there looking at each other. "Umm, let's go play with your toys and give your father some time to talk to Meelah, okay?"

I examined the little girl's face. "And what's your name?"

"Her name is Feliza. Your aunt named her. Donna was at the prison visiting the night I went into labor. She was there at the hospital with me. They let her take my baby home instead of putting her in the foster care system." Meelah tried not to cry. "I knew you would take care of her for me if you knew, but you needed time to recover."

I looked at Meelah. That was why she'd stayed away from me. She was pregnant. She was afraid her aunt Troy would send someone after her. She wasn't trying to go through what she went through when she was pregnant with our other baby. I remembered the pain of losing Magic. Something even a bullet couldn't erase.

I looked Feliza over. "What's her full name?"

"Feliza Emilia Gonzales," Meelah told me.

I glanced at her. She'd found out I'd legally changed my name back to Emilio Zachariah Gonzales. That was who I was. I wasn't a Reel, and I wasn't ready to be a Romano just yet.

"She looks just like you." Meelah admired the two of us standing before her. She gasped a little as I grabbed her body to mine. "So, I heard you divorced Snow White. I see you got your kids. They need you."

"We need to fix this. We can't keep running from each other, or should I say, you can't keep running from me," I told her.

Meelah nodded. "I won't run."

"We surrendered and sacrificed too much to be together to now be apart. It's been seven years, li'l baby," I told her as tears slid down her face. It made her cry even more when Feliza held her face to dry her tears.

"You sure you want me? I know you have a girl by now. Where the hoes at?" Meelah rolled her eyes a little.

"You don't see my brothers sitting in there?" I grinned.

"Fuck you, Emilio." Roxyn laughed. "Don't nobody want Eminem but you, Meelah."

"So, you here to fuckin' stay this time?" I asked her and kissed her forehead.

Meelah kissed my chin. "My bags are in the car."

We'd been through everything designed to rip us apart. I was glad Meelah came back to me because I was going to rip a hole through every city looking for her. It wasn't going to be easy, but we were going to get through it together. I never knew how the girl of my dreams would look, but I definitely knew how I would feel when I found her. I knew she'd make me fight for her and bring the beast out of me. I knew she'd challenge my strength. She'd make me chase her. I knew when I met Meelah that she'd change my life. All I had to do next was convince her to change her last name, too.